Candlewood Lake

More books by Penny C. Sansevieri

Nonfiction

From Book to Bestseller

(PublishingGold.com, Inc. 2005)

No More Rejections: Get Published Today!

(PublishingGold.com, Inc. 2005)

No More Rejections: Get Published Today!

(Infinity Publishing 2002, 2003)

Get Published! An author's guide to the online publishing revolution

(1st Books, 2001)

Fiction

The Cliffhanger (iUniverse, Inc., 2000)

Candlewood Lake

Penny C. Sansevieri

iUniverse, Inc.
New York Lincoln Shanghai

Candlewood Lake

iUniverse books may be ordered through booksellers or by contacting:

iUniverse
2021 Pine Lake Road, Suite 100
Lincoln, NE 68512
www.iuniverse.com
1-800-Authors (1-800-288-4677)

Love by Roy Croft
Let It Be Me by the Everly Brothers 1959
Traces sun by the Classics IV 1969
Fire and Rain written and sung by James Taylor 1970

ISBN-13: 978-0-595-35129-9 (pbk)
ISBN-13: 978-0-595-79830-8 (ebk)
ISBN-10: 0-595-35129-8 (pbk)
ISBN-10: 0-595-79830-6 (ebk)

Printed in the United States of America

For my Mom and Dad and the memories they made on Candlewood Lake

Acknowledgements

Where does one begin thanking everyone who in their own ways, both big and small, contributed to the successful completion of this book? Of all the chapters in this book, this is perhaps the most challenging to write. There are my dear friends who have never wavered in their encouragement and support of me. I love you all.

My editors. First Martha Wallace who took a great idea and turned it into a great story. With great love, care and talent she helped me bring these characters to life. My gratitude for her hard work can not be expressed in mere words except to say, thank you, without your guidance this book would not have been possible. To Jeniffer Thompson who, through her own gifted eye for editing and story-telling helped bring an amazing polish to this book and with her own dash of wisdom and guidance helped to finally give me a publishable product.

To everyone who calls Candlewood Lake home, past, present and future, this story is for you and I thank you for your kindness and generosity as we dug through hours of research to make this book as accurate as possible. I would like to especially thank Linda Fox, Director of the New Fairfield Free Public Library and Lyn Sheaffer of the New Fairfield United Methodist Church for the time they spent helping us through our research to make the details of this book as accurate as possible. Thank you for your openness and willingness to share this information with me.

To my mother who's encouragement, guidance, and belief in my work has kept me going through some of the most challenging times of my life. Thank you mom for traveling back with me to Candlewood Lake and for telling me your story, which inspired me to write this one. And finally to my father, who died long before this book was done and who will never see the bit of himself I've woven into this, or the gratitude I have for him for teaching me how to tell a story, and for being the best storyteller I've ever known. I will miss you all the days of my life.

CHAPTER 1

1980

If someone had asked Justin VanSant what one single thing had changed his life, he would have answered without hesitation: "The day my best friend's mother took her own life." It was the one moment that had turned everything in his simple existence into a complicated and irresolvable mess.

For most of us, the changes that affect our lives are comprised of small moments that often slip by unnoticed. Justin, however, was all too aware of the change, the moment his quiet life in New Fairfield, Connecticut, had turned into something entirely unbearable. Now, he felt like the party guest who had overstayed his welcome and he was eager to grab his coat and leave.

He could still remember the moment it happened. They were standing by the lake, sheltered under a grove of trees; the sparkle of the moonlight sprinkled diamonds on the water. He'd dreamt of kissing Eve nearly his entire life. Justin could feel his heart pounding in the back of his throat. His lips were a breath from hers when the rustling in the woods startled them both. Then the voice, calling to them, they needed to get back to town as quickly as possible. Billy's mother was dead. She'd been found beside an empty bottle of pills.

Justin studied the tarmac outside the airplane window. A deep voice welcomed him aboard flight 89 bound for Los Angeles while passengers continued to push up the aisles, hoisting their hand baggage into the narrow overhead compartments. His lips curved into a small, sad smile. After ten years, he was finally leaving the party.

❧ ❧ ❧

1971

The Indian summer was finally beginning to succumb to the crispness of fall. The warm air was tinged by a cool October breeze, and the trees surrounding Candlewood Lake were once again in flame. A mockingbird sang a tune of farewell before it was time to head south; a sorrowful stolen repertoire of a summer gone by. The wind whipped through the oak trees tugging the red and gold leaves from their branches, dancing with them as they floated to the ground.

Nate Parsons lived in a modest colonial home on a large parcel of land. Like most homes that bordered the lake, it was built in the shade of the tall maples that generously filled the area. Nate had by all accounts the largest pile of freshly raked leaves anyone had ever seen. Neatly gathered together in a tempting array of yellows and reds, it was all a young boy could do not to give into his carnal urge and hurl himself into it.

"You know Billy, we really shouldn't be doing this," Justin's voice was anxious, his eyes darting up and down the street.

"Aw, come on Jus, where's your sense of adventure?" Billy's face filled with the excitement of someone who had just stumbled upon a pot of gold. There, before him was the largest gold mine he'd found so far.

He stopped, placing his books at his feet he smiled over to Justin who watched him in angst. Justin hated it when Billy got that look in his eye. It could only mean trouble.

"Watch me turn this pile inside out."

"I wouldn't do that if I were you Billy," Justin cautioned, clutching his worn blue folder closer to his chest.

Billy limbered up, preparing for his jump. "Thing is, you aren't me and 'sides, one of us has to be the adventurer." Billy delivered his comment and rushed his twelve-year-old body headlong into the colorful pile that exploded around him. Billy's laughter muffled by a thousand dead leaves.

Justin's eyes darted off the house like moths off a window. He was certain Nate Parsons was home and in a moment would come bounding out of his house, yelling at the top of his lungs. Nate disliked intruders and everyone knew it. Billy continued to splash around in the now diminishing pile. Soon, there was nothing left of the old man's hard work.

Nate Parsons heard the laughter and knew that someone was up to no good. He was aging more rapidly than he'd care to admit. And at sixty-five, he could barely move without his arthritis rearing its ugly head. Nate drew himself up from his chair and lumbered painfully through the house. The young laughter became louder as he neared the front door. Through a side panel window he saw that no good Billy Freeman ruin all of his hard work while his little bookworm friend Justin VanSant looked on. "No good rug rats," he mumbled as he reached for his jacket, "never had any use for those no good boys."

"Come on Jus, it's fun!" Billy called to his friend.

"I-I'm fine right here," he said nervously. "You know we should rake this back up Billy."

His dark haired friend stopped what he was doing and stared at him in amazement, "Yer kidding right?"

"No, Billy, I'm not kidding. This isn't right, poor Mr. Parsons is elderly and this probably took him all day."

"You're goddamned right it took me all day!" A voice boomed from behind him. Nate Parsons' hands were clenched into angry fists as he marched across the lawn. Billy scurried to his feet, dusting the debris from his blue jeans.

"Sir, we're very sorry about the mess but we'll clean it up." Justin's voice was contrite.

"Right again boy, rakes are in the back. Now hurry before I call Shep."

"What would you call the police for? We didn't do nothin' wrong!" Shep was Senior Constable for the village of New Fairfield, he and Nate were good friends. Billy was certain that Shep would arrest them just to do Nate a favor, law or no.

Nate's worn face grimaced into an almost sadistic smile. "Ever heard of trespassin' boy?"

Eve Phillips wandered slowly up Nate's street, watching from a distance as the elderly man waved his angry fist at two boys. Eve had been enrolled in the fourth grade at New Fairfield Elementary for only a month now, but knew who the boys were. The two sixth graders were always seen together. And while she had never spoken with them, she'd overheard the girls in her class coo over Billy's good looks and listen to their dreamy tales of taping anonymous notes to his locker. He was by far the most popular boy and athlete in the sixth grade. She knew very little about his friend though, only that his name was Justin and that he was his quiet sidekick. She continued to walk as she watched both boys retrieve rakes from the back yard and commence the repair of Nate's precious pile.

"I dunno man; I think we should just leave. I mean what's the old man gonna do after all?"

Justin threw his slender body into his work. "He'll call Shep that's what, then he'll call our folks."

Billy shrugged, "I suppose." He continued, oblivious to the lanky young girl that approached them. Her hair, that fell in sheets of gold down her back wafted behind her as she walked. When Justin looked up, he knew he'd seen a goddess, a young girl who showed the promise of great beauty in her perfectly sculpted face that smiled to greet him.

"Hi," she offered timidly, almost sorry that she'd interrupted them. Billy looked up, his face showing the displeasure he felt inside.

"Hello." Justin smiled back at her offering her an outstretched hand just as his mother had always taught him to do. Eve took it warily; she thought hand shaking was only for adults.

"I'm Eve, Eve Phillips. My family just moved here."

"My name is Justin and this is my friend Billy."

"Yes, I…" she stopped herself before admitting that she'd heard of him. "Yes, I've seen you both around school."

Billy frowned, "Funny, we haven't seen you and I pretty much know everyone there."

"Well, I don't really know anyone and I kind of keep to myself trying to catch up on school work, we worked at a different pace where I was from."

"Where's that?" Suddenly, Justin wanted to know everything about her.

"Michigan. My parents moved for my father's job."

"How do ya' like it so far?" Billy threw her a handsome athletic smile.

"I like it fine."

"Sounds to me like you're a bit of a bookworm, so's Jus here, you two oughta hit it off just fine." Billy raked again, wanting to get this chore over with.

Justin blushed at his friend's comment. He hated the reference. Sure, he studied a lot, maybe more than most. But he had great plans and his parents had high hopes of their son attending the same college they did: Harvard. Only perfect students get into a college like that they would say. That made Justin study even harder.

"Can I help?" Eve inquired.

"Old man Parson might have another rake in the back," Billy said without looking up, "be our guest."

CHAPTER 2

Eve and her family lived in a house like many in Connecticut. It was a large white colonial with a thick front porch that wrapped protectively around the home. It boasted four bedrooms and two baths. Like most homes in New Fairfield it sat perched on the perimeter of Candlewood Lake offering a spectacular view. In the early mornings she could stand on the porch and watch as lone fishermen climbed in their boats in hopes of impressing their families with a fresh catch for dinner. "Daddy look!" She would call to him and together they would watch the daily ritual. It was her favorite moment of the day.

"Momma!" she called as she entered their home. The house was quiet. From the hallway, Eve could see into the backyard where her mother sat playing with her little brother. Teddy's fifth birthday had arrived three days prior amid hundreds of colorful balloons and a clown who painted faces. Despite the fact that she and her family were newcomers, it had been a festive afternoon, the town was friendly and welcoming of strangers and their house and yard were filled with children, some with colorful designs on their small faces, running and yelling as their parents looked on hoping they'd work off their sugar highs.

The scent of cinnamon filled the air as Eve headed to the kitchen in search of a batch of freshly baked cookies. She popped a round buttery cookie in her mouth and went outside to join her mother and Teddy before beginning her homework.

Eve was pleased to have made two new friends that day. Until that afternoon, Eve spent most of her after school hours alone. Although she had made a few new girlfriends, they seemed less interested in adventures than they were in some silly singing group called The Beatles.

"Hi honey," her mother greeted her warmly. Judith was a petite blond with an infectious smile. That was what had drawn Edward Phillips to her, as he said, a smile that lit up her face. Her father always joked that it was a good thing Eve had inherited her mother's striking features. Judith and Edward had the customary yearlong courtship before Edward announced his plans to marry her, but really, he'd known the moment he'd laid eyes on her. Together, they struggled through the first few years of marital bliss, the paychecks that often did not cover their expenses, a baby that came quite unexpectedly and, shortly after Eve was born, the shut down of the factory where Ed worked. It had been a long cold winter that year in Michigan, but somehow, they had survived. There were plenty of jobs for someone as skilled as he was and soon, Ed was employed again and the Phillips family was back on track. Then, last year, he'd been offered the chance to head up a factory opening in Connecticut. It was the opportunity of a lifetime and after discussing it with his wife they both agreed it was something neither of them could turn down. New Fairfield was a prominent part of the country, a place where they both longed to raise their children in.

Eve wandered out of the house, down the steps and onto the grass. Her mother was pushing Teddy on the new swing set their father had bought him for his birthday.

"Hi Mom," she replied, finishing her treat.

"How was school? Did you make any new friends today?" Judith hoped that each day would bring her daughter closer to settling into her new environment. It was tougher for kids, she knew. Most families in New Fairfield were well established and their families had known each other for years.

Eve smiled, "As a matter of fact, I did make a new friend today. Two actually. Billy and Justin, I met them walking home."

Teddy giggled on the swing, his arms outstretched to Eve, "Nice boys?" her mother asked cautiously. Ed often accused her of being overprotective.

"Of course they're nice mom, I helped them rake leaves."

"Rake leaves?" Judy stopped pushing her son and he jumped from the swing into his sisters arms. "Evie!" he shouted.

"Hi sweet pea," she smiled and kissed his soft, warm cheek. "Yea, well Billy was jumping in the pile and this old guy got really upset at them, so they cleaned up their mess. I helped."

"That was nice of you Eve."

"Well, I couldn't just walk away and leave them. 'Sides, it was nice getting to know them."

"What are their last names?" Her mother inquired.

Eve thought for a moment, "Um, Billy Freeman and Justin…uh, VanSant, yeah that's it."

Judith arched an eyebrow, she'd heard of the VanSant's at the local grocery store, Grand Union. They were an affluent couple, both Harvard graduates. His father was a lawyer and his mother had been a nurse until they got married. She'd seen Mary VanSant once at the local green grocer when Mary had taken a moment to introduce herself. Judy had found her warm and genuine and had immediately liked her. She knew little of the other boy's family though and made a mental note to ask around about them. One couldn't be too careful after all.

❧ ❧ ❧

Justin lay upstairs on his neatly made bed, his eyes eagerly scanning the pages of the book in front of him. He lingered here and there, on sentences that were too complex for his young mind. But continued to read on, riveted by the words that came to life in front of him. Hemingway was by far his favorite writer, and he was thrilled when his father had brought the book home for him to read. Lying on his stomach, Justin kicked his legs up behind him, his feet intertwined, thoughtfully rocking back and forth. The memory of the angry Mr. Parsons was already fading into a distant corner of his mind. With the help of their new friend, they had managed to restore the pile to Mr. Parsons liking.

Outside, he could hear his father's car hit the gravel driveway as he arrived home. The screen on the front door clicked open and closed as his mother headed outside to meet him.

His father was finishing up a high profile trial in the city; it would be a turning point in his career he'd told them all proudly. The trial had gone on quite unexpectedly for nearly three months now, causing Karl VanSant to overnight in New York more than he planned. But he promised his wife and son that as soon as it was over, they would take a trip somewhere, just the three of them.

Justin could hear the muffled voices of his parents and he quickly finished up the chapter, eager to hear his father's stories of the trial. To Justin, they were almost as riveting as Hemingway. He closed the book, gingerly running his hands over the cover. Justin thought of his own attempts at writing. His short stories, the ones he didn't dare show anyone. They were westerns mostly, tales of a lone sheriff protecting his town. Justin knew it was a silly way to pass the time, but he enjoyed the feel of the words as they escaped his pen, one by one forming sentences, paragraphs and shaping into stories no one would read.

"Well, today was another harsh one." Karl VanSant dropped his long, lean body into his comfortable maroon leather wing chair as he set his briefcase down beside him. Mary followed him into his den, remembering when she had planned to convert it into a playroom for their yet unborn child. But when Karl accepted a position in one of New York's well-respected criminal law firms, she felt that the room should be his. He would be stepping from corporate and estate law to the more demanding requirements of a personal injury and criminal trial lawyer and she wanted him to have a retreat after an arduous day in court. Here amid the dark wood paneling, oversized cherry wood desk and book cases neatly filled with law books and an occasional novel, Karl would seek some much needed solitude after a difficult trial, or prepare for his next big case.

"Can I fix you a drink honey?" Mary asked, brushing the hair off his forehead.

He took her hand and stroked it gently. "Yes, but only if you fix one for yourself and come sit with me for a while."

"Dinner is…"

Karl pulled his wife down onto his lap and placed a hungry kiss on her mouth. "Dinner be damned, I haven't seen my family in three days." His voice was muffled against her lips.

"Fine," she laughed, "you win again Mr. VanSant, I'll sit with you, but only for a moment. I've got something special for dinner and I don't want it to burn."

Reluctantly, Mary pulled herself from her husband's arms. The small rolling cart she had refinished made a wonderful mini bar. She picked up a thick glass and dropped in several ice cubes.

"Hi dad!" Justin smiled as he strolled into the room.

"Son, join your mother and I, we're just catching up."

Justin sat down on the ottoman at his father's feet. "How is the case going?"

"Well, you know I can't divulge too much, but suffice it to say I think we'll have this wrapped up by the end of the week."

"Really? That soon?" Mary, handed her husband a glass, thoughtfully sipping on her own, before sitting down on the thick armrest of her husband's chair, "why that's wonderful."

"Yes, it is going better than we hoped. I got my hands on some new evidence that is indisputable, they're going to exonerate my guy, that's for certain."

Justin listened eagerly, he loved his father's stories and after a big case, Karl would often spend hours with his son explaining all the nuances of it, hoping to inspire a future legal career.

"So, son, how was your day?"

"Well," he hesitated, "Billy got into some trouble. I was with him, but I didn't do anything."

Karl's eyes narrowed. "That Freeman boy you mean? Are you still hanging out with him?"

Justin drew in a nervous breath, he liked Billy, but his parents thought otherwise, "I am still hanging out with him, I really like him dad. He's nice, just, I don't know, he just likes to do stuff he's not supposed to."

"That's not a good thing. I've seen many people cross the courtroom who wanted to do silly, seemingly innocent things that were wrong."

"Karl! He's just a boy, he's not a criminal." Mary touched his shoulder lightly.

"No, you're right and I didn't mean to infer that he was. I just mean that he might be a bad influence for you son."

"I don't do the stuff that he does, I tried to stop him, but he didn't listen. For the most part, he's really kind of cool. All the girls at school like him."

Karl rested an understanding hand on his son's knee, "It's nice to be with someone who is popular isn't it?"

Justin nodded.

"So tell us what happened today that got Billy in trouble."

"Well," he began tentatively, "Billy jumped in Mr. Parson's leaf pile and he came out and got really mad and we had to fix it."

"So you put everything back the way it was?" Karl asked sipping his scotch.

"Yes, we did and this new girl at school came by and helped us too."

"Really, what's her name?" Mary asked, shifting her weight on the arm rest.

"Eve, Eve Phillips. Her family just moved here. She's really nice." Justin smiled broadly, thinking of the fun they had had even if they were repairing Billy's mess under the wary eye of old man Parsons.

"Oh, I think I met her mother," Mary remembered. "I spoke with her briefly in the store one day, very nice lady. They moved here so her husband could head up Brunson's."

Karl nodded, "Well, good, glad to hear you're making new friends. We'll have to invite Eve and her parents over for dinner some evening," he said to his wife more than to his son. At her husband's words, she was up like a shot.

"I've got to go check on dinner." She said over her shoulder.

❧ ❧ ❧

Billy wandered up his driveway and spotted his older brother Duane hanging all over Rebecca Owen, his new girlfriend. His face contorted in disgust and he was certain he'd lose that peanut butter and jelly sandwich he'd eaten for lunch.

"Hey Duane," Billy climbed up the small set of wooden stairs and stood on the porch, his brother did not acknowledge him, he was too engrossed in Rebecca's cheap perfume.

"Do you think you can pull your tongue out of her ear long enough to say hi to your little brother?"

"Get outta here." Duane said, irritated at Billy's timing.

"What's Ma gonna think if she sees you out here like this?"

"Ma ain't home."

"Hey Billy," Rebecca smiled over her boyfriend's shoulder.

"Hey Beck," Billy blushed, "sorry if I'm disturbing you guys."

"You're not disturbing us," she smiled sweetly, pulling herself out of her boyfriend's grip, seemingly relieved at the intrusion. "Come and sit on the porch, Duane was just going to run inside and get some lemonade. Billy honey, would you like some?" Her lips drew up into a smile. Billy noticed the remnants of lipstick that smudged the corners of them. No doubt the rest of it had been eaten off by his brother's hungry mouth.

"Sure!" Setting his backpack down he seated himself on the porch swing. Rebecca ran a set of newly polished nails through her hair, letting her auburn curls drift to her shoulders. Billy loved to watch her do this, so much so that he didn't even notice Duane turn and head inside, slamming the screen door behind him and shifting himself in his pants.

"So how was school today Billy?" Rebecca asked, crossing her shapely legs. She wore a pair of jean shorts that cut off just above her thigh and a hot pink top that set off the remnants of her summer tan.

"It was good, you know, school," Billy shrugged.

"Do you have any homework?"

"Some." Again, he shrugged, wiping his sweaty palms off on his jeans.

"Well, you should always remember to do your homework. Would you like me to help you with it?"

"No!" A booming voice came from inside the house. Duane kicked the screen door open, holding three tall glasses of lemonade in his hands.

"Come on Duane; let's help the kid do his homework."

Billy took his glass from Duane and sighed. He hated it when she called him a kid. He wasn't a kid; he was twelve and only six years younger than her.

"He can do his own homework, now scram!" Duane nodded to the house and Billy stepped off the swing, smiling to Rebecca as he did.

Her thin fingers touched the collar of his shirt, "Sorry Billy," she smiled sweetly.

"'S'all right." He shrugged, slipping past Duane who quickly took his place on the swing.

CHAPTER 3

"Man, why'd ya hafta go do that for?" Billy shuffled his feet on the pavement and stuck his hands deeper into his pockets. He and Justin watched together as Eve walked away across the playground.

"Because she's nice and she doesn't know anyone and I thought it would be nice to invite her to hang out with us."

Billy rolled his eyes, "But it's just us guys Jus, and I like it that way. What are we supposed to talk about in front of a girl?"

Justin moved his eyes off Eve and turned back to his friend. "The same stuff we've always talked about." His hand reached up to shoo away the annoying buzz of a mosquito. The end of the recess bell rang and both boys followed the crowd of children back into the aging brick building. They lapsed into a comfortable silence. Billy knew it would be rude to un-invite her now, all the same, he preferred to not hang out with girls. It would ruin his image.

"Hey, I need to get something out of my locker." Justin and Billy headed over to the yellow bank of lockers that filled one of the interior walls.

The hallway was filled with the shuffle of feet and the hum of young voices. Billy stood quietly acknowledging some friends with a slight nod as they passed through the halls. Justin dug deep under a stack of books as a thin blue book slid from the top of his pile and hit the floor. Billy reached to pick it up, "Oh, man, Hemingway? Are you outta your mind?"

Quickly, Justin grabbed the book and shoved it under a folder, closing his locker door, "I happen to like reading it," he said defiantly.

"But man, it's no wonder everyone thinks you're a nerd, walkin' around readin' that? Come on, you can do better."

"Oh, and I suppose your sports fan magazines and the occasional stolen Playboy would be a step up?"

Billy rolled his eyes. "Whatever, just don't blame me if you never get a girlfriend; girls don't like guys that read."

"I don't care about girls." Annoyed, Justin adjusted the folders in front of him.

"Sure you do, as a matter of fact, I think there's one girl in particular that interests you, little Miss Evie. That's why you invited her to hang out with us tomorrow afternoon isn't it?" A comic grin filled Billy's face as he teased his friend.

"No! I just thought it would be a nice thing to do, now come on we're going to be late for class."

"Fine, whatever, but I still don't think it's cool hanging out with a girl."

Justin sat at the end of the pier, his feet swung over the side, dangling in the cool water. He rubbed his hands restlessly across his jeans, which he'd rolled up carefully to avoid getting wet. His feet kicked back and forth through the water in a gentle rhythmic motion. A boat sailed quietly past him and Justin raised a courteous hand to the skipper who returned his gesture. The lake was calm this time of year; the tourists that filled this area in the summer had now retreated back to their lives, leaving their Candlewood Lake memories in their photo albums. Some would return the following year, while others would seek out another part of the country to spend their summer vacations.

Justin's eyes ran across the length of the lake and then subconsciously, he reached into his backpack, pulling out his well-guarded Hemingway novel. He looked back into the woods and with no sight of Billy or Eve he opened it to the spot marked by a scrap of notepaper. His eyes devoured the words in front of him, entranced again in the story of the old fisherman.

"Hi Justin." A young female voice startled him from his pages. The book slammed shut with a clap. Justin twisted up to look at her, the sun filtered through the trees, illuminating a halo like circle around her golden hair. His hands self-consciously tried to cover the title of the book, but it was too late. A curious hand reached down and gently pulled it from his grip.

"What are you reading?"

Justin didn't reply. Girls don't like guys that read. Billy's words echoed in his head.

"Hemingway! Wow! You must be really smart. My dad tried to read him to me one night, but I could never understand it." Kicking off her sandals, Eve sat down beside him, folding her flowery summer dress beneath her.

"It's my dad's book." Justin replied timidly as he watched her hands slip through the pages. Eve looked up from the book and caught Justin's gaze, closing the book, her eyes drifted across the lake.

"You are so lucky to have been born here. What a beautiful place. I never knew there was a place like this."

"What do you mean, you didn't have a lake where you came from?"

"Well, sort of, but nothing like this. I'm glad we moved here."

"So am I," Justin smiled slightly.

"Justin, wasn't Billy supposed to join us?"

"Yeah, he probably got held up somewhere."

"Say, would you read to me from your book?"

Justin's eyes opened wide, "Really?" he asked, "You mean it?"

"Sure." A small laugh bubbled up from her throat at Justin's excitement, "I'd love to hear you read Hemingway."

Carefully, Justin picked the book up from her lap and then turned the pages until he found the perfect section to read. As the words escaped his lips, Eve watched him and then turned her attention back to the lake, letting the story of the old man and the sea overtake her. She could almost see Santiago holding on to the fish with all his might. The cool breeze that swept in off the lake caressed her face and played with the tendrils of her hair. Justin's voice continued its animated reading and the story played itself out before her.

Justin could barely contain his excitement as he continued through the story. He was reading from one of his favorite books to the most beautiful girl he'd ever seen.

It was by all accounts, a perfect moment.

Billy never showed up to join them, Justin was certain it was because he was upset he invited Eve. Billy could be so pigheaded sometimes.

CHAPTER 4

"Billy, now listen here. You're going with me to see Maggie. I've made you an appointment!"

Billy leaned against the car, his folded arms pressed to his chest, "But mom, I made plans already, and I hate going to that girlie place!"

"That's too bad, I told you about this before you left for school this morning, maybe this will teach you to listen when I talk to you." Victoria Freeman snapped open the car door and slid in behind the steering wheel. She leaned over to unlatch the passenger seat while her reluctant son stood by.

"Get in!" she fumed, her hands were gripping the steering wheel with such a force, it was turning her knuckles white. Billy caught a glint of something in her eye and he knew better than to try and push her any further. She might start having one of her dark moods and Billy wanted to avoid that at all costs. She hadn't had a dark mood in a while and Billy hoped she wouldn't.

Victoria soon forgot her anger and chatted with her son during the short drive to Maggie Owen's hair salon. *Curl Up and Dye* was a busy four-chair shop, offering all the latest in hairstyles and equipment. Maggie insisted on only the best for her customers. Victoria turned into the newly striped parking lot and found a spot right up front.

"We're here!" Her voice was light and happy. She enjoyed her visits to the salon; Maggie always had the best gossip and seemed to know the most interesting people. Billy followed his mother into the shop. Once inside, they were greeted by the buzz of hairdryers and the hum of voices swapping stories. Billy despised getting a haircut here, but his mother was always adamant about supervising how her youngest child looked.

"Vickie!" Maggie called out over the din. "I'll be right with you!" Even after twenty years of living in Connecticut, Maggie's southern drawl was still evident.

Victoria offered a smile and a slight wave and seated herself in one of the padded, pink chairs. Maggie had owned *Curl Up and Dye* for nearly eighteen years. When she first moved to New Fairfield, she'd arrived full of hope and thankful to be away from her parents constant nagging that she should settle down with some nice young southern boy. The thought of ending up like her mother was more than Maggie could bear, so she packed up her one pink vinyl overnight bag and left for New York to become a Broadway star. After spending two months in the city trying for audition after audition, her money ran out and so did her patience. She followed a tip from a friend about a great summer job at a lake resort, and once she left the city she never went back. She started a life all her own, soon she had a small cottage on the quiet lake front and more friends than she'd ever known.

"Becky! So good to see you here helping your mother!" Victoria twisted herself in her chair to smile at the young woman.

Rebecca looked up from her shampoo, "Yes, well, she's just getting so busy these days."

"Looks like you have a talent for this work."

"It must run in the family!" Maggie chimed in putting the finishing touches on a wash and set.

Billy fidgeted in his chair, he thought of his friends and knew Justin would be upset. But he would understand, Justin always did.

"All right Billy, why don't you come over here and we'll get you washed up," Rebecca smiled.

Billy got up and walked over to her, a smile stole across his face. Getting his hair washed by Becky was the only good thing about this. Billy leaned his head back into the basin and Becky ran her red painted fingernails through his hair, massaging his scalp.

"So how's it goin' Billy?" She asked, smacking a piece of gum between her teeth.

"Good, real good."

"School all right? Do you have homework today?"

"Yeah, but I'll do it later when I get back." Billy found himself unable to say anything funny or smart whenever he was around her.

"So, I might stop by later today to see Duane, you think he'll be home?"

"Yeah, I guess, I don't know."

Becky ran her hands through his hair, washing it clean. Billy was disappointed when it was over.

"All right, looks like you're ready for me," Maggie waved him over. Victoria took advantage of an empty seat beside them.

"So what's new Maggie?" She asked.

Maggie combed thoughtfully through Billy's thick black hair. "Got a nice head of hair on you boy, some girl's gonna love runnin' her fingers through it someday."

Billy squirmed in his seat, wishing the whole mess was over.

"So Vickie, what do you think about my Becky datin' your boy?"

"Oh, Duane just thinks she's the best thing Maggie, I have never seen him like this!"

"Well who knows, maybe someday we'll be in-laws!" Maggie threw her head back in laughter. She was a tall wiry thing, all teeth and bones, and when she laughed, even slightly, it shook her entire body.

"Well I don't know about that, I think Duane might be a ways off from marriage."

"So, how's Terry doin'?"

"Good, you know I can't believe they've both graduated already. It's hard to believe that my boys are eighteen!"

"And you don't look a day over thirty!" Maggie smiled. "They do grow up fast don't they?"

"Yes, they do. Terry's even considering Harvard; he got accepted there you know? Full scholarship," Victoria beamed.

"You're kiddin', why that's just great!"

"I can't believe how different Duane and Terrence are for being identical twins, they couldn't be more contrary."

"Well, that's good when you think about it right? I mean how else would you be able to tell them apart?"

A smile tugged on Victoria's lips. Thankfully she felt like smiling today, sometimes an eternity would go by before she felt a happy moment. She learned to cherish them before the dark ones would appear and take control of her mind.

CHAPTER 5

It was the summer of 1949 when Victoria met her husband. Hank had come to Shreveport, Maine in search of a summer job. Fishing boats paid extremely well and he was saving up to buy a car. Victoria was an Esler back then and the Esler family was one of Maine's oldest and most wealthy residents. They had high hopes that their only daughter would marry one of the well-to-do men in the area, but their dreams of a lavish wedding vanished the day Hank Freeman sauntered into town.

The afternoon had been a great success for Hank, he had landed a job, made a new friend and now, he was beginning to discover the beauty that was Shreveport. Hank leaned his tall, athletic frame against a lamppost. A bottle of Coke dangled between his fingers. Every now and again he would lift the sweaty hour-shaped glass to his mouth and take a sip. All without taking his clear blue eyes off the blond across the street. He'd watched her pull up to the corner soda shop on a shiny red bicycle, soon she was surrounded by a crowd of her giggling friends and deep in conversation, they entered Ruth Anne's Sodas & Sweets. Hank could still see her, sitting with her back to him, her curly blond hair bouncing off her shoulders each time she laughed. Finally, he got up the courage to walk across the street and meet the girl of his dreams.

The soda shop was filled with the sounds of laughter and Perry Como, whose smooth deep voice wafted from a worn jukebox. Hank twirled the Coke bottle in his hand, then nervously ran his fingers through his short, cropped black hair. He walked past their table first, when he was certain he was a safe enough distance away, he turned to look over his shoulder. He was shocked to find the woman of his dreams looking right at him, a slight smile tugging at her crimson lips.

Hank thought back to that day often. It reminded him of the moment. The one everyone gets, that once in a lifetime feeling when everything seems to fall into place with a large and obvious "click." The one moment when everything seems exactly as it should be, exactly perfect. That was Hank Freeman's one moment of perfection. The one he would hang onto when Victoria's mind would cloud over and she would no longer be the woman he fell in love with on that summer's day. When she would become someone he did not know, and could not love.

🍁 🍁 🍁

Hank pulled into his driveway, threw his truck into park and slipped out of the driver's seat. His heavy construction boots pushed into the gravel, making a grinding sound.

"Looks like you got a haircut son," Hank smiled. Billy was sitting on the front porch swing, his eyes focused on his hands that he'd tucked between his thighs.

"Yeah, sure did." Billy still didn't look up.

Hank's heavy boots thudded across the wooden porch; he sat down next to his youngest son, pushing the swing back as he did.

"Well from the looks of things, I'd say you lost your best friend in the process."

Billy tilted is head up to his father, "I didn't lose him, but I'm sure Justin's mad at me. I was supposed to meet him today and mom just up and took me to Maggie's. Then when we got there, she forgot I was even around and spent the whole time gossiping!"

Hank threw a protective arm around his son who was already the spitting image of his father, "Well, son, you know that's what ladies like to do. They like to gossip. Besides you needed a haircut and I'm sure Justin will understand."

Billy shrugged his small shoulders, "Yeah, I guess."

"Now, how about we see what your mother's making for dinner."

"Pot roast," Victoria smiled from the front door.

"Hello Vic, looks like you spent some time in Maggie's chair too." Hank got up, pecking his wife on the cheek. The scent of freshly washed hair tingled his senses.

"You smell great," he breathed into her ear.

"Don't mess up my hair."

Hank reached a long arm around her waist, pulling her closer, "I wouldn't think of it."

CHAPTER 6

Judith hoped that her afternoon of charity work would help ingratiate her with the women of New Fairfield, Connecticut. She drove her blue Cutlass across the narrow blacktop road flanked on either side by naked trees with sharp, angry looking branches.

Every month, the Women's Club would meet to work on some sort of charity function. This time it was holiday care packages for the troops in Vietnam. Mary VanSant had extended an invitation to New Fairfield's newest addition and Judy gladly accepted. She'd never been a part of such an elite group of people before and she was itching to make a good impression.

The meeting and care package assembly would take place this month at the New Fairfield Inn. It was owned by a wispy, young Belgian woman who bore a striking resemblance to Ingrid Bergman and her often inebriated Swedish husband who could out cook any Manhattan chef, even if he was dead drunk.

Judy pushed through the heavy oak door and was immediately met with the buzz of twenty different conversations going on at the same time. A ring of laughter lifted above the voices. It was a loud, braying laugh, the kind that belonged in a bar, not at a woman's charity function. She heard it again, this time it seemed even louder.

"Mags, you got one hell of a wit about you, you do…" the voice got closer, and Judy could see a woman almost stagger out of the crowded room.

"Well, who do we have here?" the woman's thick hands flew to her full hips, she took her stance, narrowing her eyes to gaze at the stranger.

Judy fumbled with the latch on her purse, "I'm Judith Phillips, Mary VanSant asked me to join you today."

A sweaty hand reached up and slapped Judy on the shoulders, sending her in a slight stumble forward.

"Well, glad ta have you here! My name's Bernice, but everyone calls me Bernie. Can I call you Judy?" She leaned in closer, pursing her red lips together as if she were about to confide her deepest secrets, "No one here stands on ceremony you see. We're just all tryin' to do what we can for our boys overseas."

"Judy, so glad you could make it!" Mary VanSant's voice rose above the din. Judy turned to see Mary in the hall, a bright, welcoming smile on her face.

"Thank you for inviting me."

"I see you've met Bernie." Mary said, her voice hinted the faintest chuckle.

"Yep, we've met," Bernie announced, "well, I better git back to my post. Gotta keep these women in line. Pleasure to meet you, we're glad to have the extra set of hands." Bernice turned her generous body and headed back down the hall to check on everyone's work.

"You must forgive Bernie, she doesn't mean to be so abrasive, that's just her way." Mary's face filled with a warmth Judy had come to expect.

"No, it's fine, she's very nice. Just a bit…uh…"

"Startling?"

"Yes, that's it, startling."

A laugh erupted from Mary's throat, "Well, that's Bernie for you. Come on, I want you to meet everyone…"

"Vhy Mary, who do ve have here?" A sweet thickly accented voice asked. Charlotte Verhoeve stepped lightly across the polished wood floors of the entryway.

"Charlotte, this is Judy Phillips, she and her family just moved to the area."

"Velcome Judy!" The blond woman smiled. She did indeed bear a striking resemblance to Ingrid Bergman, Judy noted.

"Charlotte and her husband were kind enough to open up their bed & breakfast to us for this event."

A glamorous smile filled her face. "Oh, it's nothing, Sven and I were happy to help."

"Speaking of which, where is Sven?" Mary asked with some hesitation.

"Oh, are you kidding? He wouldn't be caught dead in a room full of vomen. He's in the kitchen making some finger sandwiches for everyone. Say, vhy don't I take Judy on a tour?"

"Great," Mary smiled, "I'll meet you in the dining room when you're done."

By the time Judy and Charlotte returned from their tour, Sven had readied several plates of his best finger sandwiches and several pots of steaming Earl Gray.

"Judy, this is my husband, Sven." She smiled, reaching for his hand.

He held out the other to Judy. "Pleased to make your acquaintance."

"Nice to meet you as well, you have a lovely place here." Judy could smell the faintest scent of bourbon on his breath, and a twinkle of something in his eye she could not place.

"Yes, well we're very proud of it."

Charlotte touched her husband's cheek with a light kiss, "Thank you for doing all of this dahling!"

"Anything for my beautiful wife." He smiled to Judy. She sensed the two were very much in love, but from what she'd gathered from bits and pieces of overheard conversations, their marriage was a stormy one.

"Everyone!" Charlotte called out over the crowd, "My husband has made us all something to eat and I'd like to introduce you to our newest member, Judy Phillips!"

Heads turned and suddenly, Judy felt the awkwardness of it rise up from her toes. She fumbled with her purse, managing a weak, "thank you" as the women applauded both for the sandwiches and for their group's newest member. Mary emerged from the crowd to rescue her new friend.

"Come on, there's someone else I want you to meet." She took her arm gently and led her to an open seat at one of the round tables that filled the dining room of the Inn.

"Well, it's our newest member, come to sit at our table!" Bernice announced.

"Judy, this is Vickie, Billy's mom."

"Hello, nice to meet you," Vickie smiled, looking up from her work. "We're glad to have your help."

"It's nice to meet you as well. I'm glad Mary asked me to join you all," Judy sat down in one of the wooden chairs. "I guess our children are becoming quite good friends."

"Oh, goodness," Mary chimed in, "Justin does nothing else but talk about Eve. He's quite taken with your daughter." She winked.

Vickie smiled to herself remembering Billy's initial reaction to their newest friend. To him, she was just another annoying girl.

"Yeah, I see them together all the time!" Bernie smiled. Charlotte was coming around with the tray of sandwiches and Bernie quickly reached for one, "This sure was great of Sven to do this for us," she smiled.

"Vel, anything for the cause you know." Charlotte bent to offer a sandwich to the rest of the table.

"Well, you know it's a sad, sad thing we're doin' makin' these boxes for those poor boys overseas. They're dyin' off faster than we can ship 'em over."

"Yes," Vickie added, "it's a very sad war."

"All these young men…" Mary sighed, feeling grateful that Justin was too young to be drafted.

"Well, even though the President says they are reducing troops, it seems like they're takin' more every day," Bernie arched an eyebrow. "Say, aren't your two boys eighteen now?"

Vickie ran her tongue over her bottom lip, "Yes, they are."

"Well, seems to me they'll be callin' them soon enough." Bernie felt Mary's hand on her arm. "Wasn't their birthday number 55 in this year's lottery?

"No, they won't be calling them over!" Vickie's voice quivered in fear and dread, despair settled into her words, "they just won't!"

"Vickie, I'm certain you're right," Mary soothed, resting a protective hand on her friend's shoulder. "Why the draft board is only calling the top ten or fifteen percent these days."

"Vic, I'm sorry, I shouldna said that, it was wrong of me. They're not takin' every eighteen year old, 'specially in this part of the country," Bernie said, her tone hushed. "And they're callin' less and less of 'em."

Judy sat quietly listening to the conversation unfold. The rattle in Vickie's voice was evident, but Mary's quiet words seemed to have a calming effect on her.

"Well, ladies, mind if I join you?" Maggie Owen smiled, pulling up an extra chair. Everyone was glad for the interruption. "I'm sorry, did I walk in on something?" Tension slid across the table, Vickie did not look up from her work; Maggie noticed her hands trembling.

"No, of course not, please join us. Say, have you met Judy Phillips?"

"Not officially, no," Maggie smiled. "It's a pleasure to meet you."

"Maggie here has the best hair shop in the New Fairfield area," Mary explained.

"Thanks, and I'll tell you what, if you stop by sometime I'll give you a free hair cut. It'll be my way of saying welcome to Candlewood Lake."

"Thank you Maggie! I'll call to make an appointment next week."

"Great, then we can really get to know one another." Maggie reached for an empty box and began filling it with gifts from home.

"I have to warn you," Mary began teasingly, "Maggie here knows all the best gossip in town. If it doesn't make the newspaper, I can guarantee you Maggie will know about it."

"Well ain't that the truth!" Bernie threw her head back in laughter. "Say, is that daughter of yours still datin' Duane?"

"Yes," Maggie smiled, "if we're lucky, maybe Vickie and I will be in-laws before too long."

"Is it that serious?" Mary asked, picking at her sandwich.

"Well, Duane's been dating her for about six months now, but he thinks the world of her." A hesitant smile crept across Vickie's face, temporarily diminishing her feelings of dread.

"Well, my Becky just thinks the sun sets and rises on him, I tell you. He makes her happier than I've ever seen her."

"Now Vic, what about Terry, is he still goin' out with that Stanhope girl?"

"Yes," Vickie said proudly. The Stanhopes were one of the areas oldest and most prominent families, "they've been going out for three months now."

"Wow, now wouldn't that be somethin' if they got hitched." Bernie pushed another filled box aside.

"Well, it's a bit too early for that I think, I'm just glad they've both found such nice young women." The feeling that threatened to engulf her had diminished, and quietly she took a calming sip of her tea.

The conversation remained intentionally light. All further thoughts of boys being drafted were left unsaid.

CHAPTER 7

The letters arrived on the same bright, spring day. They didn't even have the decency to send them a day apart. In crisp, smooth, sterile envelopes they sat, unwelcome and obtrusive on her kitchen table. Victoria Freeman gazed at them mutely.

Both names were typed in uneven lettering, Duane Phillip Freeman on one and Terrance Parker Freeman on the other. She had no idea how long she sat silently in her uncomfortable chair, staring at them. But the minutes slipped painfully past her, like swallowing pills one at a time.

"Hey Momma, whatcha doin'?"

Suddenly, she was yanked from her dark thoughts by Terry who strolled into the bright kitchen, a winsome smile on his face.

Victoria turned her face up, in a slow, almost painful motion. Her eyes were clouded and urgent.

"Hey, what's this?" Asking the question he already instinctively knew, his hand reached for one of the official envelopes. But his movement was stopped quickly by his mother's desperate reach.

"No, son you don't have to go!" Her voice brittle from disuse and dread, she wrapped her thin fingers around his hand.

Terry sat down beside her, gently running a protective arm around her shoulders. She felt little comfort in his reassuring gesture. She could feel the needles of tears pricking her eyes and reluctantly she let one slide down her face.

"Boys go over there and die! Hundreds of them every day! You can go to Canada, get far away from here."

"Momma, then where would I be? Alone in a foreign country, running away from my duty."

Victoria bit her bottom lip until she thought it would bleed. She was disappointed that it didn't.

"They can't take you both away. Not at the same time." Her voice had dulled to a barely inaudible whisper.

"Hey! What's going on here?" Duane's voice boomed from the door, Billy trailed closely behind.

"Yeah, what's up…?" Billy's grin slid from his face when he saw his mother.

Terry shot both of them a warning look, "Duane it looks like we've been drafted. Momma's very upset about this." He added quickly, knowing how excited his brother would be about the news.

"I'm sorry you're upset Momma, but we'll be fine. Terry and I, we'll look out for one another. 'Sides, you should be proud, we're goin' to defend our country."

"What about me?" Billy's voice was thick with disenchantment. "They can't take both of you and leave me!"

"You're too young, besides, you need to stay here and look after momma for us." Terry was fingering the edge of the envelope as though it were some complicated puzzle.

Billy scuffed his feet against the newly polished floor, digging his hands into his pockets, "I never get to have any fun!" his words trailed behind him as he pushed through the kitchen door.

He stood on their gravel driveway, trying to decide where to go. He kicked a pebble with his worn shoe and watched it skitter away in fear. He wanted to go to war, he wanted to fight and shoot guns. It looked fun on TV. Momma would just never understand, he huffed. Let them go, who cares! The angry thought scurried through his mind as he strode the familiar route into town.

Finley's Sweet Shoppe was the best place to go when one was feeling blue. Billy pushed open the worn door. Over his head, a rusty bell tinkled announcing a new arrival. The delicious swirling aromas of a hundred sugary sweet treats tickled his nose. Glass cases enticingly filled with every imaginable chocolate sat waiting to cheer him up.

Lloyd Finley walked from his small back office to greet his new customer. In his forty years of owning a candy shop he had acquired the skill of a seasoned bartender and knew when one of his customers needed cheering up. Lloyd leaned his stocky five-foot eight frame on the glass case that was mesmerizing the young boy.

"Billy Freeman, what can I do for you today?" Lloyd said in a voice filled with a thick Irish lilt. He peered at Billy through the thin glasses that dangled precariously at the end of his nose.

"Just lookin' Mr. Finley."

"Now, Billy, you seem kind of down, if you don't mind me saying."

Billy stuck his hands deeper into his pockets, "My brothers are goin' off to fight in Nam, and I have to stay home." His voice was as monotone as if he were reading from a scrap of paper he'd found beneath his shoe.

"Aye, and you want to go too, is that it lad?"

Billy knew he'd come to the right place. Mr. Finley always understood any problems a boy might have.

"Yeah," Billy gave in reluctantly, "I kinda do."

"Well, I've got just the thing, candy for the brave ones that have to stay behind."

"Brave?" A light filled Billy's tanned face.

"Well, of course," Finley smiled. "You didn't know? By special order of the President of the United States no less. One brave son must stay home to guard his family."

Billy eyed him suspiciously, "You joshin' me right?"

The shopkeepers face curved into a mischievous smile, "Well, perhaps just a bit, but you are still a brave soul, Billy Freeman." Finley reached into the case, pulling a dark lump of caramel, peanuts and chocolate carefully from the stack of newly arrived treats.

"I just got these in today, and I've needed someone to try them for me."

Billy's hand opened, and in one hungry movement, the piece disappeared. It filled his mouth, spreading its sweet richness onto his tongue. Suddenly, his life clicked back into place. Lloyd Finley could see the chocolate work it's magic again. Even though he'd observed hundreds, maybe thousands of children in his years of owning Finley's Sweet Shoppe, he never tired of seeing the expression on their young faces when the seductive tastes took hold of them, transforming a dark mood into youthful euphoria.

Billy sucked and chewed, letting the slippery caramel slide down his throat.

"This is the best Mr. Finley!" he said, finally able to speak.

"Good lad! Then I can sell them in my shop, because you know I only sell the best. Here, why don't you try another one, make sure they all taste the same." Seeing Billy Freeman's angst over his brother's departure evaporate with each swirl of chocolate made the arthritic pain in his back vanish. He wanted none of the silly medicine his doctor kept prescribing. The only medicine Lloyd Finley needed was a satisfied customer.

CHAPTER 8

Victoria twisted restlessly on the mattress in an attempt to gain some comfort. Beside her, Hank's breathing was deep and even. As much as she had willed sleep to take her the night before, it had come only in brief fleeting moments of seconds and sometimes minutes. Her foot brushed his strong calf and rested there, enjoying the warmth of his body. She felt only a vague reassurance having him beside her. As much as he wanted to, he would never be able to understand what it felt like for a mother to lose her sons. Nor would he ever be able to understand the dark, swirling thoughts that consumed her mind.

"Did you sleep much?" his voice was velvety rough and thick with sleep.

"No." The word was a barely audible hiss. Hank rolled over, throwing a well-toned arm around her delicate shoulder and spooning her body.

"Hon, they're gonna be fine. This is just something they have to do." Hank could feel her body tense.

"They don't have to do anything. They can get away from here. Far away."

"Then you'd never see them anyway." His breath was warm on her neck, his body relishing the feel of her velvet skin against his.

"Yes, but at least I would know that they're safe. Instead of in some Godforsaken country."

"Vic, what kind of a life would they have and what kind of an example would they be setting for their families, running away like that?"

Victoria shrugged him off her, she was in no mood for his idle reasoning. "You just want to boast to your friends that you have two sons fighting in this damned war, that's all."

His fist hit the pillow. "No damn it, that's not it. Look, it's not like we're the only ones that are going through this. Two other families from here are sending their sons off too. You're not being singled out here Vic, this isn't some conspiracy against you."

Victoria swung her legs over the side of the bed, "I've told you that's not what I think! It's unfair. Just terribly unfair! And now we have to spend their last day home at some damned send-off lunch!"

Hank fell back into bed. It was useless arguing with her at this point. He watched his wife shrug into her robe, fastening it around her tiny waist.

"Honey, please, for everyone's sake. Let's not make their final day at home unpleasant ok?"

Victoria paused at the door, "I will try Hank. I'm going downstairs to make breakfast." She swept out of the room and Hank was left alone with his thoughts and the remnants of the angry conversation she left behind.

The morning sun leaked in through the gaps in Billy's bedroom curtains. He kicked his young legs deeper under the covers, drawing the quilt farther over his shoulders. The scent of their traditional Sunday morning breakfast crept up the stairs, tendrils of it wafting under his door to invade his senses. He breathed in the delicious aroma, which served to momentarily dispel the depressive state that had infested their home since his brothers had been drafted.

The past few weeks had been sickeningly somber. His mother's unstable moods came with more frequency and several times he'd arrive home from school to find her locked behind her bedroom door. Her sobs could be heard throughout the house.

Reminding himself that today was the day of the big send off luncheon he quickly wiggled out of his sheets and ran down the stairs to the kitchen.

"Good morning Mom," Billy placed a light kiss on her cheek. He could taste the salt from her tears. He hoped that soon, this would all be over and they could return to some sort of a normal life again. Although with Duane and Terry heading off to war, he doubted anything would ever be normal again.

"Good morning sweetheart, breakfast is nearly ready." Victoria feigned a smile. The pan in front of her popped and sizzled and she tried to focus all her attention into the black skillet.

Pulling a chair out from under the table he sat down and fiddled with the flowery placemat. He heard his brothers on the stairs, their identical smiling faces appearing in the doorway at the same time.

"Good morning Momma!" Terry smiled, wrapping his arms around her shoulders; he placed a thoughtful kiss on her cheek. The guilt of his relief that soon this would all be over, washed over him. He knew he could not stand spending another day or night in that house listening to his Mom wail and sob, and making promises to her he knew he would never be able to keep, all the while trying to pretend none of this scared the crap out of him.

Duane followed his brother's lead, hugging his mother and gently kissing her on the cheek. "Hey Momma…" his words trailed off after tasting her salty cheek. Like his brother, he wanted this all to be over soon. "I'm going to pick up Rebecca this morning so she can go with us to mass, is that ok?"

"That's fine Duane, Terry will Olivia be joining us as well?" Victoria said hopefully.

Terry sat down beside his brother. "No, mom you know her family never misses service at United Methodist."

"Well, I would think considering the circumstances they would make an exception." Terry rolled his eyes and Billy chuckled silently.

"Mom, it's been their families' church for hundreds of years, I don't expect them to change just for me. Besides she and her family will join us at the luncheon afterward."

"Oh, good!" A sincere smile filled Victoria's face.

Duane frowned. "You know, I wish you would make a fuss like that over Becky's family. I know they're not Stanhopes but we've been dating for a while and you've never even invited her mother over to the house."

Victoria turned the flame off under the skillet and threw two slices of bread into the toaster. "You know I like Maggie, she's a good friend…"

"But she's not a Stanhope…" Duane shuffled his feet impatiently.

"Who's not a Stanhope?" Hank entered the fragrant kitchen, picking up bits of the conversation.

"Becky and her mom," Billy said, filling in the gaps for his father. "Duane thinks that Mom likes Olivia more because she's loaded." Billy threw his head back in a mock regal fashion.

"William!" Victoria spun around.

"That'll be enough of that," Hank grinned, he'd heard this same conversation many times, but now it was a refreshing change to the discussions of the past weeks.

"Good morning Vickie."

"'Morning Hank." Victoria breathed a sigh that curled inward. Their last day together had already begun.

❧ ❧ ❧

The Freemans pulled up to the church, crammed into the family's faded blue station wagon. Billy sat wedged uncomfortably between his parents, while his brothers and Rebecca sat quietly in back. The parking lot of St. Edward the Confessor Catholic Church was nearly filled to capacity. New Fairfield was sending four of its finest young men off to war the following day, and everyone wanted to pray for their safe return.

"Looks like it'll be a full house today," Hank remarked stepping from the car. "You boys should feel honored," he continued, "this is all for you."

An irritated puff of air escaped his wife's lips, but she refrained from commenting.

Billy freed himself from the confines of the front seat, bolting from it as though he were shot from a canon. "I'll see you inside," he called over his shoulder, "I'm goin' to find my friends."

Hank and Victoria watched their son race between the parked cars across the dirt parking lot, "Let him," Hank reached for his wife's hand. "He needs something normal in his life right now."

Victoria only shrugged; she knew her husband was right. If she was going to preserve the day, she needed to keep her paranoia in check.

Rebecca clutched Duane's hand tightly as they followed Hank, Victoria and Terry up to the church. The family was welcomed immediately by Father Matthew.

"It's so good to have so many people here today," Father Matthew threw them a warm smile as he shook first Hank's hand, then his sons'.

"Yes, Father, it's really great to see everyone here to support us," Duane replied.

"And how are you doing Victoria?" Father Matthew asked soothingly.

"Fine Father, we're holding up."

The priest could see the gaping holes in her composure and the darkness that hovered along the edges of her smile. A gentle arm went over her shoulders. "Why don't you come inside for a moment so we can talk before mass begins."

Victoria smiled willingly and followed behind him, up the stone stairs and into the sanctuary.

"Dad, Beck and I would like to walk around for a bit, we'll be back," Duane pulled his girlfriend with him, not waiting for his father's reply.

"Those two would probably rather be any place but here," Hank shrugged, placing a hand on Terry's shoulder. "Come on son, let's go say hi to some folks."

Over his father's shoulder, Terry could see a fringe of blond hair as a young woman pushed through the group of people who crowded the walkway.

"Terrance!" she called out in her cultured voice.

"Dad, look, it's Olivia. I wonder what she's doing here."

Terry stepped out to meet her, "Olivia? What's going on? Is everything all right?"

Olivia raised a delicate hand to push a strand of blond hair back in place. "Yes, everything is fine, Father said I could attend your church since it's a special occasion and all. Hello, Mr. Freeman," Olivia smiled with perfect teeth, her bright blue eyes sparkled and Hank could see how smitten she was with his son.

"Good to see you again, glad you could join us today."

"Yes sir, I am too. My parents will be attending the gathering this afternoon."

"Well, I'm sure glad to see you," Terry clutched her hand, the sweet smell of her wafted in his direction and suddenly, he was happy. Olivia had a way of making him happy without knowing why. "Dad, we're gonna go for a walk ok?"

"Sure son," Hank nodded to an already absent Terry.

CHAPTER 9

The following morning, Billy stood, surrounded by his family, on an uneven sidewalk, waiting for the bus to arrive: the bus that would carry his brothers off to war at precisely 8:15 a.m. The orders were non-negotiable. They would spend six weeks in the sweaty bowels of some desert army camp learning how to hold a gun, before being shipped off to the wet jungles of Vietnam.

Even though U.S. troops were slowly being removed from Southeast Asia, New Fairfield woke to find four of its fine young men standing amid their families waiting to be shipped off to war. The same three families who had beamed with pride as they watched their sons graduate less than a year ago. There would be no fanfare for them when they graduated from boot camp. Only a quick call made on a well-worn pay phone followed by a loud uncomfortable flight that would seem to last an eternity.

Victoria stood behind dark, concealing glasses in interminable silence. A shaky and unstable hand played with the fringe of her favorite blue flower print dress. She raised her tear-swollen eyes to focus again on her boys, both of them looking tall and handsome in their freshly pressed shirts, crisp new jeans and stiff white sneakers. At their feet, regulation green duffels sat stuffed with new stationery, family photographs and other personal reminders of home.

Except for the occasional hushed whispers Duane and Rebecca shared, no one spoke a word. Rebecca tugged lightly on the French twist Duane was so fond of. Becky could feel the tendrils of a headache forming at her temples. She wasn't sure if it was from the hairdo, or from tossing around with Duane in the backseat of his father's car the night before. She reached a freshly manicured hand out for his, remembering the feel of his weight on her and the urgent way he had thrashed around inside of her most of the night. He'd discussed their future with some trepidation and she could sense the uncertainty in his voice. Becky had tried to convince him that nothing would change. She certainly didn't want to hear a hundred promises he was not yet prepared to keep; spoken by a man chased with the urgency of leaving home to fight a war he knew little about.

A faded green bus cranked loudly as it turned the corner onto Brush Hill Road. Terry inhaled slowly in hopes that a deep breath would calm the nervous seed of tension growing in his stomach. A flood of emotion washed over him bringing with it both relief and guilt as he clutched Olivia's hand tighter in his. He heard a muffled sob escape his mother's lips as the bus stuttered to a screeching stop. The driver, unsmiling, cranked the door open and with a gush of wind it stood wide like a gaping mouth waiting to swallow them all whole. In one last act of bravery, Terry was the first to throw his duffel over his shoulder while his brother shoved his tongue down Becky's mouth one last time.

Terry looked down at his little brother, "Look out for Momma, ok?"

"I will; you better write."

"I'll write everyday, I promise."

Billy felt his body tense and quickly wrapped himself around Terry as though he were hanging on to a life preserver. Suddenly, he realized he would be alone in the house. The only brother left, at least for a while.

He needed his friends. He wished they were with him right now; it would make all of this seem a bit easier.

"I'll be back before you know it." Reluctantly, Terry extracted himself from his brother's grip, spotting the bus driver's impatient look. Terry wrapped an arm around his mother, steadying her as her tears fell out from underneath the rim of her glasses.

"It's gonna be all right Momma. I'll be home soon, I promise." How many times had he said this same sentence in the past week? Fifty, a hundred, he'd lost count.

"Dad," Terry began, reaching for his father's hand but Hank pulled his son closer, reaching his arm around him in a surprisingly emotional gesture.

"Good luck son, make us proud." His voice was steady as his large hands delivered a gentle slap on Terry's back.

"I will Dad." Terry felt his voice crack, and knew it was time to go before the exterior he'd worked so hard to protect, crumbled at his feet.

He kissed Olivia tenderly. "I'll be back," he whispered as a tear slid down her cheek.

"I know. You always keep your promises, Terrance Freeman."

Becky watched as Duane followed his brother onto the bus. Her eyes burned bright with unshed tears. She could not allow herself to cry, at least not yet. She wanted to see her boyfriend off with dignity, to hell with everything after that. Two more reluctant recruits stepped aboard and with a clap, the door shut and the bus sputtered back to life, pulling away from the curb. In a cloud of exhaust, they were gone, smiling and waving out the window as the bus turned the corner and headed out of town.

Billy sprinted from the sorry scene as soon as the bus was out of sight. Justin and Eve had promised to meet him at the pier and he could hardly wait to see them and pretend this day had never happened.

❧ ❧ ❧

Justin and Eve sat leaning against a thick oak that shadowed the small pier that the three friends had dubbed as "theirs," the earth was cool beneath them. Eve picked up a bright red leaf and studied it carefully. Billy promised the moment he could get away he would join them with stories of what it was like to watch your brothers go off to war.

"Do you think they'll be safe?" Eve hugged her knees closer to her chest.

"Of course they'll be safe and home before you know it. This war won't last much longer," Justin soothed.

"But I hear terrible things, they say boys are dying in the jungles. It's so scary."

"Evie, war is a terrible thing. And a lot of people have lost their lives already. But I'm certain that Terry and Duane will come home safely."

Eve bit down on her bottom lip, "What if they don't, what will we do? What will Billy do?"

Justin turned to her, resting a hand on her arm. "You can't talk like that, especially not in front of Billy or his family. This is going to be hard enough on them."

"I know, I guess, I just, don't feel safe anymore. I felt so safe here, like nothing could hurt us or touch us. That feeling is gone."

"You're still safe." Justin's voice was almost an inaudible whisper, but he knew in his heart how she felt. No one ever thought the ugly hand of war would have such a far reach, especially not the Freemans.

A crush of leaves and a holler from the woods told them that Billy had arrived. Their conversation would end.

"Hey guys, what's up?" Billy was out of breath, dressed in a pair of black pants and his Sunday jacket.

"We're just waiting for you Billy boy, so how did it go?"

An impatient puff of air escaped his lips, and he dropped himself onto the soft ground. Forgetting for a moment his mother's certain wrath when she realized he'd sat in the dirt wearing his only pair of good trousers.

"Man, am I glad that's over!"

"What happened?" Eve tried to feign a smile.

"Oh, you know it was just like we wus goin' to a funeral. Everyone all somber, like they were never coming home or something. The only one who seemed like he wasn't about to roll over and die was my dad. Mom's been in one of her moods ever since this happened, crying all the time. Locking herself in her room. It's weird, it's like she's someone else and not my mom."

"She's probably depressed, I'm sure she'll snap out of it in time."

"Yeah, Jus, time…how much more time does she need? My dad's been sleeping on the couch 'cause she locks him out of their room. She threw a fit because Duane and Terry refused to head for Canada. Can you imagine? She wanted them to just go somewhere and hide!"

Eve watched as Billy told his story, she couldn't imagine what he must have been going through this whole time, and he never let on until now.

"Billy, look, you've got to understand how tough this must be on her. She's sending her two sons off to fight a war a million miles away," Justin offered.

Billy said nothing. Instead, he began picking acorns off the ground and tossing them in the air. "I wanted to go," he said finally.

The sun angled sharply through the trees, and for a moment, none of them spoke. The only sound to be heard was the occasional flutter of a bird as it moved from one tree to the next. It was enough for Billy to know he had a place to go, a place that wasn't filled with the talk of war unless he wanted to discuss it. A place where he could forget for a moment the damaged home he would eventually have to return to.

"Hey, guys, I got an idea…why don't we see if we can borrow a boat from old man Ritter's dock and sail on the lake for a while?"

"You think he'll let us?" Eve asked.

"Sure, he's done it before. 'Sides, Justin's a good sailor, he knows boats and Ritter trusts him with anything. So what do you say Jus? Are you game?"

"Sure," Justin smiled, "sounds like a great idea."

CHAPTER 10

The town of New Fairfield did not see any more Army buses leave for the rest of the spring and early summer. And by July of 1972, the residents of Candlewood Lake breathed a collective sigh of relief as the days ticked by without any new letters arriving in unsuspecting mailboxes. The *News-Times* had been running a separate section dedicated to the area's military boys. The topics were a potpourri of rank changes, medals earned, and sometimes, stories from the front line. Bittersweet recounts of a war no one wanted and a fight they weren't winning.

July Fourth arrived to announce that the summer was already half over. It was a blistering hot day. But the residents of Candlewood Lake refused to let a heat wave keep them from their celebration and this year was especially important. In honor of the war effort, Earl and Abigail Stanhope opened their twenty-five acre property to the town for a picnic the likes of which no one had ever seen before. There were clowns and face painters for the children, a magic show and even a petting zoo and pony rides. One of the area's favorite bands played current hits like "Maggie May" and "Joy to the World", that even had the grandparents dancing.

The graceful Stanhope property was filled with the hum of voices, the laughter of children and the smell of mouthwatering barbecue. The picnic was exactly what the town needed and the grand finale was something Earl had worked diligently on. He had planned it to perfection, a fireworks show to end all shows, he had promised, a salute to their young men.

"You know," Bernice lifted a glass of lemonade to her lips, "this is the best darned party this town has ever seen. Earl's really outdone himself."

"Yes, he has." Judy held a hand over her brow, trying to keep an eye on Teddy.

"Looks like your youngest is havin' the time of his life," Bernice smiled. In the distance, she could see the boy, his face filled with art, enthralled by a disappearing rabbit.

"Hey, you two, happy Fourth!" Mary walked up to them, weaving her way through the crowd of people.

"Yes, same to you, where's that lawyer husband of yours?"

"He went to join the softball game and Justin sprinted from the car the minute we stopped to go find Eve and Billy."

"Well, that's just fine, you come sit with us. Vic should be around here somewhere, got to keep my eye on that girl, she's still pretty fragile."

"I went to see her last week," Mary remembered, "she just seemed so lost. I don't know what else I can do for her."

"She just needs time…" Judy offered.

"Time? She's had months. I told her she oughta snap out of it by now. She's got that husband of hers runnin' circles not sure which end is up with her. Wouldn't surprise me none if he left her."

"Bernice! You shouldn't say something like that. Why if Hank left that would certainly be the death of her," Mary shook her head, she loved Bernice, but she certainly did not mince words.

"Sorry, honey, I just calls 'em likes I sees 'em." Bernice picked up her glass, nodded to the women, and strode off in the direction of the barbecue pit.

♣ ♣ ♣

"This is the greatest isn't it?" Billy sunk his teeth into a foot-long hot dog.

"Yeah, this was pretty great of the Stanhopes to do this," Justin commented.

"So, Billy, is Olivia really dating your brother?" Eve questioned.

"Yeah, last time I checked. I guess she's all caught up in his letters now. She sent portions of them to the paper so they could reprint them. Seems kind of creepy to me."

Eve picked at her coleslaw. "Why, it seems pretty romantic if you ask me."

Billy rolled his eyes, "Figures, you'd think it was romantic. It's just that, well takin' some guy's letters and puttin' them in the paper like that, like he's dead or something."

"I'm sure that's not what Olivia meant by doing that. I think she probably just wanted to share them with the community," Justin added.

"Whatever. It's just a chick thing…oh, sorry Eve, I told you I wouldn't call girls chicks anymore…I slipped." A Cheshire grin stole across Billy's face as he smiled up at Eve.

"No harm done, Billy."

"So guys, I got a great idea for the fireworks. Why don't we take old man Ritter's boat out on the lake, we can get a great view from there."

"That sounds great!" Eve sipped her lemonade, and looked to Justin for his approval.

"Sure," he shrugged, "I could stand a sail, it's been a while and it will probably be a perfect night for it too."

"Ladies and Gentlemen," surrounded by his wife and daughter, Earl Stanhope stood proudly up on stage. "I just wanted to say, I'm thrilled we could all be here today to commemorate this Independence Day and remember our boys in Vietnam!"

The crowd broke out into a thunderous roar, Earl Stanhope lifted his hands in the air to try and quiet everyone, but it only seemed to encourage them more.

"We have a duty to our young men overseas. A duty to not let them be forgotten, a duty to support them no matter what happens!"

A cheer reverberated through the crowd. Hats flew up in the air, flags waved and mothers welled up with tears. At that moment, the band returned with their rendition of "It's a Grand Old Flag." Behind them, the skies lit up with soaring rockets and bursts of reds, whites and blues.

"Wow! Evie, did you see that?" Justin pulled the oar up into the boat. They had found their perfect spot.

"This is amazing, you were right, Billy. This is so cool!"

The sky exploded into a fiery rainbow of purples, yellows, pinks and blues. Sparkles formed a perfect circle then dipped their glittering heads to the earth as they raced to the ground. But before the perfect night sky could darken, another array of color filled the blackness. When the band played the "Battle Hymn of the Republic," Eve could feel her skin tingle and her eyes fill with tears. As if they were perfectly trained dancers, the fireworks kept time with each note. The colors of the sky reflected onto the lake, splashing it with oranges, whites and reds.

They sat perfectly still in the boat, each lost in their own private moments. Billy thought of his brothers so far away and wished they could be here to see this. Eve watched the sky, wiping an occasional tear now and then and Justin could not take his eyes off the reflection of the colors on her face.

1980

Justin studied the tarmac as the plane pulled away from the gate. Memories of the last nine years continued to flood his mind. He recalled the Halloween after Billy's brothers went off to war when he'd secretly nominated Eve for Queen of the Halloween Carnival. Much to her own embarrassment she'd won and no one ever knew that Justin's vote had been the one that put the plastic crown with pasted rubies on her head. That night, the three of them had buried a time capsule under their favorite tree. Each had contributed their own memories to it, pieces of a journal, notes to the future, whatever they could think of.

For the third year in a row, Justin had dressed as a western sheriff, and Billy had laughed at him. "Every year the same thing gets boring," he'd said. "Why don't you go as a pirate or something exciting like that?" But Justin didn't want exciting, he wanted to be a sheriff, the one who kept peace in the town. The person everyone turned to in need.

Justin snorted slightly, 'Look where it's gotten me,' he thought as his plane lined up for departure.

CHAPTER 11

Victoria had just set an empty cup in the sink when the phone rang. She looked over at it warily. She had barely slept again the night before and the last thing she wanted was to spend an hour on the phone with a concerned neighbor telling her everything would be all right. Her boys were gone, and nothing would be all right again. She knew though that if she didn't pick up, she'd have to face whoever it was at Charlotte and Sven's Christmas Eve party later that day anyway.

"Hello?" she said reluctantly.

"Mom, it's me Duane!"

Her heart leapt at the sound of his voice. The static almost made it indiscernible, but she would know her own son if he were calling her from the moon.

"Duane!" Her voice trembled with relief. Warm tears slid from her eyes, her breath came in gasps. "Where is Terrance? Is everything all right?" For a moment, panic curled through her body. Why were they permitted to call home? Was something wrong?

"Yes, Mom, everything is fine. We just wanted to call to wish you a Merry Christmas."

Merry Christmas, she thought blankly. There was nothing merry about this holiday. Not a damned thing.

"It's so good to hear your voice," she said as her own voice filled with tears.

"Momma, please don't cry…" Duane's voice cracked, "I miss you, we both do. How are Dad and Billy?"

"They're fine, they miss you. We all do. But they're not home; I know your father will want to talk to you both. Can you call again tomorrow?"

She could hear the heavy sigh in Duane's voice, "No, Ma, that's why we're calling today. We have to head out, deeper into the jungle. We won't be able to call again for a long time, but remember, we'll both be home in a couple of months—our tour of duty only lasts one year."

"But it's Christmas," Victoria insisted.

"Not here, Ma."

There was a lightness about Victoria and by the time she and Hank pulled up to the New Fairfield Inn, a radiant glow had flushed her cheeks.

"Honey, it's good to see you so happy," Hank smiled, leaning over the seat to kiss his wife on her warm face. For the first time since their sons departed, Victoria turned her head and returned his kiss. A light, soft press of her lips against his.

"Our boys are fine," she said determinedly. "And they'll be coming home soon."

"I wish I could have spoken with them," Hank's voice filled with regret.

"I wish you could have too," she said softly.

Still leaned across the seat, Hank kissed her again, this time with more urgency. "We don't have to stay long," he murmured in her ear.

Charlotte and Sven's annual Christmas party brought together about three hundred people under their well-decorated roof. Charlotte would spend weeks organizing the event, picking the exact right tree for the foyer, the perfect decorations, while her husband prepared the menu to sheer culinary perfection. Their parties were legendary and no one lucky enough to receive an invite would miss them.

The exterior of the B&B was fringed in white twinkling lights. Inside, the same white lights covered the towering tree, and peeked out from the garland that Charlotte had twisted around the banister. A fire crackled and popped from the large fireplace and the voice of Johnny Mathis floated above the hum of voices and laughter.

Victoria and Hank handed their coats to the hat check girl and disappeared into the crowd of people that filled the dining room. Tables and chairs had been removed, and waiters wove through the guests passing warm hors d'oeuvres.

"Vic! Darlin'! So great to see you!" Bernice pushed herself through the crowd of people, "Hank, you look as handsome as ever and Vickie, why honey you're positively radiant!"

"Thanks, Bernie." Victoria smiled, "I spoke to the boys this afternoon."

"You what?" Bernice looked up to Hank, who nodded in affirmation. "Why, that's just great! Mary!" Bernice turned her head to where she'd left her friend. In a moment, Mary and Karl had joined them.

"Where's Judy and her husband?"

"Right here!" Judith smiled, tugging Ed along behind her. Judith leaned in to hug Victoria and Mary. "Merry Christmas!" They exchanged.

"The boys called from Nam today!" Bernice announced, interrupting their greeting.

Mary placed an arm on Victoria's shoulder. "That's wonderful Vickie, you must be so pleased."

Victoria could only nod, forcing back her tears. Hank placed an understanding arm around her shoulders. "It's really wonderful Mary, they're safe and coming home in a few months. We have a lot to be thankful for this Christmas." As he said the words, he realized his wife would have normally disputed them. But not now; not tonight. For a moment, the dark veil that had covered them had lifted and he knew he had his wife back for however long it would last.

♣ ♣ ♣

Billy threw a tennis ball absentmindedly into the air. It hit the ceiling a few times with a soft tap and then sped back into his hands. Eve's room was a bit too girlie for his tastes, even as he lay on her bed staring at the ceiling he felt uncomfortable among the pink bedding and soft lace drapes.

"So, are we gonna just sit up here all night or what?" he asked impatiently, the ball tapped the ceiling again.

Justin had just spent fifteen minutes setting up their board game. Irritated, he looked up at his friend, "Look, Eve will be back any minute with hot chocolate for us and she wants to play this game. I think we should, it's her house after all."

"Yeah, and it's Christmas Eve and our folks are out having fun and we're stuck at Eve's with a baby sitter…"

The door pushed open and Violet inserted her head into the room, forcing him to break off his sentence. "Here we are!" the baby sitter smiled holding two cups of steaming chocolate milk. Eve beamed behind her, it was clear that she enjoyed having both the boys over for the evening. Violet set the heavy mugs down with a thud on Eve's dresser.

"Ok," Violet smiled, "I'll leave you three for now. I'll just be downstairs if you need anything." She turned her head of thick red curls and walked out the door not closing it completely.

"Justin," Eve clapped, "you set up the entire game! That was very nice of you."

"Thanks," he blushed, "I can't wait to play this. Come on Billy." He motioned to his friend who rolled his eyes and swung his feet over the bed.

"I wanna be the king," Billy motioned, picking up his game piece.

At ten o'clock, the three weary children headed downstairs to say goodnight to Violet. The plan was that each boy would stay over and their parents would retrieve them first thing on Christmas morning. When they arrived at the bottom of the stairs, they found Violet curled up asleep on the couch; the once roaring fire was now just a tiny smear of flames.

"Hey look!" Justin pointed to the window, "It stopped snowing!"

"So?" Billy shrugged.

"Well, it's Christmas Eve, why don't we head outside and make snow angels?"

Billy rolled his eyes. "What?"

"Snow angels, Justin that's a great idea!" Eve pushed past them both, grabbing her thick jacket off the coat rack. "Come on Billy, it'll be fun!"

"All right, I guess we could go outside for a while."

"Then we can exchange presents," Justin said softly.

"Presents?!" The look of panic on Billy's face told Justin he'd been correct to get an extra gift for Eve, assuming he would forget that it was only proper to bring a gift for their new friend.

"Don't worry," he leaned into his friend, "I got it covered."

"You're the best, man." Billy slapped him on the back and then followed Eve out the door and into the night.

CHAPTER 12

They called them the death watch. The men who came in unmarked cars, dressed in uniform with somber faces. The men who brought news that a son, husband or father would not be returning home. Men who stood on the doorstep of a home, with curt apologies and official letters. Who walked away, leaving gasps of agony in the doorways behind them. Who slipped into their cars and sped away before the grief caught up to them.

It was a gray February Sunday in New Fairfield and in the Freeman household. A brief smear of sunlight streaked the kitchen window and Victoria sat silently with her needlepoint at the table. She hadn't slept well the night before and the tedious work seemed to calm her nerves. The dreams had come back; the slow, painful, torturous dreams that left her feeling raw and empty. She was running through the jungle again, through the thick brush chasing after her sons. Trying to catch up with them, but no matter how hard she ran; she could never find them. Then, she came upon the field, the one she always dreaded. It was a field filled with lifeless bodies, riddled with bullets. She stepped over the bodies looking for them, praying they weren't there but before she could finish her search she would wake to a violent thunder clap and find herself twisted in her sheets, sweaty and exhausted. Victoria could never sleep after those dreams; she'd usually creep out of bed to head downstairs and make herself a cup of tea. But even that hadn't calmed her in the wee hours before dawn. Last night's dream had been different. Usually her running was accompanied by silence, this time she could hear the machine guns and the cries for help from her boys. This time, she could see them fall to the ground in lifeless, bloody heaps.

Victoria pierced the cloth with a length of green yarn; she could hear her husband in the living room, the television on. He had just snapped open the paper when a sound outside got her attention. It was the sound of gravel crunching under a set of tires. The needle she'd been holding pricked her finger and a drop of blood pushed to the surface. Two pairs of footsteps crunched over the driveway and up the walk. An uneasy feeling settled in the pit of her stomach, heavy and obtrusive. She forgot her finger and the blood dripped down her hand and onto her needlepoint. She barely heard the knock at the door.

"Hank!" she called in a voice that wasn't hers. Her hand trembled and the blood spilled onto her dress, the red dot expanding, burning the delicate blue edges of the flowers imprinted on the cloth. Hank walked into the kitchen, still holding his paper. He looked at his wife who sat motionless staring through the window.

"Honey what's wrong?" his answer was another knock on the door, this time more forceful than the one before. Hank walked back to the front door and reaching for the handle, he pulled it open. In an instant he heard a piercing scream behind him as his wife sank into the wall. The men stood there, filling their doorway.

"We're very sorry, Mr. and Mrs. Freeman. But we've come to tell you your son has been killed."

Duane Phillip Freeman was flown home by a planeload of strangers. Men who did nothing else but return sons home to their families. The wooden box that held his body sat in a row of wooden boxes, all young boys who were coming home for the last time. Men who would never again feel wet grass beneath their feet, or the final embrace of a loved one. They would never again know the warm nuzzle of a dog, the taste of ice cream on a warm day or the feel of a warm summer sun as it colored their skin.

The next month, the US military began to pull their troops out of Vietnam.

❧ ❧ ❧

Terrance arrived home the day his brother was to be buried, honorably discharged early by the Army. Fueled by his loss and the experience of war, Terry wasted no time in asking Olivia Stanhope to be his wife. Terry had wanted to get married in a small, quick ceremony. But given the Stanhope's extended family and business associates, this proved to be impossible. There were nearly five hundred people at the wedding and reception.

Terry's wedding was the only thing to lift Victoria's spirits in a long while. Most of her days were spent in the quiet darkness of her mind and the occasional thought that her son was alive, but lost and hungry in the jungles of Vietnam. These rationalizations gave her a glimmer of hope, until she remembered that unlike some young men, they'd found Duane's body lifeless and intact. Then, the sorrow would set in and she'd lock herself away for days at a time without eating or speaking to anyone. Despite Hank's best efforts, Victoria barely acknowledged him. He hadn't done enough to try and keep her boys safe and now one of them was gone. It was his fault, she reasoned with herself, his fault that one of her sons was gone. And it was shortly after Terry's wedding that Hank found himself in a bar, seeking solace there when none could be found at home.

CHAPTER 13

The summer sun beat down on the town of New Fairfield with a relentless force. The sun burned leaves and turned blades of grass into tiny hot knives. It had been the longest record heat wave since New Fairfield had started keeping track nearly fifty years before. A faded yellow school bus filled with teenagers headed for Mountain State Park lumbered down the street, sounds of laughter and excited chatter spilled from the windows. This was the annual teen camping trip sponsored by United Methodist Church and Billy, Justin and Eve all crowded into one seat. Eve sat on the aisle, her small hand gripping the seat beneath her.

"Eve, are you sure you're ok?" Justin leaned into her gently. Eve nodded, insisting she was fine but Justin did not believe her. She'd been quiet and pale ever since they'd boarded the bus.

"Hey," Billy began, "you got that hippie mix you promised to bring, Jus?"

Justin pulled his attention from Eve and unzipped his backpack. "It's granola trail mix. Here you go. Eve would you like some?"

"No—No thank you, I'm fine. That dried fruit looks like dead bugs, though."

Billy quickly grabbed a handful. "So, how long till we're there?" he asked.

"It's an hour to the lake and the camp is another fifteen minutes from there."

"Geesh, and it's hotter than blazes on this bus man." Billy popped a large fistful into his mouth and then garbled, "Mmmm, yummy bugs!" as Eve made a pained face.

"It will go by quickly," Justin said, his attention still on Eve. She was clutching her stomach and staring at the floor. "If you need to stop, you just say the word," he said softly.

"Thanks," she managed.

That evening, Eve did not join the group for dinner. Instead she stayed in her tent, curled up on the bed clutching her stomach.

❖ ❖ ❖

The following morning, the pain subsided enough to encourage her to keep her commitment to Billy and Justin to go with them on a mountain hike. The center of the camp was designated by the flagpole. Everyone who was going on the walk was asked to meet there by nine o'clock. A group of excited young adults filled the area, but Eve spotted her friends right away.

"Hi guys!" she waived. Both of them smiled when they saw her and Justin's face filled with an obvious look of relief.

"Glad you're feeling better," he smiled.

"Yes, I am actually. Good thing or I'm sure they would have sent me home."

The guided hike took a narrow trail up the side of the mountain. Billy, Eve and Justin brought up the rear of the group. The day was warm and the path baked on the unshaded side of the hill.

"This was a dumb idea," Billy lamented, rolling his eyes and smiling at a cute girl as the guide stopped again to explain what Indian guides had looked for when hunting for food. "Whatever," he sighed. "It's not like we'll ever have to hunt our own food again."

"It's interesting, Billy. It teaches us how primitive man lived when there was no running water or electricity."

Billy picked up a long stick and began dragging it behind him in the hot dirt. "Want me to carry that backpack a while, Jus?" He pointed his stick at the pack on his friend's back.

Justin shrugged, readjusting it. "No, it's fine. Thanks though."

"What the heck you got in there?" Billy asked, turning back to return the smile of a petite brunette farther up ahead.

"Stuff, you know. First aid in case one of us gets hurt, water, snacks. Just stuff."

"But we're only out here for the day. It's not like we're staying overnight."

"My father has always taught me to be prepared, and Mom made me promise to take the pack whenever we went hiking."

Billy only nodded, distracted again by the smiling brunette. "Say, you guys don't mind if I head up a ways do you?"

"No," Justin smiled, "go ahead." Billy pushed through the group of kids and Justin watched him until he tapped the object of his attention on the shoulder.

"He's never without an admirer is he?" Justin turned to Eve who walked silently beside him. "Eve? Are you ok?" Her face had gone pale again, and her hand rested on her stomach.

"I thought I was better, Justin. I'm sorry, do you mind if we sit down for a few minutes?" Eve did not wait for his reply, but dropped herself onto a fallen tree trunk. The pain seared through her again, and she tried to force herself not to double over.

"No, not at all. We can catch up to the group." Justin slid the pack to the ground and sat down beside her.

"Eve, are you sure you're all right? Maybe I should tell the group to stop, we might need to head back."

"No!" she said abruptly, "I don't want to ruin everyone's afternoon. It'll pass in just a minute, I promise." The next pain bent her in two. Justin felt powerless and stupid when all he could think to do was gently stroke her hair, all the while watching from out of the corner of his eye as the group vanished around a corner.

"I need to go to the bathroom, Justin. Wait for me, I'll be right back." In one swift movement she was up off the tree trunk and charging into the woods.

Justin waited for what seemed like an eternity. Finally, he could stand it no longer. He got up and headed after her into the woods. She had been gone too long, something must be terribly wrong he thought.

"Eve!" Dried leaves and twigs snapped under his feet as he wandered through the thick trees. Suddenly, he heard a cry, muffled at first, coming from behind a clump of trees.

"Eve, it's me. Are you ok?" He continued to walk, but Eve did not reply. "Eve, I'm going to come around and see if you need help all right?" Cautiously, he rounded the trees. When he did, he saw her lying on her side, curled into a ball. Her pants were loose around her waist. She was covered in blood.

"I'm bleeding…" she said softly. "It hurts so bad. I had no idea it would hurt this bad, Justin."

Justin knelt down beside her; pulling his pack off his shoulders he quickly unzipped it. "It's going to be all right," he soothed, "did you fall? Did you cut yourself?"

Eve bit her bottom lip. "No, it's…it's different. It came from here." She pointed a shaky hand to the spot between her legs as she watched her friend blush. "I'm sorry. I tried to clean it up, but then the pain started."

Justin dug through his bag, "It's ok Eve. It's a very natural thing. My mother was a nurse, she told me all about this. Look, I can make something for you, something for you to wear until we can get you back to camp." Justin pulled a small zippered bag from his pack, it was filled with gauze. Then, he reached in again and pulled a pair of swimming trunks out.

"I want you to put these on," he pushed the trunks into her hand, "and take this gauze and…and…" Justin could not manage another word.

"I know." Eve nodded.

"When you're done with that, we'll head to the river. It can't be too far from here and we'll wash your clothes. Then we'll head back down the mountain before anyone misses us. Are you feeling up to that?"

Eve nodded, and Justin moved himself away so she could change. Soon, they were on their way to find the river.

"Are you ok?" Justin inquired.

"Yes, I'm fine," Eve managed a smile. "Is it much farther?"

"I didn't think it was this far to be honest with you, Eve. But I'm certain it's up ahead. The river runs parallel to the walking path so if we keep heading in this direction we should find it in no time."

After an hour of walking, they could hear the water as it rushed down the mountain. The river was wide at this point, much wider than Justin had remembered it when his father had taken him fishing here some years back. Soon Eve was knee deep in the water scrubbing her pants.

"I'm so embarrassed, Justin. I can't believe this happened today of all days."

Justin followed her into the river. "Don't be embarrassed, it's perfectly natural. It means you're a woman now." The words fell from his mouth before he could stop them; he felt his face burn as he saw Eve look up at him and smile.

"You're my best friend, Justin. Thank you for understanding."

"So, we should think about heading back soon," he looked to the sun as it began to dip behind the trees, thankful he was able to change the direction of the conversation. "No doubt we're already missed."

"Good idea. The pain seems to be gone, I think I can walk faster now."

They headed toward the path, but after an hour and a half of walking, darkness was beginning to seep into the forest and the walking path was fading out of sight.

"Justin, it's getting awfully dark. Are you sure we're going in the right direction?"

"No, I'm not. I thought we were but now, losing daylight has got me turned around. I'm so sorry, Eve. We should be there soon, I promise." But another forty-five minutes of walking drove them only deeper into the dark woods.

"Justin, I'm scared." Eve pulled his hand into hers.

"I know. Eve, I'm sorry. I'm afraid we're lost."

❧ ❧ ❧

Mary and Judith sat on uncomfortable chairs looking anxiously around the bustling constable's office. A phone rang and someone yanked it off its cradle. Several men were bent over a worn map of Mohawk Mountain State Forest talking in muffled voices. Occasionally one of them would point at something on the map and the rest would nod. Several search parties had already been dispatched and a few more were being assembled. Their husbands had gone out with the first search team and Hank would be joining the next one. The door to Constable Shep Holden's office was closed but both women could catch an occasional bit of conversation that dripped through the door. Both of them heard the word "mountain lion" at the same time and Judith inhaled sharply.

"Justin knows what to do, Judy," Mary soothed. "Karl has taken him on hundreds of survival walks and his backpack is full of enough food for at least a day and a night."

"She's right you know Mrs. Phillips," Constable Holden stood before them, a tall, thin man with a weathered face and sharp, blue eyes. He dug his hands deep into his pockets and smiled a cautiously comforting smile, "I've been on enough hikes with him and Karl to know that he's well trained for this type of thing. Besides, we have every available state highway patrolman, including your husbands out combing those woods. We'll find them before much longer, I'm sure of that."

Judith finally spoke, her voice shook with emotion, "But what about the mountain lions?"

"There haven't been any sightings this year, Mrs. Phillips. We're certain they've left the area, probably in search of some place less populated."

Judith did not seem to find that consoling.

❧ ❧ ❧

Justin pushed a stick into the fire. It was a roaring blaze that filled the pit he'd dug. The woods around them were completely dark. Justin had no idea where they were. But he knew that by now, someone was bound to be looking for them. He hoped the fire would help to speed their rescue. Eve was worried, but Justin knew she was trying to keep a brave face despite her angst.

"I think my pants are dry now." Eve ran her hand along the fabric and walked over to a cluster of bushes to slip them back on.

"Are you hungry, Evie?" Justin asked. "I think I have some beef jerky and some more granola."

"Yeah, sure. That would be great." Eve's voice was filled with unease. Justin handed her the bag of granola. "You should rest, get some sleep Evie."

"What if someone comes looking for us?"

"I'll stay awake," Justin smiled. True to his word, he stayed awake for most of the night watching Eve as she slept with her head on his backpack, curled into a ball on a bed of leaves. He poked the fire occasionally to keep it burning and a couple of times he got up to gather more wood, never letting Eve out of his sight for a moment. When the early morning sun pushed up the curtain of darkness he heard the distant crunch of shoes. Gently, Justin tapped Eve's shoulder.

"What is it?" she asked, her voice thick with sleep.

"I think someone's coming." Justin answered cautiously. Eve sat up straight at his words. She could hear it too, faintly at first then it grew louder: voices calling their names!

❧ ❧ ❧

A group of eight men pressed through the forest, crumpling leaves and fallen branches beneath their feet. Ed Phillips and Karl VanSant were among the group that had been searching without sleep for the missing children.

"Eve! Evie!!" Edward's voice was hoarse from calling. Karl watched the man intently, he knew Ed wasn't used to this kind of physical exertion and combined with the worry for his daughter, it was only accelerating his fatigue.

"We should rest for a moment," Karl offered.

"I can't rest, my daughter's been out here all night. God knows what's happened to her," Edward stuck out his chin defiantly and pushed past him. Karl knew Ed was uncertain over his claims that Justin knew what to do and while Karl was still worried, he knew the overnight camping trips were probably paying off.

They both saw it at once, a pair of hands waving through the thick brush.

"Eve!" Ed's voice sounded as he raced to her. Karl and the rest of the men were on his heels.

♣ ♣ ♣

"You're a real hero," Billy's feet dangled easily off the edge of the pier, his toes dipped into the cool water.

"I suppose," Justin shrugged. He really didn't get what all the commotion had been about. He'd been on the front page of the local paper. A black and white picture of him and Eve, wrapped in blankets standing by the constable's station. Mr. Finley had cut it out and taped it to his cash register for all the kids to see. For once in his life, he was the most popular kid in school.

"I don't get why you're so quiet 'bout this, it's really somethin' man, you stayin' awake all night to protect Eve. Building a fire, it's really amazing. I don't know if I could have done the same," Billy fell silent. Justin knew his friend had confessed something he would never admit to anyone else.

"It really wasn't anything. I just did what my dad taught me. Besides, Eve's our friend, I'm sure you would have done the same."

Billy didn't answer. He stared into the lake silently watching the ripple of the water. "I felt bad. I went ahead to talk to that girl and left the two of you. If you were never found, I would never have forgiven myself."

Justin turned to look at his friend. "Don't be silly, it wasn't your fault. It wasn't anyone's fault. It just happened."

Billy pushed his toes back and forth through the water. "That's why I admire you Jus, you're just being who you are. You're a hero and you could care less."

CHAPTER 14

Billy loved the smell of the football field. Scents of hotdogs, sweat, and cotton candy mixed together in an almost aphrodisiacal way. The grass was short and soft beneath his shoes as he pressed down on the green carpet and walked out onto the field. The bleachers were filled with screaming fans. This was the big playoff game and Billy was New Fairfield High School's star quarterback. He loved it. He loved every heart-pounding minute of it. The game, the feeling of victory, of being a part of a winning team but most of all, Billy loved to feel adored. And he was, whether it was the fans, or the teachers that let him slide on his tests, or the cheerleaders in their skirts that barely covered their bottoms…they all adored him. He was Billy Freeman, star quarterback and The Rebels' only hope for victory this season.

From the field, Billy spotted Justin and Eve in their usual seats and he threw them a quick wave knowing that he was about to demolish the opposing team and win the game for his school. They were only one point behind, a field goal would not only set them ahead but in the last 15 seconds of the game, it would win them the season. Suddenly Billy was rushing forward; somewhere off in the distance he could hear the crowds screaming his name. He pushed through the other team, circling one of them, until the goal line was in his sight and then he rushed toward it with the power of a locomotive; he was virtually unstoppable. Suddenly Billy stopped and he spotted the scoreboard. His team had won, as he'd predicted. Just then he was lifted off the ground and hoisted onto the shoulders of his teammates. The cheerleaders were smiling at him; he was sure to get laid tonight.

From the stands, Justin watched his friend revel in his moment of glory. It was rare that he saw Billy exude such carnal happiness as when he was on the football field, preferably winning. It was the love of Billy's life. There were even whispers of Billy going pro someday. Justin hoped he would, Billy needed something really good to happen to him, but right now Justin knew it was enough that they'd won the season. For now, but Billy's thirst for adoration wouldn't stop there. It seemed that it wasn't until his feet touched the field that Billy truly came to life. Anything off the field was just existing.

❦ ❦ ❦

The locker room was packed with half-naked young men cheering the one man who'd brought them to victory. Billy's smile never left his face and his hair stuck to his scalp from the gallons of Gatorade that had been tossed on him. Justin observed him from the edge of the lockers near the entrance, he'd promised his friend he would go with him to an after-game party his team was having. Even though Justin wasn't particularly comfortable being surrounded by jocks he knew it meant a lot to his friend. After about thirty minutes, it looked like Billy was finally ready to leave. "I'll meet you out back," the jock smiled. "Why don't you bring the car around?"

"Sure," Justin smiled. The locker room was nearly empty now. Most of the team had already left for the party but Justin knew Billy wanted to get there last and make an entrance. He left the room quickly to get his father's car.

Billy stood in the night air waiting for his friend when he heard someone call his name, "Hey, Freeman." The voice came from behind the dumpster in the alley. Billy turned to face four of the players from the opposing team.

"We seen what you did," one of them said. "You don't play fair Freeman, you took a field goal that was supposed to be ours and now you need to pay."

Suddenly Billy was surrounded. He felt an odd twitch in the pit of his stomach. Fear? No way. Not him. Still, the twitch grew stronger.

"We're here to teach 'ya a lesson," another one said, "fuckin' star quarterbacks like you deserve to be taught a lesson."

The four young men walked steadily toward Billy, backing him up to the wall. A fist flew to his face but Billy deflected it with his arm as another hit his stomach. It was a dead on punch that forced all the air out of his lungs and sent him reeling. Then another to his head, his eyes seemed to splinter in pain and for a minute he couldn't see. He tried to defend himself but his fists kept slicing through the cool night air. The boys were pounding on him now. Billy slammed a fist into a stomach but another punch sent him face first into the gravel. Off in the distance Billy could hear a car approaching, closer and closer until it screeched to a halt.

"Stop it!" It was Justin's voice he heard. Oh, thank God, he thought. He wasn't sure how much more of the pounding he could take. The young men stopped for a moment to see who had just arrived.

"Well if it's not his buddy Pansy-boy!" one of them yelled. "Let's take him down."

Justin felt his stomach twist in fear. "I wouldn't try that," he wasn't sure if he was able to hide the tremor in his voice, "I've already called the police, and they are on their way. You can beat me to a pulp if you want, but they will probably catch you doing it."

"Fuckin' Shep won't do anything!" They were headed toward him now; Justin could see Billy try to push himself up off the ground.

"Probably not," Justin replied watching the boys get closer. "He'll just arrest you, probably keep you overnight, maybe longer, tell your parents and the school. There will be no more football for you."

Suddenly one of them spotted a set of headlights that seemed to be headed for the alley. "Shep!" he yelled and the other guys followed him as he raced through the alley, behind the dumpster and out of sight. Justin looked behind him and saw the unsuspecting car was making a U-turn in the parking lot and had already headed off for home. The timing of it, however, couldn't be denied. Billy was on his feet now. Justin spotted the beginnings of a shiner.

"You all right?" he asked, offering a hand to his friend.

Billy refused it. "Fine," he said in a soft voice.

"Come on, get in the car." Billy obeyed his friend and opened the passenger door, dropping himself on the vinyl seat.

"Fuck," he said as the pain of his bruised ribs seared through him.

Justin slid into the driver's seat, and decided not to start the car. "You going to be ok? Maybe we should take you to the hospital."

"Hell no, man. Are you kidding? I'd never live that down. I'm the fuckin' quarterback for Christ's sake, a real fuckin' hero who can't even defend himself in a fight."

"There were four of them Billy, you were outnumbered. No one could expect you to defend yourself against that."

Billy sighed against the window, "Doesn't matter, no one will understand."

"I'm sorry man."

"Don't be, you probably saved my life, no telling what those assholes would have done if you hadn't showed up. And what happened to Shep? We should get out of here before he gets here."

"I lied," Justin smiled.

A tired snort came from Billy's lips. "Good one. I didn't know you had it in you, Jus."

"I'm just glad you're ok."

"Yeah, I'm fine, but I'll be better once I get those assholes back for what they did."

"Just leave it alone Billy, you don't need the trouble."

"What are you sayin'? That I should just let this slide like some friggin' pansy-ass milk-toast?"

"Yes, that's exactly what I'm saying. You'll be more of a man if you just let them fester in their loss. That's all this is you know; a bunch of sore losers."

Billy began to grow impatient. "You think you're so smart Justin, but some things you just don't understand."

Justin turned in his seat. "You're right Billy. Honestly, I don't know the first thing about football, I go to watch you but I have no idea what a field pass is, hell, I barely know what a touchdown is. But I know a stupid thing and going after those goons would be stupid."

"What the fuck ever," Billy raised a hand to his face, touching the bruise on his eye.

"No, I'm serious Bill, don't do it, don't go after them or you'll have more trouble and I…"

"What? You won't be there to save me?" Billy's voice raised an octave or two, and Justin could tell he was getting mad.

"Why are you upset with me?" he questioned.

Billy shook his head. "I'm not. Look man, I'm sorry, it's just that, I dunno. You always seem to have all the answers and I always end up being the dumb ass. Even tonight, here I was in the middle of a fight but who comes to save me…"

"Pansy-boy?" Justin asked, feeling equally impatient.

"No, man, I'd never call you that…it's just…well…."

"Listen, we're almost out of high school, you're going to have to get over the star quarterback thing. Once we get to college it will all be different, I know how you love being adored but one day it will all go away and you'll just be Billy Freeman."

"It doesn't have to end, I can play football in college. If I go."

Justin didn't reply for a moment, he knew that Billy's family might not have the money needed to send him to anything other than a community college and no one cared about football there. "I'm just saying that it's time you got some other interests."

"Like what maybe? Maybe I should start dating and get ready to settle down. Hell, maybe I'll start dating Eve."

"I wasn't talking about Eve." Justin tried to hide his growing irritation, but Billy didn't miss the change in inflection in his friend's voice.

"I'm sorry, pal, did I touch on a sore subject?" Billy taunted, now this was getting fun.

"Yeah, maybe I should date Eve, maybe even do her, I bet she'd love to have her first time be at the hands of a star quarterback."

"Leave Eve out of this, you've never been interested in her that way."

"But you have, haven't you?"

"Just drop it, Billy. We're talking about you and your issue with being idolized."

A smile returned to Billy's face. "No, we're done talkin' about that, now we're talking about you wanting to do Eve."

"I don't, damn it! It's not like that, I lo—." Justin's sentence dropped off. He turned away from Billy, afraid of the truth that nearly spilled from his lips.

"You love her? Man I had no idea." Billy looked over at his friend, "Listen, Jus, why don't you tell her?"

"I can't," Justin whispered.

"Oh, man, have you got it bad or what?"

"Forget it."

"Yeah, and if you don't speak up, she'll forget you and you'll lose her."

"Billy, damn it, I don't want to talk about Eve. I want to talk about you and make sure you don't go after those guys that beat you up tonight."

Beat you up, the phrase lingered in Billy's mind. Loser. Beat up loser. That's what he was, a failed loser with a crazy mother, and he couldn't even defend himself. And his perfect bookish friend had saved him. Again. Ever so smart and perfect Justin. Justin who would go off to some fancy college and no doubt end up marrying Eve and having a perfect-fucking life with perfect children in a perfect-fucking house. Billy turned to the window and gazed out into the darkened alley. He didn't have any time for this condescending bullshit. He needed to get drunk. If he wanted a "talking to" he could get that at home.

Billy pushed open the passenger door. "I'm outta here," he said as his bruised body lurched from the car.

"Where are you going?" Justin yelled after him.

"To my fucking party. I don't have time for this crap and my perfect-fucking friend and his words of friggin' wisdom. Next time let them beat me to a pulp, at least I'd be able to keep my friggin' dignity that way."

Justin yelled for him to stop, but his friend was already gone. And with that, Billy pulled a single thread from the fabric of their friendship that was slowly and silently starting to unravel.

Thread by thread, row by row.

CHAPTER 15

Eve pushed her chair closer to the table as she watched her mother remove the skillet from the stove and scoop some fluffy scrambled eggs onto a plate. Judith handed the plate to her husband. "Thank you, dear," he smiled, folding the morning paper in quarters and setting it down beside his plate. "So, what are you doing today, Eve?"

"I'm spending the day with Billy and Justin. We're going out on old man Ritter's boat and sail on the lake."

"I can hardly believe those boys are less than a month away from graduation," Judith said, cracking two more eggs into a pan.

"Yes, well soon our very own Evie will be following them. Two more years for you young lady, then it's off to college." Her father smiled.

College, she thought. That was what she wanted most in the world.

"Hardly, Edward," Judith shook her head. "She'll no doubt get married first. College will have to wait."

"Mom," Eve didn't even bother to hide the impatience in her voice, "I'm not getting married right away. I want to finish school first."

"You know, nice boys won't wait around for a girl to get an education first. You're going to have to snatch up someone like Billy Freeman right away or he'll be gone."

Eve rolled her eyes toward the ceiling. Her mother set down a plate of eggs in front of her but Eve ignored them, "I don't want to date Billy, mother. I've told you that a hundred times. Besides," she added reluctantly, "he's not even interested in me, he just sees me as a friend."

Judith sat down at the table. "You'll have to make him see you as someone other than just a friend if you want to catch him."

"But that's just it Mom, I don't want to catch him."

"Then Justin perhaps? He's a good catch too, very smart."

"Judy…" her husband's voice was low and cautioning. They'd had this discussion many times, but it seemed to occur more frequently since Eve's sixteenth birthday.

Judith's head snapped to face her husband, "What?" On the opposite side of the table, Teddy giggled at them.

"I don't have to choose," Eve said ignoring them both, "they're both my friends, why can't you just leave it at that?" Eve shoved her chair back, kissed her father on the cheek and sped through the kitchen and out the front door without so much as a goodbye to her mother. Sometimes, Eve thought, that woman could be infuriating.

Eve raced to meet her friends. The day was already warm, not even June and yet it promised to be a wonderful summer. Soon, the tourists will begin to arrive, Eve thought as she pushed through the forest to the edge of the lake where the boys promised to wait for her. Her mother's words still echoed in her head. Her mother would never understand her, Eve was certain of that. It was all about doing the proper thing with her, and Eve doubted that she'd ever lived a true honest day in her life.

"This was really a great idea," Eve smiled. Leaning her head back she closed her eyes to the bright noon sun and felt the warm glow on her face as the boat rocked gently back and forth. "In another month the tourists will be swarming and there'll be no room for us."

"Yes, and then after that I head off to college," Justin said, feeling the sting of missing her already piercing his heart. He dropped his hand in the cool water to try and distract himself from his pain.

Eve snapped her head forward and said, "How far away will you be going?"

"I've been accepted at Princeton," he said almost in a whisper.

Billy snorted, "Princeton. You'll be too good to hang out with us then, never you mind Evie," Billy smiled throwing his arm around her shoulders, "I'm not going anywhere. Once Justin leaves it'll just be you and me." Billy knew that would get to his friend, and he itched to tease him while he still had the chance.

"I'll be home every weekend," Justin said in his own defense.

"But it won't be the same, Justin," Eve offered, nudging Billy's arm from her shoulder.

"Things change, Bug, there's nothing we can do about it. All we can do is change with it."

"Who says things have to change?" Billy began impatiently. "Things can stay the same if we want them to. I mean you don't have to go away, I'm staying here, so is Eve."

Justin realized the motivation behind his friend's comment; so much had changed in Billy's life he couldn't blame him for wanting to hang on to the status quo. "My aunt is coming for a visit," Justin said, changing the subject. He saw the tension in his friend's face fade slightly.

"I didn't know you had an aunt?" Eve questioned.

"Well, she doesn't come around too often. In fact, I haven't seen her since before you moved here, Eve. She's a bit of, uh, well…."

"I hear she's pretty wild," Billy smiled, feeling comfortable again with the conversation.

"I guess you could say that," Justin admitted reluctantly. "She and my dad don't quite see eye to eye on things."

"What do you mean by wild, Billy?" Eve asked, this aunt of Justin's sounded intriguing to her.

"Wild, I dunno. I overheard it in the Grand Union the other day. Justin's mom and my mom were talking. She was saying she was worried her sister in-law would get herself into trouble if she stayed here. She said that 'she finds trouble wherever she goes,' I'm pretty sure that's what she said."

Justin shrugged looking at Eve who listened with intent fascination. "He's right, my Aunt Willie has gotten herself into some strange situations."

"Willie? What kind of name is Willie?" Eve asked.

"It's from Wilhelmina, but she's never called that. Well, except for my father, he still refers to her as Wilhelmina."

"Oh, well she sounds fascinating," Eve smiled, anxious to meet this Willie person.

"I like her. She's fun, and funny and she's a good person. In the end, that's all that matters."

The conversation subsided and Billy pulled out his fishing rod. After baiting the hook, he dropped the line into the water while his two friends silently watched. The fish weren't biting, but Billy didn't mind. He was where he wanted to be; with his two best friends, in a boat on Candlewood Lake.

CHAPTER 16

Mary was preparing the guest room while her husband looked on. "It'll be fine," she said tucking the bed sheets in.

"I'm not so certain about that. I mean we haven't seen her in what, ten years and now she decides to pay us a visit? I think she's in trouble."

Mary stood up, planting her hands on her hips. "Look, dear, Willie's not always in trouble. That's just your point of view. She's a lively woman who's had scads of boyfriends and has never been married. Besides, she says she's coming to see her nephew graduate."

"She drinks," Karl offered.

"So do you, so do I. Does that make me a harlot?"

"Mary! Please, you know I don't think my sister is a harlot, I just worry about her."

Mary thoughtfully smoothed the pillows before placing them on the bed, "Your whole family has been worried about her at one time or another. And yes, I'll agree that she has given them reason to worry but for goodness sake, just try and enjoy her while she's here. If something happens, then we'll deal with it. Until then, let's not borrow trouble, ok?" Mary placed a light kiss on her husband's cheek.

Karl dug his hands deeper into is pockets, "Fine. You're right as usual my love."

Willie sped through the center of town in her baby blue '67 Chevy convertible. Her red hair was tucked inside a silk scarf that waved behind her like a victory flag. A long cigarette dangled between her fingers. Every now and then she would take a drag on it, leaving the bright red imprint of her lips around the filter. Willie could hardly believe she was actually going to visit her brother. The man who'd spent his life looking down his nose at her. Still, she wanted to see her only nephew on his big day and besides, now was a pretty good time to get out of town anyway.

Willie pulled into the long driveway of her brother's home. She envied his stability and there were times when she wished she'd settled down and had a few children. But settling wasn't Willie's nature. She was hard-wired for adventure; that was certain. As she slowed her car, she saw her brother and his wife in the doorway waving at her. They seem friendly enough, she thought, as she hoped for the best, and strode from her car.

♣ ♣ ♣

"So, sugar, what'chya up to this summer?" Willie winked at her nephew who sat across from her at the New Fairfield Inn where Karl had taken them to dinner.

"Justin's going to Princeton," Karl said proudly before his son had a chance to speak.

Willie nodded, smiling in Justin's direction, "Well, that's great Justin, I'm really proud of my nephew, but what are you doing this summer? You know, for fun."

Justin thought for a moment, somehow he was certain his adventures would pale in comparison to his Aunt Willie's, "Um, well, I spend a lot of time with my friends...Billy and Eve."

Willie nodded her head in Justin's direction, "Well, Eve...now that's more like it..." she smiled knowing she was onto something. Plucking a cigarette from her silver plated case she continued, "So, hon, tell me more about this Eve person."

"Well, maybe you can meet her sometime?" Justin offered, looking anxiously at his mother. Conversations about Eve always made him nervous.

Willie smiled, resting an elbow on the table. "Well, sugar, I'd love to meet her but why don't you tell me about her first."

Justin's face softened and Willie knew she was right, her nephew was in love. "She's wonderful," he said softly as though he were afraid someone might overhear.

Willie took a long drag from her cigarette, letting the smoke curl around her face, "Ah, wonderful." She patted his hand across the table. "Sounds to me like someone has a little crush…."

"Uh, so Willie," Mary interrupted, seeing the discomfort on her son's face, "so what are your plans while you're in town?"

Willie took the hint. "Well, I didn't get to see too much of this place the last time I was here, I was hoping to maybe do some sightseeing, tourist stuff, you know."

"Sightseeing?" Karl asked, his voice hinted of sarcasm.

Willie took the challenge, "Yes, Karl, sightseeing. It's not all drinking and sex with me you know, occasionally I do have to come up for air."

"Wilhelmina!" Karl scolded, his wife blushed beside him.

Willie threw her head back in laughter. "Oh, brother dear, I've missed you so. You are just a gem, an absolute gem."

When the check arrived, Karl took it and headed up to the register to pay the bill.

"I'm sorry Mary," Willie said when her brother was out of earshot, "I'm really trying but Karl's gotta give me a chance."

Mary smiled and patted Willie's arm, "I'll talk to him tonight," she soothed. "He just doesn't understand you, Willie."

Willie cocked her chin. "He doesn't need to understand me, he just needs to accept me." Willie stepped from the table; her stiletto heals clicking on the hardwood floors as she headed past her brother and out the door.

"I'm going for a walk," Willie announced when everyone was outside.

Karl frowned. "What, you're not coming home with us?"

"Not just yet, I just need some fresh air. Don't worry about me I know my way around."

"I'll leave a key under the flower pot by the front door," Mary said, knowing Willie wasn't planning on getting home anytime soon.

"Thanks." Willie winked at her, "Justin, I'll see you in the morning."

"All right, Aunt Willie, have a good time. Do you want me to go with you?"

"No, your Aunt Wilhelmina will be fine," Karl said, sliding into the car.

Willie watched them as they drove out of sight and then she looked around, wondering where she could find the nearest bar.

CHAPTER 17

Hank pushed the door open to Phil's bar. The sound of voices and clinking glasses met him at the door. He needed a drink, a quiet lonely drink at the bar, and he needed one bad. Life at home hadn't improved since Duane died; in fact it had gone from bad to worse. Victoria hardly noticed him. Her lucid moments grew fewer and fewer and they hadn't made love in so long he couldn't even remember what it felt like to hold her.

He slid onto a bar stool and ordered a double shot of whiskey. He loved Vic, he really did, but she refused to get better and he was done trying. The only thing she cared about was mourning her dead son. Duane had been his son too, he thought as he watched the bartender set the drink down in front of him. Hank grabbed it and threw his head back. The brown liquid slid down his throat, burning a path on its way. He ordered another and drank the second one with the same fervor. He didn't even notice when the tall slender redhead walked into the bar.

Willie opened the door to Phil's, quickly surveying the territory. Three men playing pool, a girl and a guy dancing to some tune on the juke box, and the tables were filled with people drinking and laughing. She wove her way through the tables, ignoring the glances from the men eyeing her tight fitting black pants and even tighter red sweater. Willie found an open spot at the bar and sat down.

Hank glanced over at her for a moment and then quickly went back to his drink. Willie noticed him immediately, for one because he was the most handsome man in the bar and for two because she'd seen that look on her own face once or twice. That look of sheer despair.

"Hi sugar," she smiled at the bartender, "I'll have a martini, and add an extra olive in there would'cha?" The bartender grinned at his pretty customer and quickly went to go fix her drink. Willie pulled her cigarette case from her purse, "Want one?" She asked Hank.

"No thanks," Hank didn't even look up, just waved his hand at her, "I don't smoke."

"Don't mind if I do, do you sugar?"

"It's a free country." Hank sipped at his whiskey, he could feel the first two taking effect. His entire body felt warm, like he was swimming in a pool of tepid water.

"I 'spose it is," Willie smiled, "even in a place like New Fairfield."

"You not from around here?" The last thing Hank wanted to do was engage someone in conversation, but he found the sound of a friendly woman's voice oddly comforting, even if she was a stranger.

Willie shook her head and moved her barstool closer to Hank's. "No, I'm not, I'm here visiting my brother and his family. Name's Willie."

Hank turned his face, suddenly aware of how close she was. He could smell her perfume, the faint scent of it mixing with the smell of the evening air she'd brought in with her.

"Hank." He threw her a big, toothy all-American boy smile and Willie thought she'd died and gone to heaven.

"Well, nice to meet you Hank." Willie took her drink from the bartender who looked disappointed that she hardly noticed him. Willie looked over her shoulder at the couple on the dance floor, "Care to dance?" She ventured.

Hank frowned, "Dance? Now?"

"No, sugar, I thought I'd ask you to dance and maybe we could wait till next spring," Willie laughed. "Of course now, silly. No time like the present. Besides, it looks like you could use some female companionship."

"I'm married," Hank said with a hint of finality.

"I'm not proposin' sugar, just asking for a dance."

Without thinking, Hank reached out for her arm, pulling her from the barstool. Nat King Cole's smooth voice drifted from the worn speakers. Hank wrapped his arms around Willie's tiny waist as she cupped his neck with her hands. Suddenly, a feeling Hank had forgotten washed over him, the feel of another woman, the softness of her smile, the subtle curves of her body. God, how he'd missed that. Hank bent his head farther down until his hot breath was caressing Willie's ear.

"Let's get out of here right now," he whispered.

❧ ❧ ❧

Hank pulled his car into the driveway of the Sleepy 8 motel on the far outskirts of New Fairfield. He was certain this was a safe enough distance from town. Hell, who was he kidding? He wasn't certain about anything anymore and certainly not of this fiery woman who sat in his car.

"You ok, honey?" she smiled sweetly.

As ok as I can be, he thought, taking a stranger to a motel room. Hanks hands still gripped the steering wheel, as if he could still force himself to put the car back in drive and leave the redhead behind. A delicate hand with red painted nails covered his own.

"It's ok, sugar, I know this isn't easy for you. And if you want to leave, that's ok. But I know you're in pain, a lot of pain. I know heartache when I see it."

Hank turned to look at her, his vision was clouded a bit from the drinks and her face blurred as though he were looking at her through bubbled glass, but still he could see she was beautiful. He reached over and pulled her closer, pressing his lips to hers. Willie's mouth parted, letting his tongue inside. Slowly, he pulled away. "Let's get a room." Hank whispered, his voice thick with desire.

The rooms at the Sleepy 8 were as Hank expected, dull and sparse. But there was a bed and that was all they needed. They entered the room quietly, neither of them even bothering to turn on the light. Hank stood for a moment inside the darkened room, fumbling with his thoughts.

"I don't know why I'm doing this," Hank said, sorry the moment the words escaped his mouth.

Willie's hands flew to her hips, a teasing smile tugged at her lips. "Well, thanks a million sugar."

"No, no that's not what I meant." Hank shook his head and sat down on the faded blue bed spread, "I just, I've never done this…and, I'm married."

"I know you are," Willie sat down beside him, "and sometimes marriages have problems, and husbands stray." Willie cocked her head, "Sugar, if you think I'm lookin' for some kind of commitment from you, you can forget it. I mean no offense, you're easy on the eyes and I imagine what's under that shirt ain't too bad either. But I just got out of a bad relationship, actually that's puttin' it mildly." She waved the thought away with her hand, "Anyway, what I'm sayin' is that sometimes two people just need to be together. That's it."

Hank looked at her longingly. He wanted nothing more than to lift that sweater over her head and feel the warm tingle of her skin beneath his hands. As if reading his mind, Willie took his hand and placed it underneath her sweater. Hank felt her skin, the silkiness of it, how she responded to his touch. God, it had been years since he'd felt a woman respond to him. Hank pushed her back onto the bed and soon their clothes were scattered around them. Hank's body pressed and molded itself to hers. Then, he plunged into her, stopping short of releasing himself at the sheer ecstasy of feeling another human being.

♣ ♣ ♣

When Willie woke around 2 a.m., Hank was curled around her and she could feel his warm breath in her hair.

"Hello," he said, softly sensing she was awake.

"Hello yourself." Willie turned to face him, "Did you sleep well?"

"Not at all, but that's not necessarily a bad thing," Willie frowned and he continued, "I haven't been this close to another human being in so long, I didn't want to sleep through a moment of it."

Unable to speak, Willie kissed him lightly on the mouth.

"I have to go," he whispered. "But I want to see you again." The words were out before he could stop them. Yes, he did want to see her again. But he wondered if she would. It was, after all, just a one night stand.

"I'd like to see you again too." Willie replied with a smile, "I'll have to sneak around my brother, he's a bit of a prude, but I do want to see you again."

"By the way, I never asked you, Willie," Hank said snuggling closer, he wanted her again at least once more before he went home to Victoria, "who are you staying with?"

"Karl VanSant is my brother."

"Jesus..." The word escaped Hank's lips.

"Do you know him?" she asked.

Hank's lips curled into a half smile. "You could say that," he replied, "this is going to be complicated you know?"

"I know," Willie said feeling his mouth on hers again.

CHAPTER 18

Hank and Willie continued to meet in motels far outside of town, where Hank was certain no one would know them. Their affair brought Hank a comfort he'd never known and a passion he'd missed. It only took him a week to realize he'd fallen madly in love with Justin's aunt.

On the day of his son's graduation, Hank and Willie stopped for a bite in a local diner after their early morning romp. A quick scan of the restaurant told Hank it was filled with travelers and truckers and certainly no one would recognize him. Content with his observations, he and Willie took a booth in the back.

"Just a quick breakfast ok, Will? Then I've got to go to my son's graduation."

"I know, I promised Justin I'd be there as well," Willie smiled opening the menu.

Bernie loved antiquing and on this particular day, her morning treasure hunt had been quite successful. Thanks to a tip from a friend about an antique shop in one of the adjacent towns, she had discovered an old 45 rpm record player, a German made cuckoo clock, and a perfect match for one of her end tables. Digging through old trinkets gave Bernie a fierce appetite, and when she spotted the sign for Ella's Diner, she didn't even hesitate. Taking the only spot left in the parking lot, Bernie assumed the place must be quite good. When she walked in, a smiling hostess seated her in the back of the restaurant in a booth by herself. The couple in the next booth was speaking in hushed tones, and being the consummate eavesdropper, Bernie strained to hear their conversation.

Willie fidgeted in her seat; reaching across the table she took Hank's hands in hers.

"I know this is difficult for you, but she needs help. You know that don't you?"

"Yes, I do. Victoria's been sick for a long time," Hank replied.

"I know you love her, but it's the best thing for her. Besides, you don't want Billy to always remember her as being this sad, sick woman, do you?"

"No, love, I don't." Hank smiled and pulled her hands to his lips, "And I want you to know that I will always love her, she's been in my life for too many years not to. But Will, I'm in love with you, you've saved my life and I can't wait to make you my wife."

Tears filled Willie's eyes remembering the moment he'd proposed to her earlier that morning, after they'd made love. He had cried, they both had.

"I can hardly believe this, Hank. I mean, I came here just for a family visit and I meet you. And I've fallen in love, for probably the first time in my life."

"I feel terrible for Vic, I really do. But this is the best thing for her, she needs full time hospital care and I'm gonna get her the best money can buy."

Bernie shook in her seat. She could hardly believe what she was hearing, and when the waitress came around to take her order, she quickly shooed her away. She knew she had to leave, as quickly as she could before they saw her and Hank realized the jig was up. Bernie slid out of her seat, dropped a dollar on the table and scurried from the restaurant, not daring to take a breath until she reached the parking lot.

Graduation ceremonies were to begin promptly at two o'clock, and Justin stood on the grass beneath the warm sun perspiring under his heavy robe. He slipped a finger under his collar, tugging it loose around his neck.

"Don't pull on your robe, Justin. You look great," Eve smiled.

"It's so hot under this thing, you can't even believe it."

Eve could only look at him, "I'm so proud of you, Jus," she said quietly. "I can't believe we're standing here, on your graduation day."

Justin fought the urge to grab and kiss her, right there with everyone milling around him. He didn't care. Instead, he just smiled at her, trying to burn every second of this into his memory.

"Hey guys!" Billy came bounding up, interrupting their moment.

"Hey Billy," Eve smiled.

"Well, we're here Jus," Billy smiled. "Thanks for all your help or I don't think I would have made it this far."

"Sure you would have," Justin said quietly, seeing his parents emerge from the crowd.

"Justin! We're so proud of you!" his father boomed. "We're proud of you too, Billy!"

"Thanks Mr. and Mrs. VanSant, say have either of you seen my parents?" he asked.

"Well, your mother came with us, but she stopped to talk to some friends. I guess your dad needed the car for something this morning. She said he'd be here shortly."

"Where's Aunt Willie?" Justin asked. "Didn't she come with you?"

"No, she said she had to get your graduation gift," Karl replied. "She'll be along shortly."

Behind them, the crowd began to disperse as the graduates were being ushered to their seats.

"Well," Justin smiled looking from Eve to Billy, "looks like that's our cue."

Quickly, Eve leaned forward to give them each a kiss on the cheek.

"Good luck guys," She smiled and turned to leave.

Justin watched her walk away.

♣ ♣ ♣

Hank stood over Willie's engine while she tried to start her car.

"I don't get it, it drove fine this morning," she said, poking her head out the car door window.

"Neither do I, but we're gonna have to get going in a minute or so, I can't miss my son's graduation." Hank dropped the hood of her car, and wiped his hands on his pants.

"Well, look, I can get a cab from here, and you go on home and change."

"No, I won't let you take a cab. Look, I'm going to talk to Victoria tomorrow anyway so it won't matter who sees us, besides, I can just say I was giving you a ride, which I am. I can drop you at your brother's and no one will even think anything of it."

Willie shrugged, "I guess you're right, this paranoia has got me second guessing everything."

Hank leaned into her, kissing her on the forehead. "You're sweet for worrying but we won't have to do this much longer. Come on, let's go."

The drive home took longer than Hank had hoped as tourist traffic was already crowding the highway. Remembering a detour, he pulled off onto a small dirt road. The ride was bumpy, but faster than the highway. Hank sped his car through the dirt and gravel along the narrow path that wound through the woods. Trees flanked either side of the car and Hank expertly avoided them as he kept both hands on the wheel concentrating on getting them back as quickly as possible. Willie clutched her seat, not wanting to tell Hank how nervous the drive made her. Suddenly the road snapped to the left and Hank forced the steering wheel to follow the curve. The wheels slipped on the gravel and the back of the car slid right. Hank could feel himself lose control of the vehicle and looked up to see a grove of trees bearing down on him. Suddenly, the car slammed into them. The sound of crushing metal was deafening in Willie's ears but then there was silence and for a moment she thought they'd both be ok save for the blistering burst of flames that threw her from the car and the explosion that swallowed it whole.

CHAPTER 19

Shep arrived at the high school with the bad news, but he decided to wait until the ceremony was over. When the caps flew into the air, he knew it was time to grab Victoria and Karl VanSant before they left for whatever graduation parties they'd planned. He spotted Victoria first, her son in tow, heading over to the cluster of trees where Shep stood. She was smiling. It was a shame, he thought, this was one of the few times he remembered seeing her smile.

"Hello Shep," she greeted him warmly, "did you see our Billy graduate?"

"I did ma'am," he forced a smile. "Congratulations Billy."

"Thank you sir," Billy smiled, unzipping his robe.

Shep spotted Karl, Mary, and Justin emerging from the crowd and decided to wait 'till they arrived before telling them what had happened.

"Hello Shep," Karl greeted him with a handshake. "What brings you here today, or do you attend every graduation?"

"Well, I wish that was the case Karl," Shep began hesitantly, he'd been the bearer of bad news more times than he cared to count, but this one seemed particularly difficult for him.

"Victoria, Mary, Karl, I have some bad news."

Victoria eyed him warily. "What bad news?" She said flatly.

"Hank and Wilhelmina have been in an accident. I'm sorry but Hank died on the way to the hospital."

A muffled scream emerged from Victoria's throat, as she grabbed Billy for support.

"What do you mean he died? How can that be?" Mary cried.

Billy was thunderstruck, his face became gray and his breath caught in his throat, "Dad can't be dead," he whispered. Justin put a hand on his friend's shoulder for support.

"He sustained some very serious injuries, he was bleeding internally. He was alive when they got there but died within minutes of them loading him into the ambulance." Shep looked at Karl, "Wilhelmina's in critical condition, you should go to her right away."

"Mary, stay here with Victoria, I'll take Justin with me," Karl said abruptly, not waiting for his wife to respond. "Come on Justin, we need to go."

"Dad, I have to stay here with Billy, I'll be there shortly."

Karl nodded in understanding and rushed to his car. Eve walked up to the group just in time to see Victoria collapse into a heap on the grass. She wailed as she hit the ground.

"What happened?" Eve asked, certain Billy's mother was having another breakdown.

Justin turned to her, fighting back hot tears, "Billy's father was killed in a car accident."

❧ ❧ ❧

"Near as we can tell, he just lost control of the car," Shep said, leaning against the stark white hospital wall. Karl, Mary, Justin and Eve stood close to Shep, taking in his every word.

"That's all I can tell you right now, but we're runnin' an investigation and I'll let you know what I find out."

"Thanks, Shep," Karl extended his hand, sensing the conversation was over.

"I sure hope your sister recovers quickly," he offered, then added, "Karl, can I have a word with you alone, for just a minute?"

"Sure," Karl nodded. "Hon, why don't you take the kids and go to the cafeteria, I'll be there in a minute."

"All right, thanks again Shep, for everything." Mary took the policeman's hand in her own and hugged it gently; then she placed a kiss on her husband's cheek and headed down the hall.

Shep looked around before beginning to speak, to make sure no one else could hear their conversation. "Karl, eh, I'm wondering, do you have any idea what your sister and Hank were doing together?"

Karl thought for a long moment, "No, Shep, no idea at all. I didn't even know that she knew him."

Shep nodded silently, gazing at his shoes as he contemplated his next words.

"Shep, what are you getting at?"

The policeman looked Karl straight in the eye, "I don't know quite how to say this other than to just say it, but we found your sister's car at the Sleepy 8 Motel not twenty miles from here. I wouldn't normally ask you know, but I could have sworn you told me she was staying with you."

Karl dug his hands into his pockets. "She was," he said quietly.

"Uh, Karl, look there's more.... When one of the other constables found her car, a chatty motel manager said he rented a room to her earlier that day, and then the next thing he knew she and some guy were out staring at the engine of her car. He said they finally gave up and left in the man's car, which would have been Hank's."

Suddenly, the attorney in Karl kicked in. "And how is this relevant to the case?"

"It isn't, Karl, I just wondered is all. Look, I don't know your sister, but I know Hank and I wouldn't blame him if he strayed on Victoria, hell no one would."

Karl could feel his throat tighten. "Are you insinuating that my sister was having an affair with Hank?"

"No, I'm not insinuating anything, but I'm telling you that if this gets out, folks around here will do the insinuating for me, you know that as well as I do. I don't plan on telling anyone and I've asked the other constables to do the same. This doesn't affect the case at all. It was an accident, but it's going in the file so it will be a matter of public record. If anyone should ever ask about this they'll no doubt have the same questions I do. I would just hate for that poor family to have anymore misery heaped on them right now."

"Look, Shep, I'm sorry. I just..."

Shep put an understanding hand on Karl's shoulder. "These things are tough, now go be with your sister, I've got some paperwork to do."

Karl watched Shep as he turned to leave. He thought long and hard about Shep's words and wondered if it could be true, if in fact Willie had been having an affair with Hank. She had been going out, but Willie always did that. She was never one to stay at home. And she had seemed different, but he couldn't quite put his finger on it. Karl turned and headed down the hall to where his sister lay sleeping. He pushed open her door and watched her for a long moment. The doctors said she'd lapsed into a coma but she was gaining strength and they were hopeful she'd come out of it very soon. The only sound in the room was the monitor that beeped behind her. Karl walked in and sat down on the uncomfortable stool beside the bed. He rested his hand on hers and stroked it gently, determined to find out exactly what had happened.

CHAPTER 20

Justin and Eve made their way out of the hospital, to find their friend who they hadn't seen for hours.

"I wonder how he's doing," Eve said, trying to keep up with Justin's quick pace.

"I don't know, he wasn't at home when I called, Olivia was there, she said Terry was bringing his mom home from the hospital. They sedated her after she collapsed."

"Justin, this is just awful! That poor family has been through so much. I couldn't even imagine losing my brother and my dad."

"I know," Justin said. Almost without realizing it, he reached for Eve's hand and held it in his own. It was comforting to him to feel the warmth of her palm in his, her fingers curled around his own. They walked together hand in hand toward the lake where they were certain they'd find their friend. Evening was beginning to fall around Candlewood Lake and the trees that surrounded the lake cast long shadows. The woods were hushed, and the only sound they heard was the crunch of ground beneath their feet.

"There he is," Justin said quietly, reluctantly releasing her hand.

Billy was sitting on the short pier, his legs dangling over the side. His back straightened when he heard his friends approach.

"Billy…" Justin said simply before sitting down beside his friend. He placed a hand on his shoulder, "I can't tell you how sorry I am."

"Is there anything we can do?" Eve asked. She sat down on the other side of Billy, placing a soft hand on his leg. Justin observed that it was the same hand he'd held only a moment before, but he quickly pushed the thought aside.

"No, there isn't..." Billy said softly, "but I'm glad you're both here. I just can't believe this is happening, that he's gone and all."

"I know, it's a terrible thing Billy," Eve said softly. "But we're both here for you." Her eyes filled with the tears that she tried to swallow. She saw Billy's chin tremble and quietly rested her head on his shoulder. "It's ok to cry you know, it really is. I mean, he was your dad after all."

Justin sat in silence as he watched Eve coax a rare emotion out of their friend and slowly the tears began to fall from his eyes. The sun dipped behind the trees, leaving a warm afterglow on the lake while the three of them sat in a comforting silence.

Billy liked the silence; he wished it could stay like that forever. He never wanted to leave and go home, because he knew if he did he'd have to take care of his mother and he wasn't up to that. He wasn't sure if he'd ever be.

It was dark when Terry finally caught up with his brother. He approached the pier where the three were sitting silently in a row.

"Billy?" Terry's voice startled them, Billy looked over his shoulder.

"Terry, what's up?" Billy asked, slowly getting to his feet.

"I've been looking all over for you. You need to get home."

"I know, I'm sorry. I just couldn't stand going back there right now. Is Ma worried?"

"Well, that's why I came to get you...Billy we need to talk." Terry looked apologetically at Justin and Eve who were standing behind their friend.

"They're my friends, you can say whatever it is in front of them."

Terry inhaled the crisp evening air deeply before he began, "It's Ma, Billy, she's had a nervous breakdown and her doctor felt it was best she go somewhere where she can get better."

"Go somewhere? Where would she go?"

"Olivia and I are taking her to Fairfield Hills in the morning. Billy, she's going to need full time care for a while and we want you to come stay with us."

Billy teetered back on his feet and for a moment he nearly couldn't get his balance. In a matter of a few hours, he'd lost his father and now his mother. He felt his throat tighten and the forest around him became thick and suffocating. "No!" the words emanated from his mouth, and trailed behind him as he raced through the woods.

Terry turned to follow his brother, but Eve stopped him. "Don't go after him, Terry. He needs to be by himself. He'll be fine. Justin and I will make sure he gets home before much longer."

Terry's mouth formed a fine thin line, as he watched Eve and Justin slowly walk the path behind his distraught brother.

CHAPTER 21

Victoria Freeman could not attend her husband's funeral. At the moment he was being laid to rest, she was sitting in the corner of a hospital room, in a white gown singing a song she remembered from her childhood. Victoria couldn't remember who had taught her the song, but a memory she believed to be her own wafted to her through a fog of medication. Her voice was brittle from disuse as she fumbled with the edging on her starched gown. Outside, the sun glared in the late June sky and somewhere miles from her hospital room, a priest was saying what a wonderful man her husband was, a husband Victoria would not remember having for some time to come.

Willie woke from her coma on the day of Hank's funeral to find her brother at her side.

"Hi..." she said, her voice raspy from lack of use.

"Hello yourself, the doctor says you're going to be fine. Just a broken arm and some bruises." Karl said, reassuringly.

Willie breathed deeply and closed her eyes again, for a moment Karl thought she'd fallen back asleep.

"Aren't you going to ask me what happened?" she asked quietly.

"I figured that could wait Will, I mean till you're stronger." Karl reached over and covered her hand with his.

"I don't think I'll ever be strong again Karl." She paused for a moment to wet her lips and then she said, "He's dead isn't he?"

"Yes, Will, Hank died on the way to the hospital."

She closed her eyes and a tear slipped out, trailing down her cheek.

"Will, I really think we should talk about this later."

"I loved him Karl," she said without opening her eyes, "and I had to watch him die."

Karl inhaled sharply, "Will, I really don't think…."

Willie opened her eyes and looked directly at her brother. "Think of me what you will Karl, but we were in love. It wasn't intentional, it just happened. It was nothing like I'd ever felt before, we were going to be married…after he…divorced his wife…."

"Will, look, the constables found your car at the motel but no one will ever know about this. Certainly not Hank's family."

"Karl you know what? Just because no one knows about it won't make it go away. I will never forget. Never." Willie reached a bandaged hand up to wipe the tears from her eyes. "He meant more to me than I can tell you, and he loved me too."

"I don't know what to say Will, except that I'm glad you're going to be ok. I know we haven't always seen eye to eye but the thought of losing you…." his words trailed off.

"I won't tell anyone," she said, ignoring his last statement. "I'll go away quietly and never return. But I will never stop loving Hank Freeman, know that. He was a good man, the best. And he did everything he could to hold that family together despite his wife's condition. He didn't deserve to die; if anyone did it was me. I've spent my life trolling through bars and getting hooked up with men who treated me like trash…."

"Don't you dare say that you should have died in that accident Will! I won't let you say that." Karl swallowed a mouthful of tears and continued, "Will, listen you were always what I could never be, a free spirit, you did whatever your heart desired and to tell the truth, I envied you that."

Willie turned her face to him, "You envied me, big brother?"

Karl nodded. "I was always expected to live my life a certain way, to do certain things and I'm not sorry I did them, I just wished once I could have done something spontaneous."

"There's still time," Willie smiled.

"No, that time has come and gone for me. There are things in my life that can't be changed. I'm so grateful for Mary and Justin, I love them more than my own life. But there are days when I would wonder where you were and what adventure you were having."

"It wasn't all fun and adventure, believe me. Sometimes I was downright scared and lonely and wishing I could have been more responsible like you."

Karl chuckled. "Funny that we never talked about this before now. Before…"

"Before a tragedy made us see clearly…" Willie continued for him. "I'm glad we had this time Karl and I hope someday you'll come out my way to visit me."

Her brother frowned. "You're leaving us?"

"Yes, I can't stay here. There will be too many questions and if I stay, the truth is bound to get out. As soon as I'm well enough I'm going. But we'll see each other again, I promise."

Karl bent down to kiss his sister's forehead. He couldn't remember how long it had been since he'd offered her such a loving gesture but he knew it was long overdue.

🍁 🍁 🍁

Karl was by every day to visit his sister. He brought a deck of cards and they would play endless games of Parcheesi and 21. They would talk about old times and old friends, and days gone by. One day he arrived with a handful of daisies to find her bed empty and his sister gone. He stood in the abandoned room for a long time. Finally, a nurse pushed the door open.

"Mr. VanSant?"

"Yes?"

"Your sister wanted me to give this to you," she passed him a crisp white envelope. "She checked out of here earlier today."

The nurse turned to leave, but Karl stayed behind reading his sister's writing while he sat on her bed, missing her terribly.

CHAPTER 22

September ushered in a loneliness that swept through Eve's soul. Justin was off to college, and Billy was doing what he could to survive. He'd started a job working at the New Fairfield Inn, but soon gave that up for a position at Earl's Garage fixing cars. Billy didn't know a lot about car repair, but he picked it up quickly. And Earl seemed pleased.

Eve had known things would change, but she never could have predicted how much. Billy's mother was still in the hospital and Billy refused to visit her. Terry had insisted that Billy come live with him and his wife, but Billy wouldn't move out of the family home. He stayed there, alone, day after day, refusing every invitation Eve and Justin offered.

Eve found herself looking forward to weekends more than she could have ever imagined. Every Friday evening she'd be waiting on the train platform, waiting for Justin to disembark. Her world would brighten the minute she'd see his smiling face exit the train, and suddenly life became a bit easier.

It was a chilly late January evening. Judith watched as her daughter pulled on her jacket and began fastening the buttons. Outside, the sky threatened to freshen the snow that already covered the ground.

"Are you going to pick up Justin, dear?" Judith asked tentatively.

Eve looked up and frowned. "Isn't that where I always go on Friday evening, Mom?"

"Yes, well I was just wondering if maybe this Friday you'd take Billy with you."

Eve shrugged. "Mom, Billy's not interested in hanging out with us. We've tried to coax him out but he's got other friends now."

"Yes, and I hear they're not the best sort. You and Justin really should try harder."

"Mom," Eve replied, her voice tight.

Her mother hadn't seen all the days she and Justin had spent trying to win Billy over, trying to find out what was going on with him. Each time he'd refused, insisting he was fine and telling them to leave. Billy's desertion hurt her more than she'd ever be able to admit. "Justin and I have done everything we can to help Billy. He simply doesn't want to be helped."

"I think he's worried because you and Justin are an item now."

Her mother's words were the last straw. "Mom, Justin and I are not an item. We're friends, that's it."

"Are you telling me you're not the slightest bit interested in Justin as, well, as a boyfriend?"

Eve pulled a scarf around her neck, tucking it into her jacket. "Mother, why are you always trying to pair me off with one of them? Can't we all just be friends?"

Judith wrung her hands. "Of course you can, I just thought, that, well…that might explain why he's not around."

"No Mom, he's not around because his father died and his mother is in the nut house."

"Eve!" Judith's hand flew to her mouth. "You should never say that!"

"What? That she's unstable? Why not? Everyone knows it. Even you know it. She's nuts, and it has messed up Billy's life. But despite that he misses her because she's still his mother."

Judith ran her hands along the pleats of her dress feeling uncomfortable with the direction the conversation was taking. "You should try harder to be his friend, Eve. That's all I'm saying."

Then her mother turned and left Eve standing in the hall. Quickly, Eve dashed out the door, not wanting to be late to meet Justin.

Justin could see her as the train cornered the bend, a small, figure on the platform, bundled in a jacket. He always enjoyed the first sight of her, the first glimpse as the train began to slow to a stop. He was usually the first passenger out of his seat and as he leapt from the train he could barely contain a smile that filled his face. Soon, he was in Eve's arms. He was home and nothing else mattered.

They had fallen into a routine. First he would drop his bag off at home and greet his parents; then the two of them would head out for dinner. Justin always picked the place and always tried to make it a special event. He'd spend most of the evening telling Eve about his week because she'd always press him for details of his college life.

"I can't wait till I go to college," she said, a dreamy expression on her face.

"I love it, Eve. I know you will too."

Suddenly, Justin looked up to see Billy enter the restaurant with a shapely blond on his arm.

"Billy!" Justin stood up and waved. Eve turned to see Billy and his date approach their table. It was the first time she'd seen Billy smile in ages. It must be the girl, she thought.

"Hey, how's my favorite couple?" he asked, shaking Justin's hand.

Couple? Eve thought, was Mom right?

"We're fine," Justin replied, "we just came in for some dinner, care to join us?"

"Uh, no, we uh, want to be alone." Billy winked and the blond who had yet to be introduced, giggled and nuzzled Billy's neck. It was obvious to Eve they'd spent more than enough time alone already.

"Oh, this is Saundra, or Sandy as she likes to be called," Billy said and before giving either of them a chance to acknowledge her, he continued. "Say, Eve, how are you these days?"

"Good, Billy. You should come around and see me sometime."

Billy nodded, "Sure, sometime soon. Ok gang, gotta go. Nice to see you again."

When he left, Eve tore off a piece of bread and then dropped it onto her plate. "This just makes me sick, Justin. He's so, so…."

"Different," he finished for her.

"What's wrong with him? We were so close, now he's just shut us out. And he thinks we're…uh, dating…"

Justin felt his heart speed up. "Yes, he does," was all he managed to say.

"Isn't there anything we can do for him?"

"Eve, I think Billy's having a rough time, not just because his mother's been sick, but he's lost touch with everything that was important to him."

"You mean like us?"

Justin nodded, "Well, that's part of it. But think about it, I mean he was a star in high school. Every girl wanted to go out with him; he was revered on the football team. Now that's over and in one fell swoop he's no longer a hero, and he's sort of lost both his parents too."

"So what can we do, Jus?"

"I don't know, but I'll try to think of something. He can't go on like this. He'll end up ruining his life."

❦ ❦ ❦

"Principal Mitchell, look, I know this is an odd request, but would you at least consider it?" Justin pleaded.

Allen Mitchell leaned forward in his favorite chair as he watched Justin pace his living room. "Look, son, I know you're worried about him, but you know all of our coaches have to have teaching credentials. I can't really make an exception."

"What if he started going to a local college to get his credentials, could he teach then or maybe be assistant coach?"

"I just don't know. We are looking for a replacement for the upcoming season, but I'm going to have to poll the faculty to see what they think."

"Principal Mitchell, anything you can do to help him would be greatly appreciated, he's just so lost, I think getting back into an environment that feels comfortable will go a long way to helping him get his life back on track."

"Justin, we all want to help Billy. He's had a rough time of it and he deserves our support." Allen stood up, taking Justin's hand he shook it firmly, "I'll do everything I can to help you out with this, Justin. You're a good friend for coming here."

A smile filled Justin's face and he knew instantly that Allen Mitchell would see to it that Billy got some sort of coaching position. "Thank you, sir, I can't tell you how much your help means to me and will mean to Billy."

CHAPTER 23

Eve stood in front of the mirror, hardly believing what she saw. Enveloped in a cream silk gown, she looked more like a bride than a graduating senior. But in fact, she was graduating and tonight was her senior prom. Eve fastened the pearl drop earrings her mother had bought her just for this occasion and pushed her long blond hair off her shoulder. She could not take her eyes off her own reflection. It was almost surreal as she contemplated leaving high school and moving on. But to what? She'd hardly given her future any thought. Her parents couldn't afford to send her to an expensive college like Princeton, so a community college would have to do for her. Her life had been so wrapped around school and Justin she'd had little time to think of anything else. And of course, there was Billy, who took her out now and then but still, it was different. He'd grown to love his assistant coaching job, and become quite good at it. Consequently, she saw him nearly every day at school. It was as though he'd never left.

Eve's thoughts drifted back to Justin. She wondered what it was they were doing. Going out all the time, seeing movies together. Just this past week, Justin had begun holding her hand. Remembering how it felt to fold her hand in his lit a tingle that crept up her spine. Was she in love? Eve had no idea. What she did know was that she was excited about tonight, and glad Justin had asked if he could be her date to her senior prom.

Mary sat on her son's bed as he fastened the bow tie around his neck. He could feel her gaze on him, penetrating the back of his neck.

"I'm going to tell her tonight, mom. I promise," he said finally.

"I'm glad, son. It's time she knows how you feel."

Justin pulled the edges of his tie, making sure they were even. "It's not that easy mom, I mean, for a while there, I thought she only had eyes for Billy. I had to be sure."

"Well, now you are and it's time you two get serious. Everyone's talking you know."

Justin turned to face her, "Mom, I never thought you cared about what people said."

Mary smiled. "I don't, I just thought you should know the whole town can tell that you two are in love."

Justin's smile faded, "Mom, I don't know how Eve feels about me. But I'll know after tonight." He bent to kiss her on the cheek. "Wish me luck."

"You don't need luck," she said following him down the stairs. "If that girl has a brain in her head, she'll love you right back." Mary watched as her son smiled, grabbed Eve's corsage, and headed out the door.

The auditorium was filled with color, music and the graduating class of 1979. Eve had tucked her hand lightly into Justin's arm and together they navigated through the droves of people that filled the room. The floor vibrated from the music of the Bee Gees and Donna Summer, and the lighted ball over the dance floor threw a sparkle of color everywhere, mimicking the movie, "*Saturday Night Fever*." In Justin's estimation, the evening had gone perfectly. They'd danced and laughed and soon, there would be nothing else left but to kiss her and tell her how he felt.

"Eve," Justin said as he watched couples begin to leave, "shall we go for a walk by the lake, there's something I need to talk to you about."

Eve frowned. "So serious, Jus, is everything ok?"

He smiled. "Yes, everything is perfect."

The night was clear and warm and the moon a full, glistening, yellow ball. Eve and Justin walked side by side, on the dirt path that wound around the lake. It was peaceful and quiet; the only sound came from the gravel beneath their feet and the occasional cooing of a night owl. Justin knew the exact place he wanted to kiss her. It was on the pier, the one they'd sat on years before as he read Hemingway to her and she listened.

"Eve, have I told you how beautiful you look tonight?"

"Yes, but I love hearing it again." She tightened her grip around his arm. "You look very handsome as well, Justin. I dare say we were the most striking couple at the prom."

Justin guided her onto the pier, feeling his heart race in his throat. After all these years, after everything they'd been through together. He was finally going to be able to tell her how he felt; he was finally going to be able to kiss her. He only prayed she'd return his gesture.

They stood together on the narrow pier, overlooking the lake.

"Justin, why have we stopped here, is everything ok?"

Justin turned to her, "Yes, Evie, everything is just perfect. Do you remember the first time we were on this pier?"

Eve smiled. "It was the day you read me Hemingway." Justin's joy was barely containable. She remembered! He thought.

"Yes," he began after collecting himself, "it was the day I read to you and you have no idea what that meant to me. What you've always meant to me, Eve." Justin pulled her to him. He could smell the sweetness of her perfume and he curled her silky hair around his fingers. He bent his head closer and watched as Eve closed her eyes in anticipation of his kiss. He held his mouth above hers, wanting to savor her breath, sharing her air. Then, their lips touched and Justin pressed his mouth to hers, softly at first then with more urgency.

A loud thud and a crackle of branches startled them both, "Jeyshus, there you guys are!" It was Shep. "I'm afraid I've got some bad news. Billy's mother is dead. Looks like suicide."

CHAPTER 24

Victoria Freeman was buried beside her husband in Mountain View Cemetery. Nearly the entire town attended the funeral mass, most of them still in shock from the news. No one could understand what had possessed Victoria to swallow an entire bottle of sleeping pills. Father Matthew decided to ignore the gossip since she had left no note, not a word that would indicate her breaking point. There was speculation of course. Some said she'd been released from the hospital too soon, but that was nearly a year ago. Others said she'd finally learned the truth about why her husband had been driving with Willie Van-Sant, but no one knew for sure.

No one, that is, except for Bernie and the few people she'd told last week. Bernie shifted her weight nervously from her heels to the balls of her feet and back again, hoping and praying that it hadn't been her careless gossip that had led to Victoria's death. But how could it? She rationalized. It had, after all, been nearly two years since Hank's death. Surely that was enough time to put a person's thoughts in order. Surely. Bernie looked around her, everywhere eyes were focused on the priest and the coffin, a white spray of flowers covering a good portion of it. Bernie's own thoughts drowned out the eulogy as she tried to remember what she'd said to the eager ears at the Grand Union.

In the weeks that followed Victoria's death, Eve never left Billy's side. Despite Terry's wish that his brother stay with him and Olivia and sell the old house, Billy insisted on staying at their home. He rarely, if ever went into the living room and made a point to only go through it when he absolutely needed to. Each time he walked through there, he did his best to ignore the spot on the floor where Terry had found their mother's body.

Beginning the day after the funeral, Eve arrived every morning at 7 a.m. to make him breakfast and help him start his day. At first, Billy didn't really want her around but then something happened, he found that he began to look forward to her visits and on the really bad days, knowing she'd be arriving was his only reason for getting out of bed.

CHAPTER 25

"You've got to talk to her," Justin's mother urged.

"No, mom, just forget it, it's fine, really." Justin pushed his half-finished bowl of cereal away. He wished he could push the image in his head away as easily, the one of Eve and Billy walking last night, hand in hand through town. Billy smiling, Eve laughing, and then the kiss. Justin could still feel the pain of it tear through him as if it had just happened.

Mary sat down beside her son. "No, honey, it's not fine. You love her, you can't let her get away. She has no idea how you feel, I'm sure if she did she would want to be with you too."

"Mom, Billy needs her. She's helping him get through the loss of his mother." Justin got up from the table, picked up his bowl and deposited it in the sink.

"Besides," he said resolutely, "Billy will eventually go back to being Billy, dating a different girl every week. You know him, this won't last long."

Mary frowned as she watched Justin walk from the room. She hoped her son was right.

It was six months later when Eve and Billy announced their engagement.

CHAPTER 26

It was 3 a.m. when Justin woke. Beads of sweat formed on his forehead and he felt as though he would be ill. The night so far had been spent in long endless hours when waking never really rolled into sleeping and thoughts never slipped into dreams. Except to form the nightmares he'd grown reluctantly accustomed to.

Eve and Billy. Their names slid through his mind, sinking in. Today was their wedding day. The day he had dreaded for months had arrived without fanfare.

How had it happened? How had she slipped away? Justin tried desperately to recall the exact moment when it had happened, but then he realized that it was a collection of moments. Little by little, she slipped painfully away. It was the Friday evenings she'd been unable to pick him up, then he would see the two of them walking hand in hand and kissing when they thought no one else was looking. Still, Billy needed her and Eve seemed to truly love him.

That was all he wanted for either of them. Happiness. The best man had won. Or had he won because Justin had thrown in the towel? If he had fought for her would Billy have won her love? And when exactly did it become a contest? The fact was, he never really believed it would go this far and by the time it did, it was too late.

Justin got up and wandered over to the window. The moon shown brightly and illuminated everything it touched with a sleek, subtle silvery glow. He knew he needed to stop wrestling with his emotions. He needed to stop revisiting his loss. He needed to suck up, and get through the day. Then it would be over. He would be far away, and would hopefully, rarely have to see them again. His plan was in place.

✦ ✦ ✦

The bride's room was a large cool, dark room with faded off-white walls. The only light came from the flickering florescent bulbs overhead and a lone window that looked out across the church parking lot. A chipped pink bud vase held a handful of dusty plastic flowers atop an old white dresser in an attempt to make the dismal room look cheery. Eve felt frail and small in the vast space. Her hand, thin and nervous, kept fidgeting with her dress, reminding hers that this was her wedding day.

The day she dreamt of all her life. Was this what she had always thought it would be like?

She couldn't remember right now. All she knew was that she was standing in front of a full-length mirror surrounded by a cloud of white. Her blond hair was twisted at the nape of her neck, a few curled tendrils fell around her face, making her look even younger than her nineteen years. Eve looked back at the young woman staring at her whom she hardly recognized.

Are you happy Eve? A voice in her head echoed.

"Of course I am," she whispered in reply.

You sure? This is what you want now isn't it?

Certainly it's what I want, it's what I've always wanted. Her hand brushed an annoying tendril of hair from her face.

Wasn't there someone else you once wanted to marry? the voice continued.

Eve shook her head, "Of course not. There's been no one else. Ever," she whispered again.

As if driven by a force she could not control, her mind wandered to a night, just about a year ago. When Justin had kissed her. So tender, yet so passionate. Not just one kiss, but several. She could feel the dizzying inertia of it again, pulling her, the weightlessness she felt surrounded by his arms.

"Stop it!" she yelled now. She was no longer whispering.

"Stop what?" Justin asked from the door.

Eve could feel her blood run cold as she stared at his reflection in the mirror. How long had he been standing there? What had he heard? Oh dear God, please let this be a dream, she thought.

"Eve?" Justin paused, closing the door with a soft click behind him, "Are you all right?"

"How long have you been standing there Justin?" she said without turning around.

"I just walked in, why?"

"No, no reason, I just uh, was, oh never mind. What are you doing here?" She turned to face him and at that moment Justin could feel the breath catch in his throat.

She looked exquisite.

He approached her slowly, taking in every moment. Standing tall and handsome in his tuxedo he towered over her; every fiber in his body cried out to touch her, to hold her. A cloud of her perfume that wafted toward him, made him weak through the knees.

"What are you doing here?" she smiled.

"I came to see the beautiful bride before she was descended upon by a thousand people. I wanted a quiet moment alone with you, Eve."

She could only nod. There was an odd, far off look in Justin's eyes she could not place. It looked almost painful and sad at the same time.

"You look stunning. Billy is a very lucky man."

"Thank you." Eve's eyes dropped to her hands. Then her face looked back up at his and her lips formed a smile as she recalled, "Do you remember the first time we all met?"

As if it was yesterday my love. He thought, and truly he did. He could still taste the air, with its pungent aroma of fall and burning leaves intermingled with the sweet scent of the lake they all loved so much. Then there was Eve, her hair long and free, floating behind her. Yes, he remembered every second since they'd met. If she'd asked him to, he could recall every single glorious day they'd spent together growing up on Candlewood Lake. Now though, it was over. They were no longer three friends. Soon Eve and Billy would be a married couple, and Justin would be their friend. There would be the birthday card, the call at Christmas, and maybe even the exchanging of packages through the mail. But nothing like it was.

Not ever again.

And that made Justin saddest of all.

Now, it was time. Time to tell her of his plans before she found out some other way. He couldn't do that to her. Justin had been accepted to the University of California in Los Angeles. He'd sought it intentionally after Billy and Eve had announced their engagement. Justin knew that although he'd been able to somehow stomach their courtship, he would never be able to watch them be blissfully happy for the rest of his life. And he could not spend his days wishing for something he would never have. He needed this break, and it would hopefully put him in the place he needed to be to further his career. That was all that mattered to him now.

"Yes, I do remember it Eve," he replied finally.

"Who would have thought that we'd be here someday huh?"

Justin inhaled deeply, "Eve, there's something I need to tell you."

The tone of his voice worried her.

"Are you all right?"

"Yes, I am, everything's fine, I just needed to tell you that I will be moving to California."

"What! Why?"

"I have been accepted to UCLA, they've got a fantastic creative writing program and if I want to become a screen writer that's where I need to be."

Tears sprung into Eve's eyes, "Justin no! You can't leave me! What will I do without you?" Tears streamed down her face now, and she dropped herself into his arms that immediately encircled her.

"Eve, please don't cry. I'll come back and visit, I promise," he lied.

"Justin, please. Won't you reconsider? I mean you're my best friend!" Eve looked up at him with the biggest doe eyes he thought he'd ever seen.

"Billy is your best friend now Eve," Justin said sternly.

"Billy's going to be my husband, but you're still my best friend."

Justin looked at her face, now red from her tears. "Eve, he needs to be your best friend. Anything less would be cheating yourself of something really fantastic."

Eve sighed, she'd never really thought of Billy as her best friend, but she supposed he was. She had no time to think about that now, she had to talk Justin out of leaving.

"Justin, please...please say you'll reconsider."

He released her now, and turned to face the bare wall behind him, "I can't Eve, this is my choice. It's for my future, I need you to understand that."

Eve looked away at the window, outside she could hear her guests pull up and get out of their cars. Hundreds of cheery voices were entering the church.

"I want you to be happy Justin. I suppose if that means going to California then..." she shrugged, in an attempt to reluctantly agree with him.

"Thank you," he said, hoping the pain he felt wasn't showing in his face. This was tearing his heart out. He supposed that it would just be a day full of that. In less than an hour he'd be standing beside Billy watching any hope of ever being with her vanish in a cloud of "I-do's".

"You promise you'll call all the time, every day?"

"Eve honey, if I call you every day, I'll spend all my tuition money on telephone bills. But I will call you, I promise."

"All right then since there's no talking you out of this, let me dry my face so no one thinks I've had second thoughts."

Have you? Damn that voice again. This time she didn't answer it, or Justin would think she was totally insane.

"Here..." Justin handed her his handkerchief.

"Thank you," she sniffled. "I'm going to miss you terribly."

"I will miss you too," he replied softly.

Suddenly, he could no longer resist. He bent his head toward her, and she stopped mid-mascara repair. His hand brushed her hair and fell to her face, caressing it softly. Cupping her chin, his lips fell to her cheek. It felt warm, and he could still taste the salt from her tears. Quietly, gently and with a tenderness that left her breathless, he kissed her. Closing his eyes he inhaled the scent of her, locking it away in his memory forever. Eve could feel his lips press on her cheek and her eyes closed as well, feeling something in the pit of her stomach that was unfamiliar to her. Then, she realized how much she longed to feel his lips on hers again. She immediately cursed herself for even entertaining a thought like that! Ignoring her desire she smiled up to him when he gradually pulled away from her, his face was only inches from her own.

"Good luck," he whispered. Then in a quick step, turned and left the room.

God, how he loved her. How he would always love her, no matter where he was or what he was doing, he knew he would remember this moment, forever. The moment before it was all over, before every waking daydream he'd had of her, every hope of them ever getting together came crashing down around him.

Eve stood for one final quiet moment alone with her thoughts. She could hardly believe what she'd just heard. Justin couldn't leave, he just couldn't! She had to find a way to talk him out of going. Certainly he was crazy to leave Princeton. He didn't have to fly cross-country to be a famous writer. As soon as she could she would sit Justin down and try to convince him to stay. But for right now she needed to focus on what she was about to do.

At that moment a barrage of people descended upon her. Her mother, followed by her nine bridesmaids filled the room with pink taffeta dresses, and seemingly endless excited chatter. Eve looked around at her entourage. Her mother had been responsible for her bridal party of nine bridesmaids, two flower girls and one ring bearer. She felt that it was important to include her cousins that might otherwise feel left out. Eve barely knew them, but they all seemed friendly enough, and happy to be a part of her day. Her wedding wasn't exactly as she'd always dreamed, but she knew that a girl's day wasn't her own. Her mother needed to put her thumbprint on it as well. She only wished now that all the pomp and circumstance was over so she could begin her life with Justin.... Her heart fell with a thud into her stomach. Of course she meant Billy! Certainly it was only more of the same wedding confusion. She shrugged it off and tried to focus on the chatter going on around her.

Eve was still lost in thought when her father entered the room. He weaved his way through the excitement and found his daughter standing by the mirror.

"Honey?" he smiled, taking her hands in his own.

Eve found her father's eyes. "Hi Daddy," she said wistfully.

"Are you ready? It's almost time."

Eve inhaled a deep breath. The smell of his cologne felt reassuring somehow.

Her father placed a loving kiss on her forehead and said: "Sweetie, it's normal to be a little nervous. All brides are nervous on their wedding day."

Her eyes flew up to meet his. He could read the relief in them. "Really?"

"Of course, it's the biggest day of your life. Billy is a good man; he'll make a fine husband. I'm certain of that."

Eve knew it too. Billy was good to her; he was good for her.

He should be your best friend. Justin's words echoed in her head.

She ignored the voice this time and hugged her father tightly. "I'm ready Daddy," she said finally, "ready to marry Billy."

Every seat in St. Edward's was filled. It was a warm, delicious summer afternoon. The sunlight that streamed in through the stained glass windows threw shades of blue, gold and green across the worn tiled floors and carved wooden pews. Billy stood in a small alcove entrance beside the altar. A thick red velvet curtain hung from its round brass hooks. He pushed it carefully aside and looked out into the church. Just about everyone in New Fairfield was there. Thank God Eve's mom had helped him get their portion of the guest list together. He knew his mother would have had a fit if anyone had been forgotten. He thought of her again, and wished with all his might that she could be there to watch him marry Eve. But he knew she was with him, somewhere she was watching. Probably a front row seat if he knew his mom. Crying and waving her handkerchief at him. He felt in his pocket for the small velvet box. It was there. He hadn't forgotten it. He should have given it to Justin, but he kept forgetting. Besides, Justin had enough on his mind. He seemed damned preoccupied these last few weeks Billy recalled. He hardly recognized his friend at all recently. But he didn't have time to think about that now. The priest walked up behind him.

"Are you ready my son?"

"Yeah, yeah I'm ready, just let me find my guys."

"They're in the men's anteroom. I've already spoken to them, they should be out shortly."

Billy smiled a broad, handsome athletic smile. "Great, how about Eve?"

"She's fine son and we'll bring her around the back so you two don't see each other."

"Do you believe in that Father? The bad luck stuff I mean?"

"Of course not my son, but it's tradition and what is a wedding if not steeped in traditions."

Billy nodded, his hands felt sweaty now. He stuck them deeper into his pockets. Justin appeared behind Father Matthew then, a look of relief swept over Billy's face. "Hey pal," he smiled over the priest's shoulder. The latter took his cue and went back to round up the rest of the men.

"How are you doing Billy?"

"Fine, just fine, well maybe a little nervous."

"You have nothing to be nervous about."

"Have you seen her?"

Yes, I have and she looks goddamn beautiful, so beautiful in fact I almost swept her away from here and married her myself. Justin could still see her in front of him, smiling and crying at the same time, Please don't go Justin! Her pleas still burned in his ears. Certainly he would have changed any plan for her. It was all he could do not to say he would stay. But then he would have to watch them, and that would have killed him for certain. It was merely self-preservation.

Billy frowned at his friend's silence, "Justin, she's still here isn't she? I mean she hasn't changed her mind or anything right?"

Justin shook off his thoughts of her, "No of course she hasn't, she's here. I was in to see her a little while ago."

"How does she look?"

"Exquisite." Was Justin's one word reply.

"Wow, that good huh?"

"Yes, Billy that good. You're a very luck man you know?"

"'Course I know, she's the best."

Justin only nodded. "The best" was not quite how he would have described her. But then, it didn't really matter anymore what he thought. He glanced down at his watch and felt an invisible hand tighten around his throat. They were thirty minutes away from becoming husband and wife.

It was nearly over.

Billy's brother Terry and Eve's brother Teddy who were groomsmen, gathered around them along with his high school teammates; the priest tried his best to keep them quiet.

"Well Justin ol' pal, I guess this is it." Billy grabbed his friend's hand and squeezed.

Justin nodded and on Father Mathew's cue, followed his friend through the velvet curtain and out into the church. In the distance, Justin could hear the organ music faintly playing a classical tune; the congregation waiting in anticipation for the bride to arrive. Soon, Justin promised himself, soon this will all be over.

He took his place beside his best friend who stood fidgeting in his rented shoes that now seemed a size too small. Then, the music began again. One by one Eve's bridesmaids walked in perfect succession up the aisle. All smiles, each of them quite pretty. Justin remembered Eve telling him years ago that if she ever got married she'd forgo tradition and have only one person stand up with her. Sad that she didn't get her wish Justin thought.

Then, he saw her again and everything seemed to stop. There was no more music, no more bridesmaids; in fact the church was entirely empty. All he could see was Eve. He could even hear the faint 'click-click' of her heals on the tile floor. She walked on her father's steadying arm up the aisle toward him.

I love you Eve, he thought. With all my heart, I love you and I always will. Be happy my love, always be happy.

As he stood there watching her get closer, he asked God to make it all go away. Please dear God, he silently prayed, make it end and give me the strength to get through this.

The last thing he remembered seeing was Eve smiling at him through her veil.

Then nothing.

He didn't even hear them say "I-do" although he knew they must have because the priest was turning them to face the crowd and the congregation cheered. God had been merciful, He'd granted his prayer. Justin remembered nothing of the service and that's just the way he wanted it.

The reception was held at the Amber Room in Danbury. It was a lavish affair, and every table was filled with a dazzling array of pink roses atop floor-length starched white table linens and crisp white napkins. Chairs were covered in white brocade and adorned with pink sashes. Candles filled the room, throwing a soft romantic glow everywhere. When Eve and Billy entered, the band flew into a rendition of "Here Comes the Bride" and everyone clapped and cheered. As Eve looked around the room she realized all of a sudden that every single one of the 350 people they'd invited must be there. Plus maybe even fifty or so more. She could hardly believe all the guests they had. And, much like her bridal entourage, she knew very few of them.

The bridal couple made their way to the elevated head table where the bridal party was already seated. Justin watched them enter, and from across the room he could see the glow on her cheeks. There was no doubt in his mind she was indeed happy.

✤ ✤ ✤

The evening rolled on and after an extravagant dinner, the dancing ensued. The band Eve's father had hired was from New York and they were quite good, sounding just like Cheap Trick and even Fleetwood Mac. There was not a space to be had on the dance floor. Justin looked at his watch, it was almost ten o'clock. He knew the reception would last only another two hours at the most. He could tolerate that, he had no choice. The Best Man couldn't very well leave the reception. So he sat at the now empty head table, sipping his beer and watching Eve and some of her school friends laugh and dance like he'd never seen her dance before. Every now and again, the glitter of her diamond wedding ring would catch his eye and the pain would sear through his heart again.

One of the bridesmaids came up to ask him to dance and he refused as he'd refused all the other requests. She rolled her eyes and left, making her way to the dance floor to find Eve.

"So what's up with Mr. Stuck Up?" she asked.

Eve frowned. "What do you mean, who?"

"Your husband's best man that's who I mean. Look at him; he just sits there like some high and mighty. I mean he's great looking and all but he won't even dance with any of us."

Eve's eyes flew to where Justin was sitting, he looked odd, she thought. Almost out of place. She excused herself from her friend and walked over to him. Justin watched his fingers intently as he drummed them on the table; he was counting the minutes 'till he could leave. He didn't see her approach him.

"Justin?" She'd startled him, she could see that.

"What?"

"You haven't budged from here since your toast. Have you forgotten your duties as Best Man?" She smiled; the champagne filled her head with a lightness she hadn't felt in a long time.

"What duties? I thought I lived up to my job title quite well."

"Yes, you did a splendid job. Now it's time for one final official act!"

"And what might that be?"

"To dance with the bride!" Eve reached down and took his hand, pulling him up from his seat.

"No Eve, I don't think that's such a good idea."

"Really, well I think it's a wonderful idea. Besides all my bridesmaids think you're rather rude, not dancing with them at all. What's gotten into you Justin?"

"I—why nothing, I just don't feel like dancing that's all."

Eve stood back, placing her hands dramatically on her hips. "Why Justin VanSant, how could you not feel like dancing on a day like this! You should be ashamed of yourself."

Justin sighed and laughed as he watched her frown. "Why Eve, you are right indeed. Today is a day of celebration isn't it? Lead the way then madam." He bowed to her formally and Eve giggled. Taking his hand again she walked him to the dance floor. It was then that the band ended their fast song and began playing a love ballad. Suddenly, the idea of dancing didn't seem too hot.

"Eve, maybe you should dance with Billy on this one."

"Oh you silly, what are you afraid of Justin? Can't dance? I know you can, we've danced before remember?"

She hadn't meant to mention it, but a slip of the tongue and suddenly there it was. The last time they'd danced together was at her senior prom the night Billy's mother was killed. It was also the night Justin had kissed her. Thank God Billy was nowhere near to hear her mention it.

Yes, he remembered, all too well. He also knew the song the band had chosen to play at the very moment they approached the dance floor, it was also the one they'd danced to that night.

I bless the day I found you,
I want to stay around you

And so I beg you, let it be me…
Each time we meet love,
I find complete love,
Without your sweet love,
What would life be?

Eve's eyes softened, they were one of only two couples on the dance floor. "Please dance with me Justin. Soon you'll be gone and we won't be able to do this for a very long time."

Never again. A thought ran through his head.

At last, Justin conceded and gently took her in his arms. Eve rested her head against his cheek and remembered how safe she'd felt that night, cradled in his strong arms. As if nothing bad could ever happen to her again. It was right after that dance, she remembered as if it were yesterday. He kissed her, outside in the cool night air. The moon was filled with light and the sky covered with bright glittering stars. She often wondered what would have happened if they hadn't gotten called away so suddenly….

She looked up to Justin then, the champagne making her words careless. He looked down at her and searched her eyes for what she was thinking, but nothing could have prepared him for what she was about to say: "Justin, do you ever wonder what would have happened to us if Billy's mother hadn't died that night?"

He almost stumbled mid-step. "Wha…What do you mean?"

"I mean what would have happened, you kissed me that night remember? Would you have kissed me again? Did you want to kiss me again?"

"Eve, we shouldn't be having this conversation."

She sighed, "Oh Justin, please, we're adults. I'm just wondering that's all."

"Well, don't wonder. It's not healthy."

"You didn't answer me."

"And I'm not going to. You're married now, what's past is past. The fact of the matter is Billy's mother did die that night so we will never know, will we? Now you are married and you two are going to have a wonderful life together. So forget about it ok!"

"Don't get mad, Justin!"

"Eve, I'm not mad. I just don't think it's appropriate to be having this discussion."

"You're probably right Justin, I just feel so comfortable with you, like I could tell you anything. I'm sorry for bringing it up."

Justin knew exactly how she felt. He could tell her anything, and if she weren't standing here dressed in white with a room full of wedding guests he would have told her how he felt. He would have told her that he loved her and that no matter what happened, he always would.

CHAPTER 27

His flight left the following morning at 9 a.m. from Hartford Airport. His parents had offered to drive him there, but he didn't want anyone to take him. He hated goodbyes. He would take the bus and that would be that. He would be gone.

Billy and Eve were leaving for their honeymoon the same day. Billy was taking her to Hawaii. Justin was certain she'd love that.

In the morning Eve woke up first. She looked over to Billy who slept soundly beside her. As she remembered the night before she felt that wave of guilt descend upon her. She knew she'd done it wrong. She hadn't pleased Billy, and truly she didn't feel that great herself. She had no idea what all the raving was about…as far as she was concerned sex was overrated. She turned on her side and winced, she still hurt. Although Billy had tried to be gentle it felt odd and uncomfortable to her. Now she almost wished she hadn't waited until their wedding night to sleep with him. All the build up, all the anticipation seemed to fly right out the window.

Eve looked at the clock. It was 5:45 a.m., and if they were going to make their flight they had better get a move on. She couldn't believe that Billy had changed their departure at the last minute. He said it would save them over five hundred dollars in air travel if they left earlier so she had reluctantly agreed. Eve wanted so much to be able to see her family before she left; her mother was hosting a brunch at her house for all the visiting family. They were supposed to open gifts then, unbeknownst to Billy who announced the change of plans during their wedding reception. Certainly she understood, she'd said. Her parents, however, had not been so understanding. Her father had even offered to give Billy the $500 difference. But Billy was too proud to accept it. The honeymoon was his responsibility and he took that very seriously. So the 8:50 a.m. flight it was then. Her mother would have to make her apologies for her at the brunch. Her family would be disappointed she knew, but they'd get over it, eventually.

Quietly, Eve got out of bed to wash and get ready for the trip. When she was done with her shower, she found Billy awake and ordering room service. Billy knew the preceding night had not lived up to her expectations. Truth be told, it hadn't lived up to his either. Not that he was that much more experienced than Eve, but certainly he'd been to bed with several girls in his time and he knew what to do. But more than anything he'd wanted this night to be special for her. She had been so wonderful to him, so understanding, so giving. But to his chagrin, she'd felt awkward and embarrassed about the whole thing. He got up from the bed and walked into the bathroom where he found Eve pensively combing her hair.

"Hon?" Billy began.

"Yes?" Eve turned to face her husband.

"I'm sorry about last night, I'm sorry if I hurt you, or disappointed you in any way."

"No Billy, it was my fault. I just got, scared I guess. It was all so strange to me. I promise next time will be better."

Billy kissed her gently, wanting to take her again, but he knew he'd better hold off. Besides, they had a plane to catch.

"It's no one's fault Eve, it happens. When we get to Hawaii you'll feel very different about it I'm sure."

Eve wasn't so certain, but she nodded in agreement anyway. She began to feel nervous; what if she could never please her husband? Would he leave her? Billy jumped in the shower behind her, feeling quite comfortable with his nakedness. Eve on the other hand did not feel at ease sharing a bathroom with a man yet. It was all so scary to her, so foreign. She wished someone would have warned her that there would be an adjustment period. That just saying "I-do" didn't magically make her the perfect wife. She had a lot to learn.

All the sudden she thought of Justin, and wished she could call and talk to him about it. She was disappointed that she'd not been able to say goodbye to him, or have the opportunity to talk him out of going to California. But she hoped she'd have the chance when she and Billy returned in a week from their honeymoon. She knew that fall semester wouldn't start for at least a month so there would be plenty of time. She was certain that Billy would want to call him from Hawaii; maybe she'd have the chance to discuss it with him then.

In less than forty-five minutes they were both showered and ready to head out. The travel agency had hired a car to take them to Hartford Airport and soon they were speeding away down the narrow blacktop Connecticut highways enroute to meet their flight.

♣ ♣ ♣

Hartford Airport was fairly crowded on that early Sunday morning. Justin grabbed a hot cup of coffee and a paper and sat himself down by gate 15 to wait for his flight.

♣ ♣ ♣

The car pulled up at precisely 8:10 a.m. and the driver assisted Billy and Eve with their luggage.

"Sir, it looks like you'll be departing from gate 16, if I may, I can take your luggage to the counter for you."

"No, that's fine, we can handle it from here." Billy grabbed a wad of bills from his pocket, peeled off a couple and handed them to the driver.

Billy and Eve made their way inside the terminal, and within a matter of minutes were at the counter checking their luggage. Eve suddenly began to forget the preceding night that had seemed to cloud their day thus far, and felt the excitement of going on her honeymoon. Reaching down to take Billy's hand in her own Eve said: "We're going to have a wonderful time in Hawaii. Thank you so much for taking us there."

Billy smiled, she was feeling better and that made him happy. He had no intention of letting anything ruin this trip for them. And soon he knew, their sex life would live up to his expectations as well.

"You're welcome honey, it's my first official act as your husband I suppose, planning and organizing this trip for us."

"Yes, it is," Eve laughed as they made their way to their gate, "and you've done a splendid job so far!"

♣ ♣ ♣

Justin sipped his coffee, absorbed in an article he was reading so that he did not notice the approaching couple. As they drew closer he could hear that familiar laugh, and discreetly he lowered his paper. His heart stopped as he spotted them, walking hand in hand through the terminal. Eve was laughing and Billy smiled beside her. They seemed like the perfect couple to any passer-by. Justin quickly raised his paper again in hopes of not disturbing them. What the hell are they doing here? he thought. The last thing he needed was to see the lovers leave on their honeymoon. Lovers, he thought. They were most certainly lovers now. The thought of it ripped through him again. Now, there was no doubt he was doing the right thing. This was just what he was trying to avoid.

"Honey where's our gate?" It was Eve speaking.

"Gate 16, right here."

Shit! Justin thought. And then, without warning, Eve plopped herself in the seat right beside him. Quietly he lowered his paper and smiled over to her. The shock was evident on her face.

"Justin? What are you doing here?"

"Come to see the newlyweds off of course!"

Billy frowned, "No way man, how did you know we changed our flight time?"

"He didn't," Eve said flatly. "He's leaving for California, aren't you Justin?"

He nodded.

"Wow man, I didn't know it was this soon. I thought we'd have some time when we got back to hang out."

"Yeah, well I kind of wanted to get there early, you know find a place to live, get used to my surroundings and all."

"Sounds to me like you couldn't wait to get out of New Fairfield."

"Eve!" Billy nudged her. "Don't give the guy a hard time, it's for his future."

"I was going to try and talk you out of this you know?" She remarked.

"Yes, I know."

"Is that why you're leaving in such secrecy? Because you didn't want me to nag you about going?"

"Eve honey, come on. Leave the guy alone. Hey Jus, let's go grab a cup of coffee, looks like you could use another. Honey, we'll be right back."

Eve shrugged and glared at Justin. How could he just leave? They were friends after all. Best friends.

"Say man, she's pretty hot about you going. What's up with that?" Billy questioned.

"Oh, you know Eve. She hates to break up the act. I told her I needed to do this and I thought she understood."

"Well, don't worry about her. She's my wife now, I'll handle her."

Justin felt a twinge; for some reason other than the obvious, he didn't like the sound of that.

They approached the vendor. "Two coffees please," Billy requested. "So, uh, Jus, can I ask you a question?"

"Sure, what's up?"

"I was just wondering, I mean, is it always so difficult for a woman on her first time?"

For a moment, Justin wasn't sure Billy meant what he thought. At least, he hoped not.

The coffee vendor handed them their cups and Billy paid him. They began to walk away from the cart. Justin remained silent, hoping he'd misunderstood.

Billy continued in Justin's silence, "I just mean that, you know, she was like afraid. I wasn't expecting that."

"Billy, look I don't really think you should be talking to me about this kind of thing."

"Hey, why the hell not, you're my friend aren't you?"

"Sure but…"

"Then as my friend I need your advice. I dare say last night was the biggest disappointment of my life. She kept saying it hurt, and I kept starting and stopping. Geesh it made me nuts."

"Did you hurt her?" Justin asked through clenched teeth.

"No, well, kind of, not intentionally of course, but I had to, you know, at least try."

"She wasn't ready Billy, you forced her to do something she wasn't ready for, that's what it sounds like to me." Justin was sorry the minute he heard himself speak. He had no right.

"Hey back off buddy, she's my wife. I only wanted your advice that's all."

"Sorry," Justin replied still visibly upset.

"I just thought maybe you could shed some light on the subject. You being you and all, you know the learned one."

"I didn't study sex in school Billy."

"Fine, I just thought that maybe…."

"Be gentle with her," Justin began, a far off look in his eyes. "Caress her, hold her, tell her how beautiful she is. Then when she is ready, when she's no longer afraid, she will let you know. Don't frighten her, and don't make her think it's her duty or some silly thing. It's an honor to be with someone like her, and you've got to make her feel that way."

Billy watched as his friend spoke, he seemed to make sense. He seemed to know what he was talking about.

"That will make her happy?"

"Put your own needs second and make her feel as though she is the most important person in your life, that nothing else matters but her; that you will cater to her every whim; that nothing matters but her happiness and satisfaction. Then you will make her happy."

"Gee, you sure sound like you know what you're talkin' about," Billy smiled.

Justin couldn't believe what had come out of his mouth; he knew for certain that he'd almost given himself away. Luckily for him, Billy was too involved in his own dilemma to pay any attention. "Sure, anyway we should get back to Eve, she looks bored."

Both men walked across the way and sat on either side of Eve. Justin wanted desperately to put his arm around her and tell her it would be all right, that last night was just unfortunate, but that he hoped from now on Billy would not push her.

Suddenly their flight was called.

"Well," Billy stood up, "I guess this is it. You are going to visit and call and stay in touch aren't you?"

"Of course," Justin lied. Eve looked downtrodden, as if she were losing her best friend.

"Bye man, take care." Billy held out his hand to his friend. "You were a great best man by the way, thanks for all your help."

Eve felt as though she were going to cry. She looked to her husband, who said he would wait by the gate for her. He wasn't sure what possessed him to do that. But he felt that Eve needed a moment alone with Justin.

They stood facing each other for a long moment.

"You'd better go, you'll miss your flight."

"I will think of you all the time."

Justin raised a hand to wipe a tear from her face. "You'd better not, it could get very crowded in that marriage of yours if you're thinking of me too much. Besides you'll have plenty to keep you busy. Even if I did stay in New Fairfield, we'd probably hardly ever see each other."

"That's not true and you know it. Justin I've decided that there's some other reason for you leaving, although I haven't figured it out yet, I will."

"I have no ulterior motives here, I assure you."

"Hold me," she sniffled. And he did, she fell into his arms like a rag doll. "Justin, I'm afraid, I don't know if I like this marriage thing. I'm scared."

Dear God, why now? he thought, in the middle of a crowded airport with a hundred people watching.

"You'll be fine, I promise you."

"I don't think so." She was crying now. Off in the distance, Billy had struck up a conversation with one of the stewardesses, unaware of what was going on right behind him.

"I don't think I can do this. Maybe I'm not meant to be married."

"Of course you are, you are meant to be loved and cherished and cared for."

"Well I don't feel very loved and cherished, I feel like I'm letting Billy down."

He tightened his arms around her. "You listen to me Bug. You could never let anyone down, do you understand that? You are a fabulous creature and any man would be so very lucky to spend his life with you."

"I hope it gets better."

"It will, I promise, give it time…" He had to get away, suddenly he felt as though the walls were caving in on him.

She pulled back from him, looked him straight in the eye and said: "I will miss you, my dearest friend. I will think of you all the time and part of me won't be complete until you return."

I love you, he wanted to say.

"I guess I've made a fool out of myself long enough, I better go now."

Justin released her. "Take care of yourself and have a wonderful trip."

"I'll try." Then Eve reached up and kissed him on the cheek, her lips seemed to burn his skin. Then she turned to her waiting husband who had ceased his conversation with the stewardess and was wondering what was keeping his wife.

Justin watched as they entered the gate, and then from the window as they crossed the tarmac to where the aircraft stood waiting. Eve waved to him until she disappeared into the plane.

Then she was gone.

Forever.

Justin turned from the window and fought back the tears.

CHAPTER 28

Justin's flight arrived uneventfully into Los Angeles International Airport later that day. It was a sunny 85 degrees in the southern California city and Justin could hardly believe the weather. There were no winters or harsh summers in California. At least, that was what the brochure said.

Quickly he exited the terminal, baggage in hand and hailed a taxi. He had booked a one week stay at the Best Western near the college and hoped that would be all it would take to find a suitable apartment in this town.

The trip through Los Angeles proved to be an education in itself. It was nothing like the state he'd just left but almost as crowded as New York City. Everywhere people were either jogging or walking out in the bright California sunshine. Everyone was in some type of summer attire, suddenly making his selection of pants and a long sleeve shirt seem inappropriate.

He arrived at the Best Western Motel, located on a very noisy intersection. Justin paid and tipped the cab driver, and headed into the office to register. A pudgy woman with angry red hair stood behind the counter, a half smoked cigarette dangling from her mouth.

"Kin I help 'ya?" she tried to smile, but failed.

"Yes, I have a reservation. The name is VanSant."

"Oh, yeah, I saw 'ya in there just a while 'go, you a college kid?"

"Yes, I'm here to attend UCLA this fall."

"Great, where 'ya from?"

"Connecticut."

"Wow, helluva long way to come for school, ain't 'cha got any schools back there?"

"Yes, actually quite a few very good ones."

"Then why did cha come all the way out tere?"

To escape a memory, he thought. "Well, UCLA offered the best program for what I needed."

"Ah, I see, what 'cha gonna be?"

"Hopefully," he smiled, "a screen writer."

The redhead threw her head back in laughter. "Got only five million of 'em in this here city, all unemployed. But good luck to 'ya." She handed him a key while he signed the credit card slip.

"Thanks," he smiled, feeling anything but welcome. He hoped she wasn't a shining example of Los Angeles hospitality.

The room was pleasant, and to Justin's surprise, quite soundproof. There was a small coffee maker, a television and a clock radio. All the comforts of home. As he unpacked he reached over and flipped on the radio. Smooth vocals seeped out of the speakers and filled the all but empty room.

Justin pulled out a few items that he would need for a couple of days, leaving the rest in his suitcase. He hesitated for a moment before pulling a manila envelope from the side pocket. Justin looked at it for a while and then, he could resist no longer. Opening the top he pulled out a glossy photograph. It was taken at Eve's sweet sixteen-birthday party. He and Billy were on either side of her. Eve's smile shined into the camera, and both boys grinned from ear to ear. Justin noticed that his arm was wrapped around her, and Eve was leaning toward him, her head almost resting on his shoulder. He had known then, that he loved her. He stared at the picture for what seemed like hours.

For a brief moment a sense of complete loneliness swept over him like the tide, leaving in its wake a salty, sticky residue of pain. The good old days were gone; his childhood had been reduced to a memory in a glossy photo. He was in a strange new world now, forging his own way for what seemed like the first time in his life. It was at the same time exciting and frightening. What if the red head had been right? He knew the odds. Writers were a dime a dozen in this town. What made him different? He sat on the bed now, still staring at the photograph. Everything seemed so simple then. He loved Eve, he had lived for Eve. And the three were best friends. He assumed they'd always be. But fate had something entirely different in store for him. He hated fate. It had a lot of nerve barging into his life and taking away the one thing he cared about. A song began to play softly in the background; it was one he knew well:

Faded photographs, covered now with lines and creases
Tickets torn in half, memories in bits and pieces

Traces of love, long ago that didn't work out right
Traces of love, with me tonight.

I close my eyes and say a prayer
That in her heart, she'll find a trace of love still there,
Somewhere

An angry hand reached out for the radio and slammed down the on button. The music was gone, only a broken silence interrupted by the muffled sound of cars speeding down La Cienaga Boulevard. Justin lifted himself from the bed. He needed to get the hell out of his room. He needed to walk and clear his head. Moreover, he needed to shake the pain that had settled into his bones over the last few days.

Justin left his motel room and wandered down the unfamiliar streets of Los Angeles. Justin could see that the area was beginning to show signs of erosion; the buildings were fading and dirty and a thin veil of traffic dust settled on everything. He was not impressed with his first sights and sounds of Southern California, and Justin needed to keep reminding himself that he was here for one purpose and one purpose only. To become the best writer he could be, and while he was at it, forget that Eve Phillips ever existed. Eve Freeman. She was Eve Freeman now. Mrs. Billy Freeman, wife of Billy. Not wife of Justin. Never his wife. Never his anything.

The street he walked on was dotted with liquor stores, thrift shops, restaurants and bars. Suddenly an unfamiliar urge took hold of him. He needed a drink, and he needed one bad. He allowed the feeling to overtake his senses and entered the first bar he came across. The flickering red light above the door read: Eddie's Place, and the sound of voices inside was the relief he desperately needed. No one looked up when he entered, and Justin quietly walked through the conversations and smoke to the bar where he ordered a scotch, neat. There was no such thing as drowning your sorrows, he knew that, but one could certainly try to soak them. The drink burned a path through his throat as it slid down; the tendrils of it tickled his mind and began to gradually numb him. Another drink, another bit of relief. Justin slid onto a worn barstool, resting his weight against the cool wooden counter. He ordered another drink and threw it back, letting it chase the rest through his system. Here he was, alone and getting drunker by the moment. But he no longer cared. Nothing mattered now. Not a god dammed thing mattered anymore.

A woman slid in beside him, but he only caught the sight of her hair. A few blond tendrils that wisped on her neck and that scent…that scent of…Eve! He thought. She'd come after him! The blond turned and smiled sweetly. His heart sank in his chest, it wasn't her. It was another mirage of her, haunting him wherever he went.

"Hi." The blond's glossy lips curved up into a seductive smile.

"Hi." Justin could feel the word slurring the tiniest bit. Good, he thought, for once in my life let me make no sense at all.

"What's your name?" A pale hand with bright pink painted nails fingered the collar of his shirt.

"Jus-Justin."

"Hi Justin, I'm Evelyn."

A hiss of air escaped his lips at the irony of it all. "Do people call you Eve?"

The blond frowned. "Sure, sometimes, mostly Evie though."

"Fucking figures." Justin mumbled into his glass, signaling the bartender.

"What?"

"No—nothing, just talking to myself."

The blond ran a hand along his back. "Can I have a drink too?"

"Sure, order whatever you want, it's on me."

"Say, I got a better idea, why don't we go somewhere else and have this drink. Somewhere quiet."

"I don't want quiet right now."

"Fine, we can sit here for a while." Her hand continued to run the length of his back, gently trying to seduce the muscles beneath his shirt.

"You look very smart, are you a student?"

"I will be, came here to go to UCLA."

"Whatcha gonna be, a doctor?" Evelyn's eyes perked up at the thought that she might be about to seduce a future surgeon or something.

"No, there will be no doctor in the VanSant family I'm afraid." Justin pulled his glass up to his lips again, sipping on it and considering his sarcastic remark.

The blond leaned in closer, "So, watcha gonna be then?"

"A writer. A godamned famous writer, that's what I'm going to be." He could hear the blond snicker under her breath.

"What's so funny?"

"Nothing. Can I have another drink?"

"Whatever you want." Justin sipped again, fingering the thin cocktail napkin.

Her lips tickled his cheek. "What I want isn't a drink," she hissed softly into his ear.

Evelyn leaned even farther into him, pressing her ample breasts into his side. Justin could feel the softness of them and the hard nipples that pressed through the thin cloth of her blouse. He felt the warmth of them spread to his groin as the blond leaned in even closer. That's what I need, he thought, a good fuck to make me forget everything.

"So, how about it? Shall we go back to my place?"

The thought of casual sex tempted his brain and disgusted him in such a way that it was almost faintly arousing. He needed to color outside the lines for once in his life, take the crayon and just fill the whole damned page with it. Fuck the lines. Fuck everything. He signaled the bartender to refill their glasses. Eddie, or whoever was pouring the drinks didn't seem to care that Justin was getting well beyond his limit. He splashed more brown fluid in both glasses and set them with a thud on the counter. Justin reached for his pocket, his movements slowing as though he were pushing through water. He had a difficult time finding his wallet. Finally a languid movement retrieved it. He paid the bartender and tipped his glass to Evelyn, who looked dismayed that her request was not immediately accepted.

"Well?" she said without picking up her drink.

"Can't, sorry."

"Why not? Is there someone else?" A delicate finger played with the rim of his collar again, not wanting to give up.

"There was," he replied flatly.

"Really, is that why you're here? Did you two break up?"

"I can't really talk about it Eve—uh, Evelyn."

"Call me Evie." Her voice was filled with a velvety roughness, like corduroy against grain.

An invisible knife seared his chest. "No, I won't call you that."

Evelyn chuckled. "Why? Was that her name or something?"

"As a matter of fact it was."

"Sorry." Evelyn retreated into herself, seeming to plot her next move. "Look, I gotta go, are you gonna go with me or not?" As she spoke, a hand moved from his collar, down his chest and between his legs; massaging him into an erection.

"I can feel you want me." Her breath was warm in his ear.

"You're a very beautiful woman and with your hand on my crotch, of course I want you."

"Are you too good for this? I promise you I will make you forget her."

"I wish you could."

When Evelyn suddenly yanked her hand away, Justin felt the slightest bit of disappointment in her retreat.

"Look, I'm not gonna spend the entire night trying to talk you into going home with me. Either you want to have sex or you don't."

When Justin did not answer, she slid off her barstool, turned in a huff and strode away. Her perfume swirled around his head and for a long intoxicated moment, he was tempted to follow her out. Instead, he fondled his sweaty glass and listened as the door slammed shut behind her. The bartender refilled his glass one more time and after throwing back the drink, he pushed himself reluctantly off the bar stool. The hours had slipped by unnoticed since he'd entered the bar and he was lucid enough to notice the crowd around him was changing.

Rough, rugged looking men covered in tattoos were surrounding the pool table and spoke in a loud raunchy language. Justin thought it best that he leave while he could still walk. Like a toddler stumbling through toilet training, he wove his way through the street language and heavy smoke to the same door the blond had disappeared through. The air outside was only faintly chilled, but already the sun had disappeared behind the tall gray buildings. Justin sank his hands deep into his pockets and checked the street to try and familiarize himself with his route home. A faint female voice came from an alley between the bar and the next building. He could hear the muffled urgency of it and slowly walked closer.

"Denny, leave me alone, I told you it's over."

"Aw, come on honey, just one more for ol' Den ok, just one more dip in the lake Evie, please?"

Justin leaned around the corner and could see the blond struggling against a man who was well over twice her size; he was dressed similarly to the men he'd just left behind at Eddie's. The old boyfriend or whoever he was held her tightly and was forcing his face to hers.

"No! No! I told you to leave me alone!"

"Listen you slut! Denny wants a little sweetness and you're gonna give it to him do you understand!" A large sweaty hand yanked apart her blouse, sending buttons flying like bullets through the air. He reached in and fondled her breasts as she tried to squirm out of his grip.

Justin could no longer sit by and watch, and with unsteady movement, he lunged at her attacker, surprising him just long enough for him to release his grip. Evelyn fell back in shock, pulling the edges of her torn blouse together as she watched Justin pin Denny to the ground. Still caught by surprise, Denny flung his arms at Justin's head, trying to knock him off, but Justin persisted, and with one targeted punch, he knocked any consciousness out of Denny.

"Oh, my God, you knocked him out!"

Justin stumbled to his feet, still reeling from his act of bravery.

"I-I, saw him, try to…I just thought you needed help."

Evelyn touched his elbow with a shaky hand, curling her fingers around it. "I did need help. Denny would have raped me right here in the alley if you hadn't come along."

"Well, I just did what anyone else would have done."

Evelyn threw her head back in laughter. "In this part of L.A., are you kidding?"

"Well, I'm not from here."

"It shows…oh, it looks like he did get you after all." Evelyn brushed a mark on his face that was beginning to change color.

"I'll be fine." Justin watched as Denny continued to lie motionless on the ground. "We should call an ambulance for him and get you the hell out of here."

"Well, let's get out of here first and call from a payphone, I don't want to be around when he wakes up." Evelyn tugged at him, pulling him along. "Say, you know you're a pretty good fighter. Do you do this much?"

"I've never fought a day in my life."

Evelyn snuggled closer to him, curling her arm around his while her breasts jiggled seductively under her blouse.

"Walk me home Justin. Please? And let me ice that bruise for you."

"Fine, let me call an ambulance for our friend first." Justin stopped at a phone booth, and dialed 911. After he made the call, Evelyn led him three short blocks away to where she lived; a small, meagerly furnished studio apartment on the third floor of a worn wooden building. The narrow staircase that led up to her room was dirty and smelled of urine and musk. There was far less soundproofing than at his motel room and Justin could hear the sound of her neighbor's television through the walls.

"He's always got that thing on. I swear I think he even sleeps with it on. Can I get you a drink?"

"I think I've had enough, but thanks anyway, I should probably go."

"No, don't go yet, stay a while, I rarely get company, besides, I want to ice that bruise for you."

Evelyn's bed was separated from the main room by a thin, faded blue curtain. Behind it, he could see her neatly made bed.

"Have a seat on the bed," Evelyn motioned from her kitchen, as she poured two drinks into paper cups and pulled a bag of frozen vegetables from the freezer. Wrapping them in a towel, she headed over to the bed, setting the cups down on her nightstand. She held the bag to his temple and he quickly took it from her.

"Look, do you mind if I change out of this blouse? It's kind of seen better days."

"Sure, no problem."

His eye quickly glanced around the room, wondering where she'd find the privacy to do that. In answer to his question, Evelyn shrugged out of her blouse, letting it fall to her feet in a bright pink puddle. She slipped out of her tight shorts as well and was soon walking to her closet in only her underwear. She pulled out a semi-sheer robe. Tugging it around her, she fastened it loosely at her waist. Justin could only watch her out of the corner of his eye as she casually strolled back over to the bed. The fabric clung to her breasts and outlined her nipples.

Evelyn sat poised on the bed as she sipped from her cup. Justin did not know if it was real or imagined, but for a moment, he thought it was Eve. Come to take him home, back where he belonged. The past two days had all been imagined; the wedding, the reception…the wedding night. None of it had really happened. But this, this was real. She was here and they were together. Justin sat down beside the blond, and an eager hand reached around her shoulders pulling her near. His lips fell to hers and his mouth, hungry for relief, devoured her in not one kiss but many, each building in intensity. The scent of sex filled the air and he could feel the heat of his passion overtake his senses. He pinched his eyes shut, pretending it was Eve he was making love to. Her name, sounded almost reverent on his lips and the blond beneath him was thankful that she was on the receiving end of his pent-up passion. Soon, they were naked, tossing and turning in a sexual storm. All the while he was aware and unaware, swimming from drunkenness to lucidity and back to drunkenness again as he thrashed inside this woman. Calling out Eve's name and clinging to what was left of her memory.

Justin woke the following morning, trying amid the fog of reluctant sobriety to remember what had happened. His head was filled with a hangover and the lower half of his body ached from second-hand sex that flooded his system. He could smell her in the room, her perfume and the antiseptic smell of alcohol. She stirred beside him as he remembered the previous night. The bar. The woman. The drinks and the anonymous sex with a stranger. The relief from his pain that had lasted only a few hours and the hellfire fury he now felt for having sunk so low.

CHAPTER 29

The sun began to set on their first full day in Hawaii. Billy took Eve's hand and walked beside her along the ocean's edge. Eve looked out over the water. It was so beautiful here, she could hardly believe it. It was an intense almost mesmerizing beauty. Everyone was tanned and smiling and always seemed to be saying "aloha" and offering some sort of exotic beverage to drink.

They had arrived without incident the day before, and after being greeted by two scantly clad Hawaiian women they were whisked off to their hotel via a black sedan. In the car, Eve held the lei to her nose and inhaled the scent of its richly colored flowers. It felt as though she were inhaling honey. She watched as the landscape zoomed by, while they sped to their destination on a narrow blacktop highway. Eve rolled down her window a bit, to feel the wind on her face. The air felt heavy, like Connecticut in the summer, yet at the same time it smelled sweet like a mixture of sugar cane, sea salt and a field of succulent tropical flowers.

Billy had booked them into the Maui Island Sheraton. It was a luxurious hotel that lived and breathed the tropical paradise. Once the car pulled up, they were immediately descended upon by uniformed bell staff who greeted them and handled their luggage. Eve was in awe of the place. The lobby was entirely open-air with large tropical plants and flowers everywhere. Huge brightly colored parrots sat claw-cuffed and perched atop elegant wrought iron trellis-like structures. Everywhere Eve looked, she could see wildly colored shirts with huge floral prints. She couldn't imagine anyone in Connecticut wearing something like that, but here it seemed entirely appropriate.

After they checked in, they were escorted to their room. The honeymoon package had included a luxurious two-room suite. It literally took Eve's breath away. It boasted a living room with a huge television and complete stereo system. It had a balcony in each room that overlooked the vast ocean. The room was decorated in muted tones and pastels. There was a wet bar, as well as a small round glass dining table complete with four wicker chairs. On the table was a large fruit basket wrapped in amber colored cellophane. The bellman quietly set the luggage down in the master bedroom and instructed Billy on the room's amenities as well as the thermostat controls. He nodded to the couple and Billy peeled off several bills that he shoved into the bellman's hand. With the click of the door, they were alone. Eve was busy exploring the rest of their suite and found that the bathroom was as exquisite as the rest of their room. It had a huge glass shower that Eve guessed would fit nearly five people and a Jacuzzi tub that would hold about the same. Billy followed her into the bathroom and Eve turned to him with a broad smile and said: "Billy, I don't know what to say. This is incredible."

She reached for his hand and pulling him closer, kissed him softly on the mouth. Billy wanted to christen their room with a lover's tryst, but he abstained to give Eve the space Justin seemed to think she needed. Instead, after a brief rest and a couple of pieces of fruit from their complimentary basket, they explored the hotel.

They left the hotel to walk along the ocean. They smiled and nodded to the other couples they met. No doubt they were newlyweds also. The island seemed to lure them one and all. Billy looked over to his wife. Her cheeks held the faintest of pink. They had been out in the sun for only an hour, and she was beginning to show signs of sunburn. While Eve needed to be careful because of her fair skin, Billy was already beginning to look like an islander. He seemed to tan almost instantly, making his bright blue eyes shine even more. Eve had not been ignorant to the fact that her husband attracted a lot of attention from the Island women. Eve shrugged it off. Yes Billy was very handsome and sometimes a little too aware of just how good-looking he was.

"What shall we do for dinner tonight?" Billy asked.

On their first night, they had dined at the open-air restaurant in the hotel and watched the sun set over the crisp blue Hawaiian ocean. It had been extremely romantic. Billy had held her hand the entire time, with Justin's words echoing in his head: Be patient with her and when she is ready you will know. When they returned to their room later that night, Billy wasn't sure what the sign would be. When he would know? Would she smile at him just so? Would she try to seduce him? He'd like to think so, but as timid as Eve was, he rather doubted it. Finally, he'd held her and kissed her deeply. She returned his kiss and Billy had suggested that he draw them a bubble bath. They continued to kiss encircled by fragrant bubbles and finally, made love for the second time between the crisp white sheets of their honeymoon bed.

"Eve?" He said again, "What about dinner tonight?"

"Let's go into Lahaina! I keep hearing about it, it's supposed to be a real native fisherman's village."

Billy smiled at her, he loved to see her excited and happy. "Of course we can, anything you want."

Their lovemaking on their first night in Maui had been better than on their wedding night. But Billy still hoped for more. He needed to remind himself that he was Eve's first, and it was up to him to teach her how he liked it. At least she had been more receptive to him and less afraid. He had entertained a terrifying thought enroute to their honeymoon that she would never warm up to him, and then what would he do?

CHAPTER 30

On his second day in the city of angels, after Justin had returned to his motel room, he began his hunt for living accommodations. To his surprise, his search took him to Santa Monica, a beachside community not far from the college. It was an entirely different world than what Justin had grown accustomed to on the East Coast. Everyone seemed laid back and easy going. He found that even midweek the beaches were quite crowded and the sidewalks packed with bicycles, roller skaters and enough bikini clad women to fill a football field. It was a new and different world to Justin.

He had originally hoped to find a small quiet apartment somewhere near campus. But after stumbling upon a one-bedroom cottage at a very reasonable rate, he signed a lease on the spot. The woman renting it to him was retired and lived in the house next door.

"To keep an eye on the place." She said warily.

She hadn't wanted to rent to a college student, but it had been on the market for quite some time and this young man seemed nice enough.

The cottage was located on Ocean Boulevard officially, but was really off the road almost entirely. In fact, the driveway from the street led you to the quaint home with a back porch that was literally on the beach. Very Californian, Justin thought. He smiled at his new landlady and somehow she knew she could trust him.

By the end of their meeting, she felt very comfortable with this newcomer and asked him to call her Adele. She was a silver haired widow who longed to live anywhere but on the beach.

"Terrible for the arthritis," she smiled. But her husband had bought it years before the affliction set in, when Santa Monica was a sleepy little town. "Now, it's overrun with string bikinis and teenagers with overactive hormones," she complained. "I'd love nothing more than to sell, but the market isn't so great and besides I'm too old and I have too many memories in this home. I raised all three of my children here you know. Lost one when he was just an infant. We've seen two dogs, four cats, God knows how many hamsters and enough goldfish to choke a horse. No, it's too much for me to give up. I'd miss all my little ghosts that remind me of what once was."

Justin smiled sympathetically at her. He admired her courage to stick it out, no matter what. She obviously had every intention of living there 'till she died. He could tell from her features that she had at one time been a strikingly attractive woman. He guessed her to be about eighty with faded gray eyes that lit up whenever she spoke of her late husband or family.

After renting the cottage, he roamed the area for a while. Familiarizing himself with his surroundings, he knew he would enjoy living in his new town. And he wondered, what Eve would have thought of it. Certainly nothing like New Fairfield with all its New England charm. Suddenly he missed her terribly. It was a feeling that overcame him so abruptly, he was entirely unprepared. But there it was. That empty hollowness he'd felt ever since he watched them board their plane. Justin knew it would take time, that only time could heal him. Although he knew he would never forget her, he realized that one day, he would be able to remember her without feeling such intense anguish. He longed for that day to come.

Justin found himself wandering the stores that stood in a row along the beach walk area. The beach bordered the walkway and there were a few wooden benches that faced the water. A couple was resting on one; he watched them as the woman nestled closer. The sun began to dip low in the sky and hues of reds and oranges spilled from its glowing center. The clouds that rested on the horizon turned from white to pink and gradually became infused with a bright fiery glow. Justin picked an empty bench and decided to take in his first California sunset.

The following morning, he checked out of the motel, and via taxi, transferred his meager belongings to his new home on Ocean Boulevard. He stopped in briefly to say hello to Adele with the intention of heading right off to campus.

"How are you planning on getting to your college?" she asked.

"Well I thought I'd check out the local bus system perhaps, or I could walk I suppose. I'm hoping to get a car very soon."

"Well, I happen to have something that just might work for you." She motioned for him to follow her as she led him to the white paneled garage that was attached to her home. She began to fumble with the door for a moment and Justin rushed to help her. "I really need to get this thing fixed," she mumbled, "it's been sticking ever since Henry died, eight years ago. I just never get around to it."

"I'd be happy to look at it for you," Justin offered as he hoisted the heavy door into place.

"That would be very sweet," Adele said softly. Once the door was up, Justin could see the white shiny two-seater convertible sitting quietly in the darkness. It seemed to be waiting for someone to take it out in the bright California sunshine. Adele sighed deeply as if she were remembering a time long past. "Henry loved this car. He bought it brand new, and it was the only new car we'd ever owned."

Justin ran his hand gently over the still glossy paint. It felt cool to his touch and looked as though it had been newly waxed. The chrome was polished to a high gloss and the red interior seemed almost brand new. Justin did not know that much about cars, but if he were to wager a guess he would have to say it was circa 1954 or so; maybe an English sports car or something.

Billy would know, he thought, and then he remembered; as if he could forget that Billy was probably pretty busy about right now. God, please don't let him screw this up. Justin prayed silently. Adele was still deep in thought while her tenant, lost in his own memories, gently slid his fingers along the smooth surface of her car.

"It is such a chore," she said wearily, "to keep this car running and polished the way Henry would have wanted it. Oh, the kids try to help you know but they get so busy. I don't have the heart to sell it so I'm hoping that while you're living here you'll drive it. It's a terrible shame for it to sit in here where no one can see it and enjoy it."

Justin could not answer at first, not really believing what she was offering. Adele walked around the car, running her hand along it the entire time. She remembered her husband sitting in it when he bought it, he was so proud. He'd taken her for a ride that day; it was a gloriously beautiful day. They drove and drove and ended up in Half Moon Bay, at least three hours up the coast. They spent the night there and drove back in the morning. Adele liked to call it their b.c. time: before children.

"Adele, I couldn't possibly accept your offer, I mean a car is a very serious matter."

She looked him straight in the eye when she said: "Yes, and you're a very serious young man. I know you will take good care of it. You'll wash it and wax it and park it in safe neighborhoods. But most of all you'll enjoy it and that's what it was meant for. Trust me when I say that you will be doing me a great favor."

Justin thought about it for a moment. He would need to pay her something for the loan of it, he knew that. Whether or not she would accept it was another story. He did need a car, and it was certainly a beautiful car to drive around in. "I am so touched by your offer Adele. I would be honored to drive your husband's car. And I promise I will take very good care of it."

Adele felt her heart almost melt beneath his warm smile. He was a Godsend, of that she was certain. It had been a terribly lonely time since Henry had died, and trying to rent the cottage had been difficult to say the least. No one respectable seemed to want it. Until Justin came around, she thought she'd never find anyone suitable. A glint of something twinkled in her eye as she said: "So, if you have a few minutes, why don't you take me for a ride. It's been years since I've sat in the passenger seat."

"I would love to," he grinned.

Adele went into the house and returned a short time later with a pink scarf secured around her coif and the keys to her husband's treasured possession, which she promptly handed to Justin. When he helped her into the car, he couldn't help but notice the distant look in her eyes. Justin slid behind the wheel as comfortable as if he'd always been driving Henry's car, and soon the engine hummed a thankful tune. They pulled out of the garage and into the bright sunlight. Justin took care in learning the feel of the automobile as he gently took her out onto the road.

As he drove along the Coast Highway he looked across at his landlady who sat smiling, her silken scarf wafting in the wind. A faint smile softened her face, and somehow she seemed to look years younger, as if the memories that replayed themselves in her mind wiped years from her life. Suddenly, she was that young girl again, sitting beside her husband as he drove them up the coast. From the radio Frank Sinatra sang: "It Was a Very Good Year," and Justin did not attempt to change the station. It seemed altogether entirely appropriate.

After they'd driven for about forty-five minutes, Adele requested that Justin take her home. She was getting tired, and suddenly the memories were becoming all too overpowering. She needed to be alone with her thoughts, and she knew that Justin had better things to do than drive a silly old woman around.

CHAPTER 31

"Justin, hi it's me Eve!"

As if he could forget the sound of her voice! Of course he knew who it was, almost even before he picked up the phone. Justin had sent them a letter, detailing his adventures so far on the West Coast and also including his telephone number. Just in case they needed to reach him, he'd told himself. But really it was for Eve, just in case…

"So," he began, trying to sound light and carefree, "how's the married woman?"

"Oh, fine, the honeymoon was great. Hawaii is incredible, you should go there someday, it's unreal. Everyone walks around wearing flower lei's and loud floral print shirts!"

"Sounds like quite a combination!" She sounded happy. It nearly killed him, but he wanted nothing more than her happiness, even if it wasn't with him.

"You know Justin, it really works there. I don't know if it's all the palm trees and the tropical setting or what, but it just works."

"So," he knew he shouldn't even go there, but he had to, "how is everything else?" It was none of his business, he was fully aware of that, even painfully so. At the same time, he needed to know that she was really ok. Then again, maybe it was his morbid way of making himself realize that there was absolutely no hope for him. Whatever his reason, she knew exactly what he meant. There was no mistaking the tone in his voice.

"Everything's fine, really, at least Billy seems happy."

Happy! He thought, he better be kissing the ground every day for the rest of his life, thanking God he has such a terrific woman. Kissing the ground, that's what he'd better be doing. A simple happy won't cut it buddy.

Bitterness.

It swept over him like the salt water he'd swam in earlier that day, leaving a sticky residue in its wake. He knew this would come and he was glad his best friends weren't around to witness it first hand.

At last, he managed a "that's good." But it was almost mumbled, and from thousands of miles away Eve could feel something was amiss.

"Justin, is everything all right? Are you happy out there, because if you're not you need to hop the first plane back this instant, do you hear me?"

"No, Bug, really I'm fine. A little homesick perhaps, but fine nonetheless. It's really wonderful out here. You and Billy would love it."

"Well, we have no plans on moving anytime soon. Billy is settling back into work, and assistant coaching for the high school football team, you know how much he loves that? And I am going to finally start taking some college classes. I just can't stay home and be a housewife."

"I imagine you can't Eve. Good for you. Sounds like Billy is doing well too. Is he home, can I talk with him?" He didn't want his conversation with Eve to end. But he knew, like everything else, it had to. Too much of her was too much.

"No, he's not. He's at the high school getting signed up and all. Starts next week." He could tell that Eve didn't sound too enthusiastic about Billy's coaching. Rightfully so, with Billy coaching after work it would certainly limit his time at home.

"He needs to stay in sports Eve."

"I know," she admitted reluctantly. "It's all part of the package as mother would say."

"She's right."

"You two are so different."

The statement hung like a thick wall between them. Why had she said it? She didn't know. It seemed appropriate, an innocent observation perhaps. A truthful observation.

"Yes, we are," he answered flatly.

"I just mean that I often wonder how the two of you became so close, being so different and all."

"Well, that's why we were so close. Our differences are what kept our friendship so interesting. Billy did a lot for me, he really toughened me up. I would have been a lonely bookworm all through school if it hadn't been for him."

"Billy said you taught him manners."

"Just some social stuff, that's all."

There was silence now; Eve could feel their conversation ending. Usually they would have chatted on for hours, but now something was different. Something had changed between them and she had no idea what it was. She began to worry, what if he had made a big mistake. Possibly the biggest mistake of his life and he was too proud to admit it. California was dangerous at times. She cringed every time she watched the news. Since they'd come home she would scan the newspapers and television news for anything on California and it wasn't hard. It seemed that every nut job, every derelict known to man would at one time or another find their way to the West Coast.

They talked for a little while longer but after Eve hung up the phone she knew with all certainty what she had to do. She had to fly out there and make sure he was all right.

Justin let the receiver glide gently back into the cradle after which he dropped himself onto his couch and sat there staring at the telephone. It was hard to believe that he had just had that conversation with Eve. Never, in all the years that he'd known her had their conversations been as curt and formal as this one. It was a painful reality he needed to face; there would be more of those types of calls he was certain. He needed to work on himself more, and get her out of his system once and for all. He committed then and there that there would be no more calls for at least a month, maybe two if he could stand it.

Back in Connecticut, Eve sat beside her phone, waiting and thinking about what she was about to do. She was certain that Billy would understand. As a matter of fact, he would insist on going with her. They were best friends after all, Justin, Billy and her. Eve picked up the phone again, and called a local travel agent. She was in luck, the agent said at the other end, airfare wars were on again. Eve wasn't sure what that meant, and she really didn't care. Eve reserved the seats for her and Billy and assured the agent that she would call back within twenty-four hours to pay for the tickets. But when she did phone back, the agent was surprised to find that only Eve would be traveling to California. Probably a newlywed spat, the agent surmised; she had assisted Billy in booking their honeymoon and knew they'd only been married for a short while. Odd, that Eve didn't want any room reservations either. She'd be staying with a friend, she insisted. The agent shrugged and followed her client's direction.

The flight would leave the day after tomorrow.

After Eve finished purchasing her ticket she felt a bit of excitement well up in her stomach. She could hardly wait to see Justin again! She wished Billy was able to go with her. But she'd forgotten all about the game he had to coach that weekend. It was a really important one, he'd insisted, and it would really hurt the team if they had to substitute him. She didn't understand, and she'd told him so. His best friend was thousands of miles away, in some sort of distress, and all he could think about was a silly football game.

"Honey, you're going. That ought to be fine, you don't need me. You and Justin always seemed to do fine without me, I mean you guys have this bond or something."

"Bond?"

"Yeah, you know? Like a girl thing, only with a guy," Billy shrugged. Whatever it was, they didn't need him. Besides he could use the time to hang with the other coaches and go out and do guy stuff.

"Well, I wish you were going. I really hate leaving you."

Billy smiled, and took her hand. She was sweet but this togetherness all the time was about to drive him batty.

"I won't whither away here, although I'm sure everyone will think I will. It's two days, hell, I can live with that. As long as you promise not to leave me and stay out there with Jus."

Eve's eyes flew open, "Never! I-I mean, I would never leave you Billy!"

He threw his head back in laughter. "I know, just teasin' that's all." With that, he turned and headed for the fridge. Assuming their conversation was over, he grabbed a cold beer and walked out to the porch to watch the sun set and relax. Eve watched him for a moment then headed upstairs to begin packing for her trip.

CHAPTER 32

By the next day, Justin had managed to rid himself of that sad, almost disparaging feeling he'd been left with after his conversation with Eve. Justin threw himself into his day, and as soon as he finished all his studies that night he went to bed. That way there was no time for thinking, for wondering, and especially for hoping.

On Friday, his last class ended at 4:30 and by five, he was home and wishing he had somewhere to go. The weekend yawned before him, like a black abyss waiting to swallow him up in a sea of memories. He needed to find a weekend job and quick, he knew that for certain. Perhaps on Saturday he would comb the area to see what he could find. Justin set his pack down on the couch, and mixed himself a quick drink of scotch and soda. It promised to be a beautiful sunset, and taking his drink with him he wandered out onto his porch. The sunsets took his breath away, and he enjoyed getting lost in them. Perhaps tonight he would find some inspiration for a new story. Justin sat down on the steps of his home, and sipped and watched as the evening unfolded and people wandered by.

Justin was just about to get up and begin studying, when the sight of a young couple caught his eye. She was petite with shimmering blond hair, and he looked tall and sturdy with sandy hair. He held her tightly to him, and what remained of the sun framed them like a golden orange halo. His head bent to kiss her, and hers fell back to welcome his lips. At that moment, their embrace became more intense; the warmth of the Indian summer igniting their passion. Justin watched the couple intently, as if he had never seen anyone kiss before. Something about the girl seemed so familiar. Maybe she shared a class with him, he wondered, and then in an instant he realized that he didn't know her at all—she looked exactly like Eve! Damn it! He scowled, "I see her everywhere!"

"Who do you see everywhere Justin?"

Justin's head spun around in the direction of her voice. As if from out of a dream, there she was, her beautiful face, her smile, her shiny golden hair flowing in the evening breeze. Damn! he thought, What the hell did I put in that drink? He turned his head away, closed his eyes, and then looked back again, hoping the image would disappear. She was still there! Standing there holding a small blue bag. She looked innocent and afraid. But he knew it was just another mirage, so he decided to ignore it.

"Justin!" she said again, "It's me! Eve…"

He looked again. Could it be? He stood up. A look of surprise engulfed his face. As he walked over to where she stood, a whiff of her perfume beckoned him closer. He stood directly in front of her now. "Eve?" he whispered. It was really her, what the hell was she doing there? Did she leave Billy, was it over? Was she coming here to be with him?

Suddenly her laughter resonated as she threw her head back. "You silly, you look so shocked! I wanted to surprise you and I've succeeded!"

"Well you certainly have! What are you doing here?" he was almost afraid to ask. He knew he wouldn't want to hear the answer and for another glorious second he could believe whatever he wanted to. Yes, I've left him Justin, I realized all of the sudden that I love you, that you're the only one I've ever loved!

"I came out here to make sure you are all right," she smiled. Suddenly, the reason seemed very silly. To fly across the country to check on a friend? You sure that's it Eve? That's the only reason? That damned voice again that echoed in her head.

"What do you mean Eve? Of course I'm all right."

"Well, you didn't sound all right when I spoke to you the other day. I got worried and thought I'd come out here to see how you are."

Justin's heart caught in his throat. He stood, dumbfounded, staring at her as if she were the last drink of water before a barren desert.

"Bug, that's awfully sweet of you. But I'm fine, really I am."

"Great," she smiled, "then for heaven's sake pour me a drink and try to convince me that you're ok because I know you better than that."

Suddenly he didn't care about the reason, all he knew was that he was with her again. She was here, right in front of him and all was well with his world again. At least until she had to leave, and he knew she would. But for now, she was here.

"Well?" she frowned. "So are you just going to stand there daydreaming or are you going to invite a lady in?"

❖ ❖ ❖

Justin woke the following morning before dawn. He had hardly slept the night before. His head felt thick and filled with the conversations of the previous night. He and Eve had stayed up late, staring at the ocean from his porch and discussing life, marriage and California. Justin remembered every word she'd said. Eve had poured her heart out to him and he wondered if she came to California because she was worried about his welfare or if she needed a friend. Whatever the reason, he didn't care. Justin flung his legs off the couch then and sat for a moment trying to clear his head. It would be another two hours at least before she woke and he knew he needed to get out of her space before his thoughts were a debilitated mess. He stood and stretched, heading for the laundry room where he quickly changed out of his pajama bottoms and into his running shorts.

The morning air felt cool and damp on his face as he ran along the ocean. The sand crunched beneath his feet. There were only a couple of other joggers out this early, and he smiled briefly as he passed them. He'd managed to convince her that the sadness she'd heard in his voice was just homesickness and nothing more. But for Eve, it was a confusing time. Some of the things she'd told him still resonated in his ears like a thunder clap or a slap in the face. As much as she tried, she felt as though she were failing Billy she admitted. Certainly, their honeymoon had been good but not great and definitely not what she'd expected.

"I feel as though I'm letting him down. I mean he doesn't say anything but he spends very little time at home you know. When he does, he seems distant. I don't know what to do to bring him closer."

Her words had made Justin want to punch his friend. Billy was a complete idiot for making her feel this way. Of course she feels insecure! He thought angrily as he put one lean leg in front of the other. But there was nothing he could do, or rather, nothing he should do. He needed to stay out of it, as far out of it as he could. But it was easier said than done. Justin had tried to comfort her and tell her it was probably her imagination and that he was certain she was doing everything right.

Justin stopped for a moment and looked over the water. The sun was beginning to rise and he could see the ocean turn from deep blue to turquoise. In that moment he felt another sadness engulf him as he realized he and Billy would never be close again. The friendship they shared was over, for now at least. There was too much bitterness in his heart. If he was truly a friend to Billy he would have sent Eve packing last night. Instead he became an audience for her woes and listened, as her husband never would, hoping beyond hope that he could steal a part of her that Billy never would. He was not a friend, at least not now anyway.

When Justin returned, Eve was preparing breakfast.

"I am amazed Justin, you have a very well stocked refrigerator."

"Well, I have Adele to thank for that."

Eve stopped what she was doing and turning her body toward him asked, "Who?"

"My landlady, a very sweet elderly woman. She loaned me a car too."

Eve laughed. "Well sounds like she's very fond of you. Why don't you go wash up and I'll finish breakfast. Hungry?"

"Famished," he answered back as he headed for the shower.

Justin spent the better part of the day introducing Eve to his new surroundings. Justin wanted to show her the sights first, but Eve insisted on seeing his college before anything else. They walked the campus for an hour or so, and Justin showed her around the impressive school. After the tour, Justin steered his convertible into Hollywood. Eve looked wide eyed at everything. Stopping just short of Hollywood Boulevard, Justin decided they would take some of it on foot. Eve was thankful she'd brought her camera with her because there were countless photo opportunities. Although she'd never been terribly enamored with movie stars in general she was intrigued by the history of the city: the people that had come here in the hopes of being discovered, the few who succeeded and the hundreds of thousands who failed. They walked the boulevard and Eve read each star along the Walk of Fame. They stopped at Grauman's Chinese Theatre and Eve insisted that Justin see if his feet were as big as John Wayne's. She was astounded to find that her own fit almost perfectly into Marilyn Monroe's.

She needed this, he thought. No doubt the pressures of married life were weighing heavily on her. She had no idea what her duties were supposed to be and true to form, Billy was no help. Eve had confessed the night before that she had no one else to turn to for guidance. She was too embarrassed to confide in her mother and not surprisingly, Judith had never discussed sex with her daughter. It just wasn't done by people of her generation. How the hell can anyone expect her to know everything! Justin thought, outraged as he watched

Eve lean forward to see if her handprints fit those of Jane Mansfield. She turned to him then, smiling as he hadn't seen her smile in a long time. It was good to see her so happy. And to a degree it was selfishly comforting to know that he was more capable than Billy to put that smile on her face.

"Look, Jus, they fit perfectly. Maybe I should pack up Billy and move to Hollywood. I seem to fit the part." She winked then and laughed, a deep happy carefree laugh that Justin loved to hear.

"Certainly, you have missed your calling. Hollywood needs you."

She sauntered up to him, lowering her eyes and tossing back her long shimmering hair, "I'm ready for my close up Mr. DeMille."

Justin burst out laughing and they stood caught up in the silliness of the moment. God, how good it was to be with her like this. He remembered the last time they'd been alone, it was just before her wedding. That day…it tore through him again and for the briefest of moments, the pain returned and then quickly subsided; but not before piercing him as it always did when the monster reared its ugly head. He'd gotten better at taming it though.

Much better.

♣ ♣ ♣

Hollywood was everything Eve had always thought it would be. Filled with an energy she had never felt before in her life, she savored the excitement like a child on Christmas morning as Justin led her on their adventure. Eve reflected that this was the last thing she expected to be doing today. She had thought for certain that her weekend would be spent consoling a poor homesick Justin and possibly coaxing him back to Candlewood Lake. But the situation was quite the opposite. Eve was pleased to see that Justin seemed well-adjusted to his life on the West Coast. Her fondest wish would have been to cart him home with her, but moreover she wanted to know he was happy.

Later that day Justin took Eve to a hideaway restaurant along the boardwalk. It served only two things; fish and chips, but after trying them, you longed for little else. They ate eagerly as the afternoon wore on. It was well past four o'clock. Justin worked over in his mind where he thought their adventure would lead them next.

He deferred to Eve. "So Bug, what would you like to do the rest of the day?"

Eve didn't even hesitate, "I'd like to go walking along the ocean. Just like they do here in California, and later I want to drink a bottle of wine together, build a bonfire and listen to the waves crash under the moonlight."

Justin could barely hide his surprise. "You seem to know exactly what you want!"

Eve nodded and bit into a french fry, "I do," she smiled. "On the way over I was reading one of those California tourist magazines and it looked so wonderful. I know you probably do that all the time, but please do it one more time for me?"

"Actually, I've never sat on the beach drinking wine and listening to the waves crash."

"Don't forget the bonfire."

"How could I? Well, my dear you may have your wish."

As they left the restaurant, he couldn't help but think how romantic it all sounded.

CHAPTER 33

The sun set over the Pacific Ocean in a gleam of yellow, orange and red. Eve thought it was the most magnificent sunset she'd ever seen. They sipped the wine, a California red, and sat beside each other on the blanket Justin had retrieved from his house. The waves crashed forcefully on the sand, and in the distance, Justin could see a bank of clouds over the ocean. He knew that was the reason for the turbulent tide; a storm out at sea. It did not look as though it would head inland as Justin continued to watch it. No doubt it would wreak its havoc and then dissipate. He soon forgot it and concentrated on the scene that surrounded him. They had walked a couple of miles down the beach to where the fire pits were. Justin had scraped together some firewood that Adele had given him as well as some kindling he found on the beach. As soon as the sun dipped lower and the air began to cool he would light the pit.

"This is really wonderful Jus, thank you for this."

"My pleasure," he said softly, and indeed it was. He watched her from the corner of his eye, but he didn't need to see her to know she was there.

Suddenly she said: "I wonder what Billy is doing right now?" It was the first time she'd mentioned his name since their talk the night before. Justin selfishly liked it like that; here Billy could not come between them…at least until now.

"Probably missing you," Justin said nearly choking on his words.

Eve sighed deeply, "Justin can I tell you something?"

"Of course, anything—you know that."

"Well it's gonna sound pretty awful."

"I doubt anything you say could sound bad."

Eve paused for a moment, staring straight into the ocean, "I'm kind of glad he's not here. I like this just you and me. Does that sound bad?"

For the longest moment, Justin did not answer her. He wanted to savor the words that now lingered in the air, glad he's not here, she'd said. Yes, he too felt the guilt wrench through him as he'd thought the same thing many times that day. It was a selfish, silly thought and certainly not something a best friend would even entertain. But yet here they were sitting on a blanket, drinking wine and watching the sunset. Justin and his best friend's wife.

Eve frowned when Justin did not answer, "Jus? You think it's awful don't you?"

He turned his head and held her eyes, "No, I don't. As a matter of fact I thought the same thing. We used to spend so much time together when we were growing up, I miss that."

Eve nodded and silently, she reached for his hand and held it in her own. It sent a shockwave of emotion through Justin and he quickly emptied his glass to wash the feelings from his mind.

The sun quickly set and the air began to chill. Justin lit the fire and they sat beside it, talking in hushed tones, sitting closely together.

This will all be over soon, he thought, and a sadness filled his soul. But for now I will enjoy every moment of this, he promised himself. I will worry about the after effects of it tomorrow. As they finished the bottle of wine, he felt his guilt about Billy dwindle. They were doing nothing wrong after all; just two friends sitting by the ocean remembering times gone by; days that would never repeat themselves and memories that would forever link them. Memories he would cherish forever.

It was getting late, and Eve began to yawn. Justin knew it was time to end their day and get her home. Together they put out the fire, folded up the blanket and began heading back to the house. They walked silently across the sand. Justin had counted three piers that they'd passed to get there. They had just passed under one. When they emerged on the other side, the glow of the moon was gone. A wind whipped up under the pier and blew at their backs. Without warning, huge pellets of rain began to fall. First only a few and then within minutes it was a full-blown downpour. Justin grabbed Eve's hand and pulled her back under the pier. By the time they were able to take cover the storm descended upon them with all of its force. Rain and wind threatened to hurl the waves even farther up the shore. Both he and Eve were soaked. He opened the blanket hoping to find a dry section. He was in luck and wrapped her in it.

"Wow, what happened?"

"It's one of those freak summer storms. I've heard we get them out here once in a while."

"I thought it never rained in Southern California," she smiled.

"Are you cold?" he asked.

She feigned a smile. "Freezing, and you must be too, here take some of this blanket."

She unfolded it from around her and reached over his shoulder to cover him, and in doing so she nudged up against him. They sat for a quiet moment listening to the storm that surrounded them. Suddenly a clap of thunder roared above them. Eve jumped.

"I hate thunder," she whispered.

Justin pulled her closer as he remembered how afraid she was of it. Her wet hair pressed against his chest, he could feel each strand of it through his shirt. The thunder tore through the sky again, leaving a flash of light in its wake. He cursed himself for not paying closer attention to the weather.

In a moment that he would remember for the rest of his life, Eve raised her face to him, smiling and shivering. She held his gaze for a long moment and searched his eyes for the answer to a yet unasked question. The rain fell around them in sheets of water, and the waves crashed fiercely against the pylons. She still held his gaze. At that instance, there was not an ounce of reason left in his body. She looked more beautiful than he'd ever seen her. And there they were, in their own little world beneath the pier.

Later he would blame it on the wine, but two and a half glasses never made anyone lose his mind. His head lowered then, and he pressed his lips to hers. Eve instinctively closed her eyes and accepted his overture. While a mixture of voices cluttered her head.

The prom.

She remembered that night too, the last time he'd kissed her. They were only kids then. Had it been only a year ago? The voices became louder now. Most of them screamed how wrong this was, only one lone voice told her how right it felt to kiss this man.

Suddenly his kiss became as urgent as the pounding rain. He wrapped his arms around her and pressed her into the sand. Eve's fingers pushed through his damp hair. Her mouth opened then, to receive his tongue that darted and danced with her own. She could smell his cologne, and his rain-soaked hair.

As abruptly as it began the rain suddenly stopped, but they remained there on the sand, locked in an embrace. There was no Billy. Suddenly, nothing else mattered but this man and this kiss.

"Oh God, Eve," he whispered, "I love you."

The words landed heavily on her ears as if someone had struck her over the head. She was suddenly shocked back into reality. Justin felt it too. He'd gone too far this time, much too far and he knew that in this very instance their friendship must end. They both stood awkwardly trying to find the words to close the gap of silence.

"I'm sorry, that should have never happened," he said contritely.

"It was my fault too Jus. Let's just go, the rain's over now."

They walked together in a weighted silence. The storm had blown over entirely, the clouds began to clear and the moon once again illuminated their path. Yet, their storm had just begun. The air between them was thick and stifling and Eve felt the sting of his kiss still on her lips.

The guilt burned a hole in her heart. Her poor sweet Billy.

The guilt intensified now.

The guilt of enjoying it; the guilt of still feeling his lips on her own.

And the guilt of wanting it too.

When they returned home they did not speak a word except for a brief almost whispered good night from Eve. Justin had wanted to apologize again, but it was apparent that Eve was overwhelmed by it all. Better to wait. Or perhaps, better to never see her again.

Had that not been his intention when he moved to California?

Eve could not get to sleep that night. She tossed and turned and wished she didn't have to face Justin in the morning. What had possessed her? How could she betray Billy in such a way? She cursed herself, and then tried to blame it on the storm, the wine, even the moonless sky. But she never blamed Justin. She could still feel his mouth on her own and it saddened her to admit no one else had ever kissed her that way. There was more emotion in that one kiss than she had ever felt before. How could that be? She thought. Why don't I feel that way when Billy kisses me? Eve felt terribly conflicted and wanted more than anything to talk to Justin. But she couldn't. In one fateful moment their relationship had forever been changed. What had he said? I love you. The words echoed like the thunder of last night's storm in her ear, I love you.

Of course he loves me, she tried to convince herself. We've been friends forever, we all love each other. I've always loved Justin, he's my best friend.

Friends don't kiss each other that way. A voice in her head reverberated.

She lay in his bed trying to make sense of what had happened. Or at least rationalize it in such a way that it made her feel less guilt. Less pain. And less wanting for more.

❧ ❧ ❧

Justin paced the living room knowing what he had to do. He certainly could not face her in the morning and deny what he'd said because he could never lie to her. He needed to be gone when she woke. This time for certain, he needed to never see her again.

❧ ❧ ❧

As morning began to ease the darkness, Eve finally dozed off. She slept for several hours, finally waking around 9 a.m. She lay in bed not wanting to face him. Finally gathering her courage, she slipped on her robe and walked out to the living room. The house was completely silent. Eve walked into the kitchen, empty as well. He probably went for a jog, she surmised. It was then that she saw the note on the counter. And she knew immediately Justin was not out running. He had left. Carefully she picked up the crisp white sheet of paper and read the familiar handwriting:

Dear Eve,

I am writing you this note, because I am too much of a coward to face you myself. I owe you that at least, but for now I feel it's best this way. I did not feel that either of us needed to face or discuss what was obviously an error in judgment and nothing more.

What happened last night shouldn't have and it's all my fault so please don't blame yourself. I got caught up in the moment, seeing you again. I don't know what it was really. Whatever it was needs to be forgotten and put aside. I want what happened last night to in no way affect your happiness with Billy. I am just a lonely college kid who made a mistake with a very dear friend and I hope that someday you can forgive me.

I have ordered a cab to pick you up and take you to the airport, everything is paid for. He will arrive around 10:30 a.m. I wish you a safe journey home and a wonderful homecoming with your husband.

Justin

Her hand shook as she finished the note. Eve could feel her heart split in two. She wanted desperately to find him, to straighten everything out face to face but God only knew where he was. She reread the note again, when suddenly she heard one of the porch planks creak. Justin! Her mind cried out.

"Knock knock!" A sweet elderly voice lilted from the other side of the door.

Eve walked over to open the door, a smiling silver haired woman stood in front of her, holding a plate covered in a towel.

"Justin stopped by earlier and said he had to leave and felt terrible about not getting you breakfast. So I told him I would make sure you ate something before you left, dear."

Eve stood without saying a word.

"Oh, my manners, you must be wondering who I am."

Eve nodded, although she was beginning to make her assumptions.

"I'm Adele, dear. Justin rents this house from me." She pushed past Eve and began to unwrap her muffins. Eve wasn't hungry, but she smiled nonetheless.

"He's such a sweet young man. I understand you two grew up together." Adele chatted on. It was just what Eve needed. A sweet caring woman bearing homemade baked goods who went on about Justin as if he were her son. If Adele sensed something was amiss between the two of them she said nothing. She began to prepare a pot of coffee and quickly shooed Eve off to shower and pack for her trip home.

While Adele was taking care of Eve as Justin knew she would, the latter sat under the same pier he'd shared with Eve the night before trying to force all thoughts of Eve back in a box. The thoughts became dangerous when they escaped. At ten-thirty he got up to head back home. She was on her way back to Billy. As his feet pushed through the sand he wished he could have woken her to tell her how much he loved her, how much he would always love her and that no one would ever love her the way he did; not even her husband. Instead he'd let her think it was the wine and nothing else. Maybe in a year or two they'd be able to laugh at it all. But he had his doubts. In fact he even doubted if he'd ever be able to see her again without remembering with pain what had happened so passionately the night before.

♣ ♣ ♣

The plane sped through the air. With every mile that she put between herself and Justin she could feel her heart ache from pain and confusion. She bit back a tear but it escaped anyway. Nothing made sense anymore except that she knew she needed to throw herself into her marriage and forget everything else. Nothing else mattered except her love for Billy. She mourned a part of their friendship she knew had died the night before. The kiss had changed everything.

If Billy ever found out....

The thought ran in a fleeting fashion through her head. She quickly brushed it aside. He never would. Never. No matter, what she had to preserve her marriage. That mattered above anything else.

Still...the memory of his passionate kiss haunted her again.

What in God's name had possessed her?

Billy was there to pick her up from the airport. He greeted her with a broad handsome smile and a bouquet of flowers.

"Hi darlin'," he whispered as she hugged his neck, "these are for you." He handed her the flowers, "I missed you."

God, he was so sweet. She didn't deserve him.

"I missed you too, I wish you could have come with me."

"I do too, so how is ol' Jus? Holding his own in California?"

Eve bit her lower lip. "Let's talk about that later, I'm exhausted from the flight, I just want to get home and curl up with my husband."

Billy smiled, certain his attempt at romance had worked. He was glad to have Eve back.

It was a forty-five minute trip to their home and Billy chatted the entire way about the game she'd missed. They'd won of course, he bragged. When he tried again to inquire about Justin, she very carefully talked about his new house and the college he was enrolled in and then reverted the subject back to the game, which she knew he would love to talk about again.

He talked sports the rest of the way home.

When they arrived, Eve was more determined than ever to rid herself of Justin's kiss and she could think of only one way to do that. Eve stood in the kitchen when Billy returned from bringing her luggage in. Her hands trembled with every move she made as her blouse fell to the floor. She wanted him to make love to her; she wanted to feel his lips instead of Justin's pressing against her mouth. She wanted to feel his arms encircle her and make her quiver. Billy dropped the bag and silently walked into the kitchen.

"Eve, what's gotten into you?" he smiled.

"I want you to make love to me."

"Right now?" his hands went up to cup her breasts; his lips found a spot on her neck he knew she loved.

"Yes, right now my darling. Make love to me, I missed you."

That afternoon on the kitchen floor, they made love more passionately than they ever had. Eve kissed him as she reclaimed her husband and rid herself of the memory of Justin's embrace.

CHAPTER 34

Justin did not return home during the holidays. His reason was simple: he'd recently gotten a part time job working for a local paper. No one wanted to work the holidays and he hoped to get some of the better stories while every other writer was taking time off. His parents were disappointed but decided to visit him instead. So they flew to California to experience their first warm Christmas.

Eve heard the news from Billy and was at the same time surprised and saddened by it. The kiss had now been months ago and she'd managed to chalk it up to the wine as Justin hoped she would. She rarely even gave it another thought, only on occasion would the memory creep up on her and demand to be relived. She missed Justin, sometimes terribly. Eve had tried calling many times but each time the phone rang and rang. It seemed that Justin was never home anymore. At last she gathered the courage to write him a long letter. In it she thanked him for his hospitality, and never once mentioned their interlude under the pier. In truth she didn't know what to say, and felt as he did; that it was better never to mention it again.

Billy called Justin on Christmas day and both he and Eve spoke to him briefly. It was the first time Eve heard his voice since she'd left California. She had so much to say, but all she could muster was one question: "Did you get my letter Jus?"

"Yes, Bug I got your letter. Everything's fine." Justin's voice was flat, as if he were speaking with a stranger. He thanked her also for the care package she'd sent filled with home made cookies and a few knick-knacks that she felt would brighten up his little home by the sea.

After Eve hung up the phone she wondered what he meant with that last comment. Did he mean everything was forgotten and restored back to its "pre-kiss" state? Eve had no idea, and did not have a chance to elaborate before Billy said his good-bye's and hung up the phone.

CHAPTER 35

By mid-February, Eve found out quite unexpectedly that she was pregnant. Her due date was early September. When Eve found out she was expecting, it terrified and delighted her at the same time. She had been working so hard at being the perfect wife for Billy and now they were starting a family. She could hardly wait to tell him. Eve raced from the doctor's office straight to New Fairfield High where Billy coached football every day after work. The high school campus looked much the same as it had when the three of them had gone there. Eve raced into the building and past the classrooms. The halls smelled of old books, peanut butter and jelly sandwiches and worn sneakers. It was an aroma that brought her back several years past, when the three of them were inseparable. Sometimes she missed that more than she cared to admit. How different everything is now, she thought.

Eve continued through the school, heading in the general direction of the football field. She could hear the sounds of the team at practice. Eve pushed through the doors, searching the field for her husband. A man sat alone in the bleachers watching the team at play, and she knew immediately it was Billy. She stepped through the doors and hurried across the track. Eve was very careful to watch her step, the last thing she needed was to trip and fall with the baby. The baby, she thought, and a smile crept over her face. She looked up to see Billy still sitting there, oblivious to anything else but his team. Eve could see one of the cheerleaders approaching him. She was tall, slender and scantly clad in a form-fitting sweater, tights and leg warmers. Eve watched as the girl eased over to him. Her heart then stopped as she saw the cheerleader reach up to caress his temple. Billy looked at her and smiled. They were saying something but Eve was too far away to hear. She stood there frozen in the grass unable to move another foot. Eve could feel the tears burn behind her eyes and she quickly turned to leave, running as fast as she could back across the field.

Eve sat in her car trying to calm herself. She was being silly, she told herself. Getting all upset because some young girl touched her husband's temple. No wait, caress would be the better word, yes caressed his temple.

Still.

She suddenly felt as though she were making too much of the entire thing now. Eve wiped a stray tear from her face and decided to find her husband again and tell him the wonderful news. Eve reached for the door handle when she saw him. Billy was there with that girl; they were laughing and carrying on as if they were a couple of teenagers. Billy did not even notice Eve sitting in their car. His attention was on Miss "Tight Sweater." Billy opened his car door on the passenger side and let her slide in. He took the driver's seat and in a flash they were off. For a moment Eve thought about following them, but then she thought better of it. No doubt there was some reasonable explanation for all of this.

No doubt.

Eve went straight home and waited for two hours until her husband arrived. When Billy opened their front door she was sitting in the living room quietly staring at the floor. She had not prepared dinner, nor made any attempt to tidy the house before he arrived. She wanted answers and she wanted them now.

"Hey baby," Billy smiled, walking over to her he kissed her lightly on the cheek. She remained unmoved; her eyes went from the floor to meet his. She needed to remain calm. There were possibly a hundred reasons for what she'd seen earlier. She tried to remind herself of that.

Billy hovered over her, waiting for a smile. "Something wrong, Eve?"

"No, uh not really. I-I have to ask you something. I went to the school earlier to tell you something very important." She hesitated for a moment before continuing. Suddenly she felt very silly; after all they'd only been married for six months! What could possibly go wrong?

Billy waited again for her to speak.

"What did you have to tell me?" He kneeled down beside her now.

"I…saw you on the field and then in the parking lot."

Billy nodded. "You saw Cheryl then," he said flatly.

Eve's chin began to quiver. Damn, why was she getting so emotional?

"Is that her name?"

"Cheryl is one of the team cheerleaders. Her ride flaked on her and so I offered to take her home."

"She seemed very, I don't know, enamored with you."

Billy smiled his broad alluring smile. "Yes, well she seems to have a bit of a crush on me. I assure you Eve I did nothing to encourage it. She's just, you know young and impressionable, me being the offensive line coach and all."

Eve nodded; she felt even sillier now. Of course he hadn't encouraged anything, what on earth was she thinking! Suddenly she felt terrible for doubting him, she felt so bad in fact that she did not inquire as to why it took him two hours to take the girl home. Whatever, she thought, it's silly, I'm pregnant and emotional and a little crazed.

Billy cupped her hands in his own. "So honey, what did you drive all the way out to the high school to tell me?"

"Well, Billy, I found out today that we are going to have a baby."

Billy furrowed his eyebrows. Baby! He thought. That was certainly the last thing he expected. A baby. Another life in this house? Now they were really married, he thought. Babies make everything more serious.

Eve waited for him to respond. "Billy? You're happy aren't you?"

"Oh, Eve of course I am happy," Billy embraced her then.

Billy took his pregnant wife out to dinner that night and then they visited her parents to share the news of the imminent arrival of their grandchild.

In the weeks that followed, Eve felt a new sense of herself. She was aware of every nuance and change that occurred in her body. She began reading everything she could on pregnancy and motherhood, and was determined to be the best mother she could be. Eve soon forgot Miss "Tight Sweater" and the whole sordid mess. Billy on the other hand knew that he needed to be more careful. It certainly wouldn't help for him to be spotted by someone who was not so easy to convince as his wife.

For a reason she did not understand, Eve put off telling Justin about the baby for several weeks. Finally, she knew she couldn't postpone it any longer before he found out from someone else. Eve knew he'd be terribly hurt if he had to hear it second hand.

Eve's pregnancy hit Justin like a Mack truck. If there had been even the slightest glimmer of hope residing somewhere in his heart, her announcement had squashed it. Had it only been a week ago when the call from Scott came? Scott had gone to school with Billy and Justin and was now considering UCLA as well. Along with his query about the college, Scott was also a plethora of information. He caught Justin up on all the goings on in New Fairfield.

"You know," Scott began, "you might want to talk to Billy soon."

"Why?" Justin questioned.

"Well, seems he's been hanging around, and all over the cheerleaders. He's been seen with them all over town too. One in particular, I mean she hangs all over him. Cheryl something or other. Seems pretty innocent, but you never know with Billy."

Justin's hand froze to the phone. Damn him! He thought bitterly. If he hurts her I swear I will kill him!

To help squelch the rumors, Justin assured his friend that Billy was totally devoted to his wife. The affections from this girl were most certainly unsolicited, Justin managed to convince him and by the end of the conversation he was satisfied that the rumors would stop there. The last thing Eve needed was to be topic of conversation at the Grand Union.

As Justin set down the phone, he prayed Billy wouldn't do anything to screw up his marriage.

Eve's pregnancy progressed with little difficulty; a few bouts of morning sickness but other than that she was a glowing example of what a young mother should look like. Eve had long since put the thoughts of Billy and that cheerleader behind her. Her whole focus was on her unborn child. While she busied herself decorating the baby's room, on the opposite coast, Justin buried himself in his work.

The *Santa Monica Times Daily* was not an extremely busy paper, but he seemed to be finding his niche. Senior Editor, Joseph Flaherty, began to notice that Justin appeared to have a knack for the more creative writing projects. He offered Justin his own weekly column, a slice of life piece: The world as viewed by the man, or woman, on the street. Or, if he chose, he could write about a hot topic, or something that was on the public mind. Joseph gave him free reign to do whatever he liked, and Justin was thrilled to accept. He was extremely pleased with his progress at the paper, and often sent articles home to share with his parents. In the evening, Justin continued to bury himself in his writing. And among that, homework, college and the newspaper, it left little time for anything else. Especially to think about how Eve must look right about now. Pregnant and beautiful no doubt, he thought.

It was around this time Justin began to develop the character Austin Wilding who was the sheriff of King's Town, a smallish town in South Carolina. It was post Civil War and Austin was desperately in love with Melanie, the beautiful young woman who lived outside of town. She resided on a farm much too large for one person to maintain. Duncan, her husband had gone off to fight the war, and now while everyone was returning, her husband had not. Austin would ride out to check on her several times a week. Of course he would never ride alone, he always took someone to keep the gossip hounds at bay. As it was he spent far too much time helping her during planting season, and when it was time for harvest he and some men from town would help her bring in her crops. He knew it would all end when the man of the house returned from the war, but as time crept on he hoped against hope that he would not. Austin felt horrible for this. Certainly he wished no one death, but he could not help his thoughts; he loved her and he believed, she shared his sentiment.

Justin realized after the first several chapters that the scenario was all too familiar, but he didn't care. It was cathartic for him if nothing else. He never planned to sell what he was writing anyway; it was only therapy. But soon his therapy turned into a full-blown novel, and then two. And as Eve gave birth to her first child, Justin gave birth to a series of adventures of the brave sheriff, Austin, loving and protecting the frail but courageous Melanie.

At seven past midnight on September 9th, 1981, Frances Ann Freeman came screaming into the world. She weighed in at six pounds, ten ounces and was certainly the most beautiful thing Eve had ever seen in her life. Her labor had been long and difficult, but now as she held her precious child in her arms, she knew it was worth every bit of pain she'd felt. Billy immediately called Justin to tell him the wonderful news. Justin sat back on his couch as he listened to his friend tell of the adventure that had ensued getting Eve to the hospital on time. Justin knew that every new father must feel the way Billy did. He'd saved the day, gotten her to the hospital in the nick of time, of course before she delivered in the car, and was the highlight of the evening news.

"What's her name?" Justin inquired. A gut wrenching pain seized his heart; it was both a mixture of joy and intense sadness: He was not the father of her first born child and never would be.

When Justin hung up the phone, he knew sleep was out of the question. He worked for several hours on his novel, in a vain attempt to live out his fantasy through a fictitious character.

❧ ❧ ❧

In April of the following year, Justin leapfrogged from his newspaper column to a job at a local television production company. Just before graduating with a Master's degree in Fine Arts, he was hired as an assistant to one of the head writers on a popular television series. He knew he had his editor to thank for this opportunity. Joseph had seen his potential and thought it was a shame to waste his talents on a newspaper read by only a few locals.

Justin went to work for a man named Vance Langdon, who was known for his brilliant work mostly on television shows and a few movies. Justin relished the time he spent in Vance's presence and was determined to learn everything he could from the man some industry insider's called "The Master."

CHAPTER 36

It was during his second month of work that he literally ran into Zoë Williams, a script girl on the set of *Little House on the Prairie*. Zoë was a tall, thin willowy blond beauty. She wore little or no make up and could be found wearing her favorite jeans nearly every day of the week. She dressed up for no one and refused to put on airs, or tolerate anyone thinking they were better than her because they were "Hollywood." She disliked Hollywood and everything about it, but the job fit into her school schedule and paid relatively well.

Zoë was one of six children, born Suzanne Marie Williams to a very religious Minnesota family. At eighteen, she changed her name and moved to California to join the revolution of young people out to save the planet. Zoë was an activist for anything she felt was a worthy cause, mostly animals and pollution and of course she was a devout vegetarian. Although she stayed in touch with her parents who constantly told her she was wasting her life, she had no intention of returning home—ever. They prayed for her, and continually kept her name on the prayer list at their church. She was the Williams' lost daughter, but thank heaven they had five other children who did not share her free spirit.

It was a Monday morning when Justin raced from Vance's office to the NBC studios in Burbank. Vance had asked him for his input on several upcoming episodes and Justin had worked all night preparing his ideas and potential story lines. Driving to work that day, he felt more alive than he had in a long time. As he sped into the parking lot, Justin did not see the bicycle crossing the driveway and with the fender of Adele's car, hooked its wheel and toppled it and its rider over. With a shriek, the young woman fell to the ground. Justin was at her side in the second it took him to throw the car into park. Luckily for him, she was more furious than she was hurt.

"Did you not see where you were going?" Zoë fumed.

"Miss, I'm so sorry, I don't know what to say, I wasn't looking."

"That's an understatement!" Zoë stood up to brush herself off and check her bike for damage, fortunately only the fender was bent.

"That's what you get for driving a car!" Zoë seethed. She hated cars and avoided them whenever she could. They were noisy and did nothing but pollute the air.

"Well how do you expect me to get around?"

"Try a bike, or public transportation."

Justin eyed her carefully and decided to let her vent.

"It's not always convenient," he replied.

"Yes, of course what's it matter if you pollute the air we breathe as long as you are not inconvenienced?"

"Look, I'm not going to argue with you about this, I'm sorry to be contributing to the end of the world as we know it but it can't be helped. I need to get to work in a timely fashion. Now if you're all right I really need to get inside."

Zoë shrugged, "I'm fine, go ahead and get to work."

"Look, if you find that you have any residual injuries, I can give you my telephone number."

"For what, a Band-Aid?"

"Look, I'm only trying to be friendly here. I may have been in a hurry but I don't think you were watching where you were going either. I don't know why you're so bitter but I would appreciate you not directing it at me. Now do you want my number or not?"

Zoë frowned. She had been rather harsh with him, but it had been a rough day so far.

"No, I'm fine, really." She paused, looked up at his smiling face and continued: "I'm sorry for treating you so badly, it's not usually my style. I've had a difficult day."

"Well look, I really do have to go, but maybe we could finish this conversation over coffee sometime?" He could hardly believe what he found himself saying, he'd been in California for almost two years and had not had a single date. But this wasn't a date, he corrected himself, only an offer to hear about her day.

Zoë's blue eyes flew up to him, "I don't think you'd be interested in hearing about my troubles."

"Fine then, it was only an offer."

He walked back around his car and got in, "I hope your day gets better," he remarked as he slipped behind the wheel and drove past her into the studio, never giving the pretty blond another thought.

Zoë watched as the tall handsome stranger pulled in and parked, she found herself already regretting not taking him up on his offer.

As Justin began his hectic day, there was little time for a thought of anything other than the television show. Justin liked it that way. He was focused and driven, just what Vance wanted in an assistant. His day was a flutter of activity and rewrites; it seemed they were always a constant. At twelve-thirty, Justin decided to take a break.

Justin walked from his small office into the hallway and slid out the side door of studio H. The streets between the various studios were teeming with people. With the fall season looming, the lot was crawling with writers of all sorts. A line of wanna-be actors was forming behind Studio 6 in response to a recent casting call. Justin never tired of the electricity he felt walking through the studio lot and even though it was only television, there were days when he felt he was at the center of one of the most exciting places on earth.

A low lying building with a green awning signaled Justin that he was almost to the cafeteria. Much like the streets he walked, the cafeteria was filled with people and the hum of conversation. He knew he needed to be more visible like this, but it was difficult. His days belonged to Vance and the series they were working on. But now it felt good to be among his peers.

The cafeteria smelled good and suddenly Justin realized how famished he was. He got in line behind someone he'd seen several times on television, but he'd be damned if he could remember his name. He listened while the man in front of him ordered. The voice…he could almost place it….

Zoë saw him immediately; she was sitting at a corner table trying to focus on the book she was reading when he entered. It was the first time she'd seen him there. She noticed he seemed to be deep in thought. No doubt he's already forgotten the incident from this morning, she thought. But he hadn't escaped her mind for a second. Placing the book on the table she got up and walked over to where Justin was about to order. She waited for a moment until he was done.

"Fancy meeting you here," she smiled. Justin's head snapped in her direction, he was still trying to remember the name of the guy in front of him and hadn't heard her approach.

When he didn't respond she continued, "I don't believe I took the time to introduce myself earlier, my name is Zoë, Zoë Williams."

He held out his hand, "Justin VanSant."

"Sounds like the name of a famous writer."

Justin looked surprised. "How did you know? I mean that I'm a writer, not hardly famous though."

"You will be someday." She smiled as if she knew all the secrets of the world, then she laughed, "I guessed, don't worry I'm not a mind reader or anything. It's just that everyone's somebody here, you know. See that guy in front of you, that's Michael Landon. So famous he can hardly leave his house, but one of the most down to earth people you could meet."

Justin listened to her in amazement. Was this the same girl he'd blown off earlier? He could hardly imagine.

"I'm sorry I was so mean to you this morning. You were right; I wasn't looking where I was going. As I mentioned, I had a bad morning."

Justin reached the register and paid for his meal.

"I've got a table in the corner, won't you join me?"

Justin looked around as if he wanted to escape. Who was this blond wisp of a woman who seemed to know all the answers? Nodding he proceeded behind Zoë to her table, still not sure why he was following her. Justin sat down across from her. He felt almost in awe of her as she gracefully found her seat with the confidence of someone who did indeed have all the answers.

"So tell me, what did happen this morning?" he asked, then quickly added with a smile, "before I knocked you off your bike I mean."

Zoë blushed as she laughed. "Well, I don't know if you'd understand."

"Try me."

"All right then, I am an advocate for wildlife, more specifically sea life. Anything to do with the ocean. It's my passion really. I am studying to be a marine biologist at UCLA."

"You're kidding!" he said stopping her, "that's where I went to school."

Zoë smiled, it was indeed a small world. She knew then that this meeting was fated long before they'd even been aware of it.

"Writing major?" she smiled knowingly.

Justin nodded; he felt a chill as if a cold draft blew in from somewhere. But it was eighty degrees outside and definitely not chilly.

"Someday you're going to write the great American novel, Justin VanSant." She mused.

"How do you know?"

"Just a feeling I get from you."

"Well, I appreciate your confidence but I can only hope that Vance will keep me on his team in the fall."

"You work with Vance Langdon?"

"Yes, I do. Have you heard of him?"

"Who hasn't, I understand he's a terrific writer although I've never seen one of his shows."

"You're kidding?"

"No, I try not to watch television unless I absolutely have to."

"Then how did you know who the guy was standing in front of me in line?"

"I'm a script girl on the set of *Little House on the Prairie*."

"Wow, a script girl. That doesn't seem like your kind of job, how did you end up doing that?"

Zoë smiled as she picked at her salad. "It pays the rent and helps me through college."

He nodded and smiled. "So you were telling me about your morning before we got sidetracked."

"Yes, well, you see I belong to a group of concerned citizens who fight for the rights of sea life; we lost an important battle this morning. We have been trying to get an off shore oil refinery shut down. It's polluting the water and every day we find all kinds of fish washing ashore because of it. But no one will listen. Everyone needs oil, and fish are expendable. What they don't realize is that pollution affects all of us, not just the fish in the sea. It affects the water we drink, the food we eat. It may only seem that a couple of fish are losing their life so we can heat our homes and drive our cars, but in the long run it's much more dangerous than that."

"So you're totally opposed to drilling for oil."

"No, not at all. I understand that it's not reasonable to ask people to stop driving. It's a way of life, it's a convenience and often times it's vital to our existence. What I'm asking is that these refineries take more precautions when drilling. There are a number of things they can do to stop the pollution they're causing, but they refuse because it will cost them more money. The less they spend on machinery and safety, the more they can pocket."

Justin finished his sandwich as he listened to this passionate girl speak. It almost made him want to fight the cause with her the way she talked about it.

"What you're saying makes perfect sense really," he replied. "I don't understand why it's not being taken to the top so to speak. Have you spoken to anyone at City Hall?"

"We're trying that too. But it's hard, we're not powerful, we don't have a voice. We're just concerned people trying to make life safer for everyone."

"Certainly they can appreciate that."

"You'd think wouldn't you? But no one cares until there's a big oil spill and hundreds of fish and birds end up washing up on shore dead from oil suffocation. It's a horrible thing and one we're trying to avoid."

"Sounds like you need a voice for your cause."

Zoë looked him straight in the eye, "What do you mean, 'a voice'?"

"Well, someone in the media who can give credence to your story. Someone people know and trust."

"Like?" Zoë waited and held her breath.

"Well, I have a friend who works at the *LA Times*. He's someone I know and trust and he may be able to get one of their star reporters to cover it for you."

"Thanks, but we've tried that. No one seems to care."

"Maybe you weren't talking to the right people."

Zoë shrugged, "I guess it can't hurt."

"No it can't. I tell you what, I've got to get back now, but I will call him later today and see what he says."

"You'd do that for me?" Zoë smiled, flattered at his offer.

"As you said, it helps everyone," Justin tried to keep his tone flat, but he was less than successful. For whatever reason he suddenly felt compelled to help with her cause.

Rethinking his tone he added quickly, "I'm happy to help you with this Zoë."

"Thank you," Zoë could feel her heart skip a beat as he stood up from the table.

"Where can I reach you?"

Quickly she scribbled her telephone number on a piece of paper and handed it to him.

"I will phone you later and let you know what he says."

"Thank you again Justin."

"Don't thank me yet. When your off shore rig is safe and the ocean is saved, then you can thank me for making a call. It was nice talking to you." He turned then and walked away.

Zoë watched him as he left the cafeteria. She heard nothing but the beating of her own heart, and in that very moment she knew that Justin would someday be someone very special to her. Possibly even someone she could fall in love with.

Justin was good to his word, as was his friend at the paper. Not only did Zoë's cause get a story, but a three-part segment on the dangers of improper drilling. The sheer pressure from the community and City Hall forced the rig to close down with a renewed commitment to reopen a more environmentally friendly one. Zoë was beyond thrilled. The morning she found out, she raced into Studio H to find Justin. It had been only a month since they met, but already she was feeling more of what she'd felt that first day in the cafeteria. Zoë raced through the building looking for his office. She found him instead on the set of *Hospital of Hope.*

Now that Justin had graduated from college, he was able to spend even more time at the studio, which pleased Vance to no end. Zoë, who was also out of school for the summer, had more time for her endless causes. The studio could go to hell, she thought, before she spent the kind of time at it that Justin did. But she respected his work, and knew he was quite good at it.

She smiled as she watched him working with one of the actors. Not wanting to disturb him, she waited far away from the set. She could tell that it was a crucial part of the filming and for now, she just wanted to observe. In the last thirty days, she'd found every excuse in the book to see or visit him. But usually she limited her visits to his lovely beach home, which was only four miles from where she shared a large five-bedroom house with several roommates. She'd found Justin to be friendly and helpful, but there always seemed to be a part of him that he reserved. Although she wasn't sure why, Zoë knew for certain that he was not dating anyone, nor that there was anyone he was particularly interested in. He was holding back for something or someone although she couldn't be sure whom or why.

"Ok folks," the director called out, "that's a wrap." On command everyone seemed to relax. Zoë knew they were filming a pilot episode for something Vance hoped would take off like *Dallas* had before. But this season the competition was steep. Zoë watched as Justin collected his papers and headed in her direction.

He looked up startled. "How long have you been standing there?"

Zoë smiled, "Not long, only a few minutes. I came to tell you some very exciting news."

Justin touched her arm and it sent a shiver down her spine. "Come back to my office, we can talk more privately there."

Once they were inside his office, Justin set down the script he was carrying along with a folder full of notes.

"So what's your exciting news?" Smiling, he leaned against his desk, folding his arms over his chest.

He looked tan and dangerously handsome to her. She almost forgot what she'd come there to tell him. "We did it! We closed them down, they announced this morning that they would close the rig and refit it!"

Justin smiled broadly. "I can't believe it! That's terrific news, see all your hard work finally paid off."

He took her hand then, meant as a friendly gesture of congratulations. But Zoë took it a step farther, leaning into him she wrapped her arms around his neck and breathed in the woodsy scent of his aftershave. Justin returned her hug, and found it not so unpleasant to fold her into his arms. Her thin but well-curved body pressed against him in such a way that he could feel her nipples penetrate his shirt. As if on cue, their faces pulled back and he found himself looking deep into her eyes. Zoë's eyelids fell and her long lashes brushed her cheeks; he could no longer resist and pressed his mouth to hers. Her kiss was as sweet, caring and gentle as she was. There was also a marked innocence about it, as if she had never been kissed by a man before. He did not open his mouth, but continued to press his lips against hers.

Suddenly, as if someone tore open his heart, he was under that pier again, kissing Eve. His sweet beloved Eve. She was everywhere, and it was raining again. He felt his hands run up her back. He kissed her with more passion now and suddenly Zoë began to wonder if she'd been wrong about Justin all along. Was he like every other man she'd met? Would he soon be demanding she return his favor? No! She knew better than that. Justin pulled away from her then, and Eve was gone. Zoë stood before him, dazed and confused by what had just happened.

"That was quite a kiss," she said to break the silence.

"I-I'm sorry I got a little carried away."

Then, Zoë knew, and she spoke, "Justin who were you kissing just then?"

His throat tightened, "What do you mean?"

"I mean it's ok, I understand, I've always felt there was someone else in your heart."

Damn her for seeing right through him, he thought. But Zoë was not one to mince words.

"You're wrong, there's no one." He turned toward his desk, no longer able to face her. He felt a delicate hand on his shoulder.

"You weren't kissing me just then. But that's ok because someday you will." Zoë turned to leave, pausing for a moment at the door. "Thank you again for your help, we couldn't have fought this battle without you." Before Justin could say another word, she was gone with a click of the door. And he was left alone with his thoughts and his ghosts.

Two days later, Zoë called him at home to invite him to a thank you dinner. He was glad she called; he missed her visits after work and their walks along the beach. He'd spent an agonizing couple of days wondering if he'd always be this crippled. He wanted a second chance, he wanted to feel alive again, but moreover, he wanted to fall in love again.

Zoë suggested that she bring the meal over to his house, so they'd have more privacy. He agreed, and on Friday evening they sat in his kitchen while she prepared one of her favorite vegetarian dishes. He avoided talking about the reason for her absence, until finally he could no longer stand the avoidance. They walked along the beach after dinner, in the opposite direction of the pier he'd shared with Eve.

"Look, about the other day. I feel that I need to apologize for the way I behaved."

"No need to say you're sorry Justin, it's really ok. I wanted to kiss you, I'm glad I kissed you."

"But I was..."

"Thinking about someone else?" she interrupted without looking at him, "I already told you I understand. I always sensed that there was someone else in your heart, now I am certain of it."

"But it's not what you think."

"How is it then Justin?" she reached for his hand, taking it in her own. He stopped and turned to face her.

"I like you Zoë, I really do. I just don't know if I am capable of this."

She smiled then, a broad understanding smile, as if she knew all of his secrets and accepted him nonetheless.

"Capable of what? Letting someone else in your heart? You know everyone comes with some sort of baggage, even though they say they don't, they do. Yours is something that is presumably still somewhat fresh and painful and eventually it will pass. I can accept that."

"What if it doesn't pass?"

"Then we'll jump off that bridge when we come to it." As Zoë reached up to stroke his hair, she knew she already loved him. "She's not here now, and for whatever reason you're not with her. Is there a chance you ever will be?" She almost feared his reply.

"Not a chance in hell," he said defeated.

"Then that's all I need to know. I trust that someday you will kiss me and only me and she will eventually turn into nothing more than a distant memory."

He doubted that, but he nodded despite what he felt. He longed for Eve to become a vague recollection, a distant someone he once loved. God, how he longed for that. He wanted desperately to be able to love this beautiful woman that stood before him.

Zoë paused for a moment, picking her words carefully, "I ask only that you respect me, and give this a try. If it doesn't work then we've had some wonderful moments."

"You're amazingly sweet Zoë," he said taking her into his arms.

"Yes, I suppose I am," she laughed. But Justin knew she was half serious. She had a confidence that he'd never known before in a woman. She went after what she wanted and she would not stop until it was hers. She had enough tenacity to save the world. Right now though he hoped she could save him.

CHAPTER 37

By November of that year, Zoë and Justin were an item. They were seen at parties together as well as on campus and at the studio. Often, when time permitted Justin would accompany Zoë to her various 'save the world meetings' as he called them. Zoë spent most evenings with Justin, they would take turns cooking and because of Zoë's dedication to being a vegetarian, Justin couldn't remember the last time he'd eaten meat. But Zoë had yet to spend the night, often she would stay late, but Justin always sent her home. It wasn't fair to let her stay, at least not until he was certain he was ready.

On Thanksgiving Justin invited Adele over to celebrate with them. Her children were in Colorado on a skiing vacation and she chose not to spend her holiday in the snow even though they had offered to pay for her ticket. Justin had managed to talk Zoë into letting him at least cook a turkey. It would be their first holiday together and that left him feeling a bit nervous. There was a certain unspoken expectation that crept up when the holidays drew near. He knew that although Zoë insisted she expected nothing, she hoped to take their relationship to the next level. She hoped that he would at last make love to her.

Later that night, after Adele left, Justin lit a fire and poured a couple of glasses of wine. Zoë busied herself in the kitchen, packing away the left overs when Justin came over to her and kissed her as he never had before. Zoë could feel it; at last it was her he was kissing. She dropped the towel she was holding and wrapped her arms around his neck. He pulled her over to the fire and handed her a glass of wine. She sipped it slowly, never letting her gaze drop from him.

"I love you Justin," she said finally. He opened his mouth to speak but she covered it with her hand, "Don't say anything, I know you don't love me yet, but someday when you're ready you will. For now it's enough that you've come this far."

He brushed her hair with his hand. How had he ever gotten so lucky, he wondered? To find such an understanding woman who sat patiently by while he fought his demons. He reached for her and kissed her again, this time with more urgency and more passion than he'd done before. It was in that moment that they both knew what would happen next.

There in front of the crackling fire, they made love. Somewhere off in the distance, the ocean roared to herald the arrival of an approaching storm. Soon thereafter, the rain began to fall around them, but warmed by their passion and the blazing fire, they were unaware of anything else but each other. Justin found a peace and understanding in Zoë he had never felt before. At last there was no torment, no anguish, no pain. Only Zoë, his sweet, caring, understanding Zoë.

CHAPTER 38

Eve pulled her car up the familiar driveway. It was a hot and humid July afternoon when she arrived at the VanSant's with toddler Frannie in tow. Eve felt an odd pang as she walked her daughter up the walkway to Justin's old house. How many times had she run up this walkway in search of her friend? It seemed now as though it was almost in another lifetime. Little Frannie seemed to take up every ounce of her time and energy. Billy helped a little, but not as much as she'd hoped he would. She'd hoped that during the summer he would take a break from coaching football. He did indeed take a break from football, only to coach some other sport. Eve had a difficult time keeping up with his schedule and then of course there was his time with "the boys." Billy insisted that after a long week of working for his family he needed some time to blow off a little steam. More often than not, he and his friends would head into Hartford for a little fun. Eve didn't like the idea of Billy going out and drinking and cavorting like a single man but she also wanted him to have his space. He was a good provider and a good husband and father. He adored Frannie and doted on her constantly. He was forever spoiling her, while he left it to Eve to be the stern one.

Frannie chattered as they approached the door. Eve was looking forward to this visit; she hadn't spent time with Justin's mom in a while. She also longed to hear the tidbits of information Mary VanSant would share about Justin's progress in the television industry. Eve spoke to Justin occasionally, but more often than not she spoke to his answering machine. She wrote him long descriptive letters of her life and Frannie's growing up, and in return she would sometimes get a letter or two. But the connection they'd once shared was no longer there. The door flew open and a well-dressed attractive woman stood smiling with her arms outstretched.

"My darling Frances, how are you?" She smiled, winking at Eve, "come in my dear." Mary bent down to pick the toddler up from the ground. "You are a picture aren't you?" she fussed. Mary wished with all her heart that Justin would at last settle down and give them a grandchild of their own. Until that time, she knew Frannie would always be there with a laugh and a smile.

Eve walked behind Mary and Frannie. It was cool inside their home, amazingly so, she thought. The house was very much the same as she remembered it. Mary and her husband had changed only a few things over the years.

"Come, let's sit in the kitchen dear, it's much cooler in there. I'll poor us some ice tea. Would you like some tea, sweet Frances? Or do you prefer juice and a cookie?" Turning to Eve she continued, "I bought whole grain cookies special for your visit, may she have one?"

Eve's face softened, it was no wonder Justin was the sweet and caring man he'd turned out to be, one look at his parents and you would know why.

"Of course she can Mary." Eve followed her host into the kitchen and sat down on a pale, yellow-padded chair. Mary was right; it was even cooler in the kitchen. She hoped she could stay for a nice long visit, drink a refreshing glass of ice tea and hear news of Justin.

They had been talking for over an hour before Mary mentioned her son. Mary came back from putting Frannie down for a nap in Justin's old crib. She kept it in her son's old room and would take it out and dust it off whenever Eve and the baby stopped by. Eve was sipping her second glass of tea when she returned. "Thank you for taking such good care of Frannie, it's very nice of you."

Mary patted her hand as she sat down. "Oh dear, it's not a bother at all, I couldn't love Frannie any more if she were my grandchild." A sad look swept over Mary's face. It could have been my grandchild, she thought, if only...quickly she brushed the thought from her head. What an odd thing to remember, she thought, after all these years she began recalling again the crush Justin had on Eve so many years ago.

Mary's look of nostalgia did not escape Eve; she wondered how much Mary knew. How much Justin told her. Although there wasn't that much to tell really. Besides, it was so long ago now.

Mary brightened when she recalled a recent conversation she'd had with her son. "I'm hopeful," Mary began smiling, "that Justin will find his happiness soon."

Eve was intrigued. "What do you mean?"

A mysterious look appeared on Mary's face, "Justin's met someone."

The words sent a wave of shock through Eve like nothing she'd felt before. "W-what do you mean?" she felt oddly distraught at the thought of it.

"Well dear, I mean that he's met a girl. A lovely young lady from California who saves oceans."

"Saves oceans? That's quite an undertaking. Is he involved with her?"

"Well, he insists that it's not serious, but I know better. There's a sound in his voice that I haven't heard in…years." She paused for a moment and then continued, "Anyway, I am hopeful, he hasn't really had time to date anyone since he's been living out there and I've been so worried about him you know?"

"We all have Mary, I wish with all my heart that he hadn't left Connecticut."

Mary sighed, suddenly her shoulders seemed heavy, "Yes, I know his father and I tried to convince him to stay but he insisted on going. Now I guess it's all turned out for the best. He says he's working with the best people in the business, which is what he always wanted."

"So how long has he been seeing this girl?" Eve asked.

"Oh, I don't know, a few months perhaps, he's very secretive about the whole thing. I asked him if she were some famous actress or something but he insists that she's just a regular girl. Moved out from Minnesota I believe, so at least I know she has values. Although from what I understand she seems to be somewhat of a free spirit. I've spoken to her once, on a Sunday morning when I called; she was there."

Eve felt herself grow the teeniest bit nauseous at the thought of Justin with another woman. She scolded herself for being so overly protective of him. She had no right, he was an adult.

"What's her name?" Eve asked finally.

"Zoë, Zoë Williams."

"What kind of name is Zoë?" Eve asked.

"Californian I suppose, she changed it when she moved out west, according to Justin. She spends all of her time studying to be a marine biologist and helping out with various causes."

There it was again, that sick to her stomach kind of feeling. At that moment Eve knew she was more than an over protective friend.

"Eve darling you're so pale!" Mary remarked. "Maybe you should lie down."

"Actually, can I use your restroom, I'm feeling a little ill. Probably the heat." Eve got up and staggered down the hall, as it began to swirl in front of her. The nausea suddenly gripped her so tightly she was almost unable to breathe. At that moment, Eve slipped into darkness as she sank to the floor.

When she woke, she found herself on Justin's old bed, a cold compress on her head. The sickly feeling was gone now; she was left only with a headache. A mild thumping at her temples. She tried to get up but had to lay down again when the thumping became more intense. Mary entered the room, carrying another compress and a glass of ice water.

"Oh, dear you're awake, you gave me such a scare. All I heard was a thud and when I went to find you, you had fainted."

"Frannie..." Eve mumbled.

"She's fine, slept right through it. Don't you worry about her, I called the doctor and he should be here shortly."

"No Mary, I don't need a doctor, I'll be fine. How long was I out?"

"Over an hour I'd say, and I insist on having the doctor take a look at you before you go home. I tried to reach Billy at his work but he'd already left, coaching something or other."

He didn't have to coach today...the thought raced through Eve's head and then left as quickly as it came.

"Well, anyway the doctor should be here any minute so you just hold on." Mary left the room to give Eve a chance to rest again before the doctor arrived.

She wanted to tell Mary that she knew full well what was wrong with her, but she thought she'd keep it secret just a little while longer. A breath of disappointment escaped her lungs. She didn't want to be pregnant right now, as horrible as it was to even entertain that thought she couldn't help it. She'd hoped to return to school and take some classes or maybe even get a part-time job. Now there would be no way she could ever do that for years. Or at least for a very long time. Billy of course would be thrilled. She cursed herself for having these thoughts, married people have babies. She thought of Justin and Zoë, two free spirits probably having the time of their lives. She pictured Zoë fighting all sorts of causes with Justin right by her side. Her hand fell to her tummy, a life inside there depended on her and she needed to remember that. No more fantasies about school, or work or what life was like in California.

Within a day Eve had confirmation that she was indeed pregnant. Billy was thrilled, and Eve was tired. This seemed to be a rougher pregnancy than her first. She was sick all the time and exhausted. Her mother and Mary came over often to help her with housework or just to look after Frannie while she napped.

After careful consideration, Mary finally decided to speak to Justin about her concerns. Eve had lost more weight than she should have and the doctor was considering hospitalizing her. Billy, however, was nowhere to be found, returning home only in time for dinner and then often heading out again. Coaching and all, he'd say. After listening to his mother Justin was furious. How could that bastard leave her in this condition! On an afternoon when he had a quiet moment at the studio he called Eve to see how she was doing.

When she answered he could hear the tendrils of exhaustion in her voice.

"Bug, it's me Jus."

Eve's spirits seemed to lift the moment she heard his voice. "Justin, it's so good to hear from you."

"I understand you've been under the weather."

"No, not under the weather, just pregnant again and sicker than I've ever felt in my entire life."

"Mom says they're thinking about hospitalizing you."

"I won't let them, who's going to take care of Frannie?"

Justin bit his lower lip, and forced himself to be kind. "How about Billy?" That idiot you're married to who can think of nothing other than himself, he wanted to add.

"Billy's got too much going on right now."

"Come on Eve, he can stop coaching for a while can't he?"

"I could never ask him to do that."

Suddenly Justin realized this was a whole different Eve than the girl he'd grown up with. She'd given up, she had no fight left in her; time, pregnancy, motherhood and that missing-in-action husband of hers had wrung it out of her.

"Eve honey, listen, I really think you should talk to him. It's his duty as a husband to be there for you."

"You're going to make someone a wonderful husband someday Jus."

He fell silent at the other end of the line. "Thank you," he said at last.

"I understand that you're dating someone. I think it's great Jus, you deserve to be happy." She felt a pain when she said that, not a physical pain, but rather a pain like someone was crushing her heart. It was hard to let him go, he'd been hers for so many years and now she had to share him, as much as she hated to admit it. She hoped that whomever he was dating was treating him right, she would have it no other way.

Justin listened while she spoke. Zoë was going to be over again tonight, they would cook dinner, talk and take one of their long walks along the beach while the sun was setting.

"Yes," he replied after a long pause, "her name is Zoë. I am seeing her, we're great friends."

"Like we were."

Justin could barely stand the conversation. He wanted to yell that it was nothing like they were. He wanted to tell her that every time he was with Zoë he felt guilty, like he was cheating on Eve. Suddenly, Justin needed to change the subject.

"I want you to take care of yourself, and believe me if you don't I will find out. You've got a new little life inside of you now."

Eve hesitated before she continued, "Justin, can I ask you something?"

"Sure Bug, anything, what is it?"

"When I first found out I was pregnant, I wished that I wasn't…is that terrible?"

Justin frowned. "Why did you wish you weren't pregnant?"

"It's so hard Jus, I can't even begin to tell you how difficult it is being a parent. Don't get me wrong, I love Frannie to pieces but I was hoping I could wait a while before having another one you know. Maybe return to school or something. I just, I've lost myself, Justin. If I'm not being a wife to Billy or a mother to Fran, I don't know who I am."

"No Bug, it's not terrible, I even think it's normal to feel that way. You give so much of yourself all the time, to everyone. You have every right to want to make a life for yourself outside of your family. To find out who Eve is again. Billy supports you in that doesn't he?" But he already knew the answer.

"Actually, I didn't tell him. I was going to, but then I found out I was pregnant again so what's the use."

"You can go back to school after the baby is born."

"There's no way Jus, what would I do with the little ones? It would be impossible."

"What about night school? Billy could watch them."

Eve shrugged and began to pick at a button on her blouse, "He'd never agree to that Jus. You know that as well as I do."

"Do you want me to talk to him?"

"Thank you, but no, it's my battle Justin, I should just forget about it entirely."

"Now listen to me Eve, don't ever forget about your own dreams, you're a valuable human being and you deserve every chance to better yourself just like everyone else."

"Thanks Jus, I hate to tell you this but I've got to go be sick now. I think this baby knows what I'm saying and its purposely making me ill to get back at me."

Justin laughed. "No Eve, I'm certain that's not it."

"Jus, thanks for calling, it was good hearing your voice again." Without waiting for his reply she hung up the phone. Justin stared at the receiver wondering how much more of this she could stand.

CHAPTER 39

It was a cool October day when Zoë happened upon the Austin Wilding books. She wasn't digging for anything in particular, she was putting away a set of freshly washed towels when she found the manuscripts hidden beneath a set of sheets. The cover said "King's Town" by Justin R. VanSant. Curious, Zoë began to read and before she realized it she was halfway through the first book. When Justin returned home that evening, she was almost finished.

"Hey Zo!" Justin smiled as he breezed through the door. It had been a good day on the set, the new series looked like it would be a runaway hit and there waiting for him was his sweet Zoë. She smiled back at him for a moment and then continued the chapter she wanted to finish.

She was sitting at the kitchen table, a cold cup of tea in front of her, engrossed in whatever she was reading. Homework, Justin assumed. He bent to kiss her cheek, "Hey babe, must be a good story."

Zoë smiled again, her hand covering the words. "It is, very good in fact."

Justin put his briefcase down and sat beside her. "Wow, what's it about?"

"The 1870s," she said simply.

Justin frowned. "What does history have to do with marine life?" He smiled, knowing she was teasing him.

"Absolutely nothing," she smiled, "but this is the best novel I've ever read and I hate historical novels."

"How did you…?"

"It was in your linen closet. Two of them in fact, I didn't think you'd mind."

"I never meant for anyone to read them."

"Honey why not, they're excellent!"

Justin shrugged, and ran his hand over the cover, "I don't know, it was just a phase."

"Well I think you should try and get these published."

"No, I don't really care for them to be honest, like I said, it was a phase."

"Did you know that Stephen King hated his first book? Threw it away in fact. His wife pulled it out of the trash and sent it to a publisher. The rest is history."

"So what are you trying to say," he smiled wryly, "you want to get married so you can publish one of my books?"

"Silly!" she leaned over and kissed him. "Actually, what I want is for you to publish it."

He shook his head and stood up from the table. How could he publish this drivel?

"Honey, why not? It's really a shame not to share this with the world."

Justin turned to face her again. "You mean I'm depriving everyone of the adventures of Austin Wilding?"

"Well, yes you are. Babe look, it can't hurt right. Why are you so opposed to this?"

"Hon, I'm not opposed to it," he sat down beside her again, covering her hands with his own, "I guess I just never thought that anyone else would ever want to read it."

"Well someone should. And if you'll let me, I'd like to show it to someone for you."

Justin watched her expression, she was almost pleading with him now. He certainly could not turn her down; besides what could it hurt? They'd never publish a silly book about a man longing for a woman he could never have anyway.

When Charlie Bellows first picked up Justin's manuscript he knew there was something different about it. In a matter of a single page he was hooked, and Charlie Bellows, Senior Editor for Bellows & Larkin Publishing, prided himself on rarely being hooked. The manuscript had arrived quite mysteriously on his desk earlier that day with a large note pinned to it from Liz, his assistant: "Urgent, please read! Charlie, this one comes highly recommended."

Recommended by whom? He thought. Oh, what the hell, it was probably Suzanne, his ex-wife and co-owner of the agency, forcing another one of her so-called manuscripts down his throat. He intended to pick it up and read the obligatory first paragraph only to slap a rejection note on it as he did all the others she sent over. Charlie knew that Suzanne wouldn't know a good manuscript from a bad one if it walked up and bit her in the ass, but this, this one was something entirely different. For a moment, he put down the page he was holding and hit the intercom button. "Lizzy, can you come in here please?"

Liz was off her chair in a moment. "Yes, sir?" she smiled from his doorway.

"Liz, come in and shut the door."

When she had, he continued: "Did my w…" he stopped himself before making that mistake. Someday he'd get used to their eight-month-old divorce. "Did Suzanne ask you to give this to me?"

"No sir." A slight smile appeared on her face.

"Then may I ask where you got it?"

"When I got in this afternoon, it was sitting on my chair with your name on it, I figured you were waiting on it." She hated lying, especially to a boss as nice as Charlie, but he hated unsolicited material and would no doubt reprimand her for it.

Charlie's brow furrowed for a moment wondering if it had been sent by an agent. He looked down at the manuscript again, searching for the agent's information. But there was none, just the name of the author: Justin VanSant.

"Hmmm," he said reading the name, his reading glasses slid farther down his nose and he pushed them back for a second. "Get this VanSant guy on the phone for me, would you please?" He handed Liz the cover sheet, "I believe these are his telephone numbers." Charlie leaned back in his seat again. "And I'd like to know how Mr. VanSant got past the receptionist long enough to deposit this on your desk. Check with the girl out front would you please?"

"Certainly," Liz nodded and scurried from his office to call her friend and tell her that her boyfriend's manuscript was a hit.

⁂

The meeting with Charlie was more than Justin could have hoped for. Charlie loved the manuscript and praised Justin for his work, then went on to tell him he would no doubt be signing the quickest book deal in the history of writing. True to his word, a freshly drawn up contract was on its way to Justin the morning after their meeting.

Bellows & Larkin rescheduled their print dates to accommodate their newest arrival. Charlie worked a huge publicity campaign and before it was even purchased by one reader, he'd already sold the movie rights to Paramount. Justin was in a complete daze. He hardly had enough time to absorb his "journals" being published. Now he was hearing words like "bestseller" and "motion picture."

He knew who he had to thank for that. Although she'd taken very little credit for it, Zoë had admitted to him that a friend of hers worked for Charlie and put the book on his desk. Charlie had inquired about it with Justin once, but Justin had insisted he did not know how his manuscript arrived there. Charlie dropped it after that, it didn't matter really. All that mattered was that Bellows and Larkin was on top of the "A" list again.

Charlie leaned back in his expensive leather chair. He smiled down at the glossy book cover, *King's Town* was going to be huge; it would make him millions. And soon, once the public was hungry for more, he would entice them with a sequel, and then another, and from there it was no telling how far Justin's little books would go. Charlie smelled a great author in Justin, the likes of which the West Coast had not seen in a long time. He was of the same caliber as James Michener, and Sidney Sheldon in his own right. But Justin, he suspected, would be even bigger than the two of them combined. Something in him screamed that this kid was on his way to being a star, and a millionaire, before he even turned forty.

Justin sat on his porch staring at the sea. He barely noticed the passers-by. He was only aware of his own thoughts and the thin slip of paper in his hand.

It was an advance check for $150,000. It had been delivered by messenger earlier that day along with a letter of congratulations and promises of many more checks to come. Justin could still not believe it. He'd known to expect a check, which according to Charlie would be substantial but only the tip of the iceberg.

Today, he was an author. For the first time in his life, he felt it. And not just because of the money. But because something he'd written without the help or collaboration of anyone else, was now published. He continued to watch the ocean as he mentally tried to catch up with the events of the past two weeks.

Already eight book signings had been scheduled in the Los Angeles and Hollywood areas and it became apparent to him that he would need to leave his job at the studio if he were going to effectively promote his book. He also needed to think about working on a third one in the series and then possibly a fourth. The motion picture would begin filming in the summer and he had to be prepared for any rewrites. Thanks to the advice Vance had given him, Justin insisted on script approval and because of this, he would need to be available and most likely on the set for a majority of the filming.

He and Zoë were leaving for Connecticut the day after tomorrow and before he left there was a mountain of work to do. They were not planning to return until after the New Year. Justin had spoken to his parents to share the good news with them and they were elated. It had also at last proved Justin's point when he'd insisted that the West Coast would bring him closer to his goals. Despite his ulterior reason for going, it had been a good decision nonetheless. He watched the ocean and spotted Zoë swimming with the tide. It was already getting cooler as winter was knocking on the Southland's door but Zoë didn't mind the chill. She longed to feel the sea water on her body and the sand in her hair. He wondered how his family would accept her; his parents knew that she was living with him now with no prospects of marriage. Zoë had made it clear that she did not want a legal commitment with him. She was fond of saying that she wanted him to stay with her because he wanted to, not because he was legally required to do so.

CHAPTER 40

Eve stood in her kitchen and watched the first snow flurry of the winter cover the ground in a blanket of white. The weather had turned cold only recently, it had been a long autumn, longer than most. But Eve was glad that winter was finally here. Her sick days were thankfully past and now as winter ushered the last bit of autumn out the door, she nearly felt reborn. Soon she and Billy would get the tree and they would spend the afternoon decorating it as had now become the tradition. Eve walked around her house, her tummy protruding out in front of her. Frannie was still asleep upstairs as Eve headed into the living room. Her newly delivered colonial style furniture sat patiently waiting to be used. The wooden living room floor bore a high polish and every picture and knickknack was in its place. At last after three years of marriage her home was in place.

Eve wanted very much to sit on her new couch, but she knew how difficult it would be for her to get out of it once she did. Smiling, she ran her hand absentmindedly over her stomach. A little foot kicked in response. The baby was kicking all the time now, making it difficult to sleep. But Eve didn't mind, she could hardly wait to meet the newest addition to the Freeman family.

Billy slept quietly as his wife wandered around their home. He had been out late again the night before. Out with friends, and a couple of people he'd never met before. He dreamt about the blond that had been so friendly with him. Her blouse had been a thin white silk that clutched her breasts, the top two buttons were open revealing a portion of her ample bosoms. She'd smiled at Billy from across the pool table and tossed her long curly blond hair across her shoulder. But in his dream she was fiddling with her buttons until they came loose; she was wearing no bra and was beside him in an instant.

Frances awoke then with a shrill cry, and Billy was pulled away from his dream by the sound of his daughter. Suddenly there was no more pool table, no more blond, only the reality of his life sinking in even deeper now. He turned his face into the pillow, hoping to drown out the sound of the crying baby, wondering when the hell Eve would quiet her down. He could hear her on the stairs, slowly making her way up. He should have gotten out of bed himself, but his hangover prevented him from doing anything other than lie there. He could feel it creep up on him now as Frannie's cry became more urgent, pounding at his temples as if someone was beating them with a hammer. Damn it, when is she going to get up here? He thought angrily as his head reverberated with each piercing scream.

As if Frannie could read his mind, she stopped. Billy felt a sense of relief wash over him as the pain in his head receded a bit. Closing his eyes he tried to remember the night before. Very little unfortunately about last night was very clear. He did though remember the blond, whatever the hell her name was. She was most certainly the most luscious creature he'd ever seen. But he knew he needed to be careful, he hoped he'd not been too obvious. If anyone had seen him, word of his encounter might get back to Eve; worse it might get back to Justin and then he'd have to deal with both of them. Damn this friendship, he thought.

Through the years although it had proved to be a source of comfort, now it was more or less a burden he carried with him. He was so sick of hearing about the goddamned good old days he could almost puke. He wished he had no ties to it, no memories of the way it used to be, or the way it should have been. And he wished more than anything that he did not live in such a small community where everybody knew everybody else's business. More than that he knew that if he set one foot on the wrong path good ol' Justin would call to set him straight. He had a lot of nerve thinking he could run his life even now.

But Billy knew what was really going on.

Downstairs now, Eve could hear the shower and began preparing her husband's breakfast. Frannie babbled from her highchair, her soft black curls framing her face, her blue eyes looking up to Eve, mesmerized by her mother's every move. As she shuffled a few dishes in the sink she thought of Billy's outing the previous night. She always wondered where he went and what he did with "the boys," but she never asked. Somehow on this morning she knew if she wasn't careful her curiosity would get the better of her.

Billy felt the aspirin begin to take effect as he descended the stairs into his life. He could smell his breakfast cooking but he wasn't hungry. He should never drink like that anymore. He silently reminded himself to call around to his friends to see if they could shed some light on the forgotten moments of the preceding night. He walked into the kitchen to find a very pregnant Eve sitting and watching Frances eat. Both looked picture perfect, and for a moment he felt the blood rise to his face as he recalled his dream. He had the perfect life, what the hell was he thinking? He loved Eve. Still something he could not control made him reach for more. He felt young and alive when women eyed him with a flirtatious smile. He felt like the Billy Freeman he was before his life became so damned complicated.

Eve smiled up from the table. "Good morning."

Billy only nodded as he took a seat at the table. Frannie reached her tiny arms out to him, but he could only smile, feeling his stomach begin to turn at the thought of eating.

"Did you have a good time last night?" Eve questioned trying to sound nonchalant.

"Yeah, sure, I guess."

She stood and went to the stove, putting eggs on his plate. "Don't you remember?" she tried to conceal the icy tone in her voice but Billy could feel her hurt.

"I'm sorry I didn't call."

"You stumbled in at 3 a.m. Do you have any idea how worried I was about you?"

"I said I was sorry."

Eve clenched her fist over the handle of the pan; she needed to take a breath and calm down. He never called, what difference would it make anyway?

"Where did you all go?"

"Some bar, next county I think."

"You don't remember that either?"

"The guys picked it, I just went along. I don't care where we drink, the beer's all the same."

Eve placed a plate in front of him and turned to clean up her daughter.

Billy moved the eggs around and picked at the bacon. The toast was dry, so he picked up the jelly jar from the table and began to spread a thick layer of apricot jam over the bread. He knew he'd better eat something or else he'd pay the price for that too.

"So, who did you go with?"

"The guys, I already told you that! Look, I will not tolerate twenty questions on this all right, I went out, I go out—it's what I do on a Friday night. You could go out too if you'd like, I won't stop you!"

Eve stood and turned to him, pointing at her belly with the baby spoon. "Like this?" she said wryly.

"Right, well whatever, point is I don't care if you go out and have fun."

"And when the hell would I have time? Between taking care of the house, the baby and you…"

Billy threw up a glare of disapproval as he continued to push his food around on his plate. "Sorry I'm so much friggin' work, Eve."

CHAPTER 41

Justin pulled his rented car into his parent's driveway, a slightly nervous Zoë beside him. Justin leaned over to kiss her cheek, trying to reassure her. Her hands clenched at her side, she watched the house as it grew larger with their approach. There were few times in her life Zoë could remember feeling this way. She wanted his parents to like her, but she was well aware how difficult it was for most to accept her lifestyle. Moreover, she did not want to hurt Justin. She knew that his parent's disapproval would do just that.

Justin took Zoë's hand as they left the car and walked up the path. Before they could even reach the front door it flung open and his mother stood smiling at them, so obviously overjoyed to see her son again. She flew into his arms and embraced him tightly, behind them, his father stood smiling. Zoë stayed at the foot of the porch steps watching the scene before her. She felt a sadness engulf her heart; her own parents would never accept her that way. Justin's mother looked over her embrace and saw Zoë.

"My dear," she smiled, "welcome to our home!" Mary released her son and threw her arms around Zoë as if she'd always known her. For a moment, Zoë thought she would cry.

The afternoon was more pleasant than Zoë could have imagined; soon her apprehension melted away. Mary was anxious to welcome Justin's girlfriend into their home and their life. And after she felt the appropriate time had passed, she broke out Justin's old photo album. It was there that Zoë first glimpsed a sight of the people she'd heard so much about, Billy and Eve.

"Is this them?" She asked pointing to a photograph of them by the lake. Eve was smiling into the camera while the boys played in the water.

Mary smiled as she thought back. "They were all inseparable. For as long as I can remember if you saw one, you saw the other two. Then of course it changed."

"What happened?" Zoë frowned.

"Billy's mother passed away. It was all different after that. Eve began spending a lot more time with Billy. They would go on long walks alone and Justin just began to feel left out." She paused for a moment, wandering in her mind back to that time, remembering how it pained Justin to watch them together. "They never intended to hurt him, or to exclude him. It just happened. Billy needed Eve desperately during that time and she wanted to be there for him, then they fell in love. It was bound to happen eventually."

The story had ended with such sadness; Zoë could feel his mother's pain. But why? She wondered. Mary folded the book and ran her hands absentmindedly over its cover. "It's a long time past now, and the three are still good friends."

"So it ended happily?"

Mary thought of the gossip she'd heard recently in town, Billy had been seen around town with some blond girl, and often enough that people were beginning to wonder. Eve was mostly left to her own devices, to struggle through her second pregnancy. It was anything but perfect, but then what was anymore? It seemed to her that the world was changing so rapidly that she could barely keep up.

Mary forgot Zoë's question when she asked: "You'll pardon my frankness, but do you think you will ever marry my son?"

Zoë's glance fell to the now closed photo album. She had known the question would surface, although she did not expect it quite so soon.

Her hands covered Mary's as she said, "I love your son with all of my heart. I could not love him any more than I do even if we were married."

"So you won't?"

"I don't need a marriage certificate to prove my devotion to Justin. I am more devoted to him than any wife could be."

"My dear I don't doubt that, I only wonder if you wouldn't consider it for Justin's sake?"

"Justin understands how I feel."

"So you wouldn't…"

Zoë smiled, "Please understand that I don't mean to offend you or Mr. VanSant. I only need to stand up for what I believe in and hope that it reflects Justin's beliefs as well. When we do not agree on something we discuss it and compromise. Trust me when I say this Mrs. VanSant, if it becomes important to Justin at some point, I would absolutely reconsider my position. But until that time, we are very happy together."

Mary smiled, realizing she was dealing with a very headstrong young woman who obviously loved her son very much. "I believe you love my son and I apologize for being so forward."

"Don't be, you're concerned for Justin and I respect that."

There was a knock at the door, interrupting their conversation. Mary had a feeling she knew who it was. Justin was in the kitchen and went to answer it, and from the living room she could hear the lilt in Eve's voice.

She stood before Justin, radiant and very pregnant. He wrapped her in his arms and held her there, remembering the last time he'd held her. It seemed like forever now and he thought that he hardly remembered it at all. But as he felt her melt into him, every memory of that night flooded back to him and took hold of his heart again leaving him breathless.

"I've missed you." She sniffled trying to hold back her tears. He felt one of his own slide down his cheek, he had missed her too. Despite all he'd tried, the moment she was in his space it was as though she'd never left. He released Eve then, gently pushing her back.

"It's good to see you Bug. You're looking healthy these days," he smiled. The floor creaked behind him and he realized that Zoë had emerged from the living room. The two women spotted each other and Justin stood back as Zoë walked through the hallway to greet the new visitor.

She outstretched her hand, "You must be Eve," she smiled.

Eve inhaled sharply, "And you must be Zoë."

"Guilty."

"It's a pleasure to meet you Zoë, I've heard a great deal about you. Although not from Justin. He likes his privacy when it comes to girlfriends, he never tells anyone anything. I have to hear it at the Grand Union."

Zoë smiled up to Justin. "Great, so the out of town girl is a topic of conversation at your local grocer."

Justin shrugged. "Small towns."

Mary turned the corner. "Eve honey, why don't you come in and get off your feet, you must be so tired."

"Yes, Mary, I am, I'd love to sit for a while."

Justin stood aside as Eve passed and he took Zoë's hand in reassurance. Thank God he had never opened up to her about Eve, this would have only served to torment her.

"Where's my precious Frannie?" Mary asked.

"She's with my mom, I wanted an afternoon just to visit. I thought we could introduce Fran later. There's always time for that."

They collected in the kitchen. Eve eased herself into a chair and pulled her sweater around her tummy. Justin watched her in awe. Certainly, he had never seen her look so beautiful as she did now. She radiated a glow that seemed to inspire and draw him closer to her.

Eve felt driven to learn all she could about Zoë, this woman who had stolen her Justin's heart. She was happy for him, but oddly enough, a small sting of jealously poked at her conscience as well. Despite her apprehensions about this free-spirited woman, she found Zoë to be genuine and caring and obviously very much in love with Justin. Often, Eve would see her caress his hand, or put a gentle hand on his leg. Eve noticed Justin's face soften when he would turn to her. At the same time he seemed terribly nervous although she couldn't imagine why.

Christmas day proved to be more difficult than Justin had anticipated. His mother had invited Eve, Billy and Frannie to spend the afternoon with them. When Justin saw Frannie for the first time, he immediately fell in love with her tousled curls and brilliant smile. He spent most of the afternoon playing with her and chasing her around the house. She giggled and screamed with delight as he chased her from room to room. Despite the laughter he shared with Eve's daughter, he felt the tension so thick he could cut it with a knife. Billy did not make it for dinner; he called to say he was running late and not to hold their holiday meal. He wanted to shout at his friend and tell him he was screwing up the best thing that had ever happened to him. He cursed his desire to protect Eve from a man who seemed to be neglecting her.

Billy finally arrived two hours late for Christmas dinner, the smell of beer on his breath. Eve forced a smile on her face and continued to act as though nothing was wrong. But Justin knew otherwise. With obvious difficulty, Eve stood up when Billy entered the VanSant home to warm him a plate of food. Billy handed out smiles and handsome apologies to everyone. He ate feverishly in the kitchen while everyone stayed and continued their conversations in the living room. Eve remained with her husband;-she was quiet as she set his steaming plate down in front of him.

"You could have been here on time."

"Let's not get into this right now hon. I'm starved."

"Where were you?" she asked quietly.

"I said, let's not get into this." He stuffed a forkful of mashed potatoes in his mouth and chomped hungrily. "You've had your precious Justin to keep you occupied, I didn't think you'd even miss me."

"Don't be silly, I wanted you here too."

Billy refused to answer her and continued to eat.

Eve stood up. "Put your plate in the sink when you're done," she said as she left the room.

Justin stood outside the door, not wanting to listen, but hearing everything. He'd been on his way to the restroom when he caught the controlled anger in her voice. He could not stop himself, and yet hated what he was doing. He wanted to strangle Billy. Instead, he waited for a minute or two until Eve was gone and walked gingerly into the kitchen, smiling at his friend.

"Hey, buddy, how's it going?"

Billy did not look up. "Fine," he replied.

"That's great, hey you know I'm dying to see the lake again, how about we go for a walk when you're done?"

"Don't feel like it."

"Oh, come on Billy, it'll be like old times."

"Old times are over buddy, hate to be the one to break it to you."

"You know what I mean Billy."

Suddenly Billy shoved his plate away. "Fuck! It seems a man can't have a quiet fucking meal around here! Fine, you want to walk, let's walk." He forced the chair out from under him and walked out the back door.

Justin raced to the living room to drop a quick "We'll be right back" and followed his old friend.

The lake was still, the trees barren. Snow cracked and moaned under their feet as they walked in silence.

"So had 'nuf of old times yet?"

"Billy, what's gotten into you?"

"What the hell do you mean?"

"You're neglecting Eve, I mean for God's sake man, she's pregnant."

"Like that's any business of yours."

"Billy, please, we used to be good friends."

"That was a long time ago."

Justin fell silent again; he wasn't sure where to take the conversation from here.

Finally, Billy spoke, "You wanna know why I missed dinner?"

"Yes, I would like to know."

"Because I'm tired of competing with you."

"What? What do you mean?"

Billy stopped, staring at the icy cold body of water. "All my life, I've been competing with you Jus, I mean for everything. You were always bright and intelligent and Eve worshiped you. Now she's stuck with me and I'm still competing."

"Eve loves you."

"Yes, but she loves you too."

Justin's heart caught in his throat. "Only as a friend."

"Sometimes I wonder about that. It's always Justin this and Justin that. I tell you man, I'm fucking sick and tired of having three people in this marriage. When your book got published she advanced ordered all these copies, you'd think she was opening her own friggin' bookstore. Said she wanted to have enough copies to pass down to our kids or some shit."

"I'm sorry that upsets you."

Billy sighed, "It's not that it upsets me, it's just hard. I do love her, but it seems like nothing I do is right. All I ask is that I get to spend some time with the boys now and then."

"But on Christmas?"

"Christmas is just like any other day. It shouldn't matter."

"It should be spent with your family."

"Yeah, you know that's another thing, I mean this whole family thing. Look how mine turned out. I just don't know if I can do this."

"Well you're just about to be a father of two, it's a hell of a time to decide this now."

"Oh, don't worry, I'll stick. I would never desert Eve; it's just so overwhelming sometimes. I feel like I haven't lived you know, I want to see things, like you are doing. Man that's like fucking unbelievable, your book being made into a movie and everything." Billy smiled at his friend for the first time in their conversation.

"Thanks, but really it's no big deal."

"No big deal, hell, I'm still coaching fuckin' high school football man. You're out makin' movies and becomin' famous. That's a big deal."

"Whatever, we were talking about Eve."

"No, you were talking about Eve, I was getting a lecture."

"I don't mean to lecture you. I'm only concerned."

"'Bout your precious Eve."

"About your wife."

Billy was silent for a moment. Both men stared out at the lake. It was pristine in its winter décor. There was not a breath of wind. Only the chill winter left in its wake. Justin thought about what he would say next, if he decided to speak at all. Billy seemed to have had his fill with their discussion.

"Come on, let's go, they'll think we got lost."

Justin did not move, finally Billy looked behind him.

"What?!" he almost sneered.

"We weren't done talking."

"I could have sworn we were."

Justin did not reply.

Billy breathed in deeply, his brows furrowed, "I'll try harder, ok? Is that what you wanted to hear?"

Finally, Justin began to walk.

🍁 🍁 🍁

Justin took Zoë to every New York tourist sight he could think of. While they ferried over to the Statue of Liberty, Zoë took in the amazing view.

"I can't believe this place exists."

"What, the statue or the city?"

"All of it," she smiled. "It's got so much energy you can just feel it walking down the streets. If I wasn't so in love with the Pacific Ocean I'd insist that we move here immediately."

Justin put his arm around her. "Well, I'm surprised to hear you say that Zo, I thought for certain you'd hate it here. So much city."

Zoë shrugged, "I could never hate a place where you grew up." She smiled.

CHAPTER 42

New Year's Eve found Eve spending the evening at home alone. She had had an uncomfortable day and wanted nothing more than to sit in her favorite chair and relax. Billy left at around 6 p.m. for a party in town, promising to be home before midnight. But Eve knew she would not see him until dawn. So there she was, the eve of a new year, alone and pregnant. Frannie fell asleep early that evening, leaving Eve to her thoughts. She wondered what Justin and Zoë were doing at that exact moment, and she wished with all her might that she could be at Justin's side, laughing and having the time of her life. Eve closed her eyes and dropped her head back onto the cushions. It was no use wishing, she had the life she wanted, a beautiful daughter and another child on the way. That was when it happened. Shortly after 9 p.m., Eve began to feel an odd pain in her abdomen. At first she ignored it, and then it became more like cramping, and more increasingly painful. By 10:30 the pain was almost unbearable. Eve was terrified, what she at first thought was false labor, she now knew was the real thing. She sat in her chair, writhing in pain. Finally, she was able to make it to the telephone to call for help. First, she dialed 911, then she called her mother. It was at that moment that her water broke.

She cried into the telephone. "But momma, it's too soon!!"

The ambulance screeched up to the hospital, and the EMTs eased their pregnant patient out. Eve was now delirious from the pain. She called for her mother, she called for Billy and she called for Justin. Eve's mother had called Mary VanSant over to watch Frannie and try to help them reach Billy. After

Mary arrived at the Freeman residence, her first call was to Justin. She knew that if anyone could find him he could. Justin was infuriated once again and apologetic to Zoë who followed him out the door of the party.

Eve's delivery was extremely difficult. The baby was two months premature, and not wanting to come out on its own. After waiting a significant amount of time, Eve's doctor decided it was time to do a caesarian.

Already Justin had spent hours searching for Billy but now he could not stand it any longer. He had no idea where Billy was and he knew he needed to get to the hospital. It was well after midnight at this point. He pulled his car over after he and Zoë visited their sixth bar to call and check on Eve. She had been wheeled into the labor room, but her mother sounded more than concerned. There were complications, the baby was too early and there had been a great deal of blood. Judith sounded fragile over the phone, as though she weren't telling him something. Justin knew he needed to get to Eve's side as quickly as he could and together with Zoë, they raced to Danbury Hospital.

At precisely 1 a.m., Eve gave birth to a son. There was no one at her side when Dr. Baker removed the child via caesarian from her belly. And there was no one at her side when her son died only minutes after being born.

Justin and Zoë raced into the hospital arriving thirty minutes after Eve lost her baby. When Justin saw Ed and Judith Phillips crying outside the delivery room he knew something was terribly wrong.

He walked up to her and put a reassuring hand on her shoulder; she turned her teary eyes up to meet his. "Oh, Justin, thank God you're here. Did you find Billy?"

He could only shake his head. "What happened?"

She tried to open her mouth, but no words came out, tears spilled from her eyes. Ed put a caring hand on his wife's shoulder: "She lost the baby, son."

Justin felt his heart rip from his chest, Oh, God, he thought, please, don't let this happen. Don't take this child from her. She doesn't deserve it. His eyes burned with tears for his beloved Eve and her lost child.

"Can I see her?"

"The doctor said we can go in in a moment, it was a difficult delivery and he's stitching her up right now and calming her down. He thought he might give her a sedative to get her through the first few hours."

Then the doctor appeared from the room, "I'm afraid we have a little bit of a problem. Mrs. Phillips, I am hoping you can help."

Her eyes flew up to him. "What else could possibly be wrong?"

For a moment the doctor looked almost embarrassed, he hesitated before continuing. "She won't let go of the baby," he said finally. "We need to retrieve the child as soon as possible. She needs someone who can help her understand we're only trying to help. She's getting very angry and hostile with the nurses. If she continues this, I fear for her sanity."

Justin spoke first, "Doctor, may I see her?"

"I don't think that's such a good idea."

"I think you should," Judith said, tears streaming from her eyes; she looked up at the doctor. "He is her best friend, if anyone can help her, Justin can."

"All right then, follow me."

Justin squeezed Zoë's hand for a moment; she smiled at him and nodded. The doctor led Justin into the delivery room. The room was stark and filled with machines that were now silent. A nurse held a watchful eye at the end of the bed that sat in the middle of the room. Beneath the thin green sheet a small form lay huddled. Justin could hear Eve whispering something almost inaudible. The doctor nodded to the nurse and she quickly disappeared.

"I didn't want to say anything in front of her parents, but I don't think she realizes yet that she lost the child. Take as long as you need, I hope you can help her."

Billy entered a bar in Hartford with several of his friends. It was now well past midnight and he knew he should have headed home a while ago. But he was having too much fun and he knew Eve would understand. Yeah, she'd probably be pissed, but eventually she'd forgive him. He bellied up to the bar to order his buddies a round of drinks when the bartender spotted him.

"Hey Billy, your buddy Justin was in here earlier looking for you. Said if I saw you I should send you to Danbury Hospital straight away. Says your wife's having the baby."

♣ ♣ ♣

The door closed behind him and Justin was alone with Eve. She was unaware that anyone had entered the room; she was whispering into the small bundle that she held lovingly. Justin approached her silently.

"Get away from me!" he heard Eve say.

Justin continued to her bed, walking around to see her face. The baby she held in her arms lay as if it were only sleeping, its angelic face peaceful. Eve held him tightly. She did not look up at Justin as he approached.

"It's me, Bug," he said finally.

Eve's eyes never left her child. She continued to whisper. "My sweet, sweet boy. My darling child, I love you so much."

Justin pulled a chair up beside her bed; he sat for a long moment watching her, tears filling his eyes. She looked so perfect holding her child. God, why did you have to take him from her? He cursed silently, hoping someone was listening.

Without looking at him she spoke, "Justin, isn't he beautiful, isn't he the most beautiful thing you've ever seen?"

He reached a hand out to touch the child's head. "Yes, he is beautiful. He's the most precious thing I've ever seen."

"See, my sweet boy, everyone loves you. Mommy loves you, Daddy loves you, Uncle Justin loves you."

Justin's hand went to stroke Eve's hair; it was damp and twisted around her head. Not the shimmering gold he remembered, but rather a dull yellow as if every bit of life had been drained from it.

"Honey, you have to let the baby go, sweetheart it's time."

"No!" she screamed and cried at the same time, "I'll never let him go, he's my baby and they want to take him from me!"

Eve's tears tore through Justin. He tried soothing her but Eve continued to cry for her lost child. Finally, he crawled up into the small bed with her and held her, spooning her body with his. Suddenly, in the stark, clinical room, Justin was overwhelmed with his love for her. It washed over him like the tide, leaving a sticky residue in its wake.

As she cried, he whispered things to her he knew she would neither hear, nor remember. "My sweet darling Eve, I am so sorry. If I could give my life so your baby would live I would do it without hesitation. I love you my darling, I always have and I always will."

Justin continued to hold her for almost an hour while Eve whispered to her son and cried.

At last, Eve's crying became more distressed. The shock of it all was beginning to wear off.

"Why?" she asked finally, her voice less than a whisper. "Why did God take him from me?"

Justin was almost relieved to hear her say that. "I don't know Bug, I really don't know. It's very unfair."

Eve sobbed. "Yes, he deserved to live! He did nothing wrong! This is my fault! I cursed him; I cursed this little being when he was inside of me. I didn't want to be pregnant and this is what I get! God's punishing me!" Her body was wracked with pain and sobbing.

"God Bug, please don't think this is your fault. You loved this child, there's a reason beyond our understanding why God took him from you. I'm so sorry, sweet Eve, so very sorry." He held her tightly as he continued. "You know sweetheart, it's time to let him go. Will you let me take him?"

"I know, I know I need to let him go. It's just that when I do, I will never see him again."

⁂

From a small window in the door a face looked in as his best friend held and comforted his wife. Billy watched the scene for less than a minute before he turned and left the hospital.

⁂

Eve was wheeled to a private room and given a sedative to help her sleep. Justin sat at the edge of her bed and watched her. Billy had arrived almost an hour ago, but no one had seen him since. He cursed his friend and knew they would have to discuss this as soon as he was certain Eve was all right. Something in the doorway caught his eye. He looked over to see Billy standing, looking lost and upset.

"I just saw him, they let me see him. He was so beautiful," Billy's voice quivered.

Justin did not have the heart to add salt to the already fresh wounds. He stood up from his chair and walked over to his friend, hugging him tightly.

"I wasn't here man, I wasn't here for her."

"She's fine now. She'll be all right. You both will. Just be there for her, help her, she'll need a lot of love and attention."

Billy nodded and released himself from his friend's hug. He took Justin's chair and watched as Eve slept through it all.

"How long will she sleep?" he asked.

"I wish I could say until the pain goes away, but I doubt there's anything that could make her sleep that long. Probably a few hours, she was pretty wiped out."

"Hey, Jus?"

"Yeah?"

"Thanks man."

Justin turned without a word and left the room. I wouldn't have had to do this if you had drug yourself away from the bar, he thought and continued walking; he needed some fresh air, to clear his head before he returned to Zoë.

It was nearing 5 a.m. when Justin pushed through the glass doors to the outside world. So much had happened in the last several hours. A soft icy snow began to fall around him. He should have stopped to get his coat, but he couldn't face Zoë yet. He needed to make sense of what happened; but there was no sense to be made. A perfectly wonderful woman had lost the thing most precious to her. She'd done nothing to deserve it, nothing. He pushed farther across the parking lot and into the thicket of trees that surrounded the hospital. The air should have chilled him to the bone, but he didn't notice. His only thought was of Eve and her baby, and her husband that had been absent through it all. Justin wasn't sure if he'd ever be able to forgive Billy for his neglect. Years ago he'd bargained with himself that as long as Billy was good to her, he could stomach his loss. But Billy hadn't lived up to his end of the bargain and now…he caught himself mid-thought, he had no right to interfere, no matter what. It was between Eve and Billy now. That was the way it needed to be. He forced his hands deeper into the pockets of his pants. The cold had a bitter bite, and he began finally to feel its chill. Turning, he headed back to the hospital to collect Zoë and head home.

When Justin returned to the waiting room he found that Zoë had gotten a ride with Ed Phillips to relieve his mother from watching Frannie. While he smiled at her thoughtfulness, he wished she had been there. After a night of confusion he wanted nothing more than to take her into his arms and press her against him.

♣ ♣ ♣

Billy wiped another tear from his cheek. Damn it! He thought. Why the hell hadn't he gone home? He couldn't remember, but he could feel the alcohol leaving tendrils of a headache in its wake.

"I'm so sorry babe, so sorry I wasn't here for you. I promise it will never happen again. I swear I'll try to be the best husband ever."

Dropping his head in his hands he wept. He wept for his deceased baby, for the pain Eve had to go through alone, and for a night he'd spent drinking and shamelessly flirting with that curvy blond. He felt the shame overtake him, felt he needed to hear her say it, that she forgave him. That she'd always forgive him. But Eve slept on, while Billy cursed himself and anything else he could think of to blame for the loss of his son.

♣ ♣ ♣

Justin offered to give Judith a ride home but she insisted on being by her daughter's side when she woke up. Before he left the hospital he called Eve and Billy's to find that his girlfriend was no longer there but at his parents' home; his mother had refused to give up her post. Karl had come to get Zoë and had taken her back to their house. When Justin arrived there he found the house empty. No doubt his father had already left for one of his early morning walks he assumed, and perhaps Zoë had gone with him. Justin left immediately and headed to the lake. There he found them, walking quietly beside each other. Zoë looked up and saw Justin, tired and pale. She fell into his arms and told him again how sorry she was for what had happened.

"I'll leave you two alone," Justin's father smiled and continued his trek around the lake.

After he was out of earshot, Justin put his arm around her and said: "Honey, I'm so sorry I left you alone so long."

"That's all right, I understand. Eve needed you. How is she?" her tone was soft.

"Pretty bad shape I'm afraid. They sedated her, and Billy finally showed up. I could have killed him."

Zoë slid her arm through his. "Where do you think he was?"

"Probably in some bar getting drunk and trying to get laid."

"Justin!"

"It's true Zo, sad but true. I'm afraid that man's going to hurt her terribly."

"You care about her don't you?"

Justin swallowed hard. "We've been friends for years."

Zoë stopped walking and stood staring at the lake inhaling the sweet scent of winter. "Is this where you all used to play, on this lake? I saw a photo of the three of you playing in the water, is this where it was taken?"

"Yes," was the only reply Justin could offer. He thought back to the days when they were young and the future seemed so certain.

"The three of you must have had some incredible times here."

"We did, it seems so long ago."

"I wish I had known you then, I feel like such an outsider here."

"Zoë, honey, I'm so sorry, I never intended for you to feel left out," Justin placed a caring hand on her shoulder.

"Justin, there's no way I can be a part of everything in your life. I knew there were parts I may never know about, or understand. That's what makes a good relationship, a little mystery. There is one thing I always knew though," she paused for a moment, realizing there was no turning back now. "I always knew no matter how much you loved me, that there was always someone else in your heart. Someone you would probably love forever. I had no idea who it was until last night."

Justin felt his breath catch in his throat. Zoë turned to him then, a thin veil of tears filling her eyes. "When I saw the way you rushed to Eve's side, I knew. I knew she was the one you loved. The one who had wounded you so much that you locked yourself away in that pretty little beach house of yours and wouldn't let anyone in. She is the one who owns part of your heart that you will never give up. I'm right aren't I?"

"I never meant to hurt you. There was never anything between us, I swear."

She tried to smile, "I'm not jealous, well perhaps a little envious that she is so special to you. But I know you love me, and for now that's all that matters. But I knew, I always knew. It was so hard for you to love me, I nearly gave up on you a hundred times, but I couldn't, I love you too much to let you go. I know we will be together as long as we decide to be, but there are no guarantees."

"Zoë, I love you so much." He placed a tender kiss on her lips; she wrapped her arms around his neck to pull him closer. At last he'd met the woman he'd always known existed.

When he released her from his embrace she asked: "Does she know?"

"No, and she never will."

"Why didn't you ever tell her?"

"She was going to marry my best friend. He had just lost his mother and he needed her."

"That's a very altruistic thing to do."

"Not really, it's what one would expect a friend to do I think."

"I mean no offense, but I don't see Billy doing something like that for you."

"He was different then." His tone was slightly impatient.

Zoë nodded and they continued their walk by the lake. While the sun rose on a brand new day and a brand new year, Justin thought about the confession he'd just made. Most women would not be quite as understanding as Zoë. Suddenly he realized how fortunate he was.

Eve pushed through the thick fog that filled her head and woke from the deep drug-induced slumber. Beside her, Billy sat holding her hand. She was surprised to see him sitting there, but tried not to let on. Her first instinct was to feel her tummy. Its flatness reminded her of what had happened less than ten hours ago. Her heart sank; she'd prayed that it had only been a dream.

"I'm so sorry I wasn't here Eve," Billy whispered.

Eve could only look at him as his voice begged her forgiveness. She knew he needed her to say that it was all right. That everything would be ok. That she understood. But Eve did not have the strength to soothe him, she could only look up at him and shudder at the intense pain she felt inside.

CHAPTER 43

Two days later, Eve was released from the hospital with a cautionary statement from her physician to watch for signs of depression or possible suicide. While "post-partum" wasn't really part of their vernacular, Eve's doctor had witnessed enough depression to know it was common in young mothers. And with a young woman facing the loss of an infant, it could be even more severe.

On the fifth of January, a funeral was held for William Jr. It was a small graveside ceremony, attended only by close family and friends. Justin and Zoë stayed for the funeral but planned to leave the following morning.

Eve felt the grief coil inside her, hot and painful. She lived from minute to minute, praying to get through the next sixty seconds, and then the next sixty after that. Her insides felt hollowed out and as she watched the tiny coffin get lowered into the dirt, grief twisted painfully around her heart, strangling it, choking it. She wished she were in that coffin instead of her son. What was there now for her? But suddenly remembering her precious Frannie, Eve steadied herself.

Frannie. She sighed, the name almost reverent on her lips. Her dear, sweet Frannie who needed her. Thank God someone did.

Mrs. VanSant held a reception at her home and several people who did not attend the funeral came by to pay their respects. Justin noticed an hour into the gathering that Billy was noticeably absent. When he asked his mother where Billy had gone, she whispered something about him checking on Frannie who was at home with the sitter. Without a thought in his head, he left to find Billy.

♣ ♣ ♣

Billy opened his third bottle of beer and threw his head back, swallowing it in big gulps. He felt a slight buzz overtake him. Burying his son had been more painful than he'd expected. He had felt several sets of accusatory eyes burn through him during the graveside service. Billy had wanted to scream at them: Yes! He knew he should have been at the hospital. He should have been the one to hold her hand when she lost the baby, not Justin. He put his mouth to the bottle and swallowed more of the liquid. Fuckin' Justin. The bitter thought punctured his mind. Always getting there at just the right moment to swoop in and save the freakin' day.

Justin strode up the porch and knocked on the door, determined to get through to his friend. There was no answer. He knocked again. Still nothing. He tried the door and it was unlocked. Carefully, he let himself in. The house was quiet. He stood in the foyer for a moment; then from the kitchen he heard a sound. The slight tap of a bottle being placed back on the table. When he turned the corner and peered around the doorway he saw Billy, his hand wrapped around the bottle in front of him. He stopped himself from lunging at him.

"So I found you," was all he said. Billy barely looked up from his drink.

"Yep, old hero boy, looks like you did."

"Everyone is wondering where you went off to."

"Everyone, or just you."

Justin pulled a chair out from the table, its legs screeched across the tile floor.

"You know I don't know what your problem is. Your son was just buried and here you are, drinking yourself into oblivion."

Billy looked up finally. His eyes were bloodshot, his face pale and drawn.

"Gee thanks pal for reminding me, you know I'd plum forgotten the kid died. Fuckin' thanks for coming over here to tell me."

Justin bit his lip. He wanted to punch Billy right off his chair.

"You want to know what my problem is?" he asked emptying the bottle. "My problem is you. Hero Justin always to the rescue, always in the right place at the right time. Always there to hold everyone's hand. While ol' fuck up Billy is out drinking again."

"And whose fault is that?"

"How the hell was I supposed to know she was having the kid? Like I got radar or something. I told her I was going out, she didn't seem to mind."

"She would have minded if she'd seen you wrapped around that young blond cheerleader."

"You don't know what you're talking about."

"No, maybe not, but enough people saw you together that night that I heard it from three different sources."

"Oh so there's sources now, what the hell are you Dick fuckin' Tracy?" Billy got up to get himself another beer. "Want one?" he asked over his shoulder. "Oh, no, I'm sorry that's right. Mr. Perfect never drinks, never does anything wrong."

"Look, Billy I didn't come here to fight, I came here to try and talk you into spending some time with your wife this afternoon. She really needs you."

"No, she doesn't need me. She needs you, her best friend Justin, that's who she wants. You're who she's always wanted. She only married me out of fuckin' pity."

Justin shook his head. "It's just the alcohol talking; she does need you Billy."

"I can't go there and face all those people."

"Why the hell not? They're there to support both you and Eve."

"No, wrong again buddy, they're there to tell Eve how sorry they are she lost her son and how much they pity her being married to a class A fuck up like me," he sneered. "'Mabel, did you hear he didn't even get there until hours after she lost the baby.'"

"That's not what they're saying at all Billy."

"Oh, come on! You know perfectly well that the whole town is just shaking their heads right now, 'Boy', they're saying, 'man's a great football player but a lousy husband!'"

"What do you care what they're saying Billy, just get over there. Man you don't even know what you've got here do you?"

"No, but apparently you do and you're going to tell me."

"Look, I'm not here to lecture you. I came over in the hopes that I could talk you into coming to the reception. If you don't go it's only going to make matters worse. But you already know that don't you?"

"Yeah, maybe I do, but I don't care. Let whatever happens, happen."

"If you're not going to do it for yourself or your son, then for God's sake man, do it for Eve at least. Do you have any idea what she went through that night?"

Billy could feel the tears burning behind his eyes. He wanted so desperately to push through his anger and listen to his friend. But he couldn't. He felt only bitterness and hostility and if he didn't direct it at Justin, whom else could he blame?

"Look, I need to ask you to leave. I can't do this, not right now."

"What the hell do you mean you can't do this? You don't have a choice, you have to do this. This is life man, not some high school play you can just walk out on when you've had enough. You need to get up off that chair and get yourself over there, Eve needs you."

"So now you're the expert on what Eve needs. She's my wife, and you'd do well to remember that," Billy said calmly. "You know, you seem awfully concerned about what Eve is going through. I'll remind you that I lost here too. I lost my son."

You selfish bastard, Justin thought, but said, "Hey man, what happened to that man who was so sorrowful in the hospital? The man who wanted nothing else but to help his wife through this terrible time?"

"I think you should go," Billy repeated.

"I'm not leaving until I take you with me. You're going over to that house, and you're going to sit beside your wife and you're going to comfort her and accept everyone's condolences."

"No, I'm happy grieving here damn it! Now get the hell out of my house like I asked you to, go back to your sweet Eve."

"She's your wife, you should be the one to stand beside her."

"You wouldn't know it to look at the situation now would 'ya! Now get out before I kick you out."

"I'm not leaving until I take you with me."

Billy stood up then, reaching over to Justin he grabbed his collar and pulled him off his chair, "Man, I asked you to leave several times, now I'm tellin' you, very nicely. Leave before you regret staying."

"I already told you, I will not leave until you…"

Billy's arm drew back, and suddenly Justin's face felt as though it were splintering in two. He fell back to the floor, hitting his head on something sharp. He didn't know what. Everything went black.

When Justin woke, his jaw was throbbing and Billy was gone. He checked upstairs for Frannie, but she was gone as well. Justin packed some ice in a towel and held it gently against his face. His head felt as though it would explode from the pain. He found some aspirin in the medicine cabinet and took four with a glass of water. The clock over the mantel told him he'd been out for about fifteen minutes and there was no sign of Billy anywhere.

Justin stood for a moment in their home, knowing it was the last time he'd ever be inside it. His friendship with Billy had ended that afternoon. Not because Billy had hit him and left him unconscious on the floor, but because it pained him too greatly to see how horribly he was treating his family. And how he was wasting probably the greatest gift of his life. And there was nothing that Justin could do to fix it.

Billy strode the path by the lake; Frannie giggled from the carry pack as she bounced up and down with his every step. Billy tried to reason away hitting his best friend, but even he couldn't come up with a decent excuse. What had happened? How had things gotten so out of control? He wanted to be a good husband, friend and father. But some sort of temptation always seemed to keep him from doing that. First he needed to talk to Eve when she returned home. Billy still had no intention of joining her at the reception, especially now that no doubt, Justin had headed over there. Everyone would want to know where he got the shiner from. He hoped his friend would be discreet, although he knew he didn't deserve it. If he was going to get a fresh start, he had a couple of things he needed to do first. One of them he would handle in the morning.

After the throbbing in his face began to subside, Justin returned to his parents' house, sneaking in through the back to avoid being asked questions about the obvious bruise that was forming. He headed upstairs where he found Zoë in his old room.

At first, she did not notice his bruised jaw. "I'm hiding up here Justin. I'm sorry it's just so sad down there and I barely know anyone. I just needed a…oh my gosh, honey what happened to you?" Getting up from where she was sitting, she walked over and reached up to his swollen face. "Did someone hit you?"

She frowned and he wrapped his hand around hers. He had not wanted to share this with anyone, but it would be too difficult to hide. He was embarrassed for Billy, embarrassed that he had sunk so low. He certainly did not want Eve to find out, it would only serve to deepen her devastation. Finally, he answered her. "Yes baby, someone did hit me. But you've got to promise to keep this to yourself, no one else can know what happened."

"It was Billy wasn't it?" Again, she made it clear how attuned she was.

"I'm afraid you're right."

"What the hell happened that made him hit you?"

Justin proceeded to tell her the entire painful story. When he was finished, Zoë could only look at him incredulously. Even Justin found it hard to believe that his once best friend, would not only hit him, but leave him lying on the kitchen floor.

"It was her choice you know, to marry him. You need to let them work this out. It's between the two of them now, you've done all you can."

"I know, you're right. I just feel like someone needs to shake him up. Eve is having to carry this entire burden alone, I just wish it could be different for her."

"I hope this doesn't sound cynical, but she isn't the first woman who's had to face a marriage alone and she won't be the last. All we can do is support her and be there for her. The rest is up to them."

They left the following morning for California. Justin did not see Eve or Billy before he left. He thought the Technicolor bruise on his face would pose too many questions he could not answer. He left a note with his mother to give to Eve, and hoped it would smooth over the fact that he hadn't said goodbye in person. He would call her the minute he and Zoë returned home. Justin was surprised at how anxious he was to return to California and resume his life there. He had once again allowed himself to get too absorbed in Eve's life. Now with his precious Zoë in tow, he knew that was completely unacceptable.

CHAPTER 44

In the days that followed the funeral, Eve found solace in her daughter. Although Billy tried to be a comforting husband, everything he did seemed ill timed and misplaced. But she allowed him to hold her and comfort her when she cried and together they spoke of their lost son. Part of her wanted desperately to scream out at him that he had not been there for her, that he had no idea how she was feeling. Instead, she remained silent and allowed him to believe that his sudden change of attitude meant the world to her. Billy made promises; he promised to spend less time coaching and more time at home. He promised to do more as a family and spend less time with his drinking buddies. Eve hoped that what he said was true. She wanted more than anything to have a husband she could depend on.

On a clear Saturday morning, Billy left very early to take care of his commitment to his wife and child. He headed down Gilloti Road and past the familiar white house with blue trim. But he did not stop there; instead he parked three doors down at his friend Jack's small home and headed through the side gate into his yard. From there Billy walked toward the wooded area that ran behind the houses on Gilloti Road. He took the familiar dirt path back up toward the little white house and when he was at the yard, he cleared the woods and scurried to the back door as quickly as he could. He knocked lightly. Billy could hear the familiar light tread of footsteps approaching. It was barely 8 a.m. and Cheryl had no doubt just woken up after a long night in any one of the local bars. When she opened the door, the only thing separating them was the flimsy screen door. Her blond hair was disheveled slightly and she wore a pink sleep shirt; the bottom dangled around her upper thigh, showing off her beautifully sculpted legs. It was all Billy could do not to yank the screen door open and reach for her. But he couldn't. Not this time.

"Billy, whatcha doin' here?" she smiled.

"I came to talk to you Cheryl."

"Well, by all means, come on in," she opened the door and he stood hesitantly in it's opening.

"I can only stay for a moment."

"Fine. Coffee?"

"No thanks."

Cheryl reached up and threw her arms around him, "Billy hon, what's up? You seem so nervous?"

Billy tried to pry her arms from around his neck. "That's what I came to talk to you about Cheryl, it's over between us, I can't see you or sleep with you anymore."

♣ ♣ ♣

Billy stood over the phone. Eve had taken Frannie to visit her parents and the house was quiet. The only sound that interrupted the silence was the faint ticking of the clock and the beating of his heart. The minutes that ticked by reminded him that he'd been debating for over an hour whether to call. It was noon in California; Justin would probably not be home anyway. That would no doubt be best. Finally, Billy dialed and the telephone at the other end began to ring. After the third ring, he heard the click of the answering machine, then a brief message promising the caller he would phone back as soon as he returned. Billy hesitated for a moment, he hated machines. "Jus, it's me Billy, hey man I called to apologize. I'm really sorry for what happened. I got a little crazy in the head when we lost the baby. Hey, I wanted to tell you that I'm takin' Eve on a trip in a few weeks. I'm surprisin' her tonight, I thought we could use a second honeymoon. Jus, I'm doin' everything I can man, I hope you know that. Take care, we'll call when we get back."

Justin listened while Billy spoke at the other end. He was in no mood to converse with his friend. As soon as Billy was done, Justin reached for the erase button and cleared the message.

❧ ❧ ❧

Justin's life was filled with everything he'd always dreamt of, and soon, everything that had happened on his trip home became a distantly painful memory. The movie now consumed all his time and fortunately, Zoë was also too busy to notice the pain that wore like a tired expression on his face. There was so much ending at once, a child's short life and a friendship that had lasted most of his lifetime. His thoughts turned again to Eve and her pain and he grimaced when he thought of the hell she must be going through and how he was amazed again at how Billy thought that a trip could replace a loving, understanding husband.

The filming of his movie had gone well initially, but when the rewrites became overwhelming, the director, Corbin Bennett, had walked off the set in a fit of creative rage. Production came to a screeching halt until both sides could agree to make the adaptation process a little less excruciating and the director was brought back under heavy warning to remain true to Justin's masterpiece. During this time, Justin was rarely home and spent a good deal of nights and weekends on the lot and traveling with them when they went on location. He was a perfectionist and everyone respected him for it. Per a well-negotiated contract, Justin oversaw every single detail, from costume design to the preliminary edits. Not a single aspect of production happened without his knowledge or careful scrutiny. Fortunately for him, he was not an unknown commodity, having made a lot of friends during his short experience in the world of television. He was allowed the lenience of a respected colleague and an outstanding author.

Finally, on a sunny Wyoming day, where they filmed their final scene, production was completed. In the midst of the heat and dust, there was an impromptu celebration among the cast and crew and bottles of Dom Perignon were opened and poured carelessly into paper cups to commemorate the occasion.

The minute production wrapped up, Justin raced home to Zoë. The separation had been long and challenging and he wanted nothing more than to nuzzle her gold hair and wrap her in his arms.

CHAPTER 45

Four years after losing Billy Jr., Eve could still feel numbness inside her that she knew would never heal. She'd become almost accustomed to it now and resigned herself to the fact that she would never stop wishing for her sweet, departed little boy or feeling the wave of grief every time she thought of him.

From his booster seat at the table, her three-year-old son giggled up at her. Nicholas was the new joy of her life. From the kitchen Eve could hear Frannie's favorite TV character on *Sesame Street*, Snuffleupagus, as her daughter sat entranced in front of the television.

Billy was still coaching each day after work. The trip to Florida had rekindled their marriage and for a while, everything seemed different. Billy had been loving, attentive and rededicated to his family. Then, slowly but surely, he found himself pulling away again. Eve felt it too, and the familiarity of a their lukewarm marriage returned.

Distracted, Eve watched her son squish his peanut butter sandwich. The night before had been the East Coast premier of Justin's second *King's Town* movie. And by all accounts, it promised to be as huge a success as his first film. Eve was so pleased for him; Justin was truly living his dream. As soon as she was done feeding the baby, she planned to call and congratulate him. How long had it been since they'd spoken? Six months perhaps, she'd lost count. She had not seen him since she lost the baby. Eve missed him terribly but knew this was for the best. Above all else, she wanted his happiness. Between Zoë and his career, he seemed to have it all.

❦ ❦ ❦

Zoë woke early that morning with the odd twinge and cramps she'd been feeling for several weeks now. It wasn't constant, just off and on, a heaviness that settled in her abdomen. It had been two months since she'd had her period and every time Zoë glanced at a calendar, she felt the elation of possibly carrying Justin's child. Justin had gone into the studio early that day to discuss the release of his latest movie and Zoë took the quiet time to reflect on the possibility that she might indeed be pregnant and what the reality of that would mean to her and her lover. Suddenly her head felt light, almost swirling and Zoë slipped out of her chair and hit the floor.

❦ ❦ ❦

The ringing of the phone startled her. "Hello?" she answered quickly, putting down Nick's dish. But instead of a response at the other end, she heard ratcheted breaths. "Hello? Who is this?" Eve repeated; a feeling of panic began to sweep over her.

"Bug, it's me Justin." He was trying to control himself, but the sound of her voice made him want to cry uncontrollably.

"Justin honey, what's wrong?"

"Oh, Evie, I don't know, I can't understand this."

She sat down now; Nick giggled and stretched his little arms toward his plate.

"Justin, please calm down and tell me what's wrong."

"It's Zoë."

Eve felt her heart catch in her chest. Oh God, she thought, Zoë left him.

"She's been diagnosed with ovarian cancer. Apparently it's fairly advanced. The doctors don't think there is anything they can do for her."

What she was hearing made her unwell. Not Zoë! She was the epitome of health.

"How?" was all she could muster. His explanation came out in tearful gasps.

"I came home yesterday…she was lying there bleeding…I rushed her to the hospital. The doctor says she must have had this for awhile…she never said anything…they're going to try surgery, but he doesn't think it will save her."

"Oh dear God, Jus, I don't know what to say. Is there anything I can do?"

"No Bug, I, I just needed someone to share this with. I can't believe this is happening to someone as wonderful as her. She's truly amazing Eve, you just will never know. No one will."

"Jus, look let me fly out there to be with you. You've got a lot to take on and I'd like to be there for you…."

"No, I can't let you do that. What about Billy and the children?"

"They'll be fine without me for a few days. I need to be there with you. When do they operate?"

"The surgery needs to be done as soon as possible, but she needs to regain her strength from the hemorrhaging. She lost a great deal of blood."

Eve felt a sadness she hadn't experienced since she lost her baby.

"Bug, look there's really no reason for you to come out here yet, we will know more after her surgery."

"Justin, I don't care, I'm coming out there anyway. I want to see her and talk to her before they operate and I want to be there for you too. Is any of her family coming out?"

"She insisted I not call them until we know more. She doesn't want them praying over her."

"All right then, tell me what hospital she's in and I'll take a cab from the airport."

"No, let me pick you up."

"You need to be by her side right now, I'm fully capable of getting myself there, don't worry about me."

Justin realized there was no arguing with her. He gave her the name of the hospital and wished her a safe trip. As he hung up the phone, he felt a sense of relief that soon he would no longer have to face this alone. In the past twenty-four hours he'd come to recognize that somewhere in the midst of trying desperately to move past Eve he had fallen deeply in love with Zoë. She had saved him, and now he prayed he could do the same for her.

Eve sat for a long moment staring out in front of her. Nick reached his little hands out, laughing and giggling. She thought of her poor dear Justin out in California and of Zoë, fighting for her life. Silently she said a prayer for both of them and then picking up the telephone again, called Billy to let him know what was going on.

CHAPTER 46

Zoë woke slowly. For the last several hours she had drifted in and out of consciousness; the medicine that dripped into her arm clouded her mind and she felt like her mouth was filled with cotton. But thankfully, the pain was gone. Zoë looked around her room. It was a cheery private room with a view of the city. Nurses were checking on her every fifteen minutes; all of them were smiling and friendly telling her how much they loved her husband's new movie. She'd wanted to correct them and mention that they were not married, but she was too exhausted to even worry about it. She learned several years ago when Justin first entered the public eye that people will think what they want, regardless of what you tell them.

When Justin and Adele arrived at the hospital, they found Zoë awake and reflecting on what had happened to her.

"Adele, it's so nice of you to visit me," Zoë smiled at the elderly woman who had come to be like a mother to both her and Justin. She reached for her wrinkled hand and took it in her own. "I'm really glad you're here. Justin, could I have a moment alone with Adele?"

Justin walked over to her bed and kissed her gently on the forehead. "Whatever you want baby. I'll be right outside if you need anything."

When she was alone with Adele she inhaled a weak breath. The old woman pulled a chair up beside the bed and stroked Zoë's hand.

"You're going to be fine you know," she smiled.

"That's very sweet of you Adele, but I don't have a good feeling about this. This is an aggressive form of cancer and the doctors aren't familiar with it. If I'd had any sense at all I would have seen a doctor ages ago but I thought those silly teas I drank would cure me." A disappointed smile formed on her face.

"That's ok dear, how were you supposed to know?"

"I've known for some time that something wasn't quite right Adele, and please don't tell Justin, he'll just blame himself. Seeing a doctor isn't one of my favorite things so I put it off."

She sighed then, "I'm not altogether certain I'll make it out of surgery and if I do, I honestly don't know that there's much they can do for me. I've done a little reading while lying here."

Tears sprang up in Adele's eyes and quickly Zoë added, "Oh dear, I didn't mean to distress you, I just wanted you to know. If something happens to me, Justin will need you. I need to know you're going to be there for him."

"Of course I will, that goes without saying. You are both like my children." Her voice sounded shaky and Zoë knew that she better not push it. She'd said what she wanted to, there was only one more thing, but that could wait.

Adele bent her head and lightly kissed the top of Zoë's pale hand.

❧ ❧ ❧

Eve arrived the following afternoon at Los Angeles International Airport and sped off in the first cab she could find. With the slightest trepidation, Justin told Zoë about Eve's arrival, emphasizing that he had in no way encouraged her to come out. "I know you didn't." Zoë had smiled. "If I wasn't secure in your love for me, I would have left long ago. Besides, you need someone by your side right now."

He fiddled with the coffeepot in the nurses' lounge. For the second night in a row, he'd slept in the hospital. The staff had rolled in a bed for him so he could share Zoë's room, but he slept little. He felt so helpless, so completely out of control.

From the doorway, Eve watched as Justin sat motionless watching Zoë sleep. Her heart sank when she saw all the machines and tubes that ran from her arms. On the flight over, she'd hoped by some miracle that the doctors had been mistaken. Some flunky in the lab had mixed up the test results and she'd get to the hospital and they would already be back home again. But she knew in her heart that was not going to happen.

She walked into the room then, and lightly rested her hand on his shoulder. He nodded to acknowledge her presence. "I'll wait for you in the hall," she said softly.

Justin emerged from the room a short time later. He looked as though he had gone several weeks without sleeping. A subtle beard was beginning to grow and his usual neatly combed hair was disheveled. Justin walked right into her arms and Eve closed herself tightly around him. "I'm so sorry Jus, so very sorry…"

His breath caught in his throat, it felt so good to have her near, to be able to rest on her friendship, at least for a while.

"When is her surgery?"

"They've scheduled it for tomorrow morning. I pray to God that she's strong enough. I think the cancer has taken its toll on her. She's very weak."

"Is there anything I can do?"

"No, Bug, really, just being here is enough."

"I'd like to see her if you think she can handle another visitor."

"Well, she's asleep now and she really needs her rest."

"Of course, then let me buy you lunch in the cafeteria."

Over lunch Justin explained to Eve that he was anxious for this specialist to arrive to assist in Zoë's operation tomorrow. He was optimistic, perhaps overly so, that this man would be the answer to his prayers. Eve picked at her sandwich and hoped that Justin would be able to handle the outcome. He said himself that the doctors were not hopeful. But she smiled and took his hand to show her support. At that moment a doctor approached their table. Justin introduced Zoë's physician, Dr. Steadler, to Eve.

"I've got good news Justin" he began, "Dr. Nelson has agreed to assist in Zoë's surgery tomorrow." He saw Justin's elation and quickly added. "You understand that while this does not change the severity of her situation, it will be good to have someone of his caliber to assist us. He has done these surgeries many times."

"What does he think about her situation?"

"Well, my office faxed her file to him. He agrees with me that the tumor is pretty advanced, but he and I both agree that we won't really know her prognosis until we operate. This is a very rare and aggressive type of cancer as you know."

"Of course, doctor, I appreciate everything you're doing for her."

"I must be going now, we've got a lot of work to do to prepare for Zoë's operation."

When he left, Justin turned to Eve, "I have a really good feeling about this Bug, she's going to be just fine, I know."

Eve smiled and hoped he was right.

❧ ❧ ❧

Eve sat quietly in a private waiting room while Justin paced in front of her. Zoë had been in surgery since 9 a.m., well over an hour now. From the doctor's estimation, they could be waiting another two hours, at least. It was a very complicated and delicate procedure they'd been told. Earlier that morning she had called Billy who wanted to fly out there to be with his friend as well. Eve promised to come home as soon as she knew everything would be all right with Zoë. They hung up without saying I love you. But Eve was used to that. Somehow, no matter how hard she tried, it seemed futile. Their marriage had become one of complacency. Most of the time it didn't bother her, but in the stark light of Justin's love for Zoë, it became ever more apparent what they were missing out on. She forced those thoughts to the back of her mind as she watched Justin walk from one side of the room to the other. She wished that someone would love her the way Justin loved Zoë. She'd never been loved like that, and she knew in her heart, that she never would.

After three hours and twenty-five minutes, both doctors emerged from the operating room. Justin looked anxious as they walked slowly into the private waiting room. Both men motioned silently for Justin to sit down and Eve knew immediately the news was not good.

Dr. Nelson began, "Justin, I'm sorry but the surgery did not go as we'd hoped."

"What do you mean?"

"The cancer was much more advanced than any of the x-rays showed, and it's spreading very quickly. We tried to remove as much of it as we could, but unfortunately, it's already begun attacking some vital organs."

"But…" Justin stammered, unable to speak, unable to grasp what he was being told. Eve rushed to his side and immediately put a protective arm around his shoulder.

"Doctor, what are you saying?"

"What we're saying is that I'm afraid Zoë is going to die, I give her a month or two at the very most, if that. What we've done should alleviate the pain so she can return home for a while, but probably only for a short time. I'm so very sorry Justin," Dr. Steadler's voice was calm.

Justin was allowed to sit by Zoë's side while she was in recovery. He held her hand and whispered things only the two of them could hear. He talked to her about taking their sail boat around the world, about spending their every waking moment on the ocean, about swimming in the Grecian waters which had always been her dream, and about seeing the coral reefs of the Caribbean. As he spoke he began making a plan for each day of the rest of her life.

CHAPTER 47

When Zoë woke after her surgery, it was Justin's face she saw. She knew without asking what had happened.

"I'm dying aren't I?" she asked quietly.

"Not if I can help it you're not."

"Babe, there's nothing you can do." In a frail voice she continued, "Justin I want to get out of here, as quickly as I can. I want to spend my final days at home with you, and I want to go sailing and feel the ocean breeze on my face."

Justin could feel the tears burning behind his eyes, cupping her hand he kissed it gently. "Anything you want my love."

"And Justin one more thing. How long do I have to live?"

"The doctors don't know." He stretched the truth, maybe for himself more than Zoë.

Then she closed her eyes and drifted back to sleep while Justin quietly let the tears flow from his eyes.

While Justin sat with Zoë, Eve dropped herself, exhausted, into an uncomfortable chair and cried for them both. The loss of Zoë would no doubt be unbearable for him. Eve felt another wave of sadness as she wondered how Billy would have handled this same situation. She remembered back to the loss of their child and felt a sharp pain as she recalled Billy's reaction to their tragedy. He was simply not equipped to handle such an ordeal. Eve got up from where she was sitting and wandered outside the building. It was a warm California day; the sun glowed and warmed everything it touched. Eve tried to shake what she was feeling but she couldn't help it. She felt jealous and ashamed at the same time. She envied the love they shared and wished she and Billy shared the same type of devotion. It was at that moment, for the first time since her marriage to Billy that she wished with all of her heart that she had chosen Justin.

As quickly as the doctors would let him, Justin checked Zoë out of the hospital and headed directly to their boat. She had asked him, begged him, to let her die surrounded by the ocean she loved so much. But even just a few short days into their sail Justin had to return her to the hospital because the pain became more than the prescription painkillers could abate. The thirty days Zoë's doctor had given her had collapsed into six and at Eve's urging, Billy and the VanSants flew in, arriving the same day as Zoë's parents.

Justin looked around Zoë's private room realizing that there was no way he could let her die in a stark white room. He asked Adele if she could run and get a few things from their home he knew Zoë would love. Her spinning fish lamp for one, the lamp he'd bought for her at a Los Angeles fair. At night she'd turn it on and their entire bedroom would be bathed in blue as the shadows of fishes swam the walls. The elderly woman sped off with the quick stride of a teenager, hoping she'd return in time with the precious possessions Justin had requested.

Justin was holding Zoë's hand when she took her last ragged breath. In a room lit only in the colors of the ocean, the shadowy shapes of fish that danced in circles on the wall. He knew when she neared the end because every memory they'd shared together came rushing back to him. Like a movie, it played out in his mind as he tried to hold onto her before she drifted away. But he could not stop the grip of death and in an instant, the light of her spirit seemed to fill the room as she bid him goodbye and headed home. In a searing flash of pain that ripped through his soul, she was gone and he was left alone still holding her hand, praying by some miracle she would return to him for just a moment. Just one more precious minute, that was all he wanted. To tell her again, how he loved her and how he would always miss her.

* * *

Justin emerged from her room a while later. Eve had only to look into his eyes to know what had happened and suddenly she could not stop herself from crying. Zoë's parents fell into tears as well and immediately ran into her room. Karl and Mary went to embrace their heartbroken son. Eve stood up; Justin stumbled from his mother's arms and fell into her, his body racked with sobs. Together they cried for his loss and for the wonderful person that was Zoë.

Billy looked on as the four mourners tried to find comfort in each other. Eve whispered something to Justin that Billy could not understand and suddenly he felt like an outsider. His need to get up and leave was almost overwhelming, but he refrained, knowing it would only serve to upset Eve and would certainly cause another argument between them. So, he waited patiently. Billy could almost feel the pain radiate off Justin while Eve held him in her arms. He wondered for a moment what it would feel like to lose someone you loved so desperately, as Justin so obviously loved Zoë. He and Eve had lost their passion somewhere along the way; maybe they had never had it. Once again, he thought, Justin had the one up on him. He had shared something with Zoë that Billy never would with his wife. Billy got up then, and walked to where they stood. Resting a hand on his friend's shoulder he mumbled a condolence but Justin was unaware of him. The only thing he felt was the searing pain of losing someone he loved so much.

CHAPTER 48

The days that followed her death were spent in a haze of pain and denial, the likes of which he had never felt before. There were nights he could not bear the scent of her, which lingered in their home as a constant, torturous reminder that she was no longer there. On those nights, he found himself taking refuge on the porch and falling into a nightmarish sleep on the cold wooden bench.

On the day of Zoë's funeral, Eve stopped by early and found Justin asleep outside. Tears sprang to her eyes as she watched him. She wished desperately that there was something she could do to ease his suffering. Perhaps she could talk Billy into leaving without her so she could stay behind and make sure Justin would be all right or at the very least help him back on his feet again. He opened his eyes then, slowly, his gaze blurry at first, fixed on Eve. She seemed to glow in the morning light, which was unfolding around her.

"What are you doing here so early?" he asked, his voice still filled with sleep.

Eve walked over to him, sitting down on the floor beneath where he slept. Her hand went up to stroke his hair. "I want to be with you as much as I can today; I know how difficult this is going to be for you. When did you get to sleep last night?"

"About an hour or so ago."

Eve sighed, remembering those nights when sleep would skillfully evade her. "I'm sorry Jus, unfortunately it gets worse before it gets better."

Justin flung his legs over the side of the bench. "That's what I hear. Care for a cup of coffee?"

"Yes, that would be great. Say Jus, why were you sleeping on the porch?"

Justin turned to her then, looking as though he'd aged ten years overnight. "The smell," he said almost in a whisper. "The smell of her gets stronger at night. She's everywhere, her scent, that sweet smell of sea salt and jasmine she used to love so much. I couldn't stand it, I had to get out."

Justin quickly busied himself in the kitchen while Eve observed all the cards and flowers that had been sent, some from people she was certain Justin did not even know.

"It's amazing being in the public eye like you are, I can't even imagine."

"Yeah, it's tough, everyone wants a piece of you. And when something like this happens, everyone wants to comfort you. Even people you don't know." Justin poured a cup of steaming coffee for Eve and himself. Handing her a cup, he stopped suddenly, as if he'd been slapped.

"I can't do this without her, Eve." His sudden stammering words startled her. His voice sounded shaky and devoid of emotion. Eve was at his side in a moment, wrapping him in a gentle hug.

"Hon, I know it seems that way right now, but eventually it will get better and you will go on. You have to, life doesn't give you another option."

"No it certainly doesn't does it? It's so unfair, so fucking unfair." Tears burned his eyes. He released himself from her arms and walked over to the window, staring outside. He was amazed and appalled that the world seemed to continue on without her. Didn't they know? It angered him as he watched a couple holding hands and laughing. In his mournful state it seemed terribly unfair that life's random choices left him without his beloved Zoë while others continued on as if she'd never existed.

"Jus, I promise you that one day you will wake up and find that the searing pain you're feeling right now has dulled a bit. And each day from then on it will get a little better. It will never go away, that I know, but it will lose its destructive grip on you."

"I don't know which was harder Eve, planning her burial or trying to talk her parents out of taking her body back to Michigan. Can you believe they wanted to go against her wishes to have her ashes scattered at sea, and bury her in Minnesota, all because they hoped it would somehow make up for her 'sinful life', as they put it! No fucking wonder she left there."

"People get very strange when someone dies. Even little Billy Jr. You wouldn't believe some of the odd things people suggested for his burial."

"God Evie, I'm so sorry you have to relive that. This must be so hard for you. I understand if you can't go to the funeral."

"Are you kidding?" Eve took his hands in her own, "You are my best friend, you have saved my life more than once, I would no sooner let you go through this without me than I would desert one of my own children. Is that clear?"

Justin bent to kiss her on the forehead. "Perfectly," he whispered.

❧ ❧ ❧

Much to the chagrin of Zoë's family, her funeral would be held on Justin's boat, the *Zoë Francis*, with her ashes scattered at sea. The funeral was only attended by her parents, Zoë's five brothers and sisters, Eve, Billy, the VanSants, and Adele. It was a perfectly warm California day, the sun shone brilliantly on the ocean as they all stood quietly by, watching Justin prepare for their departure. When they arrived at the spot Zoë had chosen, Justin turned off the engine, and carefully pulled out the urn. He held it for a moment while her family looked on. Then, he began to speak.

"Zoë was for me, a bright and shining light on what otherwise would have been a dark life. She came to me when I had lost all hope of finding love, or even making a new friend." A smile crept onto his face, "And she challenged me for that every step of the way. She was a glorious woman, who fought for the rights of every living being. Many of the creatures that swim beneath us today have her to thank for their continued existence.

"She believed in me. She forced me to publish something I thought was pretty awful, but she knew everyone else would not think so, and she was right. I loved her with my heart, my body and my mind as much as I think any one person can love another. I brought with me today something I'd like to read for you all. It's a poem I used to read to her, and I believe that it describes exactly what she meant to me." Justin inhaled deeply, gathered his strength and continued,

"I love you, not only for what you are,
But for what I am when I am with you.
I love you, not only for what
You have made of yourself,
But for what you are making of me.
I love you for the part of me
That you bring out;
I love you for putting your hand
Into my heaped-up heart
And passing over
All the foolish, weak things

That you can't help
Dimly seeing there,
And for drawing out into the light
All the beautiful belongings
That no one else had looked quite far enough
To find.
I love you because you
Are helping me to make
Of the lumber of my life
Not a tavern, but a temple;
Out of the works of my everyday
Not a reproach, but a song,
I love you, because you have done
More than any creed could have done.
To make me good, and more than any fate
Could have done to make me happy.
You have done it,
Without a touch,
Without a word,
Without a sign.
You have done it, by being yourself
Perhaps that is what being a friend means,
After all."

❖ ❖ ❖

They arrived at Justin's house where a modest buffet had been set up. Justin refused to eat. He was neither hungry, nor desirous of company. They felt like intruders to him now, he wanted nothing more than to be alone with his memories and her spirit. After a few moments of watching the women fuss around the house, he politely asked them to leave him alone. Eve balked at the idea of leaving him alone: "Jus, you can't be alone right now, look why don't we just go for a walk or something."

Justin's eyes were filled with pain when he turned to face her, "I need to be alone right now. I'm sorry I hope you all can understand that."

"Of course we do dear." Adele smiled, she hugged him briefly and then scurried from the house, "I'll be home all evening if you need anything else."

Billy took Eve's hand then, tugging her with him, "Yeah man, and we're only a phone call away."

In a moment they were gone and he was alone. The deafening sound of silence echoed like thunder in his ear. Outside the sun was beginning to dip low in the sky and already the heavens were being illuminated with the angry colors of purple, orange and red. Justin left the house and began to walk along the beach, remembering the many times he'd taken this same walk with Zoë by his side. Often, she would laugh and run ahead of him into the ocean, letting the waves splash up around her long lean legs. Today as he walked there was no laughter, only solace in the fact that now her spirit was free to spend an eternity on the beach she loved so much. Even as he walked he could feel her presence. The sun dipped farther now as he stood watching the waves crash and then retreat into the deep blue sea.

Justin stood for hours by the ocean until the darkness surrounded him completely. He was exhausted and numb, but the thought of returning to an empty house did not thrill him either. Finally, he turned and headed for home as the reality of the day at last began to settle in around him. He approached his house, which looked stark and austere against the night sky. It was cold and quiet inside as the door closed behind him with a soft click. He waited in the doorway as if at any moment she would come out of the bedroom, smiling and happy. But she did not emerge and he stood alone in a house that was filled with her presence.

CHAPTER 49

When he woke the following day, the morning assaulted him with its daunting presence, forcing him to feel the loneliness that penetrated him deeper with each passing moment. It engulfed him and left a sticky residue in its wake, a reminder that it would not be ignored. Nor would it go away. He felt numb. He felt hopeless. He felt as though he simply could not go on. Then, like a flash of salvation he remembered. The boat. The boat was always a good idea.

The ocean would help him put everything back into perspective again. Of that he was certain. He planned his day carefully and packed a small lunch and filled a canister with coffee. He wrote a quick note for Adele so she would not worry, and headed to the marina, before anyone could stop by to visit him. If he had to hear one more condolence, he knew he would scream.

The air felt cleansing on his face as he navigated the *Zoë Francis* through the calm waters of the pristine morning. The air was filled with the scent of sea water and suddenly, he felt her, she was everywhere; laughing, smiling, helping him steer the boat. He sailed for a long while, unaware of his surroundings, unaware of where he was headed. He was pulled back in time by a force stronger than one he'd ever known. Lost in the memory of her, no longer conscious of time or space. In this place in the past, there was no pain, there was only Zoë and he decided he would stay a while.

Eve did not like it, she did not like it one bit. He was in no state to be alone. "Billy, I need to stay behind for a while," Eve began slowly.

"Stay behind, what for?" Billy sounded perturbed.

"We still have no idea where Justin is."

"Justin will be fine." Clearly now, he was indeed beginning to get annoyed with this conversation.

"We don't know that honey, please, I need you to understand. Justin took off nearly two days ago and no one knows where he's gone. He's devastated with grief, God only knows what he's capable of."

"So, what the hell am I supposed to do? Just take off more time from work to look for him? I don't have that kind of time."

Eve felt the sting of his words. Their friend was missing and all he could think of was his own selfish priorities. Certainly she'd love nothing more than to rush home and hold her babies in her arms. She missed them so much she ached, but right now a life may be at stake. The life of her closest and dearest friend.

Eve wanted to tell him how self-serving she thought he was being, but then, thought better of it and continued in a soft, pleading voice, "Sweetheart, I would never ask you to stay behind. But I do need you to understand that I must stay here until Justin's been found."

"Justin! Justin! Justin! That's all I've fucking heard ever since we've been married! I'm so sick of hearing that name I can't even tell you! This marriage doesn't stand a chance as long as he's in our life!"

Eve was baffled by his shouting. "Billy, what are you talking about? Justin is our friend."

"No Eve, he's your friend. He stopped being my friend when he started being a better husband to you than I was. When his every motive was to make me look like some dumb asshole that had no idea what the fuck to say or do when our son died!!"

For a moment, Eve felt crippled, unable to speak or move. The memories that welled up inside her brought back every painful moment of losing her baby. She did not understand what Billy was talking about, nor did she care. With each passing moment, she felt her chance to find Justin slipping slowly away. She could not bear to lose someone again. She knew, simply, that she would not be able to live through it herself.

"Billy," she began warily, "I don't know what you're talking about. But I do know that our friend needs us right now, probably more than he's ever needed us and I am going to stay behind until I know he's safe. Now you can either do this with me, or go home and wait. I won't be very long, I promise."

Billy was more annoyed with her now than he'd ever been. Silently, he hoped that she'd never find her precious Justin. That would teach her.

"What the fuck ever Eve, stay behind, don't stay behind, I could give a fuck! But know that our marriage may never recover from this. I needed you by my side and you refused, so now you can live with that. Make your choice Eve, this marriage…or Justin."

"Billy, that's not fair, that is not what this is about! My God, he just lost Zoë for Christ's sake, don't you get it? Please don't make this a choice."

Billy walked over to the door, holding the handle he turned to face her, "Eve, you made your choice long ago." He slammed the door behind him; he needed a cold beer and the feel of a welcoming woman. He intended on finding both.

Eve watched the door for a long while. She didn't understand the preceding conversation. There was so much more she needed to discuss with Billy, but now was not the time. She needed to find Justin and if he wasn't going to help her, she'd have to go it alone.

❧ ❧ ❧

"Eve honey, I appreciate your dilemma but really, I have no idea where he may have gone. His note said he'd be back, but he never said when."

Eve paced Adele's warm kitchen. "I need to find him. I think he may be in trouble."

"My dear, I understand that he's grieving, but he is an excellent sailor. He knows what he's doing on the water."

"I know he does, but I also know what's going on in his heart."

Adele believed she did. She felt the connection between them as certainly as if she'd experienced it herself.

"I'm afraid for him Adele. I get the feeling he might be slipping away."

Adele was puzzled by her comment. "Whatever do you mean, dear?" she asked.

"I mean, that if we don't find him soon, we may never find him. I think he went out there to kill himself."

Adele gasped at the harsh truth of Eve's words. "I'm sorry to be so blunt," she quickly added, "but I think it's important that you realize the gravity of this situation. It's dire that we find him right away and for that, I need your help."

"But, what can I do?"

"You can start by telling me everything you know about where I might be able to rent a boat."

"Lady look, I really don't have time to go traipsing all over the ocean looking for your friend. I mean he could be halfway to Hawaii by now."

Eve refused to give up. She'd spoken to more than a dozen capable people who did not want to get caught up in her search. Time was running out though, and she could feel Justin's desperation as if it were her own.

"Look, I can pay you anything. You are my only hope, there has to be a way to narrow the search."

The elderly man eyed her sympathetically, hearing the desperation in her voice, "Missy, I'm too old to help you with this, besides it would be like looking for a needle in a haystack out there. What you need is aircraft. A plane or a helicopter. You'll never find him otherwise."

Why hadn't she thought of that before? Half the day had been wasted talking to wind-burned fishermen and unhelpful police officers who refused to file a missing persons because Justin's note said he'd return. That was enough for them.

"Thank you," she said gratefully. "Thank you for your suggestion. Can you direct me to where I might find a pilot and a private plane?"

"Sure can," he continued, pleased that he was able to be of service, "a friend of mine has his own plane. Maybe he can help. He operates out of a field not far from here."

The flight home was long and uneventful. Billy sat uncomfortably next to a woman who could not stop talking about her wonderful California vacation. Finally, he feigned sleep and found an escape from her incessant monologue. He thought of Eve, alone in a state she was still somewhat unfamiliar with, trying desperately to find her friend. While he admired her tenacity, he still struggled with his gut-wrenching jealously. And even still immersed in his anger, he felt the slightest twinge of guilt for not having stayed behind to help her. There was a time when he would have, a time when he would have lead the search himself. He understood their bond because he'd shared it once too, but that was before most of his family had died and all the disappointments had turned his life to shit. Billy rested farther back in his seat, his thoughts disturbed only by the clanking of the beverage cart as it, pushed by two attractive flight attendants, made its way ungraciously down the aisle.

✤ ✤ ✤

The *Zoë Francis* drifted steadily with the current as Justin lay motionless on her deck. The sun beat down on him reddening his skin, and he no longer felt the hunger that ripped through him, nor did he feel the thirst. Lulled by the gentle swaying of the boat, and unaware of his surroundings, Justin drifted in and out of his memories like never ending dreams that made him feel safe. Nothing or no one else mattered. At last he had found a place where the pain could not find him. He was free of it and soon he knew, that he and his precious Zoë would once again be united.

✤ ✤ ✤

The plane flew over the endless blue sea. Eve eyed each boat carefully, but as they ventured farther from the shore, the boat sightings became sparse and after an hour of flying, Eve began to lose hope. She could feel Justin's pain as certain as if it was her own. And with each passing minute, her desperation to get to him grew to a feverish peak. She wanted to yell at the pilot to fly faster, but she knew this kind man was doing his very best.

"We'll find your friend, Ma'am," the pilot said reassuringly.

"I hope you're right, J.T. I'm beginning to…." Then, she saw it. The sail boat, looking pristine and stark against the deep blue ocean that surrounded it.

"That's him!" she cried.

"Good!" the pilot said, seemingly relieved. "Now, I'll radio the Coast Guard so they can bring him back to shore."

"No!" Eve panicked, "I need to go to him, I need to do this alone."

"But Ma'am, we're hundreds of miles out to sea, it's taken him three days to get this far. It'll take you at least a day to get to him, do you really think he has that much time?"

Eve thought quickly, she didn't want him to be in the company of strangers. He needed her, not a platoon of men who knew nothing of his pain.

"This is a float plane right? Can't you land this on the ocean? If we get near enough to the boat I can…"

"Listen, I'm happy to do whatever I can, but you'd be risking your life, and I can't allow you to do that. Not on my watch anyway."

"I'll take full responsibility, I swear I will and besides, I'm a good swimmer, excellent in fact, nothing will happen I assure you."

"I'm sorry…I just…"

"NO! Please don't leave him out here, he's dying, I know he is. Even by the time the Coast Guard gets here it might be too late…if you don't land, I'll jump out anyway." Eve said defiantly.

The pilot chuckled for a moment. "I bet you would. All right then, but I don't leave until I know you're safely aboard his boat and I will radio the Coast Guard to alert them to this…."

Eve opened her mouth to speak, but he continued, "And, furthermore, you will wear a life vest, I don't care how good of a swimmer you are. You'll do what I say or I turn back right now. If you jump from this plane you'll die for sure and then what good will you do your friend?"

Eve knew he was right. "Ok, fine, we do it your way, just please hurry."

When the plane touched down on the water, Eve felt her entire body rock violently.

"Sorry." The pilot mumbled quietly as he continued to fight for control of the plane.

The water beneath them seemed to want to swallow the small plane, angered that it chose to land where it did. Eve held on to the bar over the window, keeping Justin's boat in sight and praying that the heaving would stop. It didn't, the water was choppy, and to her chagrin, she would have to swim in the upset waters to get to him.

"Put this on!" The pilot yelled over the sound of the wind and engine, handing her a deflated life vest. "When you're ready to jump, pull the tabs." He motioned to the two red tabs that stuck out from the yellow vest. Eve felt her heart thump so loudly, she thought she was having a heart attack.

"You sure you want to do this?" he yelled again.

Eve inhaled a courageous breath. "Absolutely. Just tell me what to do."

"All right, when I say go, you jump and start swimming. The water looks bad, but I don't think the current is too rough, at least not yet, if we wait much longer it will be. I think a storm is coming, all the more reason for us to call the Coast Guard instead of letting you risk your life to do this."

"I'm going to him," Eve said steadfastly. She was determined to do this and scared out of her mind at the same time. God, how she wished Billy were here, he was a much stronger swimmer than she was. She prayed she would see her precious Frannie and baby Nicholas again.

"You all right?" The pilot asked, pulling her from her thoughts of dread.

"Y-yes, yes, fine. I want to go now."

"Ok, look, when you get on the boat I want you to immediately turn on the radio. I will be in contact with you and will send the Coast Guard immediately if I don't hear from you. If you get on the boat and he can't sail it back, you'll need to let me know immediately. We need to get you both into safe waters before this storm hits."

"I understand."

He nodded, admiring her courage and wishing she wasn't about to do what he knew he could not talk her out of.

"Listen, in case…who do I contact…in case something happens?"

Eve wanted to protest that she'd be fine, but she knew he was right in asking. Without saying a word, she grabbed a pen that peered out of the door pocket beside her and wrote her home telephone number and Billy's name on a scrap of paper she found. She handed it to the pilot, "I have two babies, don't worry I won't let anything happen to me."

The pilot motioned with his arm across the great spans of the ocean. "This is a greater force than any you've ever dealt with I imagine, remember that Mother Nature is raw and brutal, don't ever assume anything when it comes to her and don't think that just because you're a mother she'll let you go home to your kids. She doesn't care about any of that, her only concern is defending her world against the intruders, us."

Eve only nodded. "Thank you for all your help. I'll see you back at shore." With that she pushed herself from the plane into the chilly waters below.

"I hope so," the pilot sighed.

Eve struggled against the current as the wind picked up some steam. She was ill prepared for swimming, her clothes as light as they were, still weighed her down. With each stroke, she fought with all her might to reach the *Zoë Francis*. Even as close as she now was she could not see Justin anywhere topside and she began to worry that perhaps, she was already too late.

Justin lay sleeping below deck. The sun had beaten him mercilessly and he was red and burned. The boat bobbed back and forth as the waves rustled beneath her. He did not hear the plane overhead, nor did he hear it land. He thought for a moment he heard someone call out his name, then he realized it must be Zoë. He would get to her, soon, he would be with her.

❧ ❧ ❧

Eve needed to conserve her energy and after trying to swim and scream his name, she finally gave up the latter and continued persistently toward her goal. Her body ached from the struggle. Finding the step ladder that reached into the water she began to climb it and fell unceremoniously onto the boat. Releasing herself from the constraints of the life jacket, she called out to Justin but there was not a sound. Her body went cold at the thought of what he might have done. Quickly, she climbed down into the vessel, still calling his name. It seemed that nothing in the galley had been touched. The only sign that someone was or had been on board was a small thermos and lunch box on the table.

"Justin!" she yelled, walking toward the master cabin. Opening the door, a sense of relief swept over her. "Justin!" she cried, "I've been so worried about you!" There was no response from the man who lay motionless on the bed. Quickly she sat down beside him, touching him lightly. She noticed he seemed to be asleep; his breathing was deep and slow. His face was burnt red and looked horribly painful. Eve worried that the intense burn she saw not only on his face but on his exposed arms and legs might have sent him into shock.

"Justin," she said trying to calm her voice, "Justin it's Evie, please wake up."

Justin groaned; a thick blackness swirled in his head. He heard a voice, thought at first it was Zoë, then he realized it wasn't her at all. Who could it be? And why were they disturbing him and Zoë? They wanted to be alone, didn't this person realize that? A hand touched him then and he felt a searing pain that shocked him into reality. Suddenly, Zoë was gone. Again.

Justin opened his eyes, staring right into Eve's caring face.

"Oh, thank God. Jus, I've been so worried about you! God, I was so afraid..." she bit back the urge to fall into tears. He needed to see her strong, he needed her to be strong right now.

"Eve? What the hell are you...how did you? Where am I?"

"You're on your boat, you've been here for three days, I was worried so I had someone bring me out here to you."

Justin tried to sit up then, but the sunburn pierced him with a pain he'd not felt before.

"God, what happened to you?"

"Honestly Eve, I don't remember...I needed to get away so I decided to take her out for a day and then..." She'd never believe him, he knew that for certain, so he decided not to tell her the truth.

"You saw her didn't you?" Eve knew the truth, even if he tried to keep it from her.

"How did you know?"

"After I lost Billy Jr., I spent days sleeping and playing with my baby in my dreams. They were so perfect I never wanted to awaken. That's how I knew you were in trouble, I sensed…" the words were more powerful than she'd ever expected. Their connection was stronger than she'd ever felt before in her life, even with Billy. Justin had indeed been slipping away, and if she hadn't gotten here when she did, he would have been lost to her forever.

Justin felt uncomfortable at her words, knowing the all powerful truth in them. A truth he had never been able to escape. He pulled himself up and threw his legs over the side of the bed, each movement causing him excruciating pain.

"We need to get you some liquids, then I need to tend to this burn."

"I'm fine," Justin insisted.

"No, you're anything but fine. But first point me to your radio before the eleventh brigade descends down on us."

"What?"

"The pilot that dropped me here said he was going to call the Coast Guard if he didn't hear from me. I need to tell him I found you and you're ok."

"You flew in?" Justin stood up, following her out of the bedroom.

"Yes," she said over her shoulder. "There was no time to hire a boat so I went the quickest way possible."

Justin grabbed her and turned her to face him. "Do you have any idea how dangerous that was? You could have gotten killed."

"It was my only choice. Besides I didn't get killed."

"What if you had? What about your children?!"

"I had to take that risk. I could not lose you." He looked at her for a long moment, grateful for her help and cursing her for her reckless decision.

"Where's Billy? Why didn't he do this?" But before she could answer, he knew what had happened.

"Billy had to go back. So I came out here by myself. Besides, you didn't even want me to do this. I can't imagine how you would have reacted if we'd both shown up."

"How could he let you do this alone?" Justin released her then, and followed her into the kitchen.

"In his defense, I don't think he thought I'd be jumping out of planes. If he did I'm sure he would have stayed." Eve looked around the kitchen for something resembling a radio. She was not altogether certain that Billy would have stayed even if he had known how she'd have to reach their friend. His jealously of Justin was far reaching. But she could not, nor would not share that with this frail man.

"Radio's over there," Justin pointed to a small alcove, "but I can send the message."

"You'll do no such thing. You'll sit down here for a moment, drink some water, and when I get done, I'm going to make you something to eat. You do have food on this boat don't you?"

"Sure, some canned stuff."

Eve nodded and went into the radio room. Minutes later she emerged after having easily found the large switch that turned on the microphone. Her pilot friend had been standing by. Eve was not certain that Justin could or should attempt to sail back to shore, but wanting to keep as few people out of the situation, she promised to radio again shortly with a status report. When she returned to the kitchen, Justin was slumped over the table. She ran to him, pressing her hand to his cheek. He was burning up. His skin felt dry and extremely hot. He was mumbling incoherently.

"Justin! Can you hear me? Can you tell me what's wrong?"

Again, he mumbled something she could not understand. His skin seemed to burn under her cool touch. Panicking, Eve began to search his cabinets for a cup; she found one and quickly filled it with water. Suddenly, Justin slipped from behind the table and collapsed onto the floor.

"Justin!!" Eve screamed. "Oh dear God, what's wrong?" But Justin did not speak; at that moment Eve realized her friend was in trouble. She had to get help. She raced to the radio room and frantically searched for the button she'd found so easily only moments before.

"Help, uh…mayday! Mayday! Please can anyone hear me?"

J.T. turned up his radio, recognizing her voice. "Eve! What happened?"

Oh thank God, she thought gratefully. "J.T., it's Justin, he's unconscious. One minute he was fine, now he's burning up."

"Could be sunstroke or worse, heatstroke. Look, I'll call for help, you just sit tight. The best thing to do is keep him cool. Remove any clothing and cover him with cool compresses. Keep refreshing them constantly as his body temperature will absorb the cool very quickly. And keep talking to him."

"But I don't think he can hear me."

"Yes, he can. He can hear you and right now the sound of your voice might be the only thing that keeps him from slipping into a coma. Do you understand what I'm saying? Look Eve, I don't want to scare you but this is a life threatening situation now. Keep him cool and keep talking to him, got it?"

"Yes." Her voice was barely audible, "I understand."

"Now I want you to keep the radio on. I'll be in touch with you soon. Over."

Eve dropped the microphone and ran back into the kitchen. Justin lay still on the floor. Eve began to strip him of his clothing. Shirt, pants, they all fell away. Still he was burning up. As quickly as she could, she gathered every towel she could find, filled the sink with cold water and submersed each of them in it. Once the towels were drenched she wrung them out one at a time and covered his body with them. They heated back up almost as quickly as she put them down. It was nearly impossible to keep up the pace, but she had to. She couldn't bear the thought of losing him. Eve spoke to him the entire time. She talked non-stop about anything and everything she could think of. Sometimes she made no sense at all. She talked of their childhood growing up together, of the kids they'd gone to school with. The "whatever happened to's", the "did you know's"; the senseless chatter that seemed to help steady her work until the sound of the radio interrupted her stream of consciousness. She gently pressed another set of cool towels on his still hot body and ran to answer J.T.'s call.

"The Coast Guard should be there shortly."

Outside, it was already beginning to show signs of darkness approaching. "What about the storm?"

"Looks like it will blow over, just some choppy tide and wind, not much more than that. How's the patient?"

"Still hot, but I'm talking up my own storm and trying to keep him cool."

"Good girl, you're saving his life you know? You were right to be concerned."

"I'm just glad I got here in time."

"Hold on, just another twenty minutes or so, and they should be there. They'll be arriving in a chopper so listen for it. They will have to airlift him to the hospital, but they do this all the time. They will take you as well, and a crew member will sail his boat home."

"Thank you J.T., I can't thank you enough. And they understand the need for discretion here?"

"Absolutely, they're pro's. Like I said, this isn't the first time they've had to pull a celebrity out of the water. Over."

Suddenly the line went dead and she was alone again with her panic. She looked over to Justin who did not show any signs of resuscitation. She rushed back into the kitchen to refresh the towels.

"You know," she said quietly, "you're famous Jus! Who would have ever thought one of the three of us would be famous? If anyone, I thought for certain Billy would end up playing pro, but he never had the fortitude to finish anything. And as for me, well, I'm about as far from stardom as one can get. But you, Jus you've really made a name for yourself in this world. Everyone knows Justin VanSant. I remember you when you had skinned up knees and you were some knock-kneed kid that couldn't climb trees. Now look at you…."

She paused for a moment from her work. He had indeed changed, she thought. They all had for that matter. Gone was the awkward boy, and in his place was a handsome, confident and presumably wealthy man who had just lost the love of his life to a great tragedy. Eve reached down to run her hands through his hair, "I love you, sweet Justin. You were always my dearest companion. I have no idea what my life would have been like without you…" her words trailed off at the sound of the helicopter above her. Tears sprang to her eyes. He would be saved, she thought thankfully, her sweet Justin would be saved.

Eve did not leave Justin's side from the time they plucked him off his boat until he arrived at the same hospital Zoë had died in only days before. And now, shrouded in almost complete darkness, she lingered by his bedside, determined to wait until he woke. The doctor had been optimistic when he told her that Justin would recover in a few days, although his overnight progress would be crucial to his complete recovery. He had been very close to slipping away entirely, and she was only grateful that by some miracle, she had managed to get to him in time. Justin stirred softly. He had not awoken since his collapse on the floor of his boat and when he did, she intended on being there for it. She had not called Billy.

In the earliest moments of dawn, Justin began to stir. Beside him, Eve slept with her hand wrapped around his and her head on a small portion of the bed. He looked over to her, trying to remember what had brought him to this point. He knew she'd come to him on the boat. But how he'd gotten off the boat or, for that matter, in this condition was beyond his recollection. Gently he stroked her hair and then fell back asleep until the day was fully dawned around him.

Eve was standing by the window when Justin finally opened his eyes. Outside another California day had already begun. "Good morning," Eve smiled.

"Hello yourself. What the hell am I doing here?" Justin felt as though his mouth were filled with cotton, it was almost impossible to speak.

"You don't remember anything?" Eve positioned herself beside his bed again, taking his hand in her own.

"Well, I remember you coming to the boat, that's about it."

"It'll come to you in time, I'm sure."

"Did we go sailing or something?"

Eve smiled half-heartedly. "No, if it were only that..."

"Evie, tell me, please I need to know..."

At that moment, the doctor entered his room. "Well, Mr. VanSant, I see we're awake this morning, how are you feeling?"

"Groggy, confused. What the hell happened?"

The doctor smiled and approached his bed. "This young lady saved your life, that's what happened. If she hadn't gotten there when she did, you wouldn't be here right now, or probably anywhere for that matter."

"You mean, I was dying? But how?"

"Sunstroke, well heatstroke actually. The two are often confused. You apparently had been lying in the sun for three days before you were found."

Gradually, the memories came back to him. Zoë. Zoë was gone. There had been the briefest of moments when he'd wanted to go with her. The memories, the boat. He'd gone there to escape the reality he'd been left with and find her again. He had found her, but it wasn't her. Just a mirage in a sea of despair for a desperate man trying to hang on to whatever he could of her.

Slowly, Justin began to speak, "I remember now."

The doctor held his chart to study it again, the vitals taken throughout the night looked promising. He was a strong man, with a will to live.

"Look, I know the loss you've suffered. I lost my wife too, several years ago, I understand the heartache you're feeling."

"I'm sorry for your loss."

"You obviously have some terrific friends," he smiled, nodding to Eve, "and an incredible career. My nurses read all of your books, sometimes to distraction," he winked. "You have a real gift."

Justin smiled, a little embarrassed by the compliments, something he was still not used to. "Now, I've got to finish my rounds, I'll be back later to check on you," the doctor smiled to Eve before he turned and left the room.

Justin gazed up to Eve. "My sweet, sweet Evie. I do remember now, you jumped from a plane to get to my boat."

Eve rolled her eyes. "Well I didn't exactly pull an Indiana Jones. I just swam to your boat from a seaplane, that's all."

"I owe you my life."

"No, you don't. I did what any good friend would do. I couldn't bear to live my life without you."

Suddenly, a rush of love that had been dormant for so many years came flooding over him. He had loved her once to distraction. Too soon, he thought, too much pain. Too many precious moments lost with his beloved Zoë. But for one fleeting second, he'd felt it again. That wave that engulfed him. Now though, it was over, neatly put back in check. Justin pulled her hand to his lips and kissed it gently. "I don't know what I'd do without you either Evie," he whispered.

CHAPTER 50

Miraculously, Justin's mishap somehow managed to stay out of the gossip columns and three days after he was admitted, his doctor willingly released him. He stressed lots of rest, plenty of fluids, and no more lone excursions out to sea, at least not for a while. Eve promised that she would see to it that he adhered to his doctor's orders. But she knew she would not be able to watch over him for much longer.

Billy was getting impatient and he wanted her home. Moreover, he wanted her away from Justin. There were several messages waiting for her at the hotel and he'd even called Adele on a few occasions to see if he could reach his wife. Much to Billy's dismay, Adele had gushed on about how Eve had saved Justin's life. Finally he could no longer take her colorful retelling of the story and, with a faint goodbye, quickly hung up the telephone.

Eve arrived home with Justin in tow. Adele had baked a casserole for him and left it warming in the oven. The scent of it greeted them when they arrived. There were fresh flowers sitting on the dining room table and for the first time since her death, they weren't for Zoë.

"It's good to be home," he sighed, letting himself sink into the couch.

Eve sat beside him, "We're all glad you're ok Jus. For a while there I wasn't sure." She grasped his hand tightly, remembering her fear again as the scene repeated itself in her mind.

"I promise to never do anything stupid like that again Evie, I don't know what came over me."

"It's called grief my friend." Her hand stroked his sandy hair, "You have no control over it when it rears its ugly head. But I promise you this, it will get better."

"I hope so. I don't know if I can stand much more of this." A slight painful smile appeared on his face. "It's like I've been socked in the gut," he continued, collecting himself, "I'm feeling kind of tired, I think I'd like to rest for a bit before we dig into whatever Adele's left for us in the kitchen."

As if on cue, the elderly woman knocked softly on the door. "May I come in?" She smiled through the screen door.

Eve stood up immediately to unlock it. "Of course you may…" she smiled and hugged Adele warmly.

"I've come to see our patient for myself."

"I'm fine Adele and thanks for leaving us dinner." The woman sat beside him, and he took her wrinkled hand in his own.

"I was very worried about you." She looked over to Eve, "we both were."

"I know and I'm sorry for causing you concern."

"Did Eve tell you what she had to go through to get to you?"

Eve opened her mouth to quiet Adele. But Justin interrupted her, "Yes, I had to pry it out of her, but she did finally own up to it. I'm still a little upset with her for risking her life like she did…but grateful to her as well. I was not ready to die, and I hope to be around for a long time yet."

"Well then," Eve smiled warmly, "if that's the case then I think you need to get your rest. Perhaps Adele would care to join us for dinner later."

"Oh, no dear, it's poker night and I'm having the girls over."

Justin chuckled. "Yes, we don't want to interrupt her poker night, I tried it once and was sorely reprimanded."

"Actually Justin, you had my group of ladies thrilled that such a handsome young man wanted to join us."

Justin kissed her on the cheek. "We promise, no interruptions tonight."

Adele left, promising to return in the morning with freshly baked muffins.

Justin headed for bed, clearly exhausted. After he retired, Eve sat nervously at the kitchen table wondering whether or not to call Billy. She knew from his messages the conversation would not be pleasant. Just then, the telephone rang. She answered. It was Billy.

"So what, you're answering his phone now?" he asked without saying hello.

Eve tried to keep her voice down, "No, we just returned home and Justin is lying down. He's quite tired."

"First off, that's not home, this is and I'm wondering when you'll be returning to it."

"Billy, I just need a few more days."

"What?! You've been there over two weeks! What the hell do you need a few more days for? He's out of the hospital right? For Christ's sake Eve, he's a grown man, he can take care of himself."

"Billy, my God, he nearly died, how can you be so insensitive?"

"Insensitive?! I think I'm very fucking sensitive when my wife stays behind to risk her own life to save a friend. What about your fucking family for Christ's sake, did you ever stop to think about us?!!" Billy was screaming now. Justin had quietly gotten up and was standing in the doorway. He could hear Billy's enraged voice across the room. Eve did not see Justin, or the concerned look on his face as he listened to her try to calm the man at the other end of the phone.

"How did you find out?" she asked.

"That old broad Justin's so sweet on told me when I called her, in all colorful fucking detail. 'She saved his life!' she said. 'You should be so proud of your wife,' she said. And here I am, three thousand miles away wonderin' if you're ever coming home from this sea adventure of yours."

"Look, I'll be home as soon as I can…" Justin stood in front of her, taking the phone from her hand.

"Billy, this is Justin."

Billy felt himself grow even more enraged at the other end of the phone, "I want to talk to my wife."

"Not if you're going to talk to her like that."

"She's my fucking wife! I can talk to her however I like!"

"What the hell happened to you man?" Justin asked. Eve bit her lip nervously, while she appreciated Justin's attempt to calm him, she knew it would only make things worse.

"What do you mean, what the hell happened to me? What the hell happened to you? Suddenly you're famous and BAM!! You're expecting everyone to be at your beck and call!"

"I never asked Eve to stay behind, but thank God she did."

"Yeah, right. She had to help her sweet Justin! Couldn't bear to leave knowing your nose wasn't wiped! Sometimes I think she married the wrong man." There was a subtle truth behind his words even Justin could not retreat from. She had married the wrong man, but that was a long time ago.

"Billy," Justin said finally after a long pause, "you're just upset, now please calm down and I'll let you talk to Eve again…."

"I'm done talkin' just send her home."

The line went dead. Justin hung up his end, deep in thought.

Billy flung the phone across the room. Fortunately, the children were at Eve's mother's house and were not present to witness his outburst. Whatever, he thought, she rescues him all on her own, like some fuckin' superwoman or something, now she's tending his wounds. What the hell does she need me for?

She didn't need him, which was precisely the problem.

The door slammed behind him when he left the house and headed for Cheryl's.

❧ ❧ ❧

"What's going on Eve?" Justin asked, his hand still on the phone.

Eve was circling the room. "Nothing…he's just upset."

"I would say upset is an understatement, Eve I heard him yelling at you from across the room. Now sit down and tell me what's going on between the two of you."

Eve didn't want to sit down, she needed to pace. "Justin, you've got too much on your mind right now to worry about…."

"Eve, please tell me…" he interrupted.

Eve deeply inhaled the scent of the room; it smelled of the gardenias in Adele's bouquet and the crisp smell of salt water. "He's insanely jealous of you. I don't know when it started, or if it's always been there and I just haven't seen it. We fought when I told him I was staying behind. I also think he might be…I don't know of course, I've never caught him, but…there's this feeling…."

Justin fought off his exhaustion and walked over to her. He stood behind her, wanting to wrap his arms around her shoulders, but there was no sense in tempting fate.

"Evie, what are trying to say? Do you think he's cheating on you?"

"I'm just so boring Jus, it's just me and my babies and he's a jock after all. Billy's always been in the spotlight, he's used to being carried on someone's shoulders after a game. Getting doused in Gatorade. Now he's just a dad, and just a husband, there's no crowd, no cheering. Just the everyday boring sounds of babies who need changing, bills that need paying and a wife who has found no place for herself in his life."

Justin spun her around. "First off, you're anything but boring. Secondly, Billy is a complete idiot if he doesn't embrace what he has with you and the kids."

"I don't know Jus, maybe it's more than he bargained for. Maybe it's not what he thought it would be."

"When is life ever what we think it will be? I mean come on Eve, didn't we both think our lives would turn out differently than they have? I mean who the hell thought that all that gibberish I used to write on note pads would ever make any sense? Who knew that the tomboy we all used to know and love, would ever end up being the best mommy and best wife in the world? No, Eve, life never turns out the way we expect, it usually turns out better than we could have ever imagined."

Eve realized again why her friend was such a revered writer. Finding the exact right word at the exact right moment had always been his forte. A tear escaped her eye and slid slowly down her cheek. Justin fought the old urge to wipe it away.

"You think he still loves me?" she said quietly, almost afraid of the answer.

"I think he worships you, but Billy is Billy, he's never been very good at showing his emotions." He smirked at the irony of it, "at least not the ones that count. Look, he's probably eaten up by what he said to you. But he'd never admit it because he's stubborn and as far as this jealously thing, I wouldn't worry too much about it. Guys are always envious of one another to some degree."

"You think we can work this out then?"

"I think you can handle anything my dear."

They lapsed into a comfortable silence as he contemplated Eve's words. Had he known their entire situation, he would have told her she deserved better, that she needed to pack up and leave him. And Eve did not disclose any more of their dark secrets to him, partially out of embarrassment. Justin knew how important marriage was to Eve. She would probably never survive a divorce and the children would grow up without a father. Perhaps any father was better than none at all. He vowed never to ask her again if she thought Billy was cheating on her. That was something she needed to answer for herself. If he was though, Justin was certain to find out. When he did, it would take an army to stop him from killing Billy.

CHAPTER 51

There was a moment before she stepped onto the plane, that Eve wanted to turn and run. The thought of returning to Connecticut brought with it a sorrow she hadn't known before. For the first time since that misplaced kiss under the pier, she and Justin had been close again. Really, really close. And she was quietly missing him, even before the plane left the ground. But moreover, she knew her trepidation came with the anger she'd felt through the phone during her last conversation with Billy.

There.

She felt it again.

That sensation that they were not alone in their marriage, that there was someone else. Quickly, she discarded the unwanted thought as paranoia. There was no one else. How could there be? They lived in a small town and certainly, someone would have seen something by now. Eve rested back in her seat. She wondered if Billy would be waiting at the airport with the children, or if he would send her mother. She'd left the message on their machine the day before and did not receive a return call. Eve decided not to push it. If no one was waiting for her at Hartford, she would simply take a taxi home.

The terminal was filled with anxious people and the excitement hung over them like the hum of electricity. Eve walked cautiously through the gate hoping to hear Nicky's raucous shout of "Mommy!" drift through the crowd. But there was nothing. No one that recognized her, no one had come for her. A wave of sadness washed over her and weakened her with a sense of despair.

❧ ❧ ❧

Trees in varying stages of autumn whipped past her as she sat quietly in the back seat of the somewhat uncomfortable cab. The seat was old and worn, and was beginning to sag in the middle. Eve leaned against the door to keep from slipping. The emptiness of her situation passed over her as a tear fell in lonely descent down her cheek. Every mile brought her closer to home. A home where she felt she was no longer wanted.

"So where'd you fly in from?" The cabbie tried again unsuccessfully to strike up a conversation with his passenger. Eve was too lost in her own world to even notice he was speaking to her. Above all else, she had wanted to save her marriage. Now she wondered if there was a marriage worth saving. She drew strength from her newfound sense of self, a person she'd stumbled across in California: someone who wanted to be loved with an endless passion and unyielding desire. And to have someone who would love her as Justin had loved Zoë; someone who would lose themselves at sea for days, hoping to find a single memory floating carelessly on the ocean.

After an hour and a half of driving and one hundred and twenty dollars in cab fare, they arrived at her home. Everything looked closed up and her heart sank even further. Where was Billy? And where the hell were her kids? Eve let the driver carry her bags to the house after which she paid and tipped him and sent him on his way.

The house was indeed closed up. Eve dug around for her keys. There was an eerie silence as she stepped inside. "Billy, Frannie, Nicky! Is anyone home?" she called, walking through her hallway into the living room. There was no answer. Eve felt a panic overtake her, her eye caught the machine; the blinking told her there was one message on it. She hit the key hoping it would be from Billy. It was her own voice that emanated from the machine. Her message telling Billy when and where she'd be arriving. Odd, she thought, that he'd left that message on there without erasing it. Quickly she picked up the telephone and dialed her mother's number. It was picked up after two rings.

"Hello?"

"Mom, it's me."

"Eve, darling, how are you and how is California? And when in God's name are you coming home?" It was good to hear her daughter's voice again. Judith sat down in a chair near the phone and leaned her ear closer to the receiver.

Her husband was preparing a late lunch for them. She watched him from her chair as he pulled plates from the cupboard.

"I just walked in the door Mom," Eve replied puzzled.

"You what? I had no idea you were coming home!" Ed turned to his wife, a questioning look on his face.

"Didn't Billy tell you? I left him a message a couple of days ago."

Judith sighed. That damned Billy, she thought. "No, he didn't, probably because he's been gone since Wednesday, said he was going on a camping trip with the guys.

Eve sighed with relief, at least now she knew where to find her children. "What guys?" she asked finally. She quickly scanned the notepad beside the telephone for any indication of where he might be.

"I don't know dear, it wasn't really my place to ask. Didn't he tell you he was going?"

"No, but…" she hesitated for a moment, "we had a bit of a falling out when I didn't come home with him."

"So he said. He told us you had to stay behind to tend to Justin. What happened?"

Tend to Justin she thought, was that as good as he could come up with? "Justin was in a pretty bad way, he almost died. It was important that I stay," she heard herself say in defense of her actions. Why the hell she felt she had to defend herself was beyond her.

"I see, well dear the children really miss you. Will you be picking them up today?" Eve could hear the weariness in her mother's voice. No doubt Frannie and Nick had tired her parents out. Nearing seventy, they were not used to running after little ones. Billy was thoughtless to leave them like that.

"Yes, I'll be right over. By the way, did Billy happen to mention when he'd be back?"

"He said sometime after the weekend."

Great, Eve thought bitterly, just great. She thanked her mom for taking care of her babies and promised to be over in a flash. She could hardly wait to hold them in her arms again.

Billy snuggled closer to the soft, warm body that lay beside him. A fire crackled and popped and they lay, wrapped around each other basking in the euphoria of satisfying sex. Going to Cheryl's parents' cabin had been a great idea; it was secluded and peaceful and gave him the time he needed to gather his thoughts.

Cheryl turned herself to face him, "Honey, I need to talk to you about something."

"What?"

"Well, it's been seven years that we've been together and I'm not getting any younger."

"What are you trying to say?" Billy frowned.

Cheryl chose her next words carefully. She knew that sooner or later that idiot wife of his would dig her own grave and now that she had, Cheryl needed to take full advantage of the situation.

"I think it's time we became legitimate." Cheryl could feel Billy tense at her words.

"What do you mean 'legitimate'?"

"Oh, for God's sake Billy, I don't mean marriage if that's what you're so afraid of. I mean I think it's time for you to leave your wife."

Billy loosened himself from her grip and sat up. "This is kind of sudden don't you think?"

"Sudden? Billy you're miserable, you have been since the day you married her, what the hell is there to keep you with her?"

"My children, I can't leave my kids."

"But Billy, we'll have our own kids someday."

Billy stood up quickly pulling on his pants. "It's not that simple Cheryl."

Cheryl watched him walk into the kitchen and take a beer from the fridge. "What's not that simple? Leaving her? You know you can't have it both ways Billy Freeman. Besides, I'm leaving Connecticut and I want you to go with me."

"Leaving, when?"

"Next June. I've been offered a job in Colorado once the summer starts, it's a good opportunity for me and I want to take it."

"But I'll be so far away from my kids."

"Oh Christ Billy, you forced me to get an abortion, you can't possibly love your kids that much if you had one of them killed."

Cheryl's words drew blood, he could feel the invisible trail trickle down his back and she took the knife and gave it a quick painful turn. Yes. He had killed one of his children, but it was just bad timing. He would never do that now.

Billy knelt beside her, "I'm sorry for that honey, I really am. I know how difficult that was for you."

"Do you?" A quick and unexpected tear fell from her eye as she recalled the moment when she knew her baby was gone, "I don't think you have any idea what I went through, what I have gone through for you. Now, I need you to do something for me, I need you to leave the life you insist makes you so unhappy and be with the person you've been fucking in secret for seven years."

The answer sat like a heavy lump in his throat. It was time to pay up. He knew the day would arrive sooner or later and certainly it would be the perfect way to finally get back at Eve and Justin for always making him feel like an outsider. He would still be able to see his kids, he was not insane or cruel, and since no one knew about Cheryl there wasn't a court in the world that would deny him the chance to be with his children.

Billy rested a hand on her creamy shoulder. "Give me time to work out the details...I promise we'll be together."

CHAPTER 52

Christmas in California arrived with little fanfare for Justin. He had promised to spend the day with Adele, but now that the day was upon him, he felt more inclined to spend it alone. The day was gray and cool and even the sea seemed upset as it pounded fiercely against the shore.

Justin realized that he could no longer live near the ocean she'd loved so much. In the weeks that followed Zoë's death, he could hear her voice in each wave that crashed onto the shore. Every inch of the home they'd shared reminded him of how alone he now was. He knew what he needed to do. He needed to seek refuge in the place he'd fled from so long ago; it was time to go home.

Adele's house was warm and filled with the scents of turkey and bread baking. He would miss the woman he'd become so fond of, and soon he would have to tell her. And, Justin would see to it that she would never have to worry about another thing as long as she lived.

Adele could see the pain on Justin's face when he arrived and she knew that Christmases were especially hard after the loss of a loved one. Gently, she rested an arm on his, "I'm glad you're here," she smiled.

"I am too, even though my first instinct was to hide beneath the covers all day."

"You know Justin, you will never stop missing her, but someday it will stop hurting when you do."

"I hope that someday comes very soon. I don't know how much longer I can take this."

"Everything reminds you of her doesn't it? It can be both a blessing and a curse. You want to surround yourself with her memory, at the same time it's a memory you almost can't stand to be around."

"That's it exactly." Justin hesitated for a moment, before he continued, "Adele, there's something I need to talk to you about."

"Why don't we sit down Justin, I take bad news better sitting down."

"How do you know it's bad?"

"Well, you're leaving aren't you? I call that bad news." Her lips curved into a secretive smile, patting his hand she continued, "I knew this day would come, you came here to try and forget Eve, you met Zoë, fell in love and now she's gone. You did what you came here to do, and God knows, you've been a blessing to me."

Adele sat down in her favorite chair, resting her weary hand on the worn arm rests.

"It's not just that, my father's health hasn't been the best as of late and I feel like I need to be there for both of them."

"Yes, you do Justin. You need to go home, but for now, you're here and it's Christmas and we need to celebrate and rejoice in all the things that have blessed us this past year."

"I am so thankful for Zoë."

"I know you are. So what happens when you return to Connecticut?"

"What do you mean?"

"Well, you were pretty lost when you arrived here. Will you be all right, I mean around Eve?"

Justin thought for a moment back to when he'd first left Connecticut and the pain he carried with him like an albatross around his neck.

"Yes," he said finally, "she's married and she has another life. But we will always be friends. Besides, I will probably live in New York City."

"Justin, if you don't mind me saying, I think Eve has feelings for you."

"I think Eve is just confused and her marriage is a bit rocky right now. I think Billy has the seven year itch or whatever you call it. But they'll be fine."

Adele looked down at the festive print of her dress. She didn't like to gossip, but she thought Eve was a remarkable woman and she felt in her heart that her marriage was far worse off than she had admitted to Justin.

"Justin, if you don't mind me saying, I get the impression that Billy is…well…cheating on her. I don't know what it is about him, but when he called here that day when you were in the hospital, he just gave me a bad feeling."

Justin ran a thoughtful hand through is hair, "I know Adele, I've been suspecting that too. I just hope they can survive it."

"They have to both want that."

"So, something smells good," Justin smiled, changing the course of their conversation. He worried about Eve, and having an outsider confirm his suspicions did nothing to alleviate his concern. Most importantly, he needed to stay out of it, especially since he would be near them again. He could not allow himself to get sucked into a situation that had been and always would be, hopeless.

"Justin, it's me Eve, I just wanted to call and wish you a very Merry Christmas. I know it's going to be tough for you this year, so if you need someone to talk to, just give me a call." Gently, Eve replaced the receiver, disappointed that she hadn't been able to speak with him.

The sounds of her children playing with their new toys drifted in from the living room. Eve stood by the telephone, listening to them play. They were the single joy in her life, the one thing that made all of what she was going through almost bearable. Since she'd returned home, Billy had been decidedly different, almost kind to her. Cordial in a way that was unfamiliar to her. It was almost as difficult to live with as his cruel words had been. Billy had inquired about Justin only once. The barrage of scornful words she'd been expecting, never manifested and she felt a strong sense that something was about to go terribly wrong.

Billy was spending less and less time at home with excuses varying from helping a friend, to coaching overtime and often, he wouldn't offer any excuses at all. Even this morning, he'd spent about an hour with the kids opening gifts and then dashed off muttering some excuse about a friend who needed his help. His lies were painfully transparent, and it was obvious that Billy no longer cared whether his reasons were accepted, even though Eve desperately wanted to believe them. She could feel her marriage crumbling beneath her, as if the ground would give way and she would fall into an abyss she feared more than anything. Eve wanted to tell Billy that she knew he was cheating on her and that it was all right as long as he didn't end their marriage. Frannie was giggling at something her brother did, and the sound of her voice tore Eve's heart in two. The children would never...suddenly, the phone rang. Eve prayed it was Billy, saying he'd be home soon, proving her fears unfounded.

"Hello?"

"Evie, it's me. How are you?"

Justin's voice sounded happy at the other end of the phone, and suddenly, she felt more alone than she had ever felt in her entire life.

"Fine, Jus, fine. How are you doing?"

"Oh, I'm ok, you know it's a difficult day, but I got your message and didn't want you to worry. Also, I have some news."

"Good I hope; I could use some good news right about now."

"Why? What's wrong?"

Eve started to tell him about Billy, but kept the secret to herself, not wanting to voice her fears aloud. It would only make it that much more real.

"Nothing…so what's your news?"

Justin did not believe her, but refrained from pushing the subject any further, "I'm moving back to the East Coast."

A flood of relief washed over her. He was coming home! Finally, Justin was coming home!

"Oh, Jus! I'm so happy, I can't even tell you. When? When are you moving?"

"Well, I'm going to call my broker next week and have him start looking for a place in Manhattan."

"New York? Why not Connecticut?"

Because, I still can't trust myself to be that close to you, he almost wanted to say. "I love the City and my publisher is there. Besides I'll still be closer than I am now."

"Thank God! Oh, Jus, I can't wait to have you around again."

"Well, it shouldn't be too much longer Bug. I'm looking forward to it too."

"Mom?" A small but strong voice said beside her. "Is that Daddy?"

"No, honey it's Uncle Justin. Do you want to say hi?"

Frannie nodded eagerly, tossing her curls as she did and taking the receiver from her mother, "Hi Uncle Justin! Thank you for the great Christmas presents. They were just what I wanted."

"You're welcome sweetheart, are you having a nice Christmas?"

"Uh, I just wish Daddy would hurry home."

"Well, I'm sure he'll be home soon."

"Ok, well, here's Mom again, bye Uncle Justin. Come and see us soon."

"I will honey, I promise."

Frannie handed the phone to her mother and raced back into the living room to see if her brother had touched any of her presents.

"Evie, you didn't tell me that Billy wasn't there. Where is he?" Justin said, irritated.

"Oh, he's helping someone fix something on their house."

"On Christmas?"

"Justin, please, let's not discuss this now."

"Are you all right?"

The caring in his voice brought the emotions to the surface and she had to fight off the tears that stung her eyes.

"Yes, I'm fine. Really I am."

Justin could hear the frailty in her voice and decided not to push it, he'd be back there soon enough and he'd have to set Billy straight once and for all.

When the conversation ended, the tears that she had so bravely fought off, fell from her eyes and she sank into a chair trying to regain herself before one of her children wandered in and saw her crying for her failed marriage.

CHAPTER 53

The apartment had been advertised as a trendy New York loft. But when Justin wandered the spacious rooms, he knew it was much more than that. The floors were all highly polished wood, expensive recessed lighting reflected off the walls and highlighted points where the previous owner had no doubt proudly displayed expensive works of art. Entering this apartment, Justin was immediately struck with the view captured by the floor to ceiling windows that ran the length of the living room wall. According to his broker, the prior owner had vacated quickly when his company relocated him, and consequently, he was eager to sell. There was a bedroom downstairs which, Justin noted, could easily be converted into an office. The upstairs bedroom took up the entire floor and the bathroom was carefully crafted to include a dual headed shower and Jacuzzi tub with a stunning view of Manhattan. Roof access was gained through the master bedroom and by the time Justin climbed the drop down staircase and looked out over the City, he knew he'd found his new home. He insisted escrow begin as quickly as possible and soon, he was moving into his new home.

It felt good to be back. Better than he'd expected it would and it was at that moment, as he walked briskly through the streets of New York, that he realized how much he had missed everything about the East Coast, even the weather. It was nearing February and a chilled wind whipped around the tall buildings, ruffling hair and playing with the edges of jackets and scarves. At this hour, the streets of New York were teeming with people heading to work. He had been back for exactly one week now, and already it felt as though he'd never left. He quickly slipped back into the life he had loved for so long. The first thing on his agenda for the day was to meet with his agent who had flown out to see him and discuss the final book in his extraordinary series of *King's Town*. Justin was almost sad that he would have to give his most beloved character a rest, but he knew too that it was time. The *King's Town* series had achieved the kind of success he never imagined it would. As he passed a Barnes & Noble, he saw a stack of his books on a tower designated as "The *King's Town*" section. It still thrilled and amazed him to see people buying his books. Justin planned to head out to Candlewood Lake that afternoon to visit his parents and stop in to see Eve and Billy. He hoped to get Billy alone, but knew better than to push anything so he would play it by ear. Still, he was determined to get to the bottom of whatever was going on, even though he knew it was really none of his business.

When Justin arrived at the train station, his parents were waiting for him. Even though he had insisted he would take a cab, they would never hear of it.

"Darling it's so wonderful to see you! Your father and I are so happy to have you home." His mother embraced him, holding on to her son tightly.

"Welcome home son," Karl VanSant smiled. He too was thrilled to have his son much closer to them.

Justin embraced him next. "How are you feeling Pop?" he inquired.

"Oh, I'm fine, you're mother exaggerates."

"I don't exaggerate, your father has not been himself recently and his doctor wants him to check into the hospital for more tests." Mary said, walking ahead of them to their car.

"Is that right, Dad? Why haven't you done that?"

"Because, it's not necessary. I'm fine, I really am." Karl opened his wife's door.

"You've not been feeling well and you know it," she said as she slid into the seat.

"Well, enough of this talk, our son is home, Mary. We should be celebrating."

"We'll talk more about this later," Justin said as he got into their car.

His father grunted as he got behind the wheel and drove toward their home.

❖ ❖ ❖

Later that afternoon, Justin borrowed his parents' car and headed off to visit Eve and Billy. Not to his surprise unfortunately, he found that Eve was home by herself, preparing an afternoon snack for her children. He could see her through the kitchen window as he walked up to their house and for a moment, his heart stopped. Every now and again, the feelings he'd hidden for years would rage to the surface, letting him know they were still there. Gone perhaps, but not forgotten.

"Justin!" Eve flung the door open, letting herself fall into his arms. "It's so good to have you back."

"Uncle Justin, Uncle Justin!" Nick squealed, running through the hall. Justin scooped him up in his arms and wrestled him to the floor in a bear hug. "Hello Nicky, how are you?" Before the little boy could answer, his sister raced up to greet him as well.

"Hello Uncle Justin, Mom said you moved back here, can we come visit you?"

Justin sat up to kiss her on the cheek as Nicholas squirmed to free himself. "Yes, you both can come visit me anytime you like."

"Now you two go eat your apples, Mommy and Uncle Justin want to talk for a moment."

Both children obeyed without question and headed for the living room where their peeled and cut apples and an episode of *Bugs Bunny* were awaiting them.

"So, Jus, how does it feel to be home?"

"Like I never left. It feels great Eve, I can't even tell you." Justin followed Eve into the kitchen. "So, where's Billy?"

"At work."

"It's freezing outside, a little cold to be doing construction isn't it?"

"I don't know;, they're doing something I guess. It's hard to keep track."

"Eve, what's going on?"

Eve pulled two mugs from the cupboard and turned a weary eye to her friend, "Justin, everything is fine, I told you."

"I thought we could tell each other everything."

"We can, and I would tell you if something was up, I really would. He's just a little distracted that's all. Ever since…"

"Ever since what Eve?"

"Ever since I got back from California he's been almost too nice, but not like a husband, more, I don't know…like a roommate or something."

"Why do you think that is?"

"I have no idea, I mean he was so upset that I stayed behind to find you and then when I got back, I expected a huge fight but he said nothing about it. Except to briefly ask how you were."

Justin thought for a moment, gently fingering the cup in front of him. "Do you want me to talk to him?"

A puff of air escaped her lips. "Are you kidding? I appreciate it, really I do, but I think he would take offense to it. You know how threatened he feels by you."

"Well, look, I wanted to run something by you anyway. I was thinking of inviting Billy into the City for a guy's night out kind of a thing. I want to try and mend fences with him you know, we've really grown apart, and maybe I can find out what's up with him too."

Eve shrugged her shoulders. "I don't know if he'll agree to it, he seems to think you're the enemy for some reason. But you can ask him. I would really love it if the two of you could be friends again."

Justin placed a hand over hers not mistaking the longing look in her eyes. "It will never be like it was, Eve. That time is gone."

"I know Jus, but everything was so great then. What the hell happened? What happened to us?" Eve held his eyes with her own. For a moment, Justin wasn't sure what she meant. Us? There was no us, never an us, always a them. Eve and Billy happily ever after. Married. End of story. Gently he slipped his hand off hers. Touching her brought it all back.

Finally, he answered her. "Time has a way of changing everything."

"I miss it. I miss all of it."

"I miss it too sometimes, but look at what we've become."

"Look at what you've become Jus, you're a world renowned author, but what am I? A housewife who hasn't slept with her husband in over a year." Her voice dropped to a barely audible whisper.

Tempting fate, Justin reached for her hands. "This is just a rough spot in your marriage that's all. It will get better, I promise it will."

Eve wrapped her hands around his, wanting desperately to believe him. But she knew in her heart that everything had already gone far beyond her control.

🍁 🍁 🍁

"Justin, honey, do you really think it's a good idea for you to get involved in their marriage like this?"

Justin paced the kitchen like a nervous cat, but he knew his mother was right. In a matter of hours he had already become intertwined with Eve's life again.

"It's just an evening out with the boys," Justin said trying to remain light-hearted.

"No, it's not and you know it. Look, I've been living here all this time while you've been gone and I caution you not to get into the middle of this."

Justin stopped his pacing for a moment and turned to his mother, her voice filled with considerable intensity.

"What do you mean?"

"I don't like gossip, you know that. But I hear things, you can't help it in this town."

"Tell me what you hear." It was more of an insistence than a request.

"Justin," she began reluctantly, "Billy's been seen around, at bars with some woman, a Cheryl I believe. She used to be a cheerleader. I think that's how they met. Anyway, a while back, several years in fact, Cheryl told Bernice that she was pregnant and that she couldn't say who the father was because he was married." Mary could see her son suck in his breath in one sharp, painful inhale.

"Where's the child now?" He slumped into a seat, anger and sadness engulfed him at the same time.

He watched as his mother fumbled nervously with the edge of the placemat. "There was never a baby. Cheryl disappeared for several days and returned, when Bernice inquired about the child, Cheryl broke into tears and never discussed it again."

"That son of a bitch!" Justin fumed.

"Look, we don't know for certain that it was his child, but like I said, they've been seen around."

"Does Eve know?"

"Not unless she's seen them together, no one has had the heart to tell her."

"You mean that this whole goddamned town knows and no one has had the guts to tell her?"

"Don't get involved in this Justin, you should not be the one to tell her."

"I cannot allow Billy to continue to make a fool of her."

"He's not, he's only making a fool of himself. Eve is a lovely woman, she deserves better than him, and eventually the truth will come out."

"Ma, why the hell am I now just hearing about this?"

"Because I knew if I told you, you'd feel obligated to say something. Now that you're back I'm certain you would have found out sooner or later. I wanted to be the one to tell you and also caution you not to say anything to her. If we're wrong then we've ruined a marriage, if we're not then she'll find out eventually."

"Ma, I can't let her find out 'eventually,' as her friend I owe her at least that."

"As her friend, or as someone who has loved her his entire life?" The memory that her words carried hung between them, solid and unyielding.

Mary's eyes filled with sympathy, as she continued, "Honey, I have watched you live in pain because of your love for her ever since I can remember. I was so thankful when you found Zoë. But now that she's gone, my fear is that through your grief, you're going to hang on to the distant hope that you can have some kind of future with Eve."

Her words sliced like a knife in his chest, reopening all the old wounds again.

"I know I can't Ma, I just cannot let anyone hurt her."

"She has to find her own way Justin, if she and Billy are destined to separate, she has to be the one to decide that. If you try to help her with this you will only end up her enemy."

Justin knew his mother was right. As difficult as it would be to step away, he needed to let Eve continue to fend for herself.

CHAPTER 54

"Billy, I'm serious now. I need you to know that I am leaving here with or without you." Cheryl paced through her kitchen annoyed by the hint of trepidation she saw in his eyes.

Billy sat at her kitchen table, fingering his wedding ring.

"Billy?"

"What?"

"Are you coming to Colorado with me or not?" Cheryl pinned him with her stare.

Billy let out a nervous sigh. "I told you I was going."

"Well, it doesn't look that way from here. When are you planning to tell her?"

"In a couple of days, the night before we leave. I tell her and then I'm gone, all right?" Her persistence was annoying him.

Cheryl dropped herself into a chair opposite him. "I'm sorry baby," she began, her lips forming a glossy pout, "it's just that we've been talkin' about this for so long and now that it's here, it just…it just seems so unreal." A red painted fingernail fingered the top button of her blouse, setting it loose. Then, another. Billy watched as Cheryl began to expose her naked breasts.

"Wanna celebrate hon?" she began, her voice filled with sex. In a moment, she was walking around the table in her alley cat pace. Billy's eyes filled with lust for her, her breasts firm and bouncing. Quickly he grabbed her and filled his mouth with one, momentarily forgetting the reprehensible task that stood ahead of him.

❦ ❦ ❦

Billy sat on the pier, overlooking Candlewood Lake. The weekend crowd had arrived and even in this early morning hour, they filled the lake with boats, inner tubes and fishing gear. It promised to be a spectacular weekend. Billy knew it was time to head back to the house.

In one graceful movement, he was up on his feet, walking steadily back across the pier, through the woods and back to the house.

It was time.

❦ ❦ ❦

Eve sat beside her husband as they drove to Amici's for dinner. She had been looking forward to this evening out since he'd suggested it several days before. Eve left her window open and the warm June air played with the tendrils of hair that fell from her chignon. It was a glorious evening and she was hopeful that Billy's attentiveness in recent days was an indication that their marriage was once again on track.

The restaurant was filled with people, tourists mostly, as Eve and Billy wove their way through the hum of voices. Their table was in a secluded area of the restaurant, dimly lit by a candle and faint ambient lighting. Billy held out his wife's chair and Eve let herself sink into the supple leather. Billy quickly ordered a bottle of their favorite wine and Eve knew that after tonight, things would be different. Their marriage would be back on track. After dinner, Billy suggested that they take a walk by the lake.

The lake was virtually abandoned at this time of night as Eve and Billy strolled through the woods near Chatterton Point. Boats bobbed quietly on the dark water and the round yellow moon lit their path. Eve took Billy's hand in hers, slipping her fingers between his own.

"Eve, we need to talk," Billy began, his voice soft and low.

"Yes, I think you're right. Billy, this evening has been great, it was wonderful of you to suggest it."

Billy pulled his hand from her grip, thrusting his hands deep into his pockets.

"Look, I brought you out here to tell you something Evie."

In the distance, she could hear an owl coo in the night air. The tone of Billy's voice made her heart skip in cautious dread, as if something bad were about to happen.

"What?" she asked, not really wanting the answer.

"Eve, it's over between us. I'm moving out tomorrow." The words, once out of his mouth, hit her with such a force she fell back, almost tripping on a tree stump.

"What?!"

"I'm leaving you. It's over. It has been for a long time; you and I both know that. It's better this way."

"Says who?" Eve tried to catch up with the thread of the conversation, but her thoughts tumbled over each other in a disarray of confusion.

Billy turned from her, facing the lake, hands still thrust into his pockets. "Don't kid yourself Eve, you would never admit to this. One of us has to be the strong one."

"The strong one?! What's so strong about leaving?"

Seconds stretched, heavy and obtrusive. Finally, he responded, his voice filled with impatience: "It's the way it has to be."

"Don't I have any say in this?" Eve bristled at his words and reached a shaky hand out to his arm, which he shrugged off.

"No Eve, it's just over. I don't want to rehash this, I don't want to have endless discussions about it. It's just the way it has to be."

"Who is she?" The shadow shrouded leaves above her head rustled in the warm wind that gently brushed her face.

"Come on Eve, don't do this to yourself."

"Do what? Learn the truth? I deserve at least that much don't you think?"

"It's no one you know."

As his words reached her ears, she felt the trees almost sway around her. The air was devoid of oxygen and Eve inhaled what she could of it, in painful stolen gulps clenching and unclenching her fists to keep her fingertips from trembling in fear and rage and pain and the deep down ragged hold of betrayal. She imagined the sensation of punching him, of taking him down, of leaving black and blue marks on each place on his body that touched the other woman. But then, her fists unclenched and all she could feel was the tired sigh whispering down her body. His betrayal hollowed her out like a reed, scraping her insides clean and empty. Winner take all.

"You bastard! Get out! Get the hell out of here, leave tonight! Do you hear me, before I go pick the kids up from my mother's I want you gone, go be with your whore whoever the fuck she is and leave us be!"

Billy turned to leave, obviously grateful that the conversation had ended. He tossed her the car keys and they hit the ground with a muffled thud. Eve fell to her knees to pick them up. Then, she let herself cry, not in empty gasping sobs, or a release of passion, but simply a stream of tears running from her eyes, down her face, down her neck, into her blouse. Beneath her hands, she could feel a million blades of grass and dirt, and her fingers dug into the soil. She looked up and already Billy was gone. Vanished into the trees. Eve fell into a ball on the ground, wiping tears from her face, leaving smudges of dirt. She lay beneath the trees in the quiet forest; the only sound to be heard was a faint whimper as she huddled to the ground wondering what would happen to her life and her children from this day forward.

Billy watched Eve from behind a thick tree. He waited until he saw her get up, and head toward their car. Then he sprinted through the woods, heading for Cheryl's house.

Eve forced a worn key into the lock and with a click, the door opened, creaking into the darkened hallway. She stood for a moment, fingernails caked with dried bits of dirt, streaks of it still smudged on her face. She fought back the bitter fury that threatened to consume her and gently clicked the door shut again. Eve dropped herself onto her porch swing and it too creaked as it rocked back and forth. A chilled wind whipped through the trees and the moon disappeared behind a thick mass of clouds. A plump raindrop splashed down, then another, darting the pavement, echoing from the surface before settling into pools on the ground. A loud and violent rumble then shook the sky and a streak of lightening tore through it, burning through the night air. It was altogether too appropriate, she thought as she gently swung back and forth while the rain pelted down around her.

Where had it gone, her dream of a perfect marriage? When had she let the denial of it all slip past her, numbing her to the fact that their relationship was over? She had buried herself in the monotonous tasks of her daily existence. After all, there was a house to be cleaned, children to be cared for, crusts to be cut off sandwiches and empty boxes of cookies to be discarded. All of it seemed trivial and silly in the light of the fact that somehow, in the midst of life itself, she'd lost her husband to someone who had probably never wiped a tiny snot-filled nose in her life.

Billy sat beside Cheryl as the plane lifted up into the air. She reached for his hand, but he pulled away, folding his arms across his chest, his gaze fixed on the window and the landscape that rushed by. He couldn't help what he was feeling, despite the woman sitting besides him who had cried happy tears when he'd pulled up in front of her house the night before.

He had wanted to say goodbye to his children, he wanted to know that Eve was all right. Despite the fact that he was no longer in love with her, he still cared about her. They'd shared so much over the many years; it would not just vanish at the end of a failed marriage. Billy wondered for a moment if he had ever loved her. Maybe for a fleeting moment, during a warm summer afternoon spent at the lake long ago. He began to negotiate with himself that he had loved her, however short-lived it may have been. At least, it made him feel somewhat less sinister. And he had stuck; he had stayed and been decent to her. In the end, all he could do was bargain with his guilty conscious that he had done all he could to make their marriage work.

Eve spent a sleepless night tossing and turning and begging for sleep to take her. But it never did. Instead, she couldn't stop herself from replaying every moment of their life together. The clock on the wall was merely a marker, a faint ticktock warning of the impending dawn of a day that would force her to face what had happened to her life.

The morning was filled with the scent of fresh rain, as Eve headed downstairs, she could smell it teasing the air. Eve brewed a pot of strong coffee and tried to gather herself before heading to her mother's house to pick up her children. She wondered where Billy was at that very moment. Then, the thought of him with that other woman made her want to retch. Would he want to see his children? Would he want to…. Suddenly, Eve was pulled from her thoughts by the ringing of the telephone.

"Hello?" She began, trying to hide the exhaustion in her voice.

"Eve, it's me, Billy."

She was silent, her heart filled with the hope that he had changed his mind. That it had been some unbelievable misunderstanding, he just needed time to think, that was all. Time away and time to think….

"Eve?" He said again. A voice in the background doing a flight announcement was a sharp reminder that it was not some big mistake. It had happened. It was happening. Billy was gone. Their marriage was over.

"Yes, I'm here."

"Eve, look, I'm headed out of town for a few days, but I'll be back so we can tell the children together."

"What? You want me to wait? What for?"

"Well, I was hoping we could. I think they should hear it from both of us."

"Since when are you an authority on what they need?"

"Look, Eve the way I see it, we can do this one of two ways. We can hate each other and drag the kids through a painful divorce and a town filled with gossip or, we can be civil to one another."

"You seem to forget, I am still reeling from your not-so-civil announcement less than twenty-four hours ago, so forgive me if I still hate you right this very moment!" Her voice cracked like ice.

"Look, Eve, I'm sorry, I just hate having those kinds of discussions."

"Right, so you want me to then wait and have you tell the kids so you can leave them crying in the dirt too?"

"Eve, I didn't mean for it to happen like that, I really didn't. I was worried about you."

A puff of air escaped her lips, sounding almost like a sarcastic laugh.

Eve coiled the phone cord around her hand, feeling the curved edges dig into her flesh. "Yeah, you were worried all right."

"Eve, look, are you gonna be ok?

"What the fuck do you care? You've got your girlfriend there with you no doubt, while I'm left here to pick up the pieces. The least you could have done was stick around for a day or two to make sure I don't slit my wrists."

"That's not funny."

"Good, it wasn't supposed to be you smug bastard."

Eve could hear him inhale an impatient breath. "So are you going to wait for me or what? I'll be back in a couple days as soon as we get, uh, I mean I get settled."

"Billy, don't try to spare my feelings now ok? I know you left me to be with her, whoever the hell she is. So why not say it? Until we get settled, we, we, we!!"

"Look, maybe this isn't the best time to talk. I'll call you later."

The line went dead in her hand, Eve dropped the phone and her hands covered her face to catch the tears that were already pouring from her eyes.

❧ ❧ ❧

Eve parked in front of her parents' home. Gripping the door latch, she inhaled deeply and then walked across the lawn and past her mother's graceful shrubbery to fetch her children. Her demeanor was calm, her smile ever-present. She would not tell her mother, she would not tell her father and she certainly would not tell her children that their father had left to live out his days with some whore. She would go about her day, and her life, God willing as if nothing had ever happened. She clenched and unclenched her fists, willing her hands to stop shaking; she wore her mask of indifference like a proud token that she had survived the night. Now she knew, she could survive anything. Sucking in a shaky breath, she pushed open the front door.

"Frannie, Nicky!" Eve called, and suddenly she realized how much she needed to see them. How much she needed to reaffirm that her life would continue. That it had to. The children raced to her, throwing their soft little arms around her neck. If she ever doubted her reason for living in the last twelve hours, she was reminded of it now. The sweetness of their hair, the scent of their skin that blended with the sugary smell of Coco Puffs still on their breath.

Eve held them both for a long time.

"How was your evening dear?" her mother asked, watching her in the hallway.

"Fine, Mom. We had a nice time." The words tore through her, but once they slipped painfully past her lips she felt confident that she could lie with the best of them. Nobody needed to know, no one would ever know.

Taking their bags, Eve ushered Nicholas and Frannie through the door. "Thanks again Mom!" she called over her shoulder.

Judith waved goodbye to her daughter and grandchildren. As she watched Eve place her children in their car seats, she couldn't help but sense that something was terribly wrong.

"How about we go for a picnic today?" Eve asked, Nicholas and Frannie cheering in unison. Eve was determined to make their day special, to make every day special for her babies. Despite their absentee father.

"Is Daddy going with us?" Frannie asked.

Eve swallowed the lump in her throat, “No honey, Daddy had to go on a trip for a few days, but he’ll be back soon.”

“I wanna see Daddy!” Nicholas’ voice shot out from the back seat, piercing her heart. “You’ll see him honey, just not today. We’re going to have a lot of fun aren’t we?”

They both uttered a desultory “ok”, and for the moment Eve’s eggshell heart breathed a sigh of relief.

The day had been better than she’d expected. They’d played in the park, ate hot dogs, candied apples and fresh lemonade. Every now and again the image of Billy and some faceless woman would dash through her mind but she quickly pushed them aside. Each time forcing them farther and farther away.

CHAPTER 55

That night brought very little relief. Eve fought off the urge to call Justin. She knew he would drop whatever he was doing and rush to her side. And while that would have been a great comfort to her, this was something she needed to work out for herself. God willing, it would be at least a few more days until everyone in town knew. But Eve doubted that she could keep her secret for much longer than that. She ran a hand across her throbbing temples, the headache from the night before had not subsided and her eyes still burned from the tears she'd cried into her pillow. It was all too horrible, the fear of being alone rattled through her. Eve pushed back the covers and went to take a long, hot shower before the children woke up.

Around her, daylight was breaking through the night sky, announcing another day. Today she would have to tell her parents, she could not put it off any longer. What Eve did not realize was that word of her breakup was already spreading through town faster than a winter flu outbreak.

It was barely 8 a.m. when the phone shrilled to life. The sound of it filled the kitchen and bounced off the bright walls. Judith picked it up on the second ring.

"Hello?"

"Judy, Bernice here. I just wanted to call you to say how sorry I am and I can't believe you didn't tell any of us. Well, I suppose it's none of our business, but still we're your friends dear, if you can't tell us, well then who can you tell?"

"Tell you what?"

A puff of air escaped Bernice's lips and pushed through the phone. "Well, about Eve and Billy of course, honey I tell you, I couldn't be sorrier. Eve deserves a whole hell of a lot better than to be left for some ex-cheerleader."

The words didn't make sense to her at first and Judy wondered if Bernice had taken to drinking. She twirled the phone cord around her fingers again and again, pulling it till she felt it tighten, then in one movement, let it go, the cool plastic snapping against the palm of her skin.

"I-I, don't know what you're talking about Bernice. Eve and Billy are just fine."

"Oh, honey, I'm so sorry, I thought you knew, I thought for sure Evie would have said something to you. Oh, gosh the poor thing must be embarrassed, well she has no reason to be, I…."

Suddenly, it all clicked into place. The sound of Eve's voice the night she called to say she wouldn't pick the children up 'till morning. Then, her demeanor when she arrived at the house. Her eyes swollen and red, Eve had insisted it was her allergies acting up again.

"Bernie, I-I have to go…please don't tell anyone else about this."

Before Bernie could respond, the phone went dead.

Judith sank into the chair beside the phone. If the ladies at the Grand Union were talking about it, no doubt so was everyone else in New Fairfield. She knew she needed to get over to see her daughter quickly and find out what was going on.

♣ ♣ ♣

"Eve, I don't understand, I mean how could you not tell me about this?"

Eve wrapped her pale hands around the warm mug of coffee for comfort. "I'm sorry Mom, I just wanted a little more time. Billy's supposed to come back today and we're going to tell the children."

"You mean Nicky and Frannie still don't know their father's left them?"

"Ssh, Mom, please, they'll hear you. No, they don't know and I want to wait for Billy to arrive to tell them."

"Why? Because you think maybe he'll change his mind?"

Eve could not answer, but the truth of it cracked her heart even further. If there was a chance, any chance at all that he would come back and they could save their marriage she wanted to take it. She could forgive him his indiscretion, she'd have to. For the children she'd have to.

Judith leaned into her daughter, covering her hands, "Eve listen, I know you want this marriage to work, but if he's met someone else you're going to have to let him go."

Eve's eyes filled with surprise. "You know about her."

Judith could only nod. "Honey, I'm afraid everyone knows."

Eve felt the rattle of her mother's words shake her to her core. Everyone knew, she thought, everyone.

"Well," she said finally, her voice heavy with exhaustion, "so much for keeping this a family secret."

"If you're worried about the town talking, they'll get over it, they always do. Besides, you're the victim here and if there's one thing this community does is stick together."

"I don't want to be pitied, Mother. And I can't let the children grow up without a father. I don't know what I'll do."

"What does Justin say about all of this? I bet he's madder than hell at Billy."

"He doesn't know yet."

"Eve, you've got to tell him, you don't want him finding out from someone else...."

"Mom, I'm really sorry you had to hear about it this way, but I can't tell Justin, he'll run to my rescue and I really need to work through this myself right now."

"Ok, but New Fairfield is a small town. He'll find out soon enough."

"I know, Mom, I'll tell him soon I promise. Now, I just have to tell Daddy."

"I'll tell him, you've had enough pressure on you today. Now, why don't you let me take the kids with me so you can have some time to yourself."

"No, Mom, Billy will be here this afternoon and I want him to see his children."

"Don't force him to stay honey, if he really wants to go."

Eve's breath was ragged with pain and her eyes seemed to vanish behind her welled up tears. "Mom, what's wrong with me, what did I do to make him want to leave me?"

Judith felt her daughter's pain rip through her, the need to be loved and the feeling of desperation when she wasn't.

"Honey, you didn't do anything. Some men just can't help themselves, his father cheated on Victoria, maybe it's just in his genes to do this. You were everything a wife should be so don't blame yourself."

Eve bit her bottom lip so hard, she tasted blood. The warm trickle was salty on her tongue. The salt of the earth. That's what Justin had called her once. A solid woman, someone real. That's what he'd said. It seemed a lifetime ago. Sometimes, it even seemed as though it had been someone else's life. The tears that filled her eyes now spilled down onto her cheeks, mixing with the blood on her lip.

"Mom, you know, Justin and I have always been the best of friends. Billy never understood that, he never understood this bond that Justin and I have. Billy didn't want me to spend time with Jus, but I had to…."

"Are you trying to say that's why Billy cheated, because he was jealous of your friendship with Justin? Why the three of you have always been friends."

"No, not those two, not for a while. Ever since…well, for a while, they've been at odds." In the midst of her sorrow, Eve could not bring herself to bring up the death of her child. She knew the mere mention of it would certainly kill her.

"Eve, honey, I don't understand, but I don't think this has anything to do with Justin," her mother soothed.

Eve sucked in a shaky breath, a sigh that curled inward. Absentmindedly, she pushed a strand of hair from her cheek and knew it was time to face the ultimate truth. Outside, the sun filled the summer sky with its warmth, the heat of it leaking through her kitchen window and breathing onto her neck.

"This is how we die," she said quietly. "Life keeps us breathless for years until we simply pass out."

♣ ♣ ♣

Billy drove his rented car down the familiar street. He'd been circling in the vicinity for a while now. He knew he needed to get this over with, but no matter how much he wanted to be with Cheryl, he wanted to be with his family too. Finally, Billy inched down his street. From a distance, he could see his daughter sitting on the porch swing with Eve, gently rocking back and forth. Nicholas was playing under the sprinklers. For a moment, everything seemed perfect. As though their lives hadn't been shattered only a few short days before. His son caught a glimpse of him first; pointing a soaking wet finger in his direction.

"Dad!" he cried, jumping up and down on the wet grass, sending splashes of water everywhere. Eve felt her heart stop, her hand tightened around the glass of lemonade she was holding and beside her, Frannie hopped off the swing, sending it rocking backward. She was already moving as soon as her feet hit the wooden porch.

"Daddy, Daddy!" she called out behind Nicholas. Eve spotted the car, which slowed to a stop in front of their house. Billy emerged, smiling as his children ran into his arms and Eve forced back a sob.

If anyone had been watching, they would have seemed like the perfect family. And perhaps they were, once.

Before life's unmerciful claws seized them and ripped them apart.

✦ ✦ ✦

Mary VanSant had heard the news of Billy's indiscretions and was not surprised that at last, his actions caught up with him. She felt only sorrow for Eve and the children and hoped that soon the gossip would stop and they could begin to find peace in their new life.

Mary was sitting at her husband's desk when the phone rang, it was Justin.

"Mom, hi, how are you?"

"I'm good honey, how is everything with you?"

"Fine, I just wanted to give you a quick call and let you know that I won't be able to make it for dinner Saturday, I'm headed out of town."

"Really? Where are you going?" she said, trying to hide the disappointment in her voice.

"A research meeting I had scheduled got rescheduled and I really have to take it. I'll be in Rome for two weeks."

"Two weeks! My goodness that's an awful long time isn't it?"

"Well, I'm doing some pretty extensive work for my next book and unfortunately, the person I need to work with had a last minute change of plans."

"Well, then you go dear and enjoy yourself. I hear Italy is beautiful this time of year," Mary said thoughtfully. It was small talk, she missed her son and wished she could see more of him, but perhaps it was better that he was headed out of town right now.

"So, how's everything going there, anything new going on?"

Mary thought for a long moment about what she should say, "No," she lied, "nothing's really happening here."

"Well, good to hear everything is status quo, look tell Dad I said hi and I'll be by the minute I get home…with any luck it won't take the full two weeks."

"All right dear, well, we love you and have a safe journey."

"I will Mom, love you too, bye."

The receiver went dead in her hand. Mary placed it carefully back on its cradle and wondered if she had done the right thing. If she'd told Justin about Eve and Billy, he would have no doubt forgone his own needs and rushed to her side. That was probably exactly what Eve needed right now, but she wasn't altogether certain it's what was right for Justin. He'd spent enough time pining for her. And if she ended up mending things with Billy, he'd certainly be devastated again. Justin had had enough loss in his life without having to face it again.

❧ ❧ ❧

"Well," Billy began, sinking into a kitchen chair, "I think that went well."

Eve stepped into the darkening room as the evening collapsed around them. She could still hear her children's cries and pleas to their father not to leave as she sent them to their bedrooms.

"I'm not sure I agree with your definition of 'going well,'" she sighed, sitting across the table from him.

"Look, I didn't expect them to be excited about it, but now at least we can begin to move on."

Billy's words pierced her heart yet again. "Yes, and you can't wait to have this entire thing over with so you can move on to your new piece of ass."

"That's not true Eve, I want to do what's right." Billy pushed back his chair, walking over to the refrigerator, he opened it, reached for a bottle of beer and pushed off the lid.

"If you wanted to do what was right you would have never left us, Billy."

"It wasn't working Eve, we've had this discussion before; it hasn't worked for a long time."

"According to you. I thought we were fine, but if you have to tell yourself we weren't to make yourself feel less guilty then by all means. I was a horrible wife, lousy in bed and just a downright bitch."

"Eve, please, we don't have to do this." Billy dropped himself back into his chair when really, the only thing he wanted to do was take his beer and leave.

"Do what Billy?! Talk about what happened? You take me to dinner and announce that you're leaving me with no further explanation? What the hell is that?"

"You know I'm not very good at this, Eve."

"Well, damn it, this is our marriage we're talking about." Warily, Eve pushed herself up. Her hands shook and she felt as though she were going to be sick. Outside the sky screamed a bright orange and purple. She leaned against the cool porcelain of the sink, holding herself up.

"You don't have to go, we can still make this work..." her voice was barely an audible whisper, "don't go, I can't do this alone...." Her tears came in a flood of emotion that drained from her eyes. "Please..." she whispered in a vulnerable voice, and then she began to sob.

"Please, Eve, don't do this. It's just gonna' make it harder." Billy threw back the last of the beer, shoving his chair behind him he went over to where she stood. A hand floated over her shaking shoulder and finally, rested there.

Eve turned and buried her face in his chest. "Billy, please, we can make this work, I'll do whatever it takes."

"Eve, look, it's not that simple. I-I'm in love with someone else, I'm so sorry. I wish it wasn't this way, but it is. I wish I could stay here and be near my kids, but I can't."

A heartbeat fluttered, followed by the gentle crashing sound of her heart breaking again.

Billy rested his head on her soft, sweet-smelling hair. Of all the things he would remember about their time together, he was certain he would never forget that. The sweet scent of her hair, it was one of the first things he'd noticed about her when they met all those years ago.

"I have to go," he whispered.

Eve held herself up against the sink as he walked through their kitchen and out of their door.

It shut behind him with a force he had not intended. She watched him leave in the dark. A shutter shot gaze, one tiny movie frame of her life inserted in the mass of frames that had proceeded it and all that would presumably follow. Suddenly, this was what it came down to, a moment in time; a brief glimpse of a future in which the movie before her projected her life onto the screen; silent, lonely and terrifying.

CHAPTER 56

It felt good to be back home, Justin thought as he maneuvered his car through the narrow streets surrounding the lake. With the top down, the warm summer air curled around him, welcoming him back. He planned to join his parents for lunch, but first he needed to make a quick stop. Justin pulled his car into Finley's Sweet Shoppe. The rusted bell still tinkled softly over the door as he entered. Lloyd Finley moved from his back room where Justin could hear the faint sounds of "*The Price Is Right*," playing in the background.

"Why, Justin, what brings you here?"

"I'm headed over to my parents house for lunch and thought I would bring something for dessert, what have you got?"

Lloyd smiled over his thin glasses. Reaching into a cabinet, he pulled out a plate filled with mounds of uneven chocolate. "How about hazelnuts covered in chocolate?" Lloyd picked one off the plate and handed it to him.

Justin let the sweetness of the chocolate melt across his tongue. "Mr. Finley, this is awesome, why not give me a pound of it."

Lloyd smiled and began measuring off the chocolates.

"So, I've been out of town for a couple of weeks, what's new around here?" Justin asked, swallowing the last of the candy.

"Well, not much I have to say." Lloyd tied the chocolate up with a fine gold ribbon he saved for his special orders, "'course, it is sad about Eve and Billy now 'tisn't it?"

"What do you mean, what happened?" Justin frowned.

"You mean, you didn't hear? I thought someone would have said something to you, you being so close to them and all." Lloyd rang up Justin's order. "Five even son."

Justin pulled a single bill from his pocket. "I have no idea what you're talking about."

"Billy left her, going on several weeks now I guess. He left town with that cheerleader girl. Real sordid lot if you ask me, but who's to say, maybe it's for the best."

Lloyd had barely finished his sentence when Justin rushed out the door, muffling a brief "thank you" for the chocolate and raced to Eve's house.

Eve was reading at her kitchen table when Justin came racing up the walkway. Frannie was at a friend's house and Nicholas was playing quietly in the living room. Slowly, her life was beginning to show signs of normalcy. She and the children had settled into a routine, not all that different from when Billy was around. She would take them to camp in the morning, pick them up in the afternoon. During the day she would clean, or sew, or work at some other busy project that kept her mind from wandering. Justin bound up the front porch steps, not even taking a moment to announce himself, he pushed through her front door and raced into the kitchen, startling Eve.

"Justin! What are you doing here? What's wrong?" The pained look on Justin's face was obvious, and she almost knew instinctively what he was about to say.

"I can't believe you didn't tell me, Eve."

"I'm sorry Justin…." She walked over to him, wrapping him with her arms. For a moment, she felt as though she would begin to cry again, then she caught herself, with the same core of bravery she'd found about a week ago. Hidden there, deep within her psyche, was the will to go on.

"Why didn't you say something Evie, I could have helped you, I could have been there for you." Justin pushed her back, staring deep into her eyes.

"I-I needed to see my way through this, by myself, before I could bring you into it. And for a while, I really didn't believe that he meant it."

Justin pulled back a chair for her, holding the corner of her arm, he settled her into it. Then, he pulled a chair for himself, pushing it close to hers.

"So, where is he now?" Justin asked gently.

Eve ran a nervous tongue across her lips, "Colorado."

"Colorado! What the hell is he doing there?"

Eve raised a finger to her lips, nodding in the direction of the living room. "That's where she is I guess, Cheryl is her name or whatever. According to what I've heard he's been seeing her for a long time. Years in fact. I had no idea…no idea Jus, do you know how stupid I felt? I suspected it, I did, but I ignored it. The whole time, I thought it was just my imagination."

Justin ran a hand down the length of her face, catching a stray tear with his thumb, "You shouldn't feel bad, you had no way of knowing. I can't believe he did this. I really can't." Justin could feel his heart burning with an anger he hadn't known since Zoë died.

"Neither can I, the children have no grasp of this. They keep asking for him, I've run out of things to tell them. As their mother, I want them to know the truth, but how can I tell them their father cheated on us? That isn't fair to a child."

"Are they in the living room?"

"Nick is, Frannie is out."

"I need to see them…" Justin said abruptly.

"Where's my main man?" Justin called as he walked through the hallway.

"Uncle Justin!" Nicholas was running with his head down, ready to tackle. Justin knelt down and embraced him.

Justin stayed longer than he should have, sharing some of his Finley's chocolate with Eve and Nick, hugging Frannie when she returned, and listening to all the latest "kid" news. He promised to return right after lunch to spend the rest of the afternoon with the children and take them all to dinner in town later. Justin decided to stay overnight at his parents' while he steered his car in their direction. He would need to spend as much time with Eve as he could, to see her through this.

"Hi Mom," he said as he placed a light kiss on her cheek.

"Honey, hi, I thought you were planning to be here earlier."

"I'm sorry Mom, I got held up, I stopped by to see Eve and the kids."

Mary's breath stopped in her throat, "So, you know."

"Yes, Mom and I'd like to know why no one told me until now. I had to find out from Finley."

Mary set down the bowl of tuna salad she was preparing and thoughtfully wiped her hand on a kitchen towel. "I'm sorry honey, I just thought Eve needed some time alone."

"You were afraid I'd get too involved weren't you?"

"I was afraid that you'd get your heart broken again if Billy came back."

"Mom, it's not like that. I mean she's my best friend. Above all else I want to be there for her. If I had known I would have never gone out of town."

"See, that's my point exactly, you have done nothing but put your life on hold in the event that Eve finally realizes she loves you too…."

"Mom, that's not true…."

"Isn't it? You had to leave your home because you couldn't take seeing them together."

"But, it turned out ok, didn't it? I'm an author, I have movies made about my books, and I'm happy."

"Are you? You've never really stopped loving Eve have you honey? And admit it, your first thought was to run to her side and protect her and maybe even, win her heart."

"Mom, please."

A gentle hand caressed his arm. "I only care about your welfare son. You have spent your life trying to hide from your broken heart. You've never stopped loving her and I suspect you never will. But you need to know that situations like this can be dangerous. You could get tangled up in her life and Billy could come back and what will you do then?"

Justin pulled his mother close to him, he loved her for her gentle heart. "I need to be her friend right now. That is what she needs. And those children…." A lump of tears grew thick in his throat, "I need to be there for them. Don't worry Mom, I'll be careful, I promise…." His words trailed off; his reassurances sounding vaguely uncertain.

Outside the sun reflected off the lake. It was a perfect day, he decided. This evening he would take Eve and the children for a sunset sail on the water and dinner at the New Fairfield Inn. He heard his mother's words of caution echo in his mind but he knew it was too late for that. In a matter of a few hours he'd already been inhaled back into her world. But that didn't matter. He'd spent his life being cautious, playing it safe. And where had it gotten him? A career maybe, the love of a woman he could not save from death and a heart so damaged he was certain it would never heal.

Justin spent the next few days with Eve and the children. He stayed in his parents' spare room, leaving early enough to help her ready the kids for day camp and see them off. On Wednesday evening, he'd promised to take them all into town for a night at the circus. Frannie and Nicholas could hardly wait.

"Eve, why don't you let me pick the kids up this afternoon?" Justin suggested. "The three of us can stop to get ice cream and you can get ready." Justin pulled two plates from the cupboard and began preparing their lunch.

Eve smiled; having Justin there the past couple of days had been a godsend. "Are you sure you don't mind?"

"Are you kidding? We'll stop for ice cream and start the adventure a little early, besides those kids deserve it and you deserve a chance to have an afternoon all to yourself."

"Justin, you're too good to me." Eve reached for his hand, covering it with her own. A sensation that he'd grown accustomed to ran through his body and shivered up his spine.

♣ ♣ ♣

"Shep, why not let me run that out for you?" Mack, the new constable-in-training, fumbled with a thick manila envelope.

Shep looked every bit of sixty-five. His face etched with forty-five years of police work. Most days it wasn't too tough, but then there were days like this when it sucked to have his job. He should have retired five years ago when he was eligible for a full pension. But he couldn't imagine his life without a badge and his days without the rigors of policing this small but growing town. Soon enough, later in the year, he'd be forced to walk anyway.

Shep reached for the envelope, taking it from his deputy as though it were on fire, and perhaps it was. "I'll deliver it Mack," he said more abruptly than he'd intended. He'd delivered stuff like this more times than he cared to remember, but this was different. This time, it nearly broke his heart.

♣ ♣ ♣

Eve rocked back and forth on the porch swing letting the sun drench her body. It was a fiercely warm day, one of the hottest all year according to the noon weather report. She held the sweaty lemonade glass in her hand, rolling it gently across her forehead. Eve closed her eyes for a brief moment, letting her mind wander and her breath go quiet. There was the faint sound of a car approaching that grew louder, then it stopped in front of her house. Eve decided to ignore it. The gentle rocking lulled her into a semi-sleep state. She could hear a car door closing, then the sound of footsteps coming up the walkway. Surprised, she peered at Shep as his heavy steps carried him near.

"Shep? What's going on? Come by for some lemonade?" Eve spotted the anxious look in his eyes and the envelope in his hand. The senior constable continued to move closer without responding. He was up on the porch, removing his hat and wiping his brow with a thick hand. Trickles of sweat poured down the side of his face.

"Shep, would you like some lemonade?"

"Eve, I'm sorry, this isn't a pleasure visit I'm afraid."

"What then? Is something wrong, has something happened to my children, to Justin?"

His hand raised in the air to quiet her fear. "No, no nothing like that. It's just that, well see I've been asked to serve you with divorce papers Eve."

The glass of lemonade slipped from her fingers and crashed into a million splintering pieces at her feet. A shard of glass nicked her leg, sending a tinge and a trickle of blood down her calf.

"Eve!" Shep reached for her, but was too late to save the glass from its demise. "I'm so sorry Eve. I hated coming out here."

Eve shook her head, reaching for the envelope. "Is this it?" All she could hear was her own staggered breathing, raspy and shallow. She inhaled air in short stolen gulps as if she'd been socked in the stomach.

Shep released the envelope to her. "I can stay if you want Eve."

"No, Shep, I guess I shouldn't be too surprised. This is what Billy wanted and the rest of us can just go to hell."

"Look, Eve, my daughter went through something just like this and it was awful, but now, she's happier than she's ever been. It will get better."

Eve fingered her ring. "Yes, I'm sure it will. But first it's gonna get a whole hell of a lot worse." In one swift movement, she was up off the swing. The trail of blood ran down her ankle and into her shoe. "I've got to go get myself cleaned up, Justin will be here with the children any minute. We're taking them to the circus tonight." Eve finished her sentence and threw her friend a painful smile. "You were only doing your job Shep," she said quietly as she pushed through the screen door. Shep watched her disappear into the house.

Eve tore open the envelope. There was a stack of neatly typed papers inside. Her name and Billy's name appeared at the top. The rest she did not bother to read. She already knew what it said. Left. Gone. Departed. Over. Done. Whatever it said, it all meant the same thing. In six months, she'd be divorced. He'd have a new life and she'd still be stuck with the old one. With a clap, she dropped the papers onto the floor and headed upstairs to take a shower.

❧ ❧ ❧

"Who wants ice cream?" Justin smiled as he loaded the children into his car.

"I do!"

"I do too! Are you gonna take us Uncle Justin?" Nicholas smiled.

"Yes, I certainly am, then we'll go get your momma and we'll all head for the circus."

The children piled eagerly into the car. Justin buckled them in and then climbed into the front seat.

They stopped at a roadside stand erected during the summer months to cater to the tourist crowd. They carried everything from hot dogs to ice cream and ice cold sodas.

"What'll it be guys?" he asked.

Frannie and Nicholas eyed the menu carefully. Pictures of each ice cream treat were painted in full color on a piece of wood that leaned against the snack shop.

After the children picked their treats, Justin found them a bench and the three of them sat enjoying the afternoon sun and licking the ice cream before it melted.

That's when he felt it. A twinge of something, then, a painful shudder. It alarmed him, and whatever it was it made him want to race to Eve's.

"You know, we should probably start heading home. Why don't we finish these in the car?" Despite the fact that he knew the leather interior of his car would not survive two sets of sticky fingers and dripping cream, he knew he had to get them home.

♣ ♣ ♣

Eve stood in her bedroom for a long moment, just staring into space. Then, in one painful searing moment, she reached for a lamp and hurled it across the room. It slammed against the wall in a shattering array of glass and plaster. Her jewelry dish was next. It too met the same fate. Soon, objects were flying everywhere. Wedding photographs, vases, lamps, even her wedding ring. Eve fell to the floor in sobs. She heard herself screaming out words and was dimly aware of not stringing them together. But they came in full force, tumbling from her lips. She called out uselessly for Justin. But no one answered. She was alone. She would always be alone. Soon, her children would grow up and leave her too. Alone, alone, alone. And everyone in town knew that she'd been left. Left for some blond cheerleader who gave great head and walked around in a skirt so tight it cut off the circulation to her brain. Eve's hand bled from the cuts of glass that were strewn across the floor. She picked one up, eyeing it for a moment. Then, gently, she placed it against her wrist and started to push it down into her flesh.

❦ ❦ ❦

The feeling grew more intense as Justin neared the house. He skidded into the driveway with the children giggling in the back seat.

"What a fun ride Uncle Justin!" Frannie smiled.

"Come on kids, we need to get inside and get ready to go!"

Justin dashed out of the car with Nick and Frannie behind him. Justin spotted the broken glass on the porch and quickly pushed through the front door. He stepped on the papers; it was obvious even without picking them up what they were.

"Eve!" he called out, trying to hide the desperation in his voice, "Eve!!"

"Mom!" Nicholas called out behind him. "Is Mom here?" he asked.

"Yes, honey, your mother is just fine. Why don't you two watch TV in the living room, I'm going to check upstairs and see if she's ready to go." Justin took the steps two at a time, noticing that her door was cracked slightly.

"Eve?" he asked, pushing it open. He fell back in shock at the sea of disaster that met his gaze. Everything that wasn't too heavy to pick up had been shattered, and there, lying on the floor was Eve, curled into a ball.

"Eve!" he blurted. Justin fell to the floor beside her. "Eve!" he reached a hand around her, pulling her up. She was unconscious and bleeding. Justin lifted her quickly, setting her down on the bed. Her arms and legs were filled with small cuts and scrapes, blood trickled from each of them. Slowly, she began to stir beneath him. Justin breathed a sigh of relief.

"What? What happened…?" she said, her voice weak and disconnected.

"I was hoping you could tell me."

The memory of it suddenly filled her head. The sound of glass crashing, shards of it flying across the room. Her screams, then….

"Oh, God Justin, I wanted to hurt myself…."

"What?"

"I don't know, I suddenly felt so alone, so desperate, I just…."

Justin gripped her arms. "You are not alone, do you understand me? You will never be alone. I will always be here for you!"

Eve threw Justin a weak smile, "I could never do that Justin, never. I could not leave my babies, or you."

It was at that very instant that Justin knew he could kiss her, he could almost feel the gentle pull of her lips as a gravitational sort of thing; stronger than any earthly force.

"I'm glad," he whispered, the relief evident in his voice. "I think we should stay in tonight."

"No! The children have been looking forward to this for days, I won't disappoint them."

"But Bug, look you're pretty scraped up and you should probably rest, you've been through a lot today."

"Justin, I got the divorce papers."

"I know, I saw them on the floor when I walked in, that's how I knew something was wrong."

"He's really done it," she mumbled ruefully. "He's gone Justin. It's over."

"I'm sorry Eve, truly I am."

Eve gathered her knees up under her chin and gazed around the room. "I'll have a lot to clean up here."

"No, you won't, I'm going to call a service to come in while we're gone. When we get home everything will be as good as new."

"Justin, no, I can't let you do that."

"You can and you will. Then, tomorrow, we'll go shopping for new, unbreakable things."

Eve smiled and threw her arms around his neck. He could feel her sweet breath on his neck and he was at once so grateful that she was ok and so certain he had never stopped loving her.

A day or so after Eve got served Justin decided to move into her guest bedroom, much to the chagrin of his mother. But Justin insisted that it was necessary, if only for a little while. "Besides, Mom," he'd insisted, "it'll give me a quiet place to finish my book." His mother had half-heartily agreed, though knowing that with every passing day Justin was digging himself deeper and deeper into Eve's life.

In the weeks that followed, Justin spent very little time in the city and more and more days at Eve's house guiding her through every painful step of her divorce. On the few occasions Billy called, he'd asked directly for his children and it was obvious that he did not wish to become embroiled in small talk or a lecture from his old friend.

CHAPTER 57

It had been almost a year since Billy left and when Justin came to town, he would, more often than not, stay in Eve's guest room. "To be near the kids," he told Eve.

Justin had left for a run earlier that morning and the house was quiet. Eve was putting laundry away when she spotted Justin's computer from out of the corner of her eye, as though she saw it for the first time. At that moment some childish desire took over. Justin would certainly be gone for over an hour, she thought. There would be plenty of time.

The computer beckoned. Putting the laundry down on his bed she eyed the computer for a second, feeling as though she were stealing cookies before dinnertime. The high-back chair Justin used still felt slightly warm as she settled into it, eager to read the final adventures of Sheriff Wilding of King's Town. She touched a button on his computer, bringing it to life. It hummed quietly, as the screen blinked awake. Suddenly, his descriptive words filled the screen as the lives of Melanie and Austin unfolded. Eve tapped the keyboard, moving through the document. When she arrived at chapter one, she quickly began to take in Justin's elegant words. Her eyes darted occasionally up from the page to reassure herself that she was still alone while she secretly stole a glance at his latest masterpiece. Eve found herself once again enraptured with the ever shifting events in the lives of the characters she had grown to love.

A glimmer of something that had escaped her previously, now presented itself in a way so obvious, it was unmistakable. There was a story within the story. With new eyes, she felt the veil lift that had cloaked her mind from the obvious familiarity of it. Her eyes flew from left to right along the page, no longer concerned that Justin could arrive at any moment. As she quickly navigated through several chapters, the knowledge of something she'd buried long ago began to float to the surface.

How could she have not known? This thought plagued her, dancing frivolously as thoughts sometimes do. Then it washed over her, all of it, every utterly painful, glorious moment and like a thunderous wave it crashed down. Her fingers brushed the keyboard in a soft, sensual movement as their touches intermingled.

Justin.

He'd sat there, his elegant hands clicking away, his heart pouring out the truth disguised behind characters that bore only a faint resemblance to reality.

In one graceful movement, she was up from her chair forgetting the computer that hummed patiently. Eve went in search of answers, in search of the truth. And she knew exactly where to find it. She was certain that the truth was buried deep beneath their favorite tree. Eve grabbed a shovel and ran.

Time stretched out before her as she ran to the lake. Her breath became shaky and unstable and with each step another memory revealed itself, another truth that had long since been dismissed. Now, all of it fell into place as it was always meant to be.

The prom.

The kiss under the pier.

The day she'd lost baby Billy.

All of it, in a sheer moment of serendipitous revelation she ran, feet barely touching the ground, guiding her to the truth.

Eve arrived at their tree breathless, her light cotton T-shirt sticking to her skin, her breath heavy with anticipation. Her shovel hit the soft, moist dirt; bits of gravel scraping as she forced it into the ground. Minutes ticked silently past as she dug into the dark earth surrounding Candlewood Lake.

Her shovel touched something. A worn rusted lid glinted in the morning sunlight. Impatient, Eve dropped to her knees digging with her hands, freeing the time capsule from the place it had been for almost twenty years. A faint smile danced on her lips as she pulled the flimsy box, caked in dirt, from the ground. The lid lifted without any trouble and in a moment, she was transported back in time, young and unafraid as she'd been, untainted by the torrents of reality. The contents felt slightly moist as she lifted them out. First, Billy's scrawled handwriting, then hers and finally, Justin's note, carefully concealed in an elegant envelope. Eve rested her back against the tree, feeling the roughness of it beneath her shirt as she tore open the envelope and pulled a simple note on the same elegant stationary. It read:

My hopes and dreams, by Justin VanSant

Someday, I want to marry Eve Phillips.
I love her.
I think she is the most beautiful girl in the world.

—Justin VanSant

The sheer simplicity of his words tore through her and the tears she'd been choking back surfaced and filled her eyes. A sweaty hand touched hers, and Eve looked up to see Justin, breath heavy from his run, standing over her.

"What are you doing here, Eve?" As he spoke, he knelt down beside her, recognizing the box he'd long forgotten about.

Eve looked up at him with the guilt of child. "I-I, just came here," Eve paused for a moment, trying to gather her speech.

"I was reading your story, and then it dawned on me. I mean—I just wondered, if it was, maybe written about me, about us and I had to come here to see what you'd written in our time capsule. You said you loved me." Eve was surprised at the hopefulness she heard in her voice. How much she wanted it to be true. How much she had always wanted it to be true.

"Eve, these notes were written a long time ago." Justin played nervously with the fringe of his shirt.

"I know, but I thought that perhaps, I mean when I thought back to all of those times..." she paused for a moment, not sure from his reaction whether she should continue. Words tumbled in her head, needing to be spoken: "All of those times we were together, when you protected me, when you kissed me under the pier in California, when you left after Billy and I married."

"I don't understand where you're headed with this Evie."

"I need to know if you love me."

She could feel his uneasiness on the other side of her question and when he did not answer her, she feared the worst. Suddenly, she felt terribly foolish.

"I'm sorry if I embarrassed you Justin." Her eyes fell to the ground as she mumbled these words, "I-I don't know what I was thinking." Picking the metal box up, she got up to leave.

From where he stood, Justin could not move. He had denied himself the hope of her for so long, that when it finally presented itself, he could only stand in disbelief. As she walked away he realized that he feared having her as much as he feared never having her.

"Eve wait," his voice was hoarse, barely audible. She stopped, but before she could turn to face him, he continued, "I wanted you to be happy, no matter what, but I couldn't stand to see you two together, so I left. It tore me apart, I loved you so much."

The words, once out of his mouth, lifted a weight from his shoulders he'd been carrying for over twenty years. Eve opened her mouth to speak, but he continued, needing to release what he'd spent his entire life trying to hide. "Eve, I loved you from the moment I laid eyes on you. I knew you needed to marry Billy, but there was no way I could stay around and watch as the two of you built your life together." His eyes held her tightly, "so I left, and tried to make my life in California, but I couldn't shake you, no matter what I did. Then, I met Zoë, and she was a salvation to me, and I loved her too, God help me I loved two women at the same time. And she knew, she knew there was someone else but she loved me anyway."

An unexpected sob escaped his lips, and a trickle of tears flowed from his eyes as he continued, "She didn't deserve to die, she is the reason I survived all those years, she is the reason I became a writer."

"Oh, Justin…" a hand, remnants of the soft soil still present, reached for his own, "I'm so sorry…" her voice was wet, choked with tears.

Justin's fingers gently touched hers, intertwining with them in an unspoken gesture of love. There was something else that he needed to say, something that should have been said years ago.

"Eve, I love you. I'm tired of running from it or living without you. Do you think you could ever love me in return?" His declaration left him feeling bare, with nowhere to hide should her answer be anything other than what he hoped.

An unsteady hand stroked away a lock of damp hair that had fallen in his face. "Justin, I don't know if I can anymore, if I have anything left inside me…I'm so afraid of losing what we have, of losing you too someday."

"I promise you will never lose me and I won't leave the way Billy did."

"I know." Eve smiled. Her eyes looked right into his soul and touched the love that had been lying dormant inside of him for years.

His hands delicately cupped her face, and his lips, warm and full of emotion, brushed her forehead.

Eve closed her eyes, relishing his touch. "Where do we go from here?" she whispered.

"Have dinner with me tonight. I want us to have a date, a real honest to God date."

A chuckle escaped her lips at the silliness of it all. They had been friends for over twenty years, now they would be lovers.

"A date then Mr. VanSant," she smiled.

"Yes, indeed. Now, I must excuse myself because I have a lot of work to do."

Eve frowned. "For what?"

"Well, our date of course." Justin pulled her hands to his lips, kissing them gently, "Now, I don't want you to worry about a thing. I will find someone to look after the children. All you have to do is be ready by seven."

A curious smile spread over her face. "Ok. I'll be ready at seven, no questions."

"Perfect, then I'm off and I'll see you later." Justin released her hands then turned and jogged back in the direction of her house.

Eve got her first surprise at around noon, announced by a sharp knock at the door. A delivery man was holding a large box secured with an expensive ribbon. She quickly shut the door, set the box on the floor and began to fumble with the ribbon. Finally, it fell in soft satin curls to the floor. She lifted the lid to reveal several layers of pink tissue paper. Eve dug as though she were looking for a buried treasure. The shimmering blue edges of a garment began to appear and Eve, still sitting on the cool wooden floor of her hallway, gently pulled the garment out to reveal a stunning midnight blue gown. She'd never seen anything like it before, let alone touched something so exquisite. A monogrammed card fell out from between the folds of the dress. It was filled with Justin's handwriting:

Eve,

I remembered seeing this gown in Bergdorf's last week and thought how stunning it would look on you. I hope you will choose to wear it this evening.

I can hardly wait.

Love,

Justin

Eve held the gown up to her, looking at her reflection in the worn hallway mirror. She would wear the dress, she decided. And hopefully he would take her dancing. She wanted to dance in it, and she wanted to feel his arms encircle her. Eve closed her eyes, and for a moment she lost herself in the memories they would make.

As Eve readied herself for their date, she felt a nervous seed of tension growing in the pit of her stomach. "I can do this," she said aloud. But the truth was, she was well out of practice. Never had a date with Billy given her this much titillating anticipation. This date was an odd culmination of twenty years of expectations and dreams long forgotten. For a moment, Eve thought back to the night Justin had escorted her to her prom. Had they not gotten called away, their lives might have been completely different. She might have married Justin, and lived happily ever after. Then again, maybe the love that they might find in each other now would be deeper and more fulfilling because it was enriched by their experiences, by their losses and by circumstances that kept them from being anything other than good friends. Good things happen slowly, someone had once told her. Good things. This was a good thing.

Eve pondered the blue gown for a moment, deciding how she would wear her hair. Finally she decided on a chignon. She brushed her hair to its fullness and then wrapped it in a twist that curled at the nape of her neck. Delicate tendrils brushed her shoulders. Eve smiled as she realized that Justin had thought of everything. There was even a pair of matching shoes in the bottom of the box and a sheer sparkling blue wrap as well. Eve added a splash of her most seductive perfume to her wrists and neck. All of it felt silly and exhilarating at the same time and the details of her life became strikingly apparent. Every moment that had led up to this one, and each that would follow.

When she was ready, she took a long deep breath and descended the stairs. Her mother was readying the children to go with her. When they heard her, they raced to see their mother.

"Mom," Nicholas cried, "you look like a queen!"

"Thank you sweetie." Eve kissed him gently on his forehead.

"Where is Justin taking you Mother? It must be someplace really special!" Frannie said fingering her mother's dress.

"Well, I don't know. Your Uncle Justin has planned this all as a surprise."

"Are you going to kiss him?" Frannie's question sent a wave of surprise through Eve.

"Yuck!" shouted Nick.

"Listen you guys, Justin and I have been friends for a very long time. We've had dinner before haven't we?"

"I guess." Frannie admitted.

"Looks like your car has pulled up," Judith announced. "I think Mr. Dream Date is here."

"All right then, you two be good for Nana ok?"

"Oh Mother, you know we love spending the night with Nana and Grampy," Frannie smiled and hugged her mother.

Eve stood up, opening the front door just as Justin emerged from a shiny black stretch limousine. He was dressed handsomely in a black tuxedo; in his arms he held a dozen long stemmed red roses. Eve walked onto the porch, closing the door behind her.

"Justin, I can't believe this. I mean the car, the dress. This is...I don't even know what to say," she smiled.

"I have waited an eternity for this moment Eve, and I wanted it to be perfect," he began, bending to place a kiss on her hand. "May I escort you to dinner?"

"Yes." She could not control the shaking in her voice, or the intense beating of her heart beneath her sheer silk dress.

"Eve?"

"Yes?"

"Are you nervous?"

"Extremely."

A laugh escaped his lips as he said: "Well then, that makes two of us."

Eve sank back into the thick leather seats of the limousine as Justin poured her glass full of champagne.

"Are you enjoying this, Eve?" he asked, filling her glass with bubbles.

"I can't even tell you how much. Now if you'd tell me where we are going, I'd be absolutely thrilled."

"Sorry, Bug, I can't tell you just yet. It's got to remain a surprise."

An hour later, they pulled up in front of a dimly lit establishment. It wasn't until Eve emerged from the car that she read the name over the door. He was taking her to Lutèce, one of New York's most exclusive restaurants.

Lutèce was filled with guests seated around intimate round tables illuminated with candles surrounded by delicately cracked globes. Eve had never been to Lutèce before, but she'd read about it often in the New York Times. The dress, the limo ride into the city and now this posh restaurant reminded Eve again of Justin's fame. Justin had enough money to do whatever he wanted, whenever he wanted and everyone seemed to know him. When they entered the restaurant, the new co-anchor of the *Today Show*, Katie Couric was in the foyer, and she stopped for a moment to tell Justin how much she was looking forward to their interview next week. Eve could hardly believe it. They passed by a table where Harrison Ford and his wife were dining and in the corner she spotted Jack Nicholson with Anjelica Houston. Eve was thankful Justin had sent her the dress; no doubt she would have worn something entirely inappropriate. As it was, she felt a bit like a wilted flower between all these finely sculpted roses. Justin seemed to sense this, as he walked behind her through the restaurant.

"Eve, you are the most beautiful woman here tonight." His breath was soft and warm on her neck. She reached a hand behind her and gently brushed his, touching his fingers. A bolt of electricity shot through her, catching in her throat.

Eve lingered over her slice of rich chocolate cake drizzled in raspberry coulis. Justin sat across from her at their intimate table, his face was bathed in candlelight and Eve thought he had never looked more handsome. Lifting her fork to his mouth, he wrapped his lips around where hers had just been, in a moment filled with intimacy and familiarity. Eve loved this feeling of sharing something so simple, yet so intensely personal. A warmth flushed her cheeks and filled her body with a longing she had never felt before, a warmth that trickled down her spine, then spread itself to her thighs, moistening her fresh cotton panties.

"What are you thinking?" Justin asked, unable to take his eyes off her.

Setting down her fork, Eve gently covered his hand with her own. "We have waited so long for this moment. I realize only now, maybe I've waited my entire life."

Justin placed a delicately sensual kiss on her hand. "I don't want to rush anything Eve. I love you and being able to share that secret is enough for me, for now."

"I appreciate your patience Justin, there's so much that has happened. But all I know is that right now, I am feeling something that I have never felt before. I never thought anything like this could exist."

His face curved into a smile at the words he never thought he would hear. "This is only the beginning Bug, this is only the beginning. Now, how about we go dancing?"

Eve thought he would never ask.

The limousine was waiting outside for them. In a moment they were seated beside each other and the car was gliding again through the busy streets of New York.

"Where are we going dancing?" Eve asked, leaning into Justin.

A protective arm wrapped around her shoulder. "You'll see."

"Another surprise?"

"You bet."

The limo stopped in front of a tall building, the driver emerged from the car to open the door for his passengers.

"But Justin," Eve frowned, "this is the Empire State building."

"Yes, it is. I remembered you telling me you've always wanted to see it."

"Yes, but…right now? I mean, isn't it closed?"

"Come on," he smiled. She felt him place a hand in the small of her back, where it had first fallen years before. All this time; an empty space back there waiting to be filled. His hand in that place felt right.

A doorman smiled at them, holding open the heavy door. "The guard will take you both straight up Mr. VanSant."

"Thank you Earl, and thanks again for staying late," Justin smiled, pushing something into the palm of his hand.

"You're most welcome sir. Good evening ma'am," he smiled, tipping his hat.

"Good evening," Eve said, a bit confused. Soon, they were speeding up the elevator and Eve could only wonder what he was up to.

They arrived several minutes later at the top of one of the tallest buildings in the city. The doors opened, and Justin immediately escorted her onto the observation deck where a small band played softly.

"Justin, what have you done?"

"Why I've rented the place for the evening. I thought it would be nicer to dance up here." Justin escorted her to a small candlelit table. A waiter seemed to emerge out of nowhere carrying a tray with two snifters of brandy and two small cups of coffee.

"Justin, I don't know what to say…" Eve could not take her eyes off the stunning view of the city.

"Don't say anything, just enjoy the evening and promise me every dance." Justin wrapped his arms around her waist, "I'll give you the world, if you'll let me Eve."

She felt the comfort of his arms, the perfect circle they formed around her waist. Eve dropped her head, resting it in the softness of his neck, his scent seducing her. Slowly, she turned to face him. In her mind, she replayed the night they stood by the lake after her prom, she was eighteen and unaware of what she was feeling dressed in her cream colored chiffon. In the instant before Justin kissed her atop the Empire State Building she realized she had fallen in love with him in that very moment on that warm June evening so many years ago. But life had gotten in the way and now, here they were, finally, together. Her breath trembled as it escaped her lips.

"I can't tell you how long I have dreamt of this moment, Evie." Her whispered name on his tongue seemed almost reverent. The air around them grew tighter, swirling with possibility. She felt dizzy with inertia. A pull, her pull, his pull, their pull together. Then, his lips crashed into hers and they were swept away in a flood of unchecked emotion. It was not one kiss, but many, building in intensity, the music floating softly behind them as the night sky erupted in a sparkle of stars.

* * *

The limo came to a smooth stop in front of Eve's house.

"Why don't we go for a walk by the lake?" Justin suggested. But Eve had other things in mind.

"We've walked around that lake enough, don't you think?" A secretive smile curved on Eve's lips stepping from the limo.

Justin hesitated before following her up the walkway. "I don't want to rush you, Eve."

She reached for him. "You're not," she whispered. Their hands clasped and fingers intertwined, he wondered what it would be like to arouse her and watch her naked body writhe in ecstasy as they brought each other to a carnal peak of intimacy. They walked inside and Justin clicked the door softly behind him.

"I want to kiss you, Eve." His voice was raw with desire.

"I hoped you would." Her head filled with a dizzy euphoria that whirled her thoughts into a heated mix of passion.

Bending his head to hers, he caught her lips with his and held them for a long, tender moment. Finally, his arms slid around her thin waist, pulling her to him, pressing her, molding her body to his own. Eve felt her lips part, welcoming his tongue into her mouth. They were breathing each other's air and exploring each other's body with their hungry fingers. She could taste the cognac and coffee on his tongue. His lips left her mouth, exploring the smoothness of her face, her neck and shoulder.

"This isn't right," he whispered, his breath still hot on her skin.

Eve struggled to recover her senses. "What do you mean?"

Justin put a breath of space between them, gathering the strength to do what he knew was right. "Not on our first date."

A nervous laugh escaped Eve's lips. "It's hardly our first date. Justin, you are the kindest, most wonderful man I have ever known." Eve paused, thoughtfully pursing her lips together. "You asked me earlier, how I felt about you. I didn't answer you then, I was too overwhelmed by what you were telling me." She took in a breath before she continued, "Justin, I love you. I believe I have always loved you."

"I love you too, Eve, more than you will ever know and more than I can ever describe."

They walked to her bedroom and their bodies fell onto the bed in a tumble of passion. Eve's wonderful new dress fell to the floor in a heap of shimmering blue. Justin's hands roamed the soft curves of her body, touching her in places she hadn't been touched in years and doing things to her no man had ever done. Her breath came in short gasps as he stroked her breasts, touching her nipples with his lips. His mouth fell to the softness of her abdomen, lingering there for a heated moment. His passion swirled around him with the force of a warm tornado. Eve's mouth was on him, and her soft lips kissing his warm skin sent a sensual shiver up his spine. He ached to be inside her, his body screaming out for release. Finally separating her thighs, he entered her and a whispered moan escaped her lips as her body rose up to meet his. Justin pushed inside of her, moving slowly at first, almost teasing her with pleasure, then his movements became more demanding as he felt her body peak in ecstasy, and suddenly his own release engulfed him, the passion for her washing over him as he felt himself explode with pleasure, his lips still on her mouth, the scent of her perfumed skin filling his senses. He was overcome with love at that moment and a fierce longing for her that only grew more intense as their love making subsided.

Justin moved gently to lie beside her, kissing her slightly damp skin.

"This is how it should be, this is how it should have always been," she said softly. "I love you, Justin, more than I thought I could ever love anyone."

"I love you too, Bug," Justin said before he kissed her and made love to her again. Eve gave into her newfound passion, letting this man she'd known all her life take her to places she'd only dreamt about. Afterwards she curled into his arms, still reeling from their intense mutual passion. Finally she said: "So, Jus tell me, how does your story end?"

She felt the gentle pull of his lips as he bent to kiss her. “They live happily ever after.”

CHAPTER 58

Eve was sitting in her kitchen when she heard a car pull into the driveway. She could hear the gravel crunch under a set of tires. Curious, she peered out her window. A tall, thin man emerged from the driver's seat. The car and the driver seemed strange but oddly familiar to her. Eve walked outside and decided to greet the stranger on her porch. The minute she stepped outside, she realized who stood before her. It was Billy.

Looking pale and horribly thin, he walked as though every step was an excruciating movement. He caught her eye, and a whisper of a smile drew the corners of his mouth up slightly. His face was no longer tanned, but almost gray. His eyes had lost their sparkle of blue, looking as gray as his skin.

"Billy? What are you doing here?"

"Hello Eve, are the children still in school?"

"Yes, for another hour."

"Then I need to talk to you before they come home. May I come in?" He was overtly cordial and the sight of him as he neared her sent a shiver of grief down her spine. Billy was sick, of that she was certain.

Eve invited him in and they sat down in what was once their living room. Billy looked around it for a long, thoughtful moment.

"You haven't changed a thing, Eve." He smiled.

"Billy, can I get you something to drink?"

"No, Eve I'm ok right now, but thank you."

This person sitting next to her was not the man she had married. He was a shadow of someone she used to know, with his fragile shape and cordial manner he was almost unrecognizable.

When Billy took her hand into his own, Eve held back a gasp at the sight of his nearly translucent skin.

"Eve, I have something to tell you. I've come home for good."

"What do you mean? Where's Cheryl?" The name on her lips hung between them like a painful reminder of days gone by.

"She's, well, we're no longer together. We haven't been for a while."

"What happened, Billy?"

"Eve, that's not important and that's not why I came to visit you today," Billy drew in a long shaky breath, "I've come home to die, Eve. I have cancer. Testicular cancer to be exact."

A hand flew to her mouth. "Oh, my God, Billy!"

"It's all right, Eve. I've made peace with the fact that I'm going to die, but when I did that, I realized that there was no place I would rather be than here with my family. I want to see my children, if they still remember me. I've been a horrible father, but I know one of the things I regret most about losing my own parents was not being able to say goodbye. That has haunted me my entire life. I couldn't do that to them. I'll be staying at Terry's place, but I'm hoping you'll bring them by, before…well, before I don't recognize them anymore."

"Billy, isn't there something we can do? I mean there are treatments."

Billy patted her hand gently. "Eve, after all I put you through, your kindness just amazes me. You were the best thing that ever happened to me, but I was too messed up to see it."

Eve ran a nervous tongue over her lips. "Billy, if you're asking me to…"

"I'm not asking you anything, Eve. I have no right to. I just want to die here, not in some strange city alone."

"Billy, what happened, between you and Cheryl I mean?"

"She couldn't handle the cancer. She left right after I was diagnosed. She wanted a stud. Not someone who was coughing up blood and would soon become an invalid."

"What about chemotherapy?"

"I tried that, I tried everything. My hair fell out, my teeth nearly fell out, but the cancer was too far gone to really do anything about it. So that's my lot in life. It's what I deserve I suppose, after I spent a lifetime not concerned with anyone but myself."

"Billy, don't say that! You are a good man and you were a good husband!"

A bony hand reached up to caress her face. "You have a terrible memory, Eve. And I'm thankful for that. Perhaps after I'm gone you'll remember only the good times, as few as they were. When you think about it, it's really kind of i-fucking-ronic isn't it? I mean I was someone who could never keep his pants on and now I couldn't get an erection if I wanted to."

"How…much, um…" A tear spilled from her eye, she couldn't bear to look at him.

"How much time have I got? Is that what you're trying to ask?"

She nodded.

"A few months at the most. One good month left I think. But good is relative of course. By good I mean that I'll still be able to pee on my own, after that it's all through a tube."

The thought of it choked the breath out of her. Eve got up and walked around the room.

"I'm sorry, Eve. There's just no good way to tell you about this. It takes some getting used to." He started to get up, "I should probably go now, and let you be. I'm sorry I just stopped by but I thought it was best."

"No Billy, let me make us some lemonade and come sit on the porch for me and wait for our children to come home. They're being dropped off today and they'll be so happy to see you. It will give us a chance to catch up too."

Billy pushed himself up from the couch, he could feel every bone in his body cry out in pain but he did his best to not let it show, "I'd like that, Eve. I'd like that very much."

It was a little over an hour before the children returned home. Eve and Billy sat talking quietly about the things that had shaped their lives since their divorce.

"So, how's Justin doing?" Billy asked finally.

"He's doing really well," Eve smiled and Billy could not mistake the glow that filled her eyes.

"You two are together aren't you?"

"Billy, I don't think…"

"What? That you should tell me? I'm happy for you, Eve. I always knew you and Justin were meant to be together. I swear he fell in love with you before he even knew what love was. If it hadn't been for me, you two would be married now."

"Billy, please. Let's not bring up the past."

"Eve, the past is all I have. Besides, my fondest memories are of the three of us growing up together."

"We did have some good times, didn't we?" Eve smiled, remembering a day, long ago when they were three kids, young, carefree and filled with hope for the future.

"They were the best. I wouldn't trade a second of it for anything in the world."

Billy fumbled with his hands, gazing out across the lake that sparkled between the trees. "Good things happen slowly and bad things happen fast. Death brings such clarity to one's life, Eve. You can't even imagine. Everything else falls away but those things that are most important. Nothing else holds any significance at all, and all of the petty concerns that we carry with us seem ridiculously stupid in light of the truth. A tragedy forces you to focus on the details you would otherwise ignore. The humblest things become so intense and so rewarding. Buying toilet paper, hearing the crispness of a newspaper when you snap it open. Watching a sunrise."

Eve pulled his hands to her heart, her eyes filled with tears that spilled down her cheeks. "You don't deserve this, no one does Billy, I'm so sorry."

"I am too, Eve. I wish I could have realized all this when it still mattered, before I left you and broke your heart. Now, all I can do is say I'm sorry and hope that someday you won't think too poorly of me and remember how selfish I was."

Eve pulled him to her, wrapping her arms around his chilled body she held him tight. They cried together and Eve realized it was the first time she'd seen him shed a tear since the day his father died.

❧ ❧ ❧

There was a moment when something told Justin not to go to Eve's house. A voice in his head cautioned him to wait. But he couldn't, he needed to see Eve. In fact he ached to see her. They had been lovers for nearly three months now and he had never known such love or pleasure in another human being in his life.

Justin turned onto her street, and slowed in front of her house. It was then that he saw it. An image that slapped him with a force so hard, he could almost feel his face begin to bleed. Eve and Billy, sitting on the porch swing, holding hands. Talking, their faces intimately close. She was smiling, he was too. Suddenly, the air was void of oxygen. Every second he sat and watched seemed like an hour, an invisible knife plunging deeper into his soul, ripping it to shreds. His heart pounded in his ears and his eyes burned wildly with unshed tears.

Then, all at once, he found himself at their wedding again, and then leaving Connecticut. There was a reason you left the first time, his mind screamed, she's not yours and she never will be. Justin watched them embrace and in a flash, he was gone. Barreling down the road, not seeing a thing but the image that played itself out over and over again in his mind. She's gone back, he thought, she's giving him another chance.

Justin drove for hours in a numb, painful state. When he finally reached his apartment again, it was well after dark and there were several messages on his machine. All of them from Eve saying she needed to talk to him. He already knew what she was going to say. He would save her the trouble of trying to explain it. In one swift movement, he picked up the machine and hurled it across the room. It struck their picture and sent it crashing to the floor in a million fragile pieces. Justin reached into the pockets of his jeans searching for his keys. They were on the bar, a heap of silver metal clustered together on a loop. Frantically, Justin began separating them, until he found it.

Her key.

He pulled it off the ring, and looked at it for one long, excruciating moment as if it was the last real thing in his life. The most important thing he was losing. In an angry hurl, it flew across the room and landed with the debris of glass and plastic.

Sleep was not something that came easily that night. Justin's mind raced with myriad possibilities, but the one that he settled on was simple. He had pushed her too hard. Eve was having doubts, understandably so. His desperate need for her had clouded his judgment and as much as it hurt him now to do so, he needed to give her space. The thought of losing her pierced his soul, but his sense of honor would not allow him to do any different. He could go away, for a while at least, and let her decide. Justin untangled himself from his bed sheets and walked into the kitchen. His shiny wooden floor felt like ice under his feet. He set a pot on for coffee and continued to think of what he had to do. Suddenly, it came to him like a flash of inspiration. He would need to go away again, to leave Candlewood Lake one last time.

Eve waited quietly in the doctor's office. He'd called her, said it was best to come in. She pulled an outdated magazine from the rack and pretended to read it. Suddenly the door swung open and Dr. Manter entered the room.

"Hello, Eve, thanks for taking the time to stop by."

"Doctor, what's wrong with me?"

"Oh, Eve, nothing's wrong with you really, except that you're pregnant."

Dr. Manter reached for Eve as she began to sway. "Are you all right?"

"Yes, yes, I'm fine. Are you sure doctor?"

"Positive, Eve. I'm surprised you had no idea about this, usually women who have been pregnant before know right away."

"I just, there's been so much happening with Billy's illness and all, I never for a moment thought…." Eve breathed in a sigh that curled inward. "How far along am I?"

"About two months."

♣ ♣ ♣

Eve raced home, lost in thought. She had to find Justin; she had to tell him. Suddenly, the memories they'd made together curled around her like a blanket. For the first time since Billy's return, she smiled, a real genuine happy smile. A baby. Their baby. She really didn't understand why he had suddenly disappeared and would not return her calls. Whether he wanted any part of her or not, he would love their child of that she was certain. A hand reached down to caress her stomach. She felt delighted and frightened at the same time as the irony of it pierced her soul. The intense joy of a new life mixed with the sorrowful grief of an impending death.

♣ ♣ ♣

The shrill ring of the phone woke her from her sad and happy thoughts. Eve got up from where she'd been sitting for over an hour lost in contemplation of how strange life could be.

"Hello." Her voice was weak. Justin heard the sadness in it and knew that his decision was the right one.

"Eve, it's me."

"Oh, Justin, I've tried to call you…it's so good to hear your voice…."

"Eve, I'm sorry for the short notice, but I have to go away for a while."

"What? Why…I mean how long will you be gone?"

"I don't know, Eve, I'm sorry. I have to do some work for my next book so I'll need to go into seclusion."

"How will I reach you?"

Justin's grip tightened around the phone, "I'll call you."

"You mean, I can't reach you? But Justin there's something important I need to tell you…."

"Eve," Justin stopped her before she had a chance to finish, "I'm sorry I have to cut you off but I have a plane to catch, I'll call you soon, I promise…."

"Justin, it's very important that I speak to you about something…."

He knew what she was going to say, he didn't need to hear it from her, "I will call you I promise and Eve I love you, I always have and I always will."

"I love you too," Eve replied as the phone went dead.

CHAPTER 59

Justin sat on a bench overlooking the Seine River. Paris was bustling under the warm autumn sun. Behind him, he could hear the click of cameras and tourists ooing and awwing over the architecture. He heard a group of Americans discussing whether they would eat lunch at one of the small cafes that dotted the Seine River or whether they would eat in the restaurant on the second level of the Eiffel Tower. Justin listened as they made the decision to climb the tower and eat at the restaurant overlooking all of Paris. He had come to France to finish his recent novel and so far, he'd made absolutely no headway. Every thought in his head was of Eve. If he closed his eyes, he could see her. She was there with him in Paris and they were experiencing it together. He'd wanted to take her there on a vacation, but his dreams for their future had been cut short by reality. Justin got up off the bench and began walking down the narrow path beside the river. A lone saxophonist played a slow, soothing version of La Vie en Rose.

Justin stood for a moment and listened to him play. Nothing made sense to him anymore. Not even his writing and certainly not his life. Instead of sticking it out and fighting for her, he'd been the noble man and walked away. Once again. Justin shoved a hand in his pocket and dropped several coins in the bucket at the saxophonist's feet. He walked past the musician, continuing down the long stretch of river. With each step, he became more certain that he'd made the wrong decision. Leaving had been a mistake. Letting Billy have her all those years ago had been a mistake as well. Justin's pace quickened as he headed back to his loft. He was done making mistakes. He only hoped now that he wasn't too late.

❧ ❧ ❧

Justin sped down the highway. He had told no one of his plans. He'd gotten the first available flight back from Paris, raced back to his loft, packed a bag and headed for the lake. He sped past the sign that announced he was entering New Fairfield County and decided he would stop at Finley's Sweet Shoppe to deliver a signed copy of his book he'd promised to Lloyd Finley months ago. He stopped his car on the gravel and quickly got out. The familiar bell tinkled overhead. Lloyd's son, who had since taken over for his father emerged from the back of the shop.

"Why Justin VanSant, how the heck are you?" Cory smiled. Justin took his outstretched hand.

"I'm good, Cory. How about you?"

"Terrific, say what brings you back home? Are you home for good?"

A secret smile played on his lips, "I hope so, Cory. Say, I brought a book for your father, can I leave it with you?"

"Sure you can, but Dad's here today. He'd never let me hear the end of it if I didn't tell him you were here. Would you mind, just for a second?"

Justin refrained from telling him what a hurry he was in. "Sure, I can wait."

"I'll be right back!" Cory turned to leave and emerged a few moments later with his father right behind him.

"Hallou Justin, how are you? Good Lord, it's great to see you again. You look well."

Justin shook Lloyd Finley's wrinkled hand. "I am well. You look good yourself."

"Oh, don't lie to me. I'm getting old, there's nothing that can be done about it. But Cory here's decided to take over for me now, so the shop will continue whether I'm here or not."

"Well, you're going to be here for a good long while I'm sure."

"Yes, well, longer in fact than poor Billy, I'm afraid." Lloyd slowly shook his head.

"What? What are you talking about? What's happened to Billy?"

Lloyd looked at him over the rim of his glasses. "Oh dear, don't you know? Why I thought that's why you came back."

Justin gripped the counter. "Know what Mr. Finley?"

"Why, Billy's got cancer I'm afraid. Not much longer to live, they're sayin'."

"What? How can that be? What kind of cancer does he have?"

Lloyd leaned into Justin. "It's in his testicles," he said quietly, as if afraid to utter the word. Then, he shook his head, "Ain't got much time. Not much time at all. But boy he sure is lucky to have Eve. She's never left his side for a minute. And she's pregnant again, they're gonna have another child. I hope he gets to see it before he dies. It's a sad thing you know. But I guess the silver lining is that they've gotten back together he and Eve. Once married always married, I guess huh?" Suddenly, Lloyd remembered himself, "Oh, Justin, I'm sorry. I know how fond you always were of her."

Lloyd Finley's words came like a bolt of lightening from out of a cloudless sky. Justin could not say a word. He could only stand there, gripping the counter. His palms sweating onto the glass. Finally, he looked up at the shop owner. "That's all right," he said quietly and then turned to leave, pushing open the door and walking out into the sunlight.

❧ ❧ ❧

Justin stood over his friend's bed, watching him sleep. After a quick visit to see his parents, he'd called Terry and asked to see Billy, but he wanted to make sure Eve would not be there. He couldn't handle seeing her, not now. Not today, maybe not ever. He'd waited too long. She'd gone back. What the hell else had he expected? He'd left without an explanation, just a last minute phone call. She had every right.

Billy exhaled a ragged breath. Justin sat down in a chair that was positioned next to the bed. Close enough to hold his hand, he thought. No doubt she'd held his hand and comforted him while their baby grew inside her. The pain of his new reality tore through him and forced a tear from his eye.

When he left, nearly an hour later, he hid his red eyes behind a pair of sunglasses, thanked Terry for his discretion and got back in his rental car. If he hurried, he could catch an afternoon flight and be back in Paris by the morning. He had work to do and a new story to write. Now, that was all he had left.

❧ ❧ ❧

Eve hooked a hand through Billy's frail arm as they slowly walked along the lake together.

"This may be my last time at Candlewood Lake." Billy said, with a matter-of-factness, as though he were commenting on the color of the sky. He could feel Eve stiffening beside him. She still did not want to accept the fact that each day brought him closer to death.

"You shouldn't say that, Billy."

"It's the truth, you know it and I know it. My time is limited now, in a few days, I won't have the strength to walk anymore and then that will be that."

"How can you say that?! How can you be so flippant about this? Why aren't you fighting it?! I don't understand, I mean at the very least for your children!"

Eve yanked her arm from his, sending Billy stumbling forward for a moment. "Look, Eve. We've been over this. No one wants me to live more than I do. But it's no use fighting the inevitable. I want to spend my final days in peace, not in denial. Don't you think it just kills me to know I will never see Frannie go on her first date, or coach Nicholas at his first softball game? I want that, more than I want my next breath. But sitting here and cursing fate is not going to give me anymore time here on earth. It's just going to make the time I have left that much more unbearable. So all I can do is leave them with a memory of their father they can be proud of. That he faced death with courage as it should be faced, instead of kicking and screaming." Billy's eyes burned with tears that streaked his face. He'd done more crying in the last thirty days than he'd done in his entire life.

"I'm sorry Billy, I just…as hard as our life was together, I'm just not ready to lose you."

Billy raised a trembling hand to her cheek, "and I'm not ready to go. If I had known I was only going to have thirty-two years, I would have lived my life so differently. But we have no way of knowing what tomorrow will bring. That is perhaps the greatest gift life has to give us. The promise of a new day and a clean slate. I'm glad for this cancer in a way. If I had to die so young, I would have rather had the time to make amends than to be gone in a second with no way to say goodbye." Suddenly, Billy stopped to look around. "You know, Eve, this is where it happened. Right here is where that vicious, cruel person did probably the worst thing of his life."

Eve stopped to realize where they were. Suddenly she could hear herself sobbing and falling to the ground, grappling for a set of keys Billy had carelessly discarded there.

"After you left," Eve began slowly, "Justin never left my side." Suddenly the memory of him flooded her mind. God, how she missed him.

"You love him don't you?"

"With my whole heart," she answered softly.

"I'm sorry he's gone away. Have you heard from him?"

Her heart fluttered painfully. "No, I haven't."

"So, he doesn't know about the baby?"

"No."

"You have to find him, you have to tell him."

"I know but if he doesn't call soon he may end up hearing it from someone else."

"Can't you leave a message with his publicist or agent or whatever he has?"

"I've left hundreds of messages. My guess is he just changed his mind about us. I do come with a lot of baggage you know."

"Are you kidding Evie? Justin adores you. There has to be some other reason, I encourage you to find out what it is. Don't wait another day. Take a lesson from me."

Eve reached a hand up, to meet his.

"Eve, I'm getting tired, but I'd like to ask you one more favor."

"Of course, anything."

"Take me to the football field."

♣ ♣ ♣

Eve and Billy spent the balance of the afternoon gazing out over the silent, neatly groomed grass. A chilled autumn wind blew through the stadium carrying with it the whisper of memories from long ago. The scents of sweat and hot dogs still lingered in the air from a game played the day before. Billy sat quietly, locking away every moment. He wasn't sure if he would be allowed to take his memories with him into death, but he wanted to have as many of them as his mind could hold just in case.

CHAPTER 60

"I want to see Justin now, can you send for him? I don't have much time left."

Eve sat in a worn chair by Billy's side, where she'd been almost day and night since he had lost the ability to walk.

"I've sent word for him already, I'm sure he'll be here any minute."

Billy stirred painfully in his bed. There were tubes running everywhere. Some fed him, while others helped him to relieve himself. He spent his days talking to Eve and dictating letters that she would someday read to their children. On good days, Nick and Frannie were able to visit their father and read to him, at least until his medicine kicked in and he was unable to discern day from night, or life from death.

Eve knew his days were growing short and every time he closed his eyes to sleep, she held her breath wondering if this would be the end.

Justin received the telegram from his manager that he was to come home immediately. His friend Billy was dying. Justin left without bothering to pack a suitcase and prayed that he wasn't too late.

Eve stood up to stretch, feeling the baby flutter inside her. She no longer heard the faint beeping of the machines that filled Billy's room; she'd learned to tune them out. It was her way of keeping her sanity through the long, seemingly endless hours as she kept a vigil by his side. Eve walked over to the window and looked out over the extensive and well manicured gardens. Pockets of bright colored flowers dotted the rich green carpet of grass, evenly trimmed hedges lined walkways and the perimeter of the grounds. Eve leaned against the window frame and watched her children run and play in the yard. They had been so good through the upheaval that had swept through their lives. They played when they were told, sat with their father and read quietly to him and other times they were just content to sit with their mother as she tried to explain what it meant to be dying. Eve looked down at her watch, it was nearly noon. Justin had called the house and told Terry that his flight would arrive into Hartford at around one thirty. His call had been cordial but brief and he hadn't asked for her at all. A faint, tired sigh escaped her lips. She missed his touch and the sound of his voice and she knew that regardless of how he felt about her, he deserved to know about his child. The door behind her opened softly and Terry entered the room.

"Eve?"

"Yes?" She answered not wanting to turn around, the sight of her children was mesmerizing and comforting at the same time.

"You should get some rest, you've been at this for days now. Why don't you go lay down until Justin gets here." Terry walked up behind her, putting a comforting hand softly on her shoulder.

♣ ♣ ♣

Justin arrived at Stanhope Manor a full two hours earlier than anyone had expected.

"Justin? We thought you would be here later, but please do come in." Olivia looked exhausted, Justin observed. Her usual neatly combed hair was pulled back in a tightly wound bun at the nape of her neck. She wore no make up and her keen fashion sense was replaced by a practical pair of slacks and a sweater.

"I'm sorry Olivia, I should have called. I was able to catch an earlier flight so I took it. If this is a bad time I can come back."

"No, Justin, this is as fine a time as any. But you need to talk to Terry first, I think he should prepare you."

Justin walked past her into the elegant foyer. "How much time has he got?"

Olivia sighed a heavy grief-filled exhale that told Justin everything he needed to know. Billy had only days, if that. "Not much. It's so hard to watch him deteriorate, Justin. I can't even tell you what it's been like." Olivia led Justin through the hall and into the expansive sitting area.

"You and Terry were kind to let him spend his last days here instead of in a sterile hospital, I know how tough that can be…." Justin dropped himself into an overstuffed chair, remembering Zoë's last few painful days.

"Oh, Justin, I'm so sorry, this must be terribly difficult for you."

"It's a difficult time for everyone, but for Billy most of all."

Olivia nodded. "I'll go get Terry."

"Olivia?"

"Yes?" she turned at the doorway.

"Where's Eve?" The question had hung in his mind ever since his plane had touched down on American soil.

"She just ran out, but she should be back soon."

Justin watched Olivia leave to find her husband. So many emotions filled his mind. He had longed for her, ached for her and hadn't gone a second without thinking of her.

❧ ❧ ❧

When Justin entered Billy's room, he realized that no amount of preparation could have prepared him to see his friend, once vital and full of health, struck down by this vicious disease. Slowly, Billy turned his head and met the face of his friend. Almost immediately tears filled his eyes and a thin hand reached out to Justin.

"I'm so glad you're here, I was afraid I wouldn't see you again."

Justin lowered himself in the same chair Eve had occupied only moments before and reached for his friend's hand.

"Hell or high water wouldn't have kept me from seeing you."

"You're a good friend, you always were. I, on the other hand, wasn't so great."

"You were a fine friend, Billy. I don't know what I would have done without you all those years I tried so desperately to fit in."

"You don't have to placate me just because I'm dying." A hoarse laugh bubbled in his throat.

Justin leaned into his friend, "I'm not, Billy. I never told you this, but do you have any idea what it meant to me to be able to hang out with the coolest kid in school? I was reading Shakespeare and Hemingway for Christ's sake! No one wanted anything to do with me until you started hanging out with me."

Billy's eyelids dropped shut and a smile tugged at the corners of his mouth. "We had some wonderful times didn't we?"

Justin swallowed the lump in his throat. "The best times, Billy."

"The three of us, we were inseparable."

"Yes, we were, Billy and I'll never forget those times we shared, not a single one."

"Will you forgive me?" Billy whispered.

"For what?"

"For being so filled with jealousy that I pushed you away and for stealing Eve."

Justin could feel the force of Billy's words like a knife through his heart. So, he had been right all those months ago. Eve had gone back to him. The thought of it made him want to scream out in pain.

"She loved you Billy and I understood why you pushed me away."

"Eve loved you, Justin, she always has and she always will. I knew that when I married her but I was too self-absorbed to admit it. Also, in my own small way I wanted revenge too. I was so envious of you, you were always so perfect. Saying the right thing, doing the right thing. Your lives could have been so different if I hadn't interfered and I'm sorry for that."

Justin gripped his friend's hand tighter. "Now, you listen to me, you did what you felt was right at the time and that's all that mattered and don't ever think that Eve didn't love you because she did, I know she did."

Billy turned his head away, his eyes closed and his breath became suddenly quiet, "Justin, I have so much I need to say, but I'm getting tired. Will you come back later? There's something I need to tell you…something about Eve."

Justin already knew what it was. No need to hear it again, he thought.

"Of course, I'll come back this evening." Justin got up to leave.

"Justin?" Billy said quietly. "Do you think I'll get into heaven?"

Justin was stopped in his tracks, suddenly the force of what was happening became all too real and his eyes filled with warm, salty tears.

"I have no doubt," he said quietly.

"I hope I do, I want to see my son again, William Jr. Do you think he'll recognize me?"

"I have a feeling he'll be waiting for you."

"I hope so, I want to see him again. I want to hold him. I wasn't there when he was born, I was out drinking. I hope I can make that up to him…." Billy mumbled before drifting off into a morphine induced sleep.

When Justin left his room, he was not expecting the wave of sadness he crashed into. Until that very moment, it hadn't sunk in completely. But now, he could sense the smell of death as it seeped from the walls in Billy's room and he knew instinctively that Billy had only hours to live.

Outside, Justin dropped to his knees by a row of finely manicured hedges and vomited; then he cried.

Sometime after Justin left, Billy dictated another letter. But he didn't have Eve write it. Instead he asked his brother to help him. This letter was one he wanted to keep between himself and Justin; a few final words of farewell to his best friend in an attempt to somehow reweave the delicate fabric of their friendship.

Eve leaned against the window frame, her eyes skimming the extensive gardens. Sometimes watching for her children, sometimes just looking for anything that could distract her from the man dying in the bed behind her. The sound of the monitor indicated that he was still alive, at least medically speaking. Billy stirred in his bed. Eve turned to see him open his eyes.

It would be the last time.

Eve immediately took her place beside him, covering his hand with her own.

In a voice almost too hoarse to speak, he whispered: "I wish there had been more time." Then, he closed his eyes and was gone.

Billy felt weightless. Almost floating. Yes, floating indeed. Suddenly the room was filled with the brightest light he'd ever seen. He looked down to see his brother rush in, and the nurse. Eve was crying. He couldn't stop himself. He couldn't go back. Someone was calling him. In the distance, he could see three blurry figures. As he drew closer, he realized they were his parents and his brother. His mother was holding William, Jr. She was smiling. It had been years since he'd seen her smile. Silently, she handed him his son and he held him for the first time.

"We've taken good care of him for you," his father said. Billy followed them through the tunnel, looking back one last time.

God, he had loved it there. He would miss them. He would miss them all.

William Hank Freeman, handsome, rugged football hero, died pale and unrecognizable in the fall of 1990. He weighed ninety pounds.

CHAPTER 61

Somewhere in the distance a phone rang. Olivia picked it up. Eve and Terry did not move from their huddled spot on the couch. He was wiping a tear from his cheek with the back of his hand. In the distance Eve could hear Olivia telling Justin there was no need to stop by, Billy was already gone. As much as Eve wanted to hear his voice, she could not muster the strength to get up off the couch. She was too tired, her body filled with a bone-deep exhaustion.

"That was Justin," Olivia announced as she entered the living room and fell into a chair opposite them. "He said he was coming by anyway." Eve did not move, but somewhere deep inside she could feel her tired heart skip a beat.

"The undertaker should be here any minute," Olivia whispered. Neither of them looked up. "Eve, honey, why don't you go lay down, you must be exhausted."

"I'm fine, really." The unwilling yawn that followed gave little credence to her insistence.

"Olivia's right, you should go lie down. You must think of the baby."

"I want to see Justin," she said quietly without looking up, "I haven't seen him since Billy returned."

Justin set the phone down and looked around his mother's kitchen as if it held the answer to his most burning question. The house was empty, his mother was out. Dinner with friends he recalled her saying. Billy was gone. Gone for good. The thought resonated through his mind like an echo through a canyon, returning and reverberating a second time in case he didn't hear it the first time. An all-too-familiar pain shot through him. The pain of loss, the pain of unspoken truths and the guilt of not saying goodbye. Eve had been with him, that's what Olivia had said. Justin closed his eyes to the searing stab of pain he felt in his chest. Eve was with him. Eve had always been with him. He should have seen that. He should have known. The door slammed behind him as he left to face her and to face his own demons one last time.

Within fifteen minutes, Justin arrived at the house. He was just in time to see the hearse back out of their driveway and head up the street. Billy is in that car, he thought. My friend is gone.

Olivia held the door for him as he entered, politely took his coat and escorted him into the living room. Justin spotted Eve immediately. Her eyes were closed, her head resting on the back of couch. She looked tired, he thought, no more than that. She looked completely exhausted.

At the sound of his step, she looked up. With great effort, Eve pushed herself up off the couch. It was the first time Justin noticed her slightly swollen belly. He tried with great effort to disguise his surprise. But the disappointment was like a sharp slap in the face. Not only had she gone back, she was now carrying Billy's child.

"Justin, it's so wonderful to see you." Eve's voice was heavy with emotion. Behind her, Olivia and Terry tried not to watch their reunion. Eve pressed herself against him, feeling the protection of his arms as they encircled her. Justin pulled her gently to him. Resting his head on her sweet-smelling hair.

"It's good to see you too, I'm just sorry it's under these circumstances."

"It's a sad day, Justin," Eve said quietly. "We've lost Billy."

"I can't even believe it," he whispered, then looked up to Terry. "I'm very sorry for your loss. It must be terribly difficult for you."

"I'm just glad he's free of his pain, and in a better place."

"Eve, you must be terribly exhausted, you should be resting."

"We've told her the same thing." Olivia smiled protectively. "But she insisted on waiting until you got here."

"I would really like to sleep in my own bed tonight." Eve nudged herself from Justin's arms, running a protective hand across her stomach. Justin couldn't help but watch her.

"Justin, maybe you can take Eve home and make sure she gets there safely?" Terry said.

"Sure, I'd be happy to. Are the children here?"

"No, they're with my mother."

"Ok, well if you're ready, we can go."

Eve nodded and walked over to Terry and Olivia. Tearfully she embraced them and then allowed Justin to gently help her out of the house and into his car.

A moment after Eve stepped into the car, she fell into a deep sleep. Justin drove carefully through the darkened streets. When they arrived at her house, he eased her from the car and carried her in and up the stairs. Eve did not wake once as he gently laid her on the bed. Justin pulled up a chair and sat beside her, just watching her sleep. Of all the things they'd shared together, he'd missed that most of all. And even as tired as she was, she still looked radiantly beautiful. Never more so than at that very moment. Billy's baby, he thought. The tears that slipped out were unexpected. He cried, for their lost love, his lost friend, a child that wasn't his and the truth that was strangling him.

The following morning, Eve woke to the smell of bacon crackling in a pan downstairs. Disoriented, she eyed her room trying to remember how she got back there. Justin! His name trickled through her mind. She had seen him last night and he'd taken her home. She remembered nothing else after getting in the car. Billy was dead. The thought sank heavily into her mind. She'd been in the room with him and watched them carry his frail body out of the house.

Eve rolled onto her side, looking at the empty chair beside her bed. Had Justin sat there? Had he pulled it up beside her bed while she was sleeping? Eve placed a tentative hand on the seat, feeling the cool cloth and wondering if he'd occupied that space. Eve pushed herself into an upright position and looked around the room once more. She could hear someone in the kitchen downstairs. Cupboards opening and closing, coffee brewing; the scents were enticing. When had she eaten last? She couldn't remember. Yesterday morning perhaps, nothing at noon. She'd left to run some errands and Justin had stopped by to see Billy. The baby…her mind reminded her. She needed to tell Justin about the baby as quickly as she could. Would he want her back? Would he change his mind about them? Did he still love her? The questions that had haunted her for the last few weeks tumbled through her mind.

Eve flung her legs over the side of the bed. She decided to shower first to rinse the fog from her head. If she were going to tell him, she needed a clear head. And maybe a little bit of lipstick. Quickly, she washed and dried her hair, applying some make up. Silly, silly, she thought. I'm just being silly. He doesn't love me anymore. He's changed his mind. I'm just too much damned work.

Now the baby. A burden for him perhaps. But not for her. Thoughtfully she ran a hand across her naked stomach. "No matter what," she soothed, "you're going to have a wonderful life, I'll see to that."

Justin pushed the scrambled eggs around in the pan, making sure they wouldn't stick. The bacon still sizzled on a low flame. Upstairs, he could hear a shower and knew Eve would be down at any minute. His heart felt thick in his chest pounding frantically in his ears. Soon, they would be alone, having breakfast. Eating together like they'd done so many times before. But now it was different. They were no longer together. Nor would they ever be again. Pleasant conversation, that's all they would share. Everything was different now. While they weren't looking, someone had wiped all the traces of their past like words from a chalkboard, leaving only a dusty residue.

The sound of her footfall on the stairs made him stiffen. Any minute now, the thought trickled through his mind.

"Good morning, Justin," she smiled. He turned to face her and was struck breathless by her beauty.

Quickly, he turned away. "I made us some breakfast, why don't you have a seat. I made decaf coffee, is that all right?"

Eve picked up on the nuance right away. "That's all I can have." She pulled a chair back and sat down. The inference was made, she should just tell him. She exhaled a nervous breath. Why was it so hard? She thought. Just tell him, she coached herself, just spit it out.

"Congratulations by the way," Justin turned, pointing a spatula at her protruding tummy.

"Thank you, Justin." She paused for a moment, selecting her words carefully, "Justin, there's something I need to tell you…it's about the baby."

He didn't want to hear her say it.

"Why don't we eat first?" He began to scoop eggs onto her plate. The toast popped up and he grabbed two warm slices.

"Justin, this has waited long enough…." Her conversation was interrupted by the doorbell.

"I'll get it," Justin said, setting a plate down in front of her.

Justin opened the door to find Judith and the children.

"Uncle Justin!!" They said at once. Frannie wrapped her arms around his neck. Justin bent to give her a kiss, and high-fived Nick.

"Hello Justin," Judith said, the hint of coolness was unmistakable in her voice. "What brings you here?"

"I, uh, picked Eve up from Terry's last night and brought her back. I didn't think she should be alone."

"Oh." Judith pushed past him into the kitchen while the children vied for his attention.

"I've missed you two." Justin sat down, while the kids scrambled into chairs around the kitchen table.

"Why have you been gone so long?" Frannie demanded.

"Will you stay with us and Mom for a while?" Nicky questioned.

Justin inhaled the scent of them; God, how he'd missed their liveliness and good cheer.

"I made breakfast, have you two eaten yet?"

"We had Coco Puffs!" Nicholas announced.

"Yea, Nana gave us Coco Puffs!" Frannie smiled and turned to her mother. "How's Daddy?"

"Honey, why don't we have breakfast first and then we can talk about Daddy in a few minutes."

Justin watched Eve with her children. Her strength left him almost breathless. Quietly, she said: "I missed you two, I'm glad you're home."

Judith silently pulled a chair back.

"Will you be staying with us for breakfast?" Justin inquired.

"Yes, if you don't mind." Judith placed a hand on her daughter's arm.

"Yes, Mom, I'd love it if you stayed a while. Thank you again for taking care of them." Then turning her attention to her children, "Tell Nana thank you."

"Thank you Nana!" they smiled together.

"You're welcome dears, come stay with me and Grampy anytime."

Justin made a plate for Judith and asked Nicholas if he wanted some eggs.

"I ate," the boy announced. "I want to go outside and play."

"All right then, go ahead," Eve shrugged.

"I have to go call Amber." With a flounce, Frannie headed upstairs.

Eve, Justin and Judith ate their breakfast making polite but uncomfortable conversation. Eve and her mother talked quietly about the funeral arrangements and who needed to be notified. Justin listened intently, wondering how Eve managed to hold it all together. No one mentioned the upcoming birth. Finally, Justin got up, stacked the empty plates in the sink and began running water.

"Justin, you don't have to do that," Judith said, standing up.

"Really, I don't mind."

"No, I insist, you made breakfast, really, why don't you just sit down."

"Well, I should be going. I have some business I need to tend to."

Eve's heart sank again. "Can't you stay for a little while?"

Justin could not look her in the eye. "No, I'm sorry, I really have to go."

"All right then, let me walk you to the door." Eve got up, despite his protests that he could make it to the door on his own.

"I need to talk to you Justin," she said while they stood in the hallway.

"Can it wait?" he asked, fumbling with the keys to his rental car.

"Not really. I think it's waited long enough."

"I'll try to stop by later."

"Promise me you will. It's really very important." Eve placed a hand on his arm. It sent chills through him.

"I can't make promises, Eve. But I will try."

Eve snaked her arms around his waist, pulling him to her. "Thank you for staying with me last night, and for taking care of me."

A flash of a memory skipped through Justin's mind. She was sleeping, and he was sitting in the chair beside her bed watching her, where he'd stayed for most of the night.

"You're welcome." The feeling of her against him was almost too much to bear. He didn't want to know the truth. It would hurt less if it was unspoken and he had no intention of returning later that day.

Eve watched through the open door as Justin drove away.

"You really shouldn't throw yourself at a man you know," her mother said sneaking up behind her. Eve quickly pressed the door shut, regarding her mother intently.

"I'm not throwing myself at him. I need to tell him about the baby."

"Why? He's shown no interest. I mean how can he not know this is his child?" Judith folded her arms impatiently across her chest. "You should look for a more stable man, like your brother Teddy, he's such a successful plastic surgeon. Why all the Palm Beach society matrons go to him, you know."

Eve ignored her mother's comment about her brother. "There has to be some misunderstanding Momma, that's the only explanation. Justin loved me, loves me…."

"Honey, I know you still love him but face it, he left you. Those Hollywood people are like that, fickle you know."

Eve hated her mother's idle assumptions that everyone who had ever lived in California was an airhead idiot who believed in UFOs and free love. Impatiently, she walked past her mother down the hall. "Justin's not like that

Momma, how many times do we have to have this conversation. He deserves to know this is his child."

"Why, so he can dutifully send a check to you every month?" Judith trailed behind her daughter.

"No Mother! Because he'll want to be a part of his child's life, regardless of how he feels about me."

"And what will everyone think, dear?" Judith raised an accusing eyebrow.

Eve turned slowly to face her mother. "Quite frankly Mother, I don't really care what anyone thinks. I love Justin and I always have. I have spent my life doing what was right and what was expected and look where it got me."

Eve did not wait for her mother to reply but walked upstairs to tell her older child that her father had died.

CHAPTER 62

The funeral was three days later. St. Edward's was filled with four hundred mourners, a dutiful ex-wife and every notable Stanhope within a hundred mile radius. A few troubled relatives from the Freeman side who seemed to only gather at funerals, sat dry-eyed in the front pews. Even the still affluent family from his mother's side managed to find their way down from Maine. They were a mixed bag of money and despair. Eve was thankful they were all sitting behind her. At least that way she couldn't see their scowling, grimacing faces as they were forced to share oxygen with those they considered lesser or perhaps unworthy of the privilege.

The priest spoke softly about forgiveness, life and death. He knew, like everyone else, that Billy hadn't been a model citizen, or a model anything for that matter. But he had managed to die better than he had lived, contrite and humbled by a life cut short.

A reception was held at Olivia and Terry's estate. People mingled and mixed, offering condolences to the family and talking in soft, respectable tones. Eve wandered amid the crowd of people. She'd been looking for Justin, but hadn't been able to spot him. Suddenly, she noticed his back to her, speaking to some distant relatives of Billy's.

She came upon the group. "Hello, forgive my intrusion, but I need to steal Justin away for just a moment."

"How nice," the spindly woman began, smiling with yellow teeth, "that you're having Billy's child. What a wonderful way to remember him by. I suppose you'll name him after his father."

"Good to see you," Eve spat, clearly annoyed. She pulled Justin's arm through the crowd. Idiot woman, she thought, first to assume this was Billy's child and then to think I would name him after my deceased ex-husband.

"Eve, what did you need?" Justin inquired, trying to free his arm from her grip.

"I told you the other day that I needed to talk to you."

"Oh, right, but do you think this is really the place…."

"It's going to have to do, Justin. You've really given me no choice. Come on, let's go outside."

Justin followed her as she wove through the crowd of people and slipped out the patio door. She headed into the back gardens, toward the maze of hedges. Eve felt her palms sweat and her heart race in her throat. When they were well out of hearing range, Eve stopped and turned slowly to him.

"Justin, there's something I need to tell you…."

Her words were interrupted by the sound of quick steps and a call of her name. "Eve, so glad I found you," Terry began slightly winded, "it's Nicky, he's pretty distraught. He's up in our room."

Eve's heart fell in her chest. Her eyes met Justin's. "Go to him," he said softly, "I'll wait here."

"Promise me, Justin. I really need to speak with you." Eve heard the pleading in her voice and didn't care.

"I will, I promise." He rested a gentle hand on her arm. "Now, go be with your son."

A slight smile crept onto her lips and with a nod she turned to follow Terry back into the house to comfort her son.

Justin sat outside under the bright blue sky, listening to the birds and the subtle hum of voices coming from inside the house. Occasionally, a mourner would venture outside for a breath of air or a cigarette. But for the most part, he was alone with his thoughts. Despite what the last few days must have been like for her, Eve looked remarkably beautiful, he thought. He closed his eyes, allowing himself to remember for a moment; a luxury he rarely allowed himself. But now, being in her presence the memories were too strong to hold back. A buzzing in his pocket made him jump, he stood up and looked around before he realized it was his phone.

He turned it on. "Hello?"

"Justin, it's Susan." It was Justin's assistant, calling from New York. From the sound of her voice, he sensed that something was wrong.

"Hi Susan, what's going on?"

"Justin, I'm so sorry to bother you on a day like this but there are some problems with production of *Tender Fury*," she said referring to the last in the series of the *King's Town* stories. "It seems there are decisions to be made and no one knows what to do. The director is threatening to walk off the set."

Again? Justin thought. It seemed as though directors did little else but yell and threaten. He wondered how movies ever got made with a tyranny of egos dominating production.

"And they need me." His words were more of a statement.

"Yes," Susan answered quietly, "I'm so sorry, I wouldn't have called you but if they don't get these rewrites we may not make the summer release."

While Justin was still trying to understand every nuance of movie production, what he did know was that a movie's success largely depended on when it was released. His movies did much better in the summer than they did in the fall. It could mean the difference of millions of dollars not just to himself, but to his staff as well.

"I'll be on the next plane out," he said simply, and after a short goodbye, folded his phone and placed it back in his pocket.

He glanced up at the house and noticed that people were beginning to leave. He stepped quickly inside and decided to look for Eve before he headed out. Justin headed to the kitchen. The catering staff was beginning to clean up. Terry stood talking to one of the guests at the breakfast table.

"Terry, I'm sorry to disturb you," Justin began, "but I've got an emergency and I've got to go."

"I think Eve needed to see you."

"I know, can you tell me where she is, I'd like to say goodbye."

"Goodbye?" Terry frowned. "Where are you going?"

"There's a problem with the screenplay of my movie and I have to fly out to LA tonight to see if I can correct it."

"Well, look, let me take you upstairs and you can see Eve before you go." Terry turned to his guest, "Will you excuse me for a moment? I'll be right back." Terry stood up and Justin followed him out of the kitchen and up two flights of stairs. He could hear Nick's shouting grow louder as he approached the room.

"Maybe this isn't such a good idea," he said tentatively. "He sounds pretty upset." Justin could hear Nick's cries for his father and felt his heart tear in his chest. He fought off the urge to run into the room and embrace them both.

"Well, let's take a peak inside and see." Terry gently pushed the door open and peered inside.

Justin could see Eve sitting on the bed, trying to calm the hysterical child. It was no use, he thought, whatever she has to say can wait. Nicholas needed her more. Justin tapped Terry on the shoulder and the two retreated into the hallway. Eve never noticed they were there.

"I'll just go Terry, thanks anyway. I'll try to call her tonight and talk to her then. Please tell her I'm sorry I had to leave so abruptly."

Terry nodded. "Sure, Justin. Travel safely."

"I will." Justin sped down the stairs, taking two at a time. He wove through the guests, stopped briefly to speak with Olivia and then he was gone.

CHAPTER 63

Eve rubbed her belly as the dawn began to gradually seep through her windows. The baby had kicked all night, leaving her little time to sleep. She knew it would be soon, any day now. All of her babies had accelerated their kicking right before they were born. As though they couldn't wait to get out into the world.

"It's not that much better out here, little one," Eve said softly. It had been five months since Billy's death. Her children were beginning to finally accept it and grieve.

Only last week, Eve had finally erased a message from Justin that he left on her machine shortly after he left on that terrible day. She knew it by heart: "Hi Eve, it's me Justin. Sorry I missed you, I know you said you needed to talk to me. I'll be gone for a while. They're having problems on the movie set, and I have to get there and see if I can help move things along. Take good care of yourself and kiss the munchkins for me…." Then the line had gone dead. Eve remembered when his messages used to end with "I love you" or some other endearment. But that was over. He'd changed his mind. And now, she was going to give birth to their child and he would never know.

With great effort, she pushed herself out of bed and splashed some chilled water onto her face. It was the time in her pregnancy when she didn't care how she looked. She was heavy and uncomfortable and sad. Sad because somewhere deep inside she had thought that telling Justin about his child would make him fall in love with her all over again. But she'd never even had the chance to tell him. There was someone she did intend to tell and she knew she needed to do it today.

It was late Saturday morning and Eve decided to make Nick and Frannie go with her instead of spending the day in front of the television, watching cartoons. When she parked in the driveway, both of them sprang out of the car and ran up the path to the VanSant residence.

Mary opened the door when she heard them drive up.

"So wonderful to see you, Eve," she smiled, embracing her. "How are you feeling, my dear?"

"Fat, and uncomfortable and ready to deliver this child."

"Come on inside, I've made us some lunch."

Mary held the door while Eve passed by her. Eve's call that day had come as somewhat of a surprise to her. But she welcomed the visitors. Waiting for word from her son made the days pass slowly. He'd left so abruptly, and she wondered if this time he'd ever return.

Eve lowered herself into one of Mary's kitchen chairs. "Have you heard anything from Justin?"

"No, not since he got back to LA. I guess they're on location and he's pretty busy." Mary thoughtfully curled the rim of her cup with a finger. "Can I get you something to drink? How about the children?"

Both women looked around the empty kitchen. Frannie and Nicholas had run into the backyard to play on the swing set Justin had built for them in the hopes that they would be spending many hours at Grandma Mary's.

"I think they're fine right now. If they get thirsty they won't hesitate to tell you."

"I miss them, Eve. You must bring them by more often. It hasn't been the same, since…" Mary broke off her sentence, "Eve, I'm sorry, I shouldn't have brought that up." Mary sat down beside her, pressing her hands onto her lap.

"It's ok, Mary. That's actually why I stopped by today. Well, sort of. Mary, there's something I need to tell you, that I need for you to know. I would have told you sooner, but I was hoping that I could tell Justin first."

Mary frowned. "What is it, dear?"

Eve ran her hands across her stomach. "I know I haven't been too forthcoming about my pregnancy…."

"Well, I think it's wonderful that you and Billy reunited…"

"Mary, that's just it. We never reunited. I allowed people to draw their own conclusions knowing what they would think."

"Why did you do that?"

"Because I wanted to be the first to tell Justin that he was going to be a father."

Mary's eyes flew open. "What? My son, your baby…?"

"Yes," Eve smiled, "and it feels so good to tell someone other than my judgmental mother."

"May I?" Mary reached out a tentative hand to Eve's stomach. Eve removed her hands. "Yes, please."

Mary felt her grandchild kick and tears spilled from her eyes. "My grandchild…Eve, you have no idea what this means to me."

Eve covered Mary's hands with her own. "No, I do know what it means to you. I'm only sorry I had to wait so long to tell you. I just, I had hoped to tell Justin first. But I know, that he's, I mean that he doesn't want to be with me, I just thought he'd want to know about his child…."

Mary withdrew her hand. She knew she had no right to interfere but as far as she was concerned this misunderstanding had gone on long enough.

"What's wrong, Mary? Is it Justin? Is he all right?"

"He saw you," she began tentatively, "with Billy I mean, on the porch swing. He said you two were…close, I guess is how he put it. It hurt him terribly to see you two, and of course he had no idea that Billy was sick. He just assumed that you two had gotten back together. Then, when everyone found out you were pregnant, we all assumed you had."

Eve sat, unable to utter a word.

"But, Mary, I mean didn't he even want to discuss it with me?"

"He backed off, he wanted to give you time to be certain that it was him you really wanted. He knew how much your marriage had meant to you."

Eve picked a strand of her hair and began to twirl it. "But Mary, we worked through that long ago, I don't understand what happened. He knew I was over my marriage."

Mary thought carefully about her next words, a hesitant tongue darted out, wetting her bottom lip. "Eve, when you married Billy years ago, it devastated Justin. I think he was terrified of going through that hell again, so he backed off."

Eve let out a sigh that curled inward. As much as she wanted to believe Mary's recount of the story, she didn't dare trust that it meant that she and Justin would simply be able to pick up where they left off. But it gave her hope at least and it was more than she'd had in a while.

❧ ❧ ❧

After weeks of rewrites and struggling to get the director's ego in check, it seemed that Justin's movie was finally back on track. Filming had taken them to some unusual places in Wyoming. Justin loved the breathtaking scenery and untouched land that dominated the better part of the state.

Justin was scheduled to return to Los Angeles in three days. After that he wasn't sure what he'd do. He had honestly not given it much thought. He knew one thing for certain though; he knew he'd never be returning to Candlewood Lake. That was in his past and now with Billy's passing he knew he could never return there. The memories were painful even at this distance, and being so close to them would make them almost unbearable.

The day before Justin was to return to Los Angeles he received a FedEx letter from his assistant. One of the set assistants delivered it to his air-conditioned trailer where he was working on his next screenplay. Inside the package he found two envelopes, one from Terry, the other sealed with his name handwritten on the front. He opened Terry's note first,

~

Dear Justin,

I hope this finds you doing well. We are adjusting to Billy's loss although it's a difficult transition of course. I'm sorry it's taken so long to get this to you but in the confusion after Billy died I'd forgotten to give this to you. He dictated this letter after your visit. He had a lot to share with you and I think he knew he'd never see you again.

Best wishes,

Terry

Justin set the second envelope on his desk and stared at it in stunned silence. Within the crisp, white envelope were his friend's final words. The thought of it shook Justin to his core. What more could Billy possibly have to say? He wondered. Carefully he slid a letter opener inside the envelope and opened it. He pulled out the fine linen paper marked with the Stanhope logo. The three typewritten pages were single spaced and Justin ran his hand along the pages before he read them. He absorbed Billy's words carefully, the impact of them shaking him to his foundation:

Dear Justin,

I don't know if I'll get to tell you this so I thought I'd put this down on paper before it's too late.

I have spent so much of my life resenting you Justin, I never really knew how to appreciate you until now. It honestly didn't start out that way. When we were young I just idolized you in my own confused way. But later I became so jealous of you I couldn't hardly stand it at times, and yet I wanted to be so much like you it hurt. Do you remember the time that you saved me from those guys who tried to beat me up after the game? I've never forgotten that, and for the longest time, I couldn't forgive you. I guess I was so filled with pent up anger and resentment that you were everything I wished I was but knew I could never be. Then, I took the one thing that I knew meant the world to you: Eve. In my own selfish mixed up way, whether consciously or unconsciously, I hoped that by taking her away from you, I could even the score in my own twisted way; that I could feel that after suffering through all of your perfection that I have finally bested you. I got what you wanted more than anything in the world. But in the end I didn't, because no matter what, she always loved you anyway even though she didn't realize it until I left her. I took Eve from you Justin, and for that I will never forgive myself. I can only hope that through this letter, I can somehow right a terrible wrong.

Justin I don't know what happened between the two of you but I know this: Eve loves you and she always has. I know you think we got back together but we never did, in fact there wasn't a day that went by that Eve didn't speak of you and didn't tell me how much she loved and missed you. She assumed of course that you decided you no longer loved her and that's why you left. I knew better though, and while I encouraged her to call you she was far too invested in my illness to even allow herself the distraction of it. And I think in her heart that she hoped you'd return to her of your own volition. But you didn't. Not that I can blame you, you've suffered through this most of your life. Watching her and me together, watching us raise our children and watching me fuck up my marriage as only I could. But now my friend it's time for you to stop being a prisoner of the past.

By the time you read this I'll be gone and it's time both of you stop paying for my selfishness. You need to be with Eve and never waste another day wondering if she loves you because she does, and she always has. So much so that she's carrying your child. Even though I'm sure most of New Fairfield thinks Eve and I reunited, it's not true. She could never have gotten back together with me after what the two of you shared.

I hope this puts an end to any misunderstanding between the two of you and I hope that in some small way, I've been able to make up for my past transgressions. If you're not by Eve's side when you're reading this, Justin, then go be with her and your new baby and start the life you were meant to lead years ago. Forgive me if you can but if you can't I understand.

I have come to realize that in the end the only thing that matters is how we loved, how we were loved, and the love we leave behind. I'm saddened by the fact that I loved very little in this life and certainly didn't give anyone much reason to love me in return. But I pray that my death bed regrets aren't too late that I can somehow bring a sparkle of love, even in some small amount to those I truly cared about.

I don't know where I'm going from here my friend, whether it be heaven or hell. I suppose that is now up to God to decide. But know this. No matter where I go, I will never forget you or the friendship we shared and the days we spent on Candlewood Lake. I will cherish them always and I hope in some small way, you will too.

I love you my friend.

Billy

Justin sat quietly reading and rereading the letter. The only sounds he heard were the quickened beating of his own heart and the distant voices of the film crew outside his trailer.

"Billy," he said in an almost reverent way, "of course I forgive you my friend. There is nothing to forgive." He waited in silence for an answer but of course there was none. Billy was gone and in his hands were his final words. How much time had they wasted misunderstanding one another? Days, months, years? It seemed so senseless to him now. He should have seen it; he should have spotted Billy's anguish and dealt with it. But he hadn't. Like a frightened boy he'd let Billy marry Eve and disappeared into his own life in California.

Justin couldn't move, he couldn't even cry as he remembered his own transgressions from so many years ago. In truth, he'd let Eve down. If he had loved her enough back then he should have fought for her instead of giving up and giving in. But he handed her over to Billy and then walked away. Suddenly the tears that were absent five months ago filled his eyes and flowed down his cheeks. So many years, he thought painfully, so many lost days.

Don't waste another minute. The voice came from nowhere. Inside his head? Perhaps? Was it Billy with one final message? Possibly. But whatever it was, Justin knew he couldn't stand to be away from Eve any longer. Already he'd wasted too much time. And in the end, the real lesson he needed to learn in life wasn't taught to him by a college professor or some other intellectual, it was taught to him by Billy. Billy who'd struggled all of his life against his own expectations and a dysfunctional family. Billy who'd met the loss of most of his relatives with a bravery Justin could never hope to muster and suddenly he admired his friend like he never had before and realized just how lucky he'd been to know him.

He pushed open his trailer door and headed for home.

CHAPTER 64

It was still cold outside but Eve couldn't stand to be cooped up for one more minute. She decided to sit on her porch swing and wait for the mailman. He would offer a smile, maybe an interesting piece of mail and certainly a bit of conversation. She was too big to drive or she'd head into town to see who was at the Grand Union. She knew it would be only days, maybe even hours before her child was born. Mary promised again to stop by as she now did every day. Ever since she'd found out she was going to be a grandmother, she'd managed to cram in nine months of grandmotherly duties in the last several days. But Eve appreciated it and wasn't sure how she could have managed to get through the final days of her pregnancy without her.

Judith had been beside herself when she found out Eve had told Mary about the child. Judith had aspirations of keeping the little secret and letting everyone think it was Billy's. But soon enough the entire town would know her daughter had given birth to her lover's baby. Eve recalled how her mother had visibly cringed when she realized the questions she'd have to answer. But Eve didn't care. She'd spent her life worried about what other people thought and now, quite frankly, she didn't give a hoot. No one had ever asked her, they all assumed. A secret smile played on her lips and Eve visualized the faces of her neighbors when they found out.

Eve spotted the mail carrier but the smile faded from her face when she realized it was a substitute. No conversation today, she thought, substitutes were always in a fiery hurry. Probably doing two routes, she assumed.

"Good afternoon ma'am." The portly man smiled at her from under the brim of his hat as he handed her a bundle of mail.

"Good afternoon. Where's Sam?"

"Fishin' I think, seems too cold to me but who knows. Anyway, have a good day." He turned and headed back down her walkway as Eve watched any hopes of conversation to stave off her boredom diminish. She glanced down at the pile in her hand, sifting through it absentmindedly. From within her belly she felt a surge of something familiar. Then a pain as she dropped the mail, doubled over and realized she had gone into labor.

♣ ♣ ♣

"Can we go any faster?" Justin leaned forward to the driver who, at his urging, was already breaking the speed limit.

"I'll do my best sir, I can't say as I blame you, with you going to be a father and all. I'd want to get home as quickly as I could too." Justin could feel the driver pressing down on the accelerator, as the black sedan sped forward.

A father, Justin thought. He was indeed going to be a father. In his own way, Billy had single-handedly righted the wrongs from so many years ago and for that Justin would forever be grateful. Who knows how long Justin would have sat stubbornly on the West Coast, assuming Eve no longer loved him. He'd been insane to think she could have ever stopped, he knew all too well what they'd shared but the scars from the past had overwhelmed rational thought and, faced with the torment of losing her again had been too much even for him.

The sedan came to a smooth stop in front of Eve's house and Justin quickly stepped from the vehicle, running up the walk.

"Eve!" he called out, knocking frantically on the door, "Eve!!" But there was no answer. Justin looked around and then darted through the side gate and into the back yard. Maybe she was back there with the children, he thought. Then a voice in his head told him to get to the hospital. Suddenly he was quite certain Eve was there, delivering their child.

♣ ♣ ♣

Eve nuzzled her daughter's soft face. Justine Mary VanSant slept soundly after her entrance into the world not an hour before. The room around her was quiet, although she expected a flood of visitors at any moment. Mary VanSant had arrived just in time to find Eve had already gone into labor. She drove them both to the hospital and then, upon Eve's urging, had gone into the delivery room with her. Eve recalled how Mary had cried when she'd held her granddaughter for the first time. A tiny hand emerged from the blanket and Eve gazed at her perfect pink baby with worshipping eyes. She wished more than anything that Justin could be here to share this moment.

And then the door to her room burst open, and her mother walked through. A smile swept across her face when she saw her daughter and the newest addition to their family.

"My dear, you look radiant!" she cooed.

"Thanks Mom, where's Dad?"

"Oh, he'll be along in a second, I think he and Karl are sharing a cigar outside." She waived a disapproving hand in front of her face, "so, may I hold my granddaughter?"

Unwillingly, Eve released her child to her mother who gently scooped her up. Justine yawned and fluttered her eyes open briefly, and then shut them again to continue her nap.

"So, have you decided on a name, Eve?"

Eve hesitated for a moment, "Yes I have, Mother."

"Well, are you going to share it with us?" She puckered her lips at the baby, "whatever will I be calling you my sweetness?"

"Justine. I've decided to name her Justine Mary VanSant."

Judith flinched at her words. Her eyes flew to her daughter. "You're kidding right? I mean why would you do that? Why not just give this child the Freeman name? Why make her an outsider?"

"She won't be an outsider, Momma and she deserves to be a VanSant. She deserves to carry her father's name."

"But Eve," her mother pleaded, sitting down at the edge of her bed, "what will everyone say once they find out she's Justin's?"

Eve rolled her eyes and wondered for a moment if her mother's obsession with public approval would ever wane. "Mom, look I'm sorry you don't approve but my decision is final. I am proud of the fact that Justin and I created this child together."

"But you aren't married to him."

Eve reached for her daughter. "Mother, this isn't the fifties anymore. These things happen."

"Not at Candlewood Lake they don't." Judith fumbled with the edging of the blanket.

"Mother please! It's a virtual Peyton Place here at times; you and I both know that. But the town has grown so much and all the new people could care less about my soap opera life. Besides, the minute I'm out of this hospital Justine and I are going to find her father and bring him home."

Judith crossed her arms in disapproval, "So, you're just going to swallow your pride and go begging for him to return?"

"Yes, Mother, I love him and that's what people in love do." Eve touched her daughter's hair.

Judith stood up. "Eve, you know I only want what's best for you. But I strongly disapprove of this whole thing, I just want you to know that."

Eve watched her daughter sleep, completely absorbed in her perfection. Like it or not, mother, quite frankly I don't really care, she thought. She refrained from commenting on her mother's disapproving tone and instead she only smiled when she heard the door to her room close behind her when she left.

Justin pushed through the doors of Danbury Hospital. A call he'd placed from the limo confirmed his suspicion, Eve was indeed delivering their baby. Without waiting for the elevator, Justin took the stairs two at a time up to the maternity ward.

"Eve Van…eh, I mean Freeman, Eve Freeman," He said quickly to the nurse behind the counter.

"Room 304," the nurse smiled, "she's just delivered."

Just delivered. Justin heard the words over and over again as he raced through the halls. Their child was born.

Their child.

Eve curled herself around her daughter. "I wish your father could be here to see you," she whispered softly as she watched Justine sleep in her arms. Eve heard the door to her room open but assuming it was a nurse, didn't bother to look.

"Papa's here now."

Then she felt a familiar hand on her shoulder and looked up. "Justin!" she exclaimed, waking their daughter from her nap.

"Yes, Eve, it's me."

The sight of him was like a bolt of thunder from out of a cloudless sky. Eve could not breathe, but it felt wonderful to be breathless. She could not move, she could only pray she wasn't imagining him standing there beside her.

"Oh, God, Eve, I've missed you so much!" Justin gasped breathlessly bending to kiss her gently on the lips.

For a long moment, she was unable to find her voice. "J-Justin? What? How did you know I was here?" she finally managed to say.

"Billy told me," he smiled.

"Billy?"

"Yes, it's a long story, Eve, but the minute I realized what a fool I'd been I raced back here as fast as I could. I thought you and Billy had gotten back together Eve, that's why I left, I was so foolish. Can you ever forgive me? I love you, Eve. I always have and I always will, forgive me for leaving you."

Eve began sobbing. "I love you too," she said through her tears. "I knew you would come home, I always knew it."

Justin pulled back from her then and placed a warm kiss on her mouth, a tender, longing and passionate kiss of sweet return.

She reached up to wipe her face. "Oh God Justin, I never got a chance to tell you. I tried, I tried so hard."

He smiled. "About our baby you mean?"

Now Eve could barely talk, her breath came in short gasps and tears flooded her eyes. "How did you know?"

"Billy." He smiled as he reached for his daughter. Eve only nodded, still unsure what he meant by that.

"Justin VanSant…I'd like you to meet your daughter, Miss Justine Mary VanSant." She handed him his daughter and he took her with shaking hands. Justine looked up at her father with blue eyes that matched his.

"Oh God Eve, she is so beautiful. I'm so sorry I missed out on your pregnancy. I should have listened, you tried to tell me, but I was too consumed with my own pain."

Eve pushed her fingers through his hair. "It's all right, it's over now and we're together and that's all that matters."

"I will never leave you or our daughter, Eve. Marry me, marry me tomorrow."

She smiled through her joyful tears. "I thought you'd never ask."

CHAPTER 65

1992

The lake was filled with summer visitors, their voices echoing across the water. Justin paddled their boat to the center of the lake. Eve watched Frannie and Nicholas as they sat on the same pier she'd shared years ago with her husband. She fingered the diamond wedding set on her hand as it glittered in the afternoon sun.

"Okay," Justin said, setting aside the oars, "we're here, now hand me our daughter so I can give her the official tour of the lake."

Eve smiled and handed the babbling, happy toddler over to him.

"Now, Jussy, I wanted to bring you here to show you where I fell in love with your mother."

Justine replied, "Da da da da," and hit her father in the nose.

Eve laughed. "In the middle of the lake?"

"No," Justin smiled, "everywhere. It wasn't one moment but a collection of a thousand moments and every place you can see and even those you can't are where I fell in love with you, over and over again. So when someone asks you, 'Mrs. VanSant, where did you and your husband first fall in love?' You can just say, at Candlewood Lake."

About the Author

Penny is the author of the Amazon.com bestselling book *The Cliffhanger*. She is also a book marketing and media relations specialist. She coaches authors on projects, manuscripts and marketing plans and instructs a variety of courses on publishing and promotion. To learn more about her upcoming events, books or promotional services, log onto her web site at www.candlewoodlakenovel.com or www.amarketingexpert.com

For more information contact: info@amarketingexpert.com

978-0-595-35129-9
0-595-35129-8

Printed in the United States
65422LVS00003B/36

9 780595 351299